Ah-Mah

BOOK ONE OF THE HEARTMIND CHRONICLES

*For Paula, a kindred soul.
With love,
Emily
5-1-05*

EMILY SEATE

WEBEUS HOUSE

AH-MAH. Copyright © 2005 by Emily Seate. All rights reserved. No part of this book may be used or reproduced in any manner whatsoever without written permission except in the case of brief quotations embodied in critical articles and reviews. For information address Webeus House, P.O. Box 330071, Fort Worth, TX 76163-0071 or www.webeushouse.com.

FIRST EDITION

Book and cover design by Janet Long

Library of Congress Control Number: 2005922844

ISBN: 0-9766635-0-3

Printed in the United States of America.

FOR STEPHEN AND MILBRA

In 1979, Ed Case of Los Angeles, California, discovered this pictograph in the tomb of Ankhmahor (about 2500 B.C.E.) in Saqqara, Egypt. In it he saw clearly the use of both hand and foot reflexology. It was a small stretch to envision the inventor of this practice as a woman in southern Egypt around 3100 B.C.E., where tradition holds that civilization developed earlier than in the north. My first foot treatment came from Ed Case, and for many months I was his last client on Fridays. Through Ed, I met Ann Ferro who became my reflexology teacher, and ultimately, my friend.

CHAPTER ONE

Remtu's Hut

In the season of Peret, Khmet kissed his wife, and set out with the horned cow for the third field south of the stone dock. Ah-mah watched her husband, the new plow with its bronze blade over his shoulder, the cow following, until both were beyond her sight. For some reason she was tempted to run after him. His body seemed so strong and erect. She chuckled when she realized where her thoughts were taking her. With a shrug, she picked up the short-handled hoe. She was breaking up the soil beneath the rosemary bush when she heard the cow bellow. Dropping the hoe, she sped across the fields.

A milling knot of field hands screened the fallen animal from sight, but moved aside when they saw her. "It was a gany, Mistress," said Shnum, referring to the deadly burrowing asp, his mouth close to her ear to be heard above the roaring animal.

"The Master?" she asked. Shnum gestured toward a group a short distance away. The man on the ground in their midst did not move. "Khmet!" she cried, and dropped to her knees beside him. The cow still bellowed in agony, but Khmet slept the sleep of death.

2

Shnum knelt beside her. "When the gany struck the cow, it fell hard, pulling the Master into the plow. He died quickly, Mistress."

"You know it was a gany?"

"Yes, Mistress."

"Then kill the cow now, Shnum. Cut it up and take the pieces into the desert so the people will not be tempted to eat it." Shnum helped her to rise. As he started toward the still bellowing animal, she stopped him with hand on arm. "We will need men to carry the Master."

"These men are willing, Mistress," he said.

She nodded, and four men bent to lift Khmet to their shoulders. Ah-mah walked with them, her hand on the shoulder of the nearest to steady herself. They had not gone far when the bellowing stopped, leaving only natural sounds, chattering birds, the wind stirring palm fronds, and the soft crunch of the feet of those who bore their Master's body across the fields.

Servants, openly weeping, waited in front of the great stone house of Ah-mah's ancestors, some reaching out to Ah-mah, others touching the body as the men carried it up the steps. At her direction, they placed Khmet on the bed where he and Ah-mah slept, where their daughter, Ak-hu, had been conceived and born. Ah-mah crumpled onto a stool beside the bed.

Alone with her husband, she took his hand in hers, her heart willing his eyes to open, his fingers to move, to give some sign of life. As his body cooled, hers did also, a trembling taking her. Old Bo, Ah-mah's house servant and friend, brought beer and made her drink it. The liquid lessened the trembling, but it did little to relieve the shock. She did not move or speak when Ak-hu rushed in, her arms reaching for her mother before she could bear to look at the still body on the bed. Ak-hu's husband, Gedju gave their infant daughter, Ah-nah, to Bo's arms. The loyal servant took the hand of

Menes, their son, and withdrew.

For the rest of that day the family stayed with Khmet. At last, Bo brought steaming water and a basket of cloths, and knowing it was time for the body to be washed, Ak-hu and Gedju went to find their children.

Stirred to action by ritual and necessity, Ah-mah chose two cloths from the basket, handing one to her servant and friend. Together they washed Khmet, Bo on one side, Ah-mah on the other.

"His face is peaceful, do you see?"

Ah-mah nodded through her tears. The sharp blade had split his head, a blackish-gray substance showing through the gash. She wiped the blood and soil away from the wound and bound it, just as she might if he were yet living. Suddenly the nape of her neck became warm, that special place where he touched her, and for just a moment, it seemed Khmet still lived.

They dressed him in his best garment, last worn when he visited the self-proclaimed ruler of Nubt. Bo went to the garden and returned with stems of rosemary twined into a wreath for his head. Great bunches of lotus blooms gathered by the field hands stood in water-filled pots around the room. Their clean fragrance seemed appropriate to Khmet, who was known for his fairness, his just ways.

Just after dawn men carried Khmet's body to the ancestral cave behind the stone house. Ah-mah, Ak-hu, Gedju, Bo, the other house servants, and the field hands followed behind carrying lotus blooms to honor this man each had reason to mourn. They placed his body on a shelf dug into the side of the cave in the midst of other shelves holding the bones of Ah-mah's ancestors, and covered it with a freshly woven mat. Upon his chest Ah-mah set a smooth river-tumbled stone that she thought was especially beautiful.

"The river has washed you, the river travels with you in the form of this stone. May you be blessed in death, Khmet, as you have blessed us with your life. Fare well, my husband. Sleep peacefully with our ancestors."

From that moment, Ah-mah could barely tolerate the house of her birth, the home of her mother, her mother's mother, and all her ancestors stretching back to a time when rain fell and the land was green. Each morning she left the house before anyone else had risen and went to the garden to work. She did not speak nor did she acknowledge those who spoke to her. Worried, Ak-hu looked for her in the garden, and found her, sitting on the ground by one of the rosemary bushes, a few forgotten weeds in one hand and a far away look in her eyes.

"Mother?"

A shudder passed over Ah-mah as she brought her attention back from wherever it had been. "Sit by me, Ak-hu. Let me touch you so my mind will stay here."

Ak-hu sat and put her arms around her mother.

"Ah, that is good, my daughter."

"Mother, are you ill?"

Ah-mah did not answer immediately. "It seems I can do nothing but remember Khmet and pull the weeds in this garden." Ak-hu started to protest, but before she could, Ah-mah continued. "I have been remembering a hut I knew as a child. An old man named Remtu lived there and took care of his garden. After he died, I could not bear the thought of anyone else living in that hut, for I loved that old man. Khmet understood and made certain no one took up residence. He also had field hands tend the garden." Then, rushing on as though pushing the words out while she could, she said "I want to go there, my daughter, to live in that hut and to tend that garden. I must go, Ak-hu. It is the only way I can heal."

"Was not the field Father was plowing near that garden?"

"Yes, Ak-hu, and that is another reason I must go. I want to be near the place where Khmet fell."

"But you are Mistress of the Land, my mother."

"You must be Mistress now, my daughter, for I cannot."

The next morning, Ah-mah wrote Ak-hu's name beneath her own on the wall of ancestors and began a life of solitude in Remtu's ancient hut. With difficulty, Ak-hu let her go, but kept a close eye, and in those first weeks sent one of the field hands or house servants with hot food each day. Often they reported finding Ah-mah sitting in the field where Khmet had fallen, and once they heard her talking to someone who was not there.

After a while, Ah-mah healed enough to cook for herself and Ak-hu sent her barley or dried lentils or an onion, not too often, but often enough to ensure that she would have plenty. Sometimes Ak-hu went herself. Then mother and daughter remembered Khmet or sat in silence, togetherness the only balm needed.

Ah-mah grew to love Remtu's hut, arranging it to express the simplicity of her life. Bunches of dried and drying herbs hung from pegs in wall and roof. Along one wall, a low bench provided storage for pots, and corners held a straw broom and a hoe. A single bed frame stood against another wall with a thick mat on its ropes, her one concession to Ak-hu who was deathly afraid of scorpions and would not sleep on a stone floor, much less the ground. Her salt box, her knife, a wooden spoon and her and Khmet's cups, she stored on a shelf Remtu had scooped out of the thick mud wall near the doorway.

The hut faced south and west from a rise one field distant from the natural levee built up through countless inundations, the top of the levee serving as a path. The garden occupied the lower ground south of the hut. Ququ trees with their palm nuts bordered the far south side of the garden, with bener and their tasty dates bordering the west side nearest the river and shading the hut in the afternoon. Remtu had planted nehet opposite the river, their nequat, or notched figs, vital to many of her remedies. An older, larger nehet stood at the end of the row near to the hut, the ground beneath it serving as her treatment room. Herbs and vegetables grew in her garden, with more than half of the space devoted to lentils, onions and garlic, the rest to herbs including thyme and rosemary. The portion of the garden nestled beside the nehets, she reserved for new plants.

The lore of using herbs for healing was passed down, along with the responsibility for the land and the title, Mistress of the Land, from mother to daughter in Ah-mah's family. Her grandmother began the search for new herbs, encouraging the masters of every caravan that came to the village of Nubt to bring new seeds or seedlings to her. Ah-mah's mother continued the search, as did Ah-mah. Now the tradition of three generations was Ak-hu's responsibility, and as her mother returned to herself, Ak-hu brought seeds or a cutting from a new herb and shared her knowledge of it. Ah-mah's grandchildren, Menes, now a boy of six inundations, and Ah-nah, a toddler of two, often accompanied their mother, Menes straying toward the river to watch any boats that might pass. Ah-nah stayed with the two women, the sound of their voices lulling her into a contented sleep. Most of these new herbs died, being too tender for the hot, dry climate, but others thrived.

As Ah-mah's zest for life returned, so did her curiosity. She became fascinated with feet, watching everyone's way of walking. "He steps harder on his right foot than his left," she would muse, or, "Look how that foot turns in, and the other steps straight." When she asked to see the feet of the few who came for herbs or tonics, most were embarrassed to show her feet that had walked in dust and mud and sometimes the dung of animals. She solved that with water and a rag which she used to wash the feet and wipe them. The water seemed to soothe the person, and the act of wiping the feet reminded Ah-mah of her rubbing ritual, invented to keep her fragile soul in her body when she first came to the hut and practiced every morning. She noticed her own tendency to dig the outside of her heels into the soil and changed the way she walked to place her feet more evenly upon the dusty path. As she touched the earth with her bare feet, solidly, evenly, she felt a different kind of balance within.

Ah-mah began this day by rubbing her smooth, brown arm from shoulder to fingertips down one side and up the other. Three times she did this, and then rubbed the other arm, down and back three times. She pushed her right hand across her stomach beneath her breasts, and returned with the left, three times. Always, as she rubbed and pushed, she breathed deeply, in and out. Sitting up, she rubbed first one leg from thigh to toes, and then the other. Finally she stood, and with both hands over her heart, said, "I am alive. I am in this world. I am ready to greet the day."

After breaking her fast, she began to weed the lentils. About half-way through her task, the ache in her back begged her to stop. "Time for a drink," she thought, and went indoors to the water jug. Pouring a cup, she sipped it as she gazed out the doorway.

A stranger walked up the path with confident strides, his skin a deeper brown than hers, nearly black, wearing a simple linen kilt from waist to knees. His stride did not break until he stood in front of the entrance to her hut where he stopped sharply and called, "Is anyone in the hut?"

"I am here," Ah-mah said as she came out from the shadows. "Who are you?"

"One who seeks your counsel," he said.

Ah-mah squinted at him. Deep brown eyes met her gaze. It did not occur to her to consider what he might think of her, her shapeless dress hanging from her shoulders, her glossy black hair sticking out all over her head. He was tall, but her forehead came above his shoulder, for she was a tall woman, with muscles on her thin body made tough and strong with use. She gestured to the shade of the large nehet. "I will bring water."

Returning to the hut, she wiped the dust out of Khmet's cup with her fingers and filled it with water. As the stranger drank, she noticed scars on his face and arms, a large one on his leg. A warrior. For whom? Or does he kill for gold? When he handed her the empty cup, their eyes met for a moment. No, he did not kill for gold. The need to kill was not in him. But his eyes did hold a secret.

She looked at him to see if he would want more water, but he did not ask, so she set the cup down and squatted beside it in the shade of the ancient tree.

"I have heard that you prepare herbs for healing," he said. Ah-mah nodded. "People speak highly of your abilities."

She frowned slightly and asked, "What is your name?"

"I am called Sept the Warrior."

"What is your ailment?" Ah-mah was anxious to get on with this.

"Today I am well and to look at me no one would know how I suffer on the days when I cannot breathe. I take in air but cannot get enough. On those days I am weak as a newborn and a warrior for no one, not even myself."

"Does the difficulty breathing come on you suddenly?"

"Often it comes at night, or I wake up with it, having had no warning."

"How long does it last?"

"Usually hours, but once it lasted a whole day. When it has gone, I am weak for a while and must rest. Not the occupation of a warrior, nor good for his reputation."

"Have you always had this ailment?"

"No."

"When did it begin? Tell me about the first time."

"A group of us were set upon by black men far to the south. I stabbed two of them and was turning around when another lunged at me, knocking me to the ground. I tried to get up, but he drove his body into me, causing bones to crack and blood to come from my mouth. My companions killed the man and carried me to the snwn who bound my chest and tended a gash in my leg. In the night I awoke suddenly, my heart pounding, unable to draw breath. I thought that black devil still sat on my chest. The more I tried to breathe, the more difficult it was to take in enough air. I was suffocating and could not imagine the cause." Ah-mah noticed that Sept grew agitated as he spoke.

"A servant realized my difficulty and woke the snwn, who came quickly with a cup from which he bade me drink, a foul tasting brew, and hard to swallow. He told the servant to sit with me and she did, patting my back and speaking soothing words. At last, my breathing eased and I fell asleep once more.

"I am no coward, but this ailment confounds me, and I do not know when it will strike again. The snwn treats me with the foul tasting potion, which I now know to be something to calm me." By this time Sept the Warrior was up and pacing. "What is wrong with me that I have become such a weakling? Could that black devil have cast some kind of evil spell on me? I have sacrificed to all the gods from here to Djeba, but to no avail. The dread of the next time haunts me; I confess I am afraid to sleep. My servant continues to watch over me at night." Whirling around to Ah-mah, the tall, young warrior, his face gray with remembered terror, said, "I implore you. Find a way to help me." Having said that, Sept dropped to the ground in front of Ah-mah and put his head in his hands.

Ah-mah reached for his cup and rose to fill it. She had an idea about the cause of his illness, but did not know how to tell him, and she wanted time to think, time to be more certain of what she suspected. Such a fine man, and the inside of him was clear except for this tiny darkness. Often, she knew, it was best to heal the ailment and not speak of the cause, but something in the young man spoke to Ah-mah's heart. She did not want to give him a temporary cure like the snwn's potion. The black warrior had robbed this man of his confidence and made him afraid. She sought a way to restore it.

Returning, she handed him the cup of water, watching his broad, open face as he drank gratefully, the water cooling him. When he had finished, he set the cup down, an expectant look on his face.

Ah-mah did not speak, but gazed intently at him, wanting to be sure of her diagnosis. Then, she went back into the hut, this time returning with a bowl of water and a rag.

"I have noticed that people like to have their feet washed," she said, as she sat before him. "I would like to wash your feet because they may reveal something about your illness."

Sept started to laugh, but seeing that she was serious, removed his sandals and stretched his legs out in front of him, leaning back on his elbows. Ah-mah dipped her hands into the bowl and let the water pour over his left foot. She rubbed the dust from it with her hands, and dried it with the rag. She did the same with the other foot, and after drying it, held both feet by the heels. The legs were even, with the heels matching. A good sign. "Why are you surprised? It is only a little darkness." Aletha. What a time for the companion who lived in her mind to appear!

"Tell me what you see in his feet," she thought to Aletha.

"Look at the calluses around the ball of his foot." Ah-mah lifted the foot slightly so she could see that part more clearly. "My, my! The calluses circle that area, but the center is soft and puffy. Could that be the area of weakness?"

"I must find a way to treat him. But for now, I will send him home to return when the sun has slept three times," Ah-mah thought to her mind companion.

"Do you think that will be long enough?"

"It must be."

Sept plainly enjoyed her touch, for his relaxation went deeper and deeper. If she kept rubbing his feet, he would soon be asleep. She drew her hands away and clasped them together in her lap.

"I must think about all you and your feet have told me," she said. "Go now, and return after the third dawn from this one. In the meantime, every night before you sleep, have your servant wash your feet and dry them as I have done. It is not a cure, but I believe it will keep you from having an attack before you return."

"Thank you, Ah-mah. I will do as you say," Sept said, and rose to leave.

Ah-mah was not sure that Sept was satisfied, but he kept his silence and so did she. She was surprised to note that her heart walked with him as he strode off.

"I must be getting old and soft in the head," she thought.

"Or younger." Aletha again. "How will you treat him? Do you know?"

Not ready to be drawn in to conversation with her unseen companion, she said, "I must finish weeding. Then I will eat, and then I will rest. We can speak again when I am resting."

Ah-mah worked hard for several hours weeding the rest of the lentil plants, noticing that the lowest pods were turning brown, and one had opened, dropping its two seeds on the ground. She would begin picking tomorrow. The reed mats she had used for drying them last year were still good. With great care, she did not think of the warrior or his ailment. His presence, his scent, his energy were still with her, and his image often came unbidden to her mind as she pulled weeds from the soil. When that happened, she would rest for a moment, stretch her back, and gaze at the path. When the image passed from her inner vision, she returned to her task, trusting her mind to work as hard as her hands.

Weeding completed, she returned to the hut. Earlier in the day she had taken dried lentils from one cloth bag and barley from another and put them into a bowl, covering them with water to soak. Now she carried a chunk of dried dung to the fire pit. Lifting the cooking pot from the embers, she put the dung on top, watching it flame up briefly as the embedded straw ignited. Inside the hut, she took salt from the salt box and added it to the lentil/barley mixture. Each time she drew salt from it, she remembered seeing her mother and grandmother do the same. She peeled the dry golden skin from an onion and chopped it, adding it and a clove of garlic to the mixture. A pinch or two of thyme completed the recipe. When the dung had burned down to coals, she took the filled bowl to the pit and poured the mixture into the cooking pot, placing it on the coals, and covering it with the clay lid. Then she went to rest beneath the nehet while the stew cooked.

When the stew was ready, she removed the lid from the pot and returned the steaming contents to the bowl. She laid the empty pot aside to scrub with sand later and put the lid over the coals. Taking the bowl to her spot beneath the branches of the tree, she dipped the stirring spoon into the stew and blew on it before putting it into her mouth, eating slowly, relishing every bite, consuming just enough to satisfy, with plenty left for the evening meal, as well as to break her fast in the morning. When she finished her portion, she spread the rag over the bowl to keep out flies and leaned back against the bole of the tree. Very soon, belly full, Ah-mah's eyes closed and she began to snore softly.

She awoke much later in the afternoon, mouth dry as dust, and went to get water, drinking one full cup and returning to the shade of the tree to sip a second as she allowed thoughts of the man and his ailment to surface, random, unconnected. Aletha had returned for the promised discussion, but stayed silent as the image in Ah-mah's mind of the man pacing beneath the tree was replaced by a toddler, not much beyond first steps. Ah-mah almost cried out a warning to the little one when her inner vision showed her a calf, perhaps seeing the boy as another calf, running up to the toddler and butting him, causing him to hit the ground with such force, the wind was knocked from his chest. As Ah-mah watched the scene play out, the little boy's eyes got bigger and bigger, and his skin turned a bluish hue. "Breathe," she thought to this child from another time. The calf, still playful, reached down with its huge pink tongue and gave the boy's face a wet swipe, causing him to cough out the breath the shock made him hold. Where are the mother and father? Just as Ah-mah had that thought, a woman and a man came running, the woman scooping the boy up in her arms, the man chasing the calf back to its mother.

Ah-mah nodded to herself. The little boy was comforted by his mother. The man responded to the servant when she stroked his back and murmured soothing words to him. The warrior sought her out, another woman, the memory of the little boy strong enough in him to make him want to consult a woman instead of a man.

The sun was lowering through the western sky when Ah-mah rose from her place beneath the tree and went into the hut for the water jar. It was half full, enough for tomorrow, but she felt like a walk. She poured the water around the nearest plants, then lifted the jar to her head and began her trek to the river, her stride that of a woman in tune with dusty paths.

CHAPTER TWO

A Dream of Feet

Ah-mah loved the river and the boats that traveled on it, carrying goods from one village to another. One passed her now, oarsmen rowing downstream with the lazy current, tempting her to follow with her gaze. Instead, she walked upstream to a place where the levee dipped, giving access to shallows created between the bank and a sandbar. Reeds and lotus edged the shallows, marking them clearly.

She pulled the shapeless dress over her head and walked into water that came to her waist, naked except for the cloth that wrapped her loins. Ah-mah leaned back into the water and floated, her eyes drinking in the deep blue sky. Returning to the bank, she retrieved a small pot brought to hold the river-washed sand she preferred to use for cleaning. She dipped handfuls into the little pot, then tilted the water jar to fill it. Grabbing her dress, she dunked it and rubbed furiously at some of the stains. Then she pulled the wet garment back over her head and let it drop to its full length just above her knee, knowing it would be dry before she reached the hut. With the sand-filled pot attached to its thong and the heavy water jar on her head, she started home. Just as she reached the path that led to Remtu's hut, she chanced to look across the river directly into the huge golden-red sun, made more tolerable to the eye as it neared the horizon.

It may have been the time of day, that magical time between light and dark, day and night, but Ah-mah fancied she saw the image of the warrior, Sept, standing directly in front of the great disk. The moment passed and she resumed walking, barely reaching the hut and divesting herself of her burdens before falling on the bed asleep.

Crickets chirped the night away, calling and answering each other in rhythm with the river frogs. Ah-mah slept deeply for most of the night, her mind playing freely in its own world. Toward morning, she began to dream.

The warrior moved through a stone village with narrow streets, and she followed. If she lost sight of him, she held her breath until she saw him again. Often it seemed he waited for her, just out of reach, but not long out of sight. He entered a courtyard and ducked under a low opening in a wall. She followed and stopped, shocked by the brightness of the room she had entered. In front of the far wall, his back to her, the warrior stooped as though to see something more clearly. When he straightened and faced her, the room abruptly went dark except for the wall behind him. Ah-mah squinted in the dream, trying to make out the image she thought she glimpsed. Suddenly, the warrior stepped aside to reveal the soles of a pair of feet outlined in vivid gold. When he moved in front of the golden feet, becoming part of the image, his golden eyes flashed in the darkness. Ah-mah cried out and awakened.

Sitting up, she drew her knees to her chest and rested her cheek on them as she recalled the dream. Then, as the night sky grew lighter in the east, she rose, neglecting her rubbing ritual for the first time since its invention. She poured water into a bowl, splashing her face and rinsing her mouth automatically, spitting the water back into the bowl. Usually, she took that water to one of her plants, but this morning, she set the bowl back on the shelf and took a filled cup with her to sip beneath the stars.

She called to Aletha in her mind, and related the dream to her.

"The feet on the wall are important." Aletha said.

"My thought as well," Ah-mah said. "Golden feet on a wall, the man in front of them. The man... Aletha! I saw him. Last evening. It seemed he stood before the sun. The golden feet, the golden sun. What could it mean?"

"The feet touch the ground, and the sun is in the sky, much like the top and the bottom of things," Aletha said.

"Top and bottom, or inside and outside. Or two sides of the same thing." Ah-mah paced under the morning stars. Suddenly, she stopped. "Could it be that something done to his feet would strengthen him?"

"No doubt. But what?"

The colors of the dawn beckoned, the ritual greeting of the day. Ah-mah whispered to her mind companion, "Be still for now, and let us welcome the morning together."

"But..."

"Shhhhh."

CHAPTER THREE

The Beginning of Healing

When Ra rose above the eastern mountains for the third time, Ah-mah was ready. Since the warrior's visit, she had treated several people, each time washing their feet, and once, rubbing and twisting the foot in a way that came to her. No matter what she did, each person whose feet she touched seemed to relax.

Ah-mah spoke often with her mind companion about the dream. "Each golden foot had toes at the top, heel at the bottom. Could the top of the foot, the toes, represent the top of the body?" she asked her unseen companion.

"And the heel the bottom?"

Ah-mah picked up a stick and drew the outline of the sole of a foot in the dirt. She stared at it, and then drew the opposing foot beside the first. Finally, she drew a line between the two feet that stretched from toe to heel.

"Imagine this line to be the spine. Could this half of the body be helped by rubbing the foot on that side? And would rubbing the other foot affect the other half of the body?"

"Of course! Now draw a line that cuts the spine in half and extends across the feet," said Aletha. "Could that be the middle of the body? The waist?"

Ah-mah drew the second line and looked at it intently, her brows knit together in concentration. "If the waist is there, then the place of breathing would be here," Ah-mah said as she pointed with her stick to the area below the toes and above the newly defined waist. Aletha seemed to peer over her shoulder. "Stop that," Ah-mah said. "Be serious. We must help this warrior, and we must do it by strengthening his place of breathing. Tell me how we will do that, even knowing where the place of breathing is on his feet."

"If I did not know better, I would say you were smitten with him."

"He is the first new person to come into my life in a long time."

"You will meet many new people in your life, dear Ah-mah."

"What do you mean?."

"You create a different future for yourself with your study of feet."

Ah-mah was silent, stunned by Aletha's words.

"Who are you, Aletha?"

"The same as I have been since the day you were born."

"You have been in my mind for as long as I can remember, but today I would not say I know you. Only that you are familiar, and most times, a great comfort to me."

Ah-mah felt Aletha's sigh in her mind. The image of a woman, tall and slim with hair the color of honey and an oddly pale complexion, teased her, the mouth seeming to form words: "I am you, Ah-mah. We are the same mind. Now, back to those feet..."

* * *

When he appeared in the distance, she was startled. She did not remember his being so tall. Putting her hand over her heart to slow its beating, she went to sit beneath the nehet to wait for him.

Sept strode up the path to the tree and bowed to Ah-mah. She motioned to him to sit in front of her and handed him Khmet's cup filled with water. The bowl of water and the rag were at hand.

"How have you fared since we last spoke?" she asked, looking into his deep brown eyes.

"I have had no attacks," he said, draining the cup and handing it back to her. "The servant washed my feet each night, and I have slept soundly, with no dreams."

"Will you lie down on this mat once more? I want to wash your feet, but I also want to treat a place on your feet. I do not know if it will be part of your cure, but it has come to me in a dream that this is something I must do."

Sept removed his sandals and lay down on the mat, while Ah-mah hastened to place her own small pillow beneath his head. Sitting at his feet, she dipped her cupped hands into the bowl, pouring water over first one foot, and then the other, wiping them with her hands before drying them with a rag. Another bowl held a measure of oil. She dipped fingers into that bowl and rubbed the oil into the left foot and then the right, concentrating on the place she and Aletha had identified as the most likely spot for the place of breathing to reside. As she worked, a kind of prayer came to her, and she said the words over and over in her mind. "Where there is need. Where there is desire. Where there is consent."

She could sense that Aletha was with her, silent and watching for a change. Ah-mah almost spoke to her inner companion, thinking to quiet her nervousness, but she did not dare take her focus from Sept.

Once she had oiled both feet and wiped off the excess, her hands slipped to the heels. Instinct told her to pull, and she did, holding the heels tightly in her hands. She released them, then pulled again. Three times she pulled on the heels, and the third time, Sept sighed loudly, as though it had been drawn from him.

The oiled feet seemed to ask for more. Stumped, Ah-mah moved both hands to the left foot and rubbed here and there, twisting and stretching it. Not enough. With her left hand as support, she began pushing her right thumb into that soft, puffy area above the invisible waistline and below the toes. Sept groaned. Ah-mah heard him, but she also felt something like sand in his foot. She pushed again with her thumb, looking for more sand. She found it, but not where she expected it to be. Sept gasped.

"Is there too much pain?" she asked.

"It feels like you are sticking thorns into my feet. Are you?"

"I am only using my thumb. If you can stand the pain, I will do more."

Sept nodded and clamped his jaws together.

"Breathe deeply and the pain will lessen," Ah-mah said. "Tell me about your travels."

Ah-mah pushed her thumb into Sept's foot, hardly listening as he talked of the river and the people he had met. She still felt for sand, and kept finding it for a time, but never in the same place. When she went back to where she had started, pushing her thumb in again and again, Sept no longer groaned or gasped, and she found no sand at all. She looked at Sept's face. No lines of worry, or pain. Her strong brown hands moved to the other foot, pushing and pushing into the place of breathing until she could find no more sand.

"Are you asleep?" she asked, softly.

"Almost. My feet are different," Sept said. "They feel alive where you pushed your thumb into them," he said.

"Good. Rest while I fetch water for you," Ah-mah said, taking Khmet's cup with her to fill from the jar. When she returned, Sept was sitting on the mat waiting for her.

He took the cup from her and drank its contents. "I do not know what you have done, but I do feel different, Ah-mah. My heart is lighter."

"The treatment is finished for today, but if you can stay longer, I would like you to tell me of your travels. I confess I did not listen carefully when you spoke earlier, and I would like to hear it all again."

A good story-teller, Sept told Ah-mah of his travels up river and down. When the sun was directly overhead, Ah-mah prepared her usual meal, with some extra lentils and barley for her guest. As she stirred the pot and then returned to sit with Sept, she noticed that her heart, too, was lighter, lighter than it had been since Khmet's death.

Sept was quick to notice her frown. "What is wrong, Ah-mah?" he asked.

"I was just thinking of my husband," Ah-mah said.

"Oh," Sept said, disappointed. Regaining his composure, he said, "Where is your husband? Working in the fields?"

"My husband is dead, Sept. Dead for two years." Almost she told him that her sojourn in Remtu's hut began with Khmet's death, but she thought better of it.

"I am sorry to hear of this," Sept said, without feeling sorry at all. "Then you live here by yourself. Are you not lonely?"

"My daughter visits me, and the people come when they have an ailment. They bring me barley and sometimes a bit of cloth or thread in exchange for my herbs and treatments. It is a good life, and I am content."

Sept was taken aback. "Forgive me, Ah-mah. I had not thought of it, but I would pay you. Is there anything you would wish from me?"

"Your illness has given me much to think about, and when you speak of your journeys, I can see in my mind the places you describe. It is a fair exchange, and nothing else is required."

Sept said nothing, for he already had something in mind for

Ah-mah, several somethings, in fact.

"Am I healed, Ah-mah?"

"I tried something with you that is new to me. I do not know if it will work." Abruptly Ah-mah changed the subject. "Could the incident with the black warrior be related to something that happened when you were very young? Do you remember a calf knocking you down?"

At first she thought he had not heard her. Then his eyes grew big as two full moons, and his hands clutched his chest. His breath came in great gasps.

"Shhhh. Shhhh. It is only a memory. There is no calf here." Ah-mah murmured to him and touched his arms and his back. "Shhhh. You are here with me, Sept. Nothing will harm you. Nothing."

He crept into her arms, and she held him until he quieted and his breathing was easy.

When he stirred, she released him. He moved out of her embrace, but stayed close.

"I am not yet healed," he said, softly.

"You have confronted the fear of a child and you have brought that fear into your man's world. Now healing can begin, for as long as the fear was buried it remained the unseen enemy. Continue having your servant wash your feet before you sleep and return to me on the seventh day from this one. It is my hope that working your feet will strengthen you so that you are no longer troubled by this memory."

Sept rose, bowed to Ah-mah, and marched off, long legs taking great bites from the path. She watched until he was no more than a stick on the horizon. He seemed to know she watched, for he turned and waved. She did not wave back in spite of Aletha's urging, but she did smile.

CHAPTER FOUR

Ah-Mah is Smitten

On the seventh morning since she had last seen him, Ah-mah stood at the doorway holding her cup, telling herself that she was thirsty, and not that she wished to watch for him. As she sipped the water, intending to make it last as long as possible, his tall frame came into view. Suddenly, the heart of a much younger woman beat inside her chest. Could Aletha be right? Was she smitten with him? In her mind she heard Aletha's "I told you!" Ah-mah snorted her disgust, and went to stand beneath the nehet.

"I am glad to see you, Ah-mah," Sept said.

Color rose in her cheeks as she handed him Khmet's cup. "When you are ready, lie down on the mat," she said. The mat and the bowl of water, the rag, and a small bowl of oil were neatly arranged, her small pillow placed on the mat where she knew his head would be.

Ah-mah dipped her hands into the bowl of water and noticed their trembling. Quickly, she whispered a plea for steady hands under her breath as she poured water over his left foot and rubbed off the dust. The more she rubbed, the steadier her hands became. By the time she poured water over the right foot and rubbed it, she was once again a healer. She reached for the rag to dry his feet and glanced at his face. His deep brown eyes startled her.

Covering her embarrassment, she said, "Today, I will look for sand over the entire foot. I want you to tell me what you feel as I work," Ah-mah said, grateful that her voice did not betray her.

Holding both heels in her hands, she pulled three times, each time holding the feet and legs stretched for a few seconds. She could see Sept relax just from the stretching. Taking the left ankle in her hands, she twisted it to loosen it, and then pulled and twisted the foot. She held the foot with one hand, a bit awkwardly at first, and beginning with the largest toe, pushed her thumb into it. Each toe followed in succession. She soon found it more comfortable to rest his heel on her knee, place her left hand behind his toes and push the toes into it. Not content with Sept's silence, she asked, "Can you feel any difference in your toes?"

His voice seemed to come from a distance. "My foot wants what you are doing."

Satisfied, she continued holding the foot with one hand, pushing in with the thumb of the other. Sometimes, when her thumb tired, she would use her strong brown fingers, digging, digging, always looking for sand. In the area under the toes where she and Aletha thought the place of breathing might be, she found some sand, but less than last time. She continued lower and lower down the foot, even pushing her thumb into his heel. By the time she got to the other foot, she was tired, but determined. She sipped water from her cup, then took the right ankle in both hands and twisted it. This time, when she stole a glance at Sept, his eyes were closed, his breathing soft and even. He was asleep.

She worked the foot thoroughly, even though her thumbs ached from the friction. When she finished pushing, she took the bowl of oil and rubbed it into the soles of his feet. The treatment completed, she chose not to wake him, but settled herself against the trunk of the tree and watched.

A fly buzzed past her face, waking her. Sept had turned over onto one side, his elbow digging into the mat, hand supporting his head, eyes looking directly into hers.

"How long have I been asleep?" Ah-mah asked.

"You were sleeping when I awoke." Turning onto his back, Sept stretched his arms over his head, and yawned. "How lazy you have made me, Ah-mah. I do not know when I have felt more content."

Always a healer, Ah-mah asked, "Is that the difference you feel this time over last?"

"Not just that. My feet felt alive where you touched them last time. This time they feel alive all over, and somehow larger. I would dance, if only I knew how." Sept grinned at her, and then, abruptly, sat up to face her. "I have brought you payment, Healer." From behind his back he pulled a box. He must have retrieved it while she slept for she had not noticed it before.

"Open it, Ah-mah. I wish to hear what you will say about the contents."

Eyes bright with anticipation, Ah-mah touched the box, running her fingers over it. The wood was smooth, like nothing she had felt before. Certainly not like the rough wood of the salt box, although the way to open it was similar. Carefully, she slid the cover back in its grooves to reveal what was inside.

On top lay a most beautiful piece of linen. She touched the finely woven cloth, marveling aloud at its softness. Finally, under Sept's watchful eyes, she lifted the cloth from the box to find that it was a dress, with tiny feet and hands painted on the front. "Oh, Sept," she said. "This is too much for the little I have done."

Sept beamed his pleasure and said, "There's more."

"More?" Ah-mah asked. She carefully folded the beautiful garment and laid it aside before looking into the box once more. This time she saw a much smaller box made of the same smooth wood. She wondered if Sept knew that the boxes alone would have been payment enough. Hugging the box to her, she pulled the lid back and gasped. Inside were beautiful copper combs and the most extraordinary necklace of green malachite. Beneath them were tiny pots of color, unguents, and a polished piece of copper with a small handle. She lifted the copper piece, catching the sun's rays and blinding herself for a moment. Sept turned it so that its reflective surface held her face. One more thing she had forgotten.

"Will you wear these things when next we meet? It would please me to see you in them." Sept said, a mischievous grin splitting his face. "They are small payment, Ah-mah. You give me hope, and more, you enable me to continue my life as a warrior."

"I will wear them the next time you come. I will wear them because it pleases you." Too late, Ah-mah realized the import of her words. She ducked her head, but not before Sept saw her reddened face.

"Ah-mah, how many times has the river blessed the land since you were born?"

Startled into response, Ah-mah said, "The river has shared itself thirty-five times since my mother bore me."

"Ah, we are not so far apart. I have thirty years."

"I would not have thought it. You are so young in appearance. I am old, Sept. Too old…"

"For me? Who knows? We might find we have more in common than ailments and treatments."

Ah-mah wanted to run away from him, to take her time and think through his words, to touch the things he had brought her, but she could not bear to lose sight of him. Shyly, she said, "I am used to being the healer, to giving orders and telling people how to mend themselves. I know how to say soft words to people in pain, but I confess I do not know what to say to you now. The gifts are more beautiful than I have beheld in a long time. I have forgotten what some of the pots contain, or what is to be done with them, but I will try to remember."

The day had neared its close when Sept, his heart fuller and his step lighter, began the trek back. As before, when he reached the furthermost horizon, he turned and waved. This time, the wave was returned.

CHAPTER FIVE
The Two Boxes

Ah-mah woke early and rushed through her ritual body rubbing. She considered skipping it, but balance was important to the body's energy. Aletha was already in her mind as she settled herself against the wall and looked up at the stars.

"The stars don't seem quite so appealing when one has boxes filled with wonders, do they?"

"My heart wants to fly from my chest, to race to where he is."

"What will you do instead?"

Not yet ready to be practical, Ah-mah thought, "He entered my dreaming last night, Aletha. My body felt such longing for him. Do I wrong Khmet with this feeling?"

Aletha hesitated before responding. "How could truth dishonor anyone? But, answer my question. What will you do since your heart cannot fly to him?"

"I shall visit my daughter, Ak-hu. She will help me remember what to do with the contents of the smaller box."

"You are going home at last!"

"Just for today," Ah-mah said, "but yes, I am going home."

When it was light enough for her to see, Ah-mah gathered herbs she thought Ak-hu might need, not remembering that the ancestral garden was much larger than her own, tying them into bundles with bits of thread and putting them into a coarse linen bag. With the same thong she had used to attach the sand pot, Ah-mah hung the bag from her waist, moving it to the side so it would not interfere with her stride. The box, with the dress and smaller box inside, she lifted to her head, and for the first time in two years, took the path that led downstream.

Nodding to the field hands, both men and women, as they smiled broadly and greeted her by the title she would always have for them, Ah-mah hugged her emotions close and relied on that long held role to sustain her. The first sight of her ancestral home took her breath. She had forgotten how extensive and commanding it was, the largest in the area, much larger than the new temple of Ra in Nubt. Built in a past too dim to be remembered, its airy rooms enclosed a central courtyard filled with trees and plants, its imposing facade dominating the land. Ah-mah felt her spirit soar with the stone columns to the lofty roof. She was pleased to see the reed mats filled with lentil pods lining both sides of the tree-lined path that led to the great stone house, the women turning the pods with long sticks.

"Mistress?" The voice was familiar, but she could not remember the name. Turning her gaze from drying lentils, Ah-mah faced not one, but half a dozen women who had come to greet her.

"Mistress, let us carry these burdens for you," the one standing directly in front of her said. Before she could speak, the bag had been undone from its thong, the box taken from her head. The women crowded around Ah-mah, touching her, welcoming her with their voices and their smiles. Suddenly, the group parted, dividing itself along the path to Ah-mah's ancestral home, urging her forward, one running up the path ahead of her to bring news of her arrival.

A boy, having already recognized her in the crowd of women, streaked toward her, crying "Na-na, Na-na!" She marveled at his size. "Menes!" she cried, holding her arms out to her grandson and enfolding him. He hugged her hard, then pushed away and took her hand, joining the women in escorting her down the path to the great house. Ak-hu, little Ah-nah holding her hand tightly, descended the steps.

"Welcome, Mother," Ak-hu said. "My heart is glad to see you here."

"I come only for a visit, since Remtu's hut has become a place of comfort I would not soon give up. But at last, I have come, and with such welcome as I never expected." To the waiting women, Ah-mah said, "I thank you for your greeting and for carrying burdens that are not yours."

The women placed the box and bag on the veranda, and left with smiles and whispers of "Mistress."

In that shy stage that often comes near the end of the second year, Ah-nah peeped at her grandmother from behind her mother's dress. Ak-hu embraced her mother, then stepped aside, revealing Ah-nah. Before she could hide again, Ah-mah swooped the girl into her arms and tickled her, causing gales of laughter as the shyness was forgotten. When the laughter subsided, Ah-mah looked into Ah-nah's eyes and smiled. "You are such a beautiful girl, my Ah-nah." Ever mindful of her grandson, she added, "You have grown so, Menes, I would not have known you. Here, take my hand so you can help me climb these steps."

Carrying Ah-nah and holding her grandson's hand, Ah-mah ascended the steps with Ak-hu. A table had been hastily set with fruit and bread fresh from the fire and cups of water from the river, whose ribbon of liquid light was visible from this vantage point. Ah-mah stood drinking in the sight of the river, and in that moment, she was once more Mistress of the Land. Ak-hu felt it, as did Menes as they stood beside Ah-mah and An-nah, the essences of all the mothers and children who preceded them seeming to radiate from the stones beneath their feet.

"I had forgotten the power of these stones, Ak-hu. I am ashamed that my grief for your father could so blind me to our inheritance."

"How can we know what is right or wrong, what honors or dishonors, when we have lost what is dear? How can we do more than follow the steps as we see them laid out in front of us?" Ak-hu asked. "But let us speak of lighter matters, my mother. Give An-nah to Bo, then come, refresh yourself with bread and fruit, and let us celebrate your return to us. Menes? You go with Bo as well."

Ah-mah hugged Bo before giving An-nah over to her. "It is good to see you, old friend," Ah-mah said. Bo's eyes glistened. Shyly, she touched Ah-mah's shoulder, acknowledging her greeting.

Ah-mah watched as Bo left with the children in tow, surprised at how old she looked. She wondered if her friend had been ill, and started to ask Ak-hu when Menes broke away from Bo's grasp and ran back to his mother, crying, "Mama, Mama! Tell Na-na about the mean man from the village!" Then, just as quickly, he ran back to Bo.

Ah-mah raised her eyebrows in question. "Rahotep. But the story can wait, my mother. Here, sit, and let us enjoy this meal together," Ak-hu replied.

"Before I forget," Ah-mah said, "will you thank Gedju for me? He has brought me dung for my fire without my asking, and before I have had need. He is a good man, my daughter."

As they ate, the women talked of the births and deaths among the servants and the field hands, the crops, the traffic on the river, and the few events of consequence in the village of Nubt, with the conversation returning at last to Rahotep.

"You are Mistress of the Land, my daughter, but now that I am healed of my grief, I would have you unburden yourself to me. Tell me about Rahotep. How many times has he come and for what purpose?"

"The first time was a month after you left. He has come six times since, each time for the same reason, although he tries to cloak his motives differently. When he came two days ago, he so angered me that I ordered him off the land."

"You are not easily angered," Ah-mah said.

"You would have felt anger, had you been here."

Ah-mah reached across the table to touch her daughter's arm. "Tell me," she said.

"He arrived at mealtime, as he always does, with his retinue of servants and guards. This time Khufer was not with him." Ah-mah noticed that Ak-hu did not give the high priest his title. "He was pleasant enough during the meal, but as we were finishing, he said to me, 'I am surprised that your fields across the blessed river from Nubt are not yet prepared for the inundation.' I replied that it was not yet time to prepare the land. 'Word came this morning that the river is rising in the south,' Rahotep said as though he knew something I did not. All might have been as dust in the wind if he had not spoken further, but he did. He said, 'I have brought gold with me to pay you for all the land along both sides of the river. I have a man ready to take charge of the land and those who work it. You could live in this house without the burden of the land.'"

Ah-mah's jaw dropped and for a moment she could not speak. "What did you do?" she asked when she had recovered.

"I stood, indicating the meal was over. Rahotep and Gedju stood as well. Gedju and I escorted Rahotep down the steps, silent until we reached the ground in front of the house. Then I turned to face him and said, 'You are no longer welcome in this house.'

"Rahotep feigned surprise, but then he smiled, and my mother, it was his smile that made me afraid."

Ah-mah was quiet, absorbing the import of her daughter's words. At last she said, "I have lived a simple life these past years, Ak-hu, and you and Gedju have allowed me to do so. Rahotep is bold and dangerous, but I believe he has met his match in this Mistress of the Land," she said, reaching across the little table to touch Ak-hu's arm.

Wanting to change the subject, Ak-hu asked, "What have you brought with you, Mother?"

"Herbs for you," Ah-mah said, reaching over to pick up the bag. She undid it and pulled out the bundles of herbs, handing each to her daughter, and keeping the bag for another trip.

"Thank you, my mother," Ak-hu said, laying the bundles aside, "but I was not speaking of herbs. What is in that box?"

With delight showing plainly on her face, Ah-mah said, "A warrior came to me with an ailment, and when I asked him to return for further treatment, he brought me this box."

Ak-hu rose and went to the box. "Is there something inside?" she asked.

"Open it and see for yourself."

Ak-hu ran her hands over the wood of the box, a light in her eyes as she felt its smoothness and slid the lid back through its grooves. "Oh, Mother," she said softly, as she touched the beautiful linen. "May I take it out?"

"Of course."

Carefully, Ak-hu drew the bundle of cloth from the box and

unfolded it. "It is a dress! Who could have known? And what is painted here on the front? Feet! And hands?" Beaming love at her mother, Ak-hu said, "The dress of a healer. Is there more to this story, Mother?"

"There is another box."

Folding the dress and laying it carefully on the stone floor, Ak-hu looked inside and drew out the smaller box, quickly opening it. "A cosmetics box!"

"Yes, a cosmetics box. I have looked and looked at the contents, but I do not know how to use them. Will you help me remember?"

Ak-hu was quiet for a moment. "You truly have forgotten? You, who taught me the art of painting the face?"

"The simple life has healed me, Ak-hu. In place of grief, I have my garden with its plants. Without a husband, I have learned to love and care for myself. To do so, I have had to forget some things and learn others."

"Then today, let us celebrate your healing and your return to us by using the contents of this box to enhance your beauty."

With practiced hands, Ak-hu began to separate the strands of Ah-mah's hair, first with her fingers, and then with one of the copper combs. She dipped the tips of her fingers into the unguent, and rubbing them together, started at Ah-mah's forehead, working it into her hair. She dipped more, and worked further, all the way to the end of each strand. When she had finished, she pulled the hair back from Ah-mah's face and fastened it there with the combs.

"Turn around," Ak-hu said. Ah-mah was so relaxed she would have preferred not to move. "Now hold your head up and keep your eyes closed."

Something cool touched her lids, first one and then the other. Ak-hu's strong fingers rubbed a sweetly scented oil onto her forehead, her nose, her cheeks, and her chin. She continued her rubbing to include the neck, both front and back, beneath the luxuriant hair. The scent invigorated Ah-mah and awakened her memory. She struggled to determine the fragrance. When Ak-hu touched her eyelids once more, she knew that her daughter applied a malachite paste. Ak-hu's finger traced around her eyes and over her eyebrows. With sure strokes, more paste was applied to her cheeks and lips.

"Open your eyes, Mother."

Ah-mah stared into the polished copper mirror Ak-hu held in front of her, then drew back until the whole of her face could be seen, framed by glossy hair pulled back with the beautiful combs.

"You have transformed me."

Ak-hu giggled. Putting her arms around Ah-mah, she whispered in her ear, "I love you so, my mother. You do not see your own beauty."

Embarrassed in front of the child she had borne, she said, "Tell me, Ak-hu, tell me true. Am I beautiful because you have painted my face and dressed my hair?"

With the wisdom that comes to each of us at need, Ak-hu said, "My work proclaims your beauty, but it is there for me every time I see you, or think of you, or remember you in my heart. My husband sees it, Mother, as do all of the people who know you and love you. Gedju hopes I will look more like you as I add years. But I am like my father, with large, sturdy bones, and a plain face." Seeing that Ah-mah was about to protest, Ak-hu continued. "Nay, Mother, I do not wish to look like you. I am content with my father's appearance, and Gedju will be also. Your beauty is unique, although An-nah has your slender bones."

Ah-mah stared thoughtfully at her daughter, drinking in the sturdiness of her face, the well-defined jaw line, the generous mouth, the deep-set, black eyes in a face wreathed with finely braided black hair.

"You are like the sacred river, who, with its many moods, nourishes the land and enables it to grow what feeds us. We do not think whether the river is beautiful, we simply depend on it to be what it is, and that in itself is beauty. You underestimate your beauty, my daughter. Your broad face is not plain, but open, just as your father's was. I know of no one else I would trust as deeply."

Ak-hu's face shone as Ah-mah drew her into an embrace, her heart filled to overflowing. "What a gift this warrior has given me! Because of two boxes, I have come home to my daughter and her children. Oh, Khmet! It is good how you live on in her."

CHAPTER SIX

Ah-Mah and Sept

The morning of the seventh day, Ah-mah, in her new dress, watched for Sept from the doorway, her hair and face transformed by the contents of the small box. The green malachite necklace kept finding its way into the hollow between her breasts. Quickly, she plucked out the beads and smoothed the dress so they stayed, for the moment, on top of it. Picking up the copper mirror in her restless fingers, she inspected her eyes. Was the line around them too thick?

"You are beautiful, Ah-mah," Aletha said to her mind. "And just in time, too. Look! He wears new clothes as well. Hmmmm. Now what should we make of that?"

"Shush!" Ah-mah thought as she stepped out of the hut to stand before it. His stride did not falter, but brought him closer and closer until he stood before her. Ah-mah could not stop staring at him, arrayed in a fine linen kilt, gold-wrapped thread creating a subtle border along the hem which just brushed his knees.

"Greetings, Ah-mah." Sept said.

"Greetings, my lord," she replied, automatically, since she had seen his finery, but had already forgotten her own.

He inspected her, up and down, and then, circled her. She wished for the ground to swallow her. She wanted him to touch her. Suddenly, against all reason, a saucy mood came over her and she said, "Do I please you?"

Jerking his gaze up from her bosom where the errant necklace had parted the dress once again, Sept said, "Your beauty takes my breath and does not want to give it back. Come, sit with me beneath the nehet."

Side by side in their finery on the reed mat, Sept spoke first. "I have learned something about you, Ah-mah," he said. "Now that I see you in this dress with your face painted so beautifully, I believe it."

"What have you learned?" Ah-mah asked softly.

"You are Mistress of the Land, ruler of all the land and people on both sides of the river. It is said that your land extends five atours to the south of Nubt and the same to the north."

"My daughter is Mistress, Sept. I gave up that title when I came to live here."

"Nevertheless, you are revered by the people. I am but a warrior, Ah-mah, employed by Rahotep." Sept bowed his head. "I have seen the great stone house of your ancestors. I cannot give you such a house with servants and fine clothing. I would give you my heart, but I fear it is not enough."

"It is more than enough, even though you are employed by Rahotep."

"Does that displease you?"

"Rahotep is ambitious. Since my daughter became Mistress, Rahotep has tried to buy the land that has been in my family for longer than any can remember."

"I did not know this, my dear Ah-mah. It is my only

employment, but I would give it up if you asked."

"I do not ask it. But be wary of your employer, Sept, and tell me of any plans that might involve my family. I do not trust Rahotep."

"I would do that even if you did not ask it. Ah-mah, will you be my wife?"

"I will, dear Sept."

"Then let us be together today, not for treatment, but for the healing your presence brings me. And let us be joined soon, my Ah-mah, for only then will my heart be at peace."

CHAPTER SEVEN

Aletha and the Keeper of Language

Seronak strode through the crowded streets of Atla, capital city of Atlantis, to the docks, with their ships from countless ports, and up the hill behind them. The hut, jammed between two others in a row of rude dwellings and perched on a rocky ledge above the docks, was in the part of Atla inhabited by the poorest day laborers. Nothing on the outside distinguished it from the others except a single rose, picked fresh that morning and clipped to the bit of rope that held the curtain back from the doorway.

The Keeper of the One had tried to disguise himself, pulling the hood of his plain, brown cloak low over his forehead, but Aletha knew him from the moment he bent his tall frame to enter her doorway. The sight of him took her breath, his vital essence preceding him, extending out from his body in waves. Aletha felt them much as sea surf crashing against rock. She breathed deeply to steady herself, and smiled at him.

"Please sit," she said, in fluent Atlantean, indicating a stool just inside the entrance. "I will be finished in a moment."

She had seen him once in the Temple of Healing, one of several imposing structures in the center of the city, his robes of office quite different from the humble brown cloak, his silver hair flying, the silver bushes of his eyebrows jutting out from the base of his high forehead, a silver beard flowing from chin to chest. He was easily the tallest man in Atlantis, and certainly the most formidable, although his power came more from the fire within him than any sizable musculature. Aletha glimpsed slender hands with long fingers as he gathered his robe and folded himself onto the stool.

Refocusing on her customer, a man who was certain his wife had a lover, but whose heart revealed his own untrustworthiness, she concluded her reading with a warning to stay close to home. He took her words to mean that he should keep an eye on his wife, but her intent was to diminish the time he would spend with his mistress. She secreted the coins the man gave her in a pocket of her robe, closing her eyes to his leaving, cleansing her heart in preparation for the one who came next. Not standing for fear of giving away the fact that she knew him, she gestured toward the vacated stool.

"Do you have a question for me?" she asked as he sat down before her.

He said nothing, but reached up with one hand to draw back his hood. She was surprised to see merriment in his face, his gray eyes, a shade lighter than her own, warm, laugh lines raying outward from them. His mouth was generous beneath the beard, his face long. She had not yet looked into his heart, and would not, unless he asked.

"A trusted friend told me of you, Mistress Aletha," he said, his voice unexpectedly deep and musical. She imagined the voice of a mountain or the great sea would be as rich were it to burst forth in song. Once he spoke, she had no defenses, nor did she feel the need for any.

"You are not Atlantean," he said, as though stating a fact.

"I am from Mu," she said.

"Mu does not exist, and has not for many years. Are you descended from survivors?"

"I was born there."

"How can this be? You are young," he said.

Aletha gazed steadily into his eyes, opening her heart to him.

"Will you not answer?" he asked, when Aletha did not speak.

Surprised that he did not read her heart, she said, "I do not know why I do not age, but it seems, at present, that I do not."

"I am told you can see into the future."

With complete honesty, Aletha said, "Nay, Lord, I but look into a person's heart. I see what is. Will you tell me your name?"

"I am Seronak, Keeper of the One. What do you see in my heart?"

"I have not looked, Lord Seronak. I do not look unless I am asked. Do you ask?"

"I do," Seronak said, and placed his hands palms up on the table.

Aletha did not touch him, but closed her eyes and placed her right hand over her heart where the aquamarine lay hidden beneath her robe. She breathed in his essence, getting to know him by his scent, his feel, his taste, letting the gemstone aid her. Her mind drifted, with no purpose other than to know him. His shielding would have been impenetrable had she attempted to thrust herself through it, but he was not prepared to thwart the gentle breeze that cooled his mind, or the whisper that entered his heart. It was a beautiful heart, with wisdom and purity in abundance. As she melded with him, a part of her understood her vulnerability to him, to his strength, which more than matched her own.

"You are afraid," she whispered, genuinely surprised. "Why? Oh.... Disaster comes to Atlantis. Soon. You are not used to being afraid. You feel responsible...for the people...for the destruction. Why would you feel responsible for something you cannot prevent? Oh.... You think you could have prevented it. Not so. Your heart knows you cannot stop the Wheel of Time."

Aletha sat back and opened her eyes. Oddly, Seronak looked smaller, diminished. "That is enough for today."

Seronak had closed his eyes as well, and when he heard her say that the session was ended, opened them slowly, his gaze seeming to return from a great distance.

"You did not speak of loneliness," he said. "You know my fear. No one else does."

Was there more? She waited.

"Atlantis will be destroyed. It will happen in my lifetime. I fear it will happen all too soon." Abruptly, Seronak changed the subject, saying, "Are you comfortable here?"

"My needs are satisfied," Aletha said.

"Perhaps it is foolishness, but I have prepared a house for you. All I ask in return is that you continue to look into my heart and tell me what you see there, holding nothing back."

"To feel the heart is natural to me, my Lord. Muans were connected through the heart from birth. To be separate, as I am now, is unnatural. I would welcome the opportunity to share what I feel in your heart, but I am not sure my doing so warrants an entire house."

"I feel a need for your presence, and your gift. You give me solace just from seeing the fear I have hidden from everyone else."

"You asked, I answered. It is what I do."

"Lady Aletha, you do not fear me." Seronak shifted on the stool before continuing. "Little is hidden from me in this city. Little except what is in my own heart. Will you allow me to present you with this small gift so I may count on you to keep me honest about my feelings? I know my mind, Lady, but I do not know my heart."

"I would be grateful for a house. Indeed, I would be grateful for your visits. The bargain seems weighted in my favor, but I will do my best for you."

"Then come. All is prepared."

The house Seronak brought her to was made of stone and sat high above the city of Atla with windows open to the ocean breezes, and heavy shutters that could be closed when the wind was too cold or harsh. He had seen to the smallest detail, even hiring a maidservant, a scrawny girl with freckles and a turned up nose, her hair in braids. "This is Nyla, Lady Aletha. She has been trained to serve you. Please let her know of anything you might need or want."

Hiding her misgivings that anyone should serve her, she asked, "Would there be a place where I could view the sea?"

Seronak beamed as he said, "Come with me, my lady, and I will show you a balcony where you can gaze at the sea to your heart's content."

The balcony extended out from her sleeping room. As soon as Seronak left, Aletha asked Nyla to help her move the bed to the center of the room so the odor of the sea would reach her, carried on the night breeze.

Aletha blossomed in her new house and her friendship with Seronak grew. Often he joined her on the balcony for long talks and even longer silences. He seemed never to tire of her stories of Mu, and recounting them brought a measure of peace to her heart, making her people seem alive again, instead of ghosts within the sea. In turn, Seronak told her of the Keepers; how they searched the universe for answers and how they sent their combined energy to wherever they deemed it was needed. Including Seronak, there were eight Keepers, not all Atlantean by birth. Seronak's father, his father's father, and on back to the dim beginnings of Atlantis, had been Keeper of the One.

She was most intrigued by the Keeper of Language, asking question after question. Seronak noticed her interest with gratitude, for the Keeper of Language grew ever more frail and there was no replacement.

"What does she do?" Aletha asked.

"She listens," Seronak said.

"To what?"

"To anything that is without a language known to us. She tunes her inner hearing to the subject, be it another race or the music of a star, and she listens carefully until she finds the pattern. Once she has the pattern, she shares it with us."

"Does she speak the language of the pattern?"

"Yes, she gives us the full intent," Seronak said.

"You misunderstand. Does she tell you with the sounds she has heard, or does she share the message using Atlantean words?"

"She speaks to us in our own language. Why do you ask?"

"I thought she might share the new language."

Seronak felt something hidden in Aletha's words, and abruptly exhibited some of the spontaneity that seemed natural to him when they were together. "How many languages do you speak, Aletha?"

"I have not thought of it. Let me see... Muan, of course, and Atlantean, Kala, Kem-t, and about a dozen more."

Seronak pulled his brows together in a frown of intense concentration, eyes closed. "Do you speak any non-human language?"

"Yes."

He opened his eyes. "Tell me," he said.

"Do you know dolphins, my Lord?"

"Those playful creatures of the sea? What do they say to you?"

"They tell me their names." In a softer voice, she continued, "I have heard the voice of one ancient tree and I dream with Hawk."

Tempted to pursue the new and intriguing subjects of dolphins and hawk dreaming and tree-speaking, Seronak remembered his purpose in asking her. "The Keeper of Language is ill, Aletha. I would like you to meet her soon," he said, temporarily forgetting that Aletha would read his heart.

"She is dying! She is dying and you want me to take her place! How could I? I have no great knowledge, no long line of Keepers from which I have descended. Besides, from all you have told me, the Keepers are a breed unto themselves, occupied with roving the stars." Aletha covered her mouth in horror when she realized the import of her words.

"We must seem aloof and out of touch to you, but we face a new challenge now, one that will require all our skill and experience. We must be whole, we must be eight, and there is no one else who can take Girda's place. I have witnessed what you do, Aletha. What would be the harm in meeting with Girda? Would it not be interesting to see what is in her heart?"

Aletha listened intently. "What is the purpose of the Keepers?" she asked.

"We act as the spiritual consciousness of the Atlantean race," was the response.

"How is that possible? Doesn't everyone have his own consciousness? Unless you know my heart, how can you speak for me?" she blurted out before she could stop herself.

Seronak was quiet, thoughtful. "Can you teach me to look into your heart?"

"It is not something I was taught."

"You lost your own people, Aletha. Atlantis is doomed, but surely our people can be saved. Help us. Help me find a way to preserve as much as possible." From the look on her face, he knew he had reached her, he knew she would help, but she was not yet ready to admit it.

"I must search my own heart. I will give you my answer in two days."

That night, she dreamed of Hawk, her messenger, and next morning, the screech of one of the original Hawk's descendants served to wake her. With Nyla's help she fashioned a thick pad for her left shoulder, his favorite perch when he was near.

She poured out her feelings to him as they looked at the distant sea. When there was nothing more to be said, she continued to stare at the sea, the faint sound of the surf comforting. Hawk waited, then cocked his head to look at her before lifting from her shoulder into the sky, his great wings beating a steady rhythm.

Aletha visited Girda, the Keeper of Language, not long after that. Seronak went with her the first time to perform an introduction where none was needed. The two women seemed to know each other, pressing their foreheads together in greeting before Seronak could open his mouth to speak. He withdrew quietly and did not return.

When Aletha saw how close to death the woman was, she and Nyla gathered their few belongings and moved to Girda's house, Nyla joining with Oranica, Girda's maidservant, to ensure both women would have every comfort and not be disturbed.

It was high summer, and the days were filled with more sunshine than was usual for this craggy, wind-swept, stormy island. Aletha often helped Girda to a couch just inside the doorway to the balcony. Girda leaned on the stronger woman, her thin body covered with a heavy cloak. Even so near to the sun's rays, Girda seemed never to be warm.

During that first week, when Girda still had not spoken except through her heart, Aletha asked her why. "Lady Girda, I have so many questions about the Keepers. Will you not answer some of them for me?"

"I have been," was the whispered reply. "Have you not heard all I have said to your mind?"

"Alas, no. I read your heart clearly and without effort, but I do not hear your thoughts."

"Forgive me, Aletha. I forgot you are not Atlantean. We depend on thoughts for communication, and rarely speak."

"All Atlanteans send thoughts?" Aletha asked.

Girda nodded. "All except those who must communicate with the many traders who sail to this island."

"Now I know why Atlanteans seemed so cold to me, not speaking unless I spoke! They were speaking to me all along; I just couldn't hear them." Aletha thought a moment before continuing. "That must mean that they thought I was Atlantean. How could that be?"

"I thought you were Atlantean," Girda said softly.

"Why would you think that?"

"You have a way about you, a calmness, and you resemble Atlanteans in your height. Coloring is not much help, since we are a diverse people, having mated with many others over time."

Aletha looked at Girda, taking in all that she had said. Girda waited, hiding nothing from Aletha. When she sensed Aletha had absorbed this new information, she asked, "Did you speak to each other in Mu, or did you already know what a person would say because of what was in the heart?"

"We did not speak often. Perhaps that is why I did not notice the absence of talking. Girda, tell me of the Keepers."

"First, go to the table and fetch the crystal lying on it."

The crystal was large, filling both Aletha's hands. She brought it to Girda, who said, "Sit, Aletha, and hold the crystal in your hands. Now imagine a crystal as tall as a man and twice as wide, the crystals that power Atlantis. Locan, Keeper of Energy, tends them and oversees their growing. He claims they sing to him."

Aletha started to say that she did hear a kind of humming from the crystal in her hands, but before she could, Girda continued, as though reading her thoughts.

"I have heard a melody from this crystal. Perhaps you hear it also? The energy of the Keepers is crystalline, Aletha. It may seem harsh to you at first, but be patient. The crystals hold a cold light, but have you noticed how this crystal warms in your hands?

"We have not had a heart person in our midst before. Does it not impress you as odd that you should enter our ranks at the time of our ending? Your energy is from the earth, your heart beats in rhythm with its cycles. Our energy is tuned to the stars, the deep cold of space. Hence, we seem cold, aloof, distant, filled with thought but not speech." Her energy spent, Girda closed her eyes and rested. Aletha thought she would sleep, but in a moment, heard Girda's whispering voice once more.

"I do not know what comes, Aletha, but the veils of life grow thinner each day for me. Through them, I see things I do not understand: Crystals, taller than any I've seen; the Keepers gathered together, not in the Crystal Room, but in a home, your home. Last night I dreamed that Seronak lost his beard. It simply slipped off his face. Threaded through everything are dolphins. Why would that be? What do dolphins have to do with the Keepers? I cannot imagine, but Aletha, you must be alert. The earth may give you messages. A chance encounter may spark your thinking along a different path. I think you are somehow a key."

For almost a week of days they talked like this, Aletha's chair scooted up next to Girda's, eyes closed, the crystal in her hands, straining to hear Girda's whispered words. It was afternoon when Hawk interrupted them, his scream reaching them from the sky. He plummeted to the edge of the balcony and stood looking at her for just a moment. Then he spread his wings and let the air beneath them lift him from the balcony, his wings beating slowly, evenly, lifting him ever higher until he was a speck. A last scream, and he was gone.

"Your Hawk is fierce. Did he bring you a message?"

"Yes, Girda," Aletha said, eyes wide with wonder. "He caused me to notice that I can hear you in my mind. How long has this been true?"

"For today at least. Forgive me, Aletha, but it is so much easier."

"Do you hear my thoughts?" she asked in her mind.

"Yes, Aletha," Girda answered in her own.

"Would you hear me if I did not hold the crystal?"

"Lay the crystal aside and see."

Aletha gently placed the crystal on the floor in front of her, for she had grown to think of it as a living thing.

"I love you, Girda." she said in her mind, and heard Girda's clear thought, "We are One."

Less than a month later, Aletha and Girda sat together just inside the balcony room; Girda determined to spend her last day on the couch. "I am so blessed!" she said to Aletha's mind. "My knowledge, my life is remembered because of you." They were her last communicated thoughts.

Aletha stayed beside her, listening as only she could to Girda's fragile heart beating more and more slowly until, at last, it stopped. A faint light rose from Girda's body. It hovered for a moment, as though reluctant to part from the human who had housed it for so long. Then it rose higher and higher, trailing thin strands. One of those strands broke away from the whole and curled around Aletha. Her heart embraced the strand, and as it did, a cloak seemed to enfold her. Without ceremony or official pronouncement, she had become the Keeper of Language.

CHAPTER EIGHT

Aletha's Shame

Aletha dreamed she flew over water, following dolphins, coming at last to the island of Mu, to the Obelon tree high on its cliff, the entrance to her Gardens. Carried on a stream of energy, her light body soared above the familiar paths. A bell sounded, its intrusive voice entering her dream and drawing her back suddenly, quickly, into her body. She stretched, arms extended out over the head of the bed with its exquisite, finely woven sheets, now rumpled and wadded. Lifting her eyelids, just a slit, she saw Nyla at the foot of her bed, a tiny crystal bell in her hand. She looked about to ring it again. Aletha opened her eyes and groaned, "I'm awake." Softening, she said, "Good morning, Nyla."

"Good morning, my lady." With experienced movements Nyla replaced the bell on its shelf and carried a basin filled with steaming water and rose petals to the low table beside Aletha's bed. Turning on her heel, she left the room, her sandals making small, slapping noises on the stone floor.

Aletha liked to be alone in the mornings, alone with the rose water, so near to the odor of the beloved Obelon tree. For a long time the memory of her Gardens, forever lost, had brought only pain, only loss, but finally, her grief went past poignancy. This morning she walked the Gardens in her mind and senses. When she reached the Obelon tree, she imagined wrapping her arms around it, as in reality, she wrapped her arms around herself, beginning the Ritual of the Body.

She hugged her tree/self for several minutes, breathing in the scent of the roses, while imagining them to be blossoms on the Obelon tree. "I am in this body. I belong in this world," she intoned the ritual words. With her left hand she moved energy from her right shoulder down her pale arm to the tips of her fingers, then back to her shoulder and across her chest. Picking up the energy with her right hand, she moved it down her left arm to her fingertips and back. Three times her hands repeated the procedure. The beginning of awakening. When she had completed the ritual exercise, her hands joined, left palm over right, both over her heart. Focusing the strength of her mind on that organ, she pulled energy into it and then out, matching her breath to its pulsing until her body began to tingle. Her breathing slowed as she calmed herself, and gathered her energies for the day.

Rising, she dipped her cupped hands into the bowl of water and tried to hold the scent against her face, still taken aback when the water ran through her fingers onto the floor. She grabbed the towel Nyla had laid by the basin, and squatted to mop up the droplets. Unnoticed, and with perfect timing, Nyla returned, bringing with her a transparent, colorless gown and arranging it carefully over the form used to display it. With deft efficiency, she untangled the bed clothes, and spread them, neatly tucking in corners so that the bed could be used for sitting during the day if need be.

During her Ritual of the Body and her sojourn in the Gardens of Mu, green had impressed itself upon Aletha's mind, as it usually did. She imagined herself wearing a green gown, and as the vision became clearer, the hue of the gown shifted from clearly transparent to pale green, to dark green, the color of the leaves on the Obelon tree. Sending a love-thought to Girda for teaching her the silent language of the mind had become part of the morning ritual as well. Nyla waited until the color was the familiar green, then slipped the gown off the form and over Aletha's head. It fell to the floor, molding gracefully to her body, no longer transparent. She sat and Nyla brushed her long tresses, the golden brown color of honey, with soothing strokes, beginning at her temple and brushing the hair back, the brush gathering the oil from her scalp and distributing it through the hair until it gleamed.

Nyla had not always known how to brush hair, nor had her timing been so in tune with that of her mistress. Aletha chuckled as she remembered when Nyla had been presented to her for the first time. All elbows and knees, Aletha thought, and chuckled again.

"What do you remember, my lady?"

"How do you know I remember?"

"When you chuckle, or smile, or laugh out loud, it is always a memory that causes you to do so."

"Really? Is that true?"

"Yes, my lady." Nyla continued her nearly automatic strokes while she observed her mistress in the looking glass above the small dressing table. Aletha's eyes were thoughtful.

"What else do you know about me, Nyla?"

Taking a deep breath for courage, Nyla released it slowly before speaking. "You are lonely. Since Lady Girda's death, you have had no one with whom you share your heart except Lord Seronak." Nyla's brush halted of its own accord as she stared intently, looking for any sign of disapproval in the reflection of her mistress' face.

"I share my heart with you, Nyla."

"You are my teacher, my mentor. I do not think I have achieved the capacity for the kind of sharing you need." To her surprise, a tear slipped from Aletha's eye and ran down her cheek.

"Forgive me, Nyla. To know someone sees my loneliness overwhelms me." Aletha sighed.

A cry from high up in the sky out her window startled them. "My non-human messenger," Aletha said. Nyla brought the thick pad for Aletha's left shoulder and strapped it into place.

Aletha stood on the balcony and sent a piercing whistle into the sky. Hawk plummeted straight to her shoulder, lifting his wings at the last moment to break the force of his fall. The magnificent bird was almost companion. She had poured out her grief to him in wordless poetry when Girda died. He seemed to have a wisdom, a knowledge of earth and sky that was beyond her reckoning. She envied him the vision of his flight, although in dreams, he occasionally took her with him. Aletha looked out at the rocky wonders of this island, but her eyes did not rest until they reached the sea at its edge. The sea, source of endless water, holding salt and minerals instead of rose petals, the odor of seaweed and fish, familiar and not unpleasant.

This morning's mental walk in the Gardens and Nyla's observation caused emotion to surface in Aletha. She searched for a word to label the emotion. The only one that seemed appropriate was "yearning." For what? For a life that was. A good life. A simpler life than in this extraordinary Atlantis with its sharp angles and hard stone. A softer life, with dirt paths underfoot and houses made from earth and wood. At times she missed the hut where Seronak found her, and the people who lived nearby. They were good people, poor but sturdy, and for the most part, honest. She missed the sounds and smells of the docks, with its multitude of diverse people and goods. A sharp wind blew continuously outside Girda's stone house, now hers, sometimes taking her breath. The Gardens had been warm, the breeze gentle. Not like Ah-mah's dry, dusty land with its hot desert winds and cool nights, but a tropical warmth that held the soft dampness from the sea in its breezes.

"There is change in the air, Hawk. Do you sense it?" Aletha spoke without expecting Hawk to. He would share his message in his own way, his own time. Now he listened, attentive to every word, every movement, looking out at the sea before them, just as she did.

"Do you dream of change, Hawk? Is there rumor in your sky world?"

The next thing Aletha knew, Nyla was shaking her shoulder and Hawk was gone. What had happened? She remembered snatches, and wanted to remember more, but Nyla kept shaking her shoulder. Aletha opened her eyes. The shaking stopped.

"My lady, are you well?" Nyla asked.

Aletha's eyes were open, but her mouth could not yet wrap itself around words. Nyla hurried back into the room to fetch a cup of water. Putting the cup to Aletha's lips, she licked her own unknowingly, silently willing her mistress to drink. A sigh escaped those unmoving lips, as Aletha crumpled in a heap. Nyla called out and a servant came running from the corridor outside Aletha's sleeping room. Together they lifted Aletha and laid her on her bed. Nyla pulled a chair up close and dismissed the man with a nod.

* * *

From the height of a cloud, she saw a great river, its ribbon dividing a brown, thirsty land. Tiny paths led from the river across the land and she was drawn to one of them and the two who walked the path, hand in hand. A man and woman, familiar to her, paid no attention as she swooped over them. Neither heard her scream before the heated currents lifted her higher and higher making the river a ribbon again. Restless, abandoned, she followed it to the sea.

High over that watery body she flew, looking, searching, thinking she spied something on a wave, finding it was not what she wanted. Where is he? In some part of her, Aletha knew she was in Hawk's dream and not her own. She flew on.

He entered her mind just before she saw him. She rested, floating on a current of air, circling as it circled. He danced in the water beneath her, leaping with the joy inherent to his species. "How old are you?" she thought to him, the question emerging from she knew not where.

"I am ancient," she heard in her mind. "I am earth and water. I am form and not-form. You are not-form and form. In your sleep time you are not-form and in your waking time you take form. I am dolphin. What are you?"

From the depths of her soul Aletha sent words to him on Hawk's piercing scream. "I am human in Hawk's dream."

* * *

When Aletha opened her eyes, she was surprised to be in her bed, Nyla dozing in a chair beside it. Closing her eyes, Aletha tried to recall her dream. Something about dolphins. Why would she dream of dolphins?

Nyla stirred, causing Aletha to open her eyes again. "Are you awake, Nyla?" she asked.

"Yes, my lady," Nyla said, stifling a yawn. Then, remembering the scare her mistress had given her, she asked, "How do you feel?"

"Rested and peaceful. Have I been asleep long?"

Nyla looked through the door to the balcony. "All morning and part of the afternoon."

"That explains why I am hungry. Let's go see what we can find to eat!"

Nothing seemed amiss with Aletha for days afterwards, but all was not well. Bits and pieces of the dream surfaced at odd times, stirring up feelings, causing acute awareness of a loss Aletha had admitted to no one.

One morning, not long after the incident, Nyla entered Aletha's room to find that she was not in her bed, but standing on the balcony looking out into the distance. Setting the bowl of steaming water and rose petals on its table, she noticed the bed had not been slept in. Aletha seemed drawn to the fragrance and came inside to sit on the bed, glancing absently at the bowl. When Nyla returned with the filmy, translucent gown, Aletha had not moved.

"My lady, are you well?" Nyla asked. Silence. Nyla moved closer to Aletha and touched her shoulder. "My lady?" Aletha shuddered, her head jerked up, and she looked at Nyla but did not see her. Then she lay back on the bed and brought her arm up to hide her eyes.

Alarmed at this unprecedented behavior and the drawn face she had glimpsed, Nyla hurried to the hallway and beckoned with her hand. A young boy came running, ready to obey instantly any command she might give to him.

"Go to the house of Lord Seronak, Keeper of the One. Tell him he is needed urgently at the house of the Lady Aletha, Keeper of Language. Go!" Nyla could not help but give him a slight push with her palm as he turned and ran down the corridor. She wished her gift of telepathy extended to Lord Seronak in that moment, so frightened was she for her mistress. Drawing a chair to her bed, Nyla sat, watchful for any sign either hidden or overt that would give her some indication of what troubled her mistress so acutely.

Seronak came within the hour, his robes hastily donned, his silver hair flying. Nyla met him at the door to Aletha's room. "What is wrong?" he asked.

"I do not know, Lord. I think you should see for yourself."

Aletha had not moved, her arm still covered her eyes. "You were right to summon me, Nyla. Now leave us, dear girl. I will call you when there is need," Seronak said.

Sitting in Nyla's vacated chair, Seronak observed Aletha closely. Her breathing seemed labored, and periodically, a sigh escaped her lips. Slow tears rolled down her cheeks from eyes still hidden by the ever present arm.

"I have lost her, Seronak."

"Who?" Seronak's deep voice was calm, and even at its softest, threatened to fill the room, just as his presence seemed to pervade its space and bring Aletha back from wherever she had gone.

"We have been together since before she was born. Now she is gone." Aletha flung the arm away from her face and sat up. Seronak was alarmed at her appearance. Her eyes were red and swollen, her energy so close to her body as to be nearly invisible. Who had she lost? And why was that person so important? A constant companion. Girda? Surely that grief had been tempered. Seronak knew of no one Aletha currently saw on a daily basis other than Nyla, and she certainly was not lost.

Carefully, gently, Seronak touched her knee. She flinched, but did not draw away. "Who have you lost, my Lady?"

Frustrated by her inability to explain what was so deep inside her, Aletha felt her emotions surge. She rose from the bed to pace the room. "I survived the loss of my homeland, my family, my people, Seronak. We speak glibly of the coming inevitable loss of Atlantis. I fear in a way others cannot. I do not wish to be forgotten. I fear this time I will be."

Seronak waited, all senses alert, listening to every word and the energy behind it, feeling Aletha circling the core of the thing that terrified her, much as her beloved Hawk circled as he looked for prey. He wished, in that moment, that he had learned to read hearts as she did.

"I am ashamed, Seronak. I am ashamed of what I have done, and devastated that I might no longer be able to do it."

Seronak's eyes clouded and misted over as he perceived the depth of her pain. He started to speak words of comfort, meaningless words, but Aletha continued.

"Long time I grieved when Mu was lost to me, hardly sane." Seronak nodded, but otherwise held himself perfectly still. "In the depths of my grief, I sent my soul roaming and connected with an unborn child in a land I did not know, a time that is yet to come. She welcomed me and I have been her other voice from earliest memory, the companion in her mind. We grew together through her childhood and budding womanhood. When she married, although I did not intrude on her intimate times with her husband, we shared secrets like giddy maidens. She bore a child, and I rejoiced, for once more I, too, had a family. When her husband died and she left her ancestral home for a gardener's hut, I was her constant companion."

A sob was torn from Aletha, and for a moment she halted, unable to speak. The pacing resumed. "I knew the moment I saw him that she would love him. I loved him, Seronak. His body, tall and muscular, his skin dark, his eyes dark pools, sensitive, strong, not the same pale eyes and skin I knew, but the same soul. Aye, I loved him, for he was my beloved, incarnate once more. I recognized his love for her before she did. I saw that he wanted her, and more, that he needed her." Aletha's voice trailed off, as she sat once more on the bed and stared into nothingness. Her voice was low when she spoke again, and Seronak strained to hear her. "Ah-mah is a beautiful soul, Seronak. I want to be with her, for she is like my child and my dearest friend, but a high wall has raised itself between me and my precious Ah-mah now that she is with Sept who was Jonat. My heart is a lump inside my chest. My body has the will to live, but I do not."

For a time Seronak and Aletha sat, Seronak's great mind rushing through a multitude of thoughts, Aletha spent with telling. Gently he pushed her shoulder so that she lay on the bed. Brushing her forehead with his lips, he said, "Sleep, Aletha. I will be here when you awaken."

Aletha did sleep, deeply, for the rest of the morning and on into the afternoon. The food and drink Nyla brought to Seronak lay untouched, his mind too busy to feel hunger or thirst. This woman had connected with someone in another time, and had stayed connected for many years. How many? Did it matter? Now the connection was broken, broken because her reincarnated husband had found her mind companion. Did she not understand the idea of reincarnation? Surely she must know that her connection with Ah-mah went far beyond chance. The Keepers must hear of this, Seronak decided. But not yet. Aletha was too fragile. How could he help restore her calm strength, strength he had grown to value, to trust, perhaps to love?

When Aletha awoke, the sun was nearing the western horizon. Seronak, knowing that sleep began healing, but answers were necessary to complete it, did not delay in asking the question paramount to Aletha's restoration. He smiled at her and took her hand before asking, "What can keep you from being lost, dear lady?" When Aletha looked at him, he saw a spark of interest, and waited.

"I do not know," Aletha said. "But, I want to."

"As you were speaking of this woman and this man, I saw feet in my mind. Feet walking a dirt path. Could those be your feet, my lady? Would you like to walk a dirt path?"

Definite interest, even curiosity filled those haunted eyes. "I had not thought of it, my Lord, but yes, I believe my feet hunger for dirt."

"I was born on an island not far from here. I return there when I need time to myself. Recently I have thought it would be pleasant to walk on its many dirt paths. The walking, the touching of the earth, clears my thinking as nothing else can. I would be honored to have you accompany me on my next visit. We could leave in a few days. Would that be agreeable to you?"

Grateful tears filled Aletha's eyes and threatened to spill down her cheeks. "That would be most agreeable."

Seronak stood and walked onto the balcony high above the city. He looked out at the rocks upon which the house was built to the sea beyond, the sky above. After a time, Aletha joined him, as he knew she would. He spoke softly, for her ears alone.

"One of my gifts as Keeper of the One is to see threads of time as they spin. I am able to follow these threads to their origins, and sometimes to what appears to be the future. Always, there are many threads, and to follow one exclusively is dangerous, since it is but one of the paths our past and present have set spinning. I see threads spinning around you, connecting you to this woman of another time, connecting you to this man of your time and her time. But more, I see that you have set something in motion that will affect Atlantis, and more specifically, the Keepers. You think you have been selfish in following need generated by grief. But I perceive a gift in what you have done.

"Come with me to the island, Aletha, and when you have walked for a while, perhaps you will feel restored enough to want to share your story with the Keepers." Seronak turned, his gaze meeting hers, as he said, "I think you will speak again with this woman from another time. It will happen when you both are ready."

CHAPTER NINE

Aletha and the Dolphin

Not long after dawn, Aletha's feet touched a new path on Seronak's island. Although faint, the tiny ribbon of dirt was easy to follow since it made its way along the most logical route to the beach below. Aletha had not worn sandals since leaving the ship, her bare feet enthralled by the dirt beneath them. Now, as she reached the sand, they fairly shouted their joy to her.

Tall rock walls extended from the beach out into the water, lowering as they reached the sea, creating a lagoon protected from the strong-surfed ocean. She dropped her garment and dove into the water. With long, sure strokes, she swam away from the beach, then turned over to float on her back.

The island restored her in ways she had not known she needed. For the first time since Mu was destroyed, she felt free from the need to survive for one more day, free to let the water support her. She had not yet restored her connection with Ah-mah, but today, that did not seem so devastating. "Dear Ah-mah," she said, sighing with the breeze.

An insistent nudge interrupted her. Glistening skin told her who it was.

"Hello!" she called in her mind, and heard a stream of clicks and a whistle. Pursing her lips, she whistled back and made clicking noises with her tongue and teeth.

"Our songs speak of you, Letha, who speaks our language," he said to her mind. "What brings you to our world?"

Ignoring the missing letter in her name, Aletha thought back to him, "I have come for the joy of it, Hukuhu."

"A good reason, but not the only one."

"Do you think of time or place? Is this the only time in which you exist? The only place?"

The dolphin did not answer, but positioned himself so that his dorsal fin extended toward her. She took it as an invitation and grabbed hold, trailing alongside him as he towed her easily out to the rocks which acted as barrier to the sea.

"You climb over rocks."

Aletha let go of the dolphin, clambered up the wet rocks and dove into the ocean on the other side. The dolphin welcomed the return of her hand to his fin, taking her into deep water and the seven other dolphins in his pod. Still holding his fin, Aletha watched as the other dolphins circled them, rhythmically diving and surfacing, diving and surfacing. Her eyes closed.

"Picture your garden," Hukuhu said to her mind.

Immediately, she saw the Obelon tree and her bench overlooking the sea. The vision captured her, seeming more vivid than before. She sat on the bench. Soon Jonat would be calling her home. As she thought it, she heard his voice, the voice she never thought to hear again.

Shift. She stood on the tallest hill on the island, her people encircling her, their arms raised skyward. Their heart energy melded with hers as they sent Earthsong to the stars.

Another shift. Aletha walked a dirt path in a dry and dusty land, a jar balanced expertly on her head, other pots and jars hanging ingeniously from thongs around her waist. Her heart was at peace, her steps sure, the river near.

All was dark. No light. Not a fearful dark. Just dark. Black. One tiny spark lit up the dark briefly, then another. Soon hundreds, thousands of sparks made the dark day.

A woman looked out to sea. Her hair, once dark blond, sported silvery threads, her face weathered by many years of watching the far horizon. A man joined her on the wooden pier built out into a lagoon. They spoke softly of other times, of a friend, and as they spoke, they looked younger. Suddenly, they were in the water with a dolphin, swimming together. The dolphin was their friend.

A great crystal stood before a table upon which lay a tall man with long silver curls. Seronak! Others surrounded the table, watching as the man was transformed into dolphin.

Aletha's hand slipped and she went under, the dolphins stopping their circling to lift her from the water. Hukuhu called to her in his mind.

"Letha?"

Aletha opened her eyes, and seeing the dorsal fin once again in front of her, took hold of it, and allowed the dolphin to tow her back toward the lagoon.

Still in the dreaming, she clambered back over the rocks into the lagoon, and allowed him to tow her nearly to the beach before she let go, paddling to stay afloat.

"Letha? Were the pictures in your mind past or future or now? Were they in this place, or in another? You are form and not-form. Will you be dolphin?"

CHAPTER TEN

The Bargain

"Oh, bother!" Ah-mah's disgust spewed the words from her mouth. She could see the priest coming straight for her door. She contemplated telling him she had been called away on some urgent errand, far away, back to her birth home or Remtu's hut, back to people she understood. "But," she thought, "I am the wife of Rahotep's Master of Guards and must treat this priest with the dignity he deserves." She chuckled. "If I did that, he would not enter my garden!"

She listened for Aletha's teasing. It did not come, and had not for the year since she and Sept had declared their love. A year of many changes, but none so devastating as that. In truth, Aletha's absence was one source of Ah-mah's foul disposition. Another was the Nubtians. With no inkling that her reputation with feet had preceded her to the village, she did not understand their demands. The lines outside their home grew ever longer, and often Ah-mah spent the entire day working the feet of as many as she could. Most of the people were healthy and had no complaint, coming only because the treatments relaxed them. Then there was the garden, continually trampled by the inconsiderate as they tried to be first in line, or at least, near the front.

Taking one last sip of water, Ah-mah set her cup down and went to the doorway. She arrived just as the priest did.

"Do you have need of me, holy one?" she asked.

"Oh, Lady, my heart is relieved to find you. I do not come for myself, but for another who is in the temple and cannot leave. He is ill and needs your help."

"Tell me about him." Ah-mah said.

"There is no time. We must return at once."

"I must know what to take with me." Ah-mah was not budging.

Seeing the set of her jaw, the priest said, "He is doubled up with pain in his stomach. He moans constantly, and cries out from time to time with the agony of it. His screams have deafened us for hours."

"Hours? What did he do before the pain started? Did he eat a meal? What did he eat? Has he been here long? Where is his home?" Ah-mah's tone demanded answers.

"He is from the great sea to the east and arrived last night having spent many days in the desert. He came to us to speak of spiritual matters, and to ask for blessing from Ra. Since he is a person of importance in his land, we prepared a feast to welcome him. We shared a roast fowl, dates, bread, and we drank some quantity of beer."

"How do you know he is important?"

"Because he showed us his seal. Also, his clothes are well made and costly, and he has many rings on his fingers."

"Wait here," Ah-mah said, and went back inside to gather her bag of herbs and potions. She thought of the patch of mint in her garden, grown from a new plant brought to her by one of the caravans, and went to cut several leafy stalks which she wrapped in clean linen, adding them to the bag hanging over her shoulder by its leather strap.

The priest waited, standing first on one foot and then the other in a kind of clumsy dance. As soon as Ah-mah emerged with her bag, he fell into step beside her, and together they hastened to the temple.

The man was doubled up in a near fetal position, his moans much softer than those described by the priest. Ah-mah knelt on the floor beside him, having removed the bag from her shoulder. Immediately, she noted the man's thinness. His hands held no extra flesh. One of the rings had fallen off, being much too large for his slender finger. When she pushed back the sleeve of his robe, his arm was bone covered by skin, but not much flesh. This "rich" man had been starving until last night's feast. She drew the linen wrapped mint from her bag.

"Bring heated water," she said. Immediately a bowl of steaming water was placed at her side by one of the well-trained priests. She put the mint into the bowl and spread one of the linen cloths flat. To the priests who hovered, watching her every move, she said, "Remove his robe."

Two priests set to the task. One rolled him while the other drew his arm from the garment, then rolled him back so the other arm could be drawn out. Even in his agony, the man resisted this undressing, confirming Ah-mah's suspicion that he wished his body to remain hidden. Ah-mah ignored the priest standing behind her who gasped when he saw the ribs of the man clearly.

His stomach was swollen from too much food too soon after his long fast.

"Bring him to a sitting position," she said.

When the priests had managed it, she dipped a cup into the bowl of hot, minty water and put it to his lips, forcing him to take several sips. When she saw he could not drink more, she bade the priests allow him to lay down. Taking one of the linen cloths, she dipped it into the hot water, holding it by the corners. "Hold him straight," she commanded. One priest moved to his head and held the man's shoulders, the other moved to his feet, and pulling on his ankles, straightened his legs. The man groaned. She knew the heat could scald his skin, but it would be temporary, and might serve to take his mind from the pain in his stomach. She was right. When she laid the hot cloth on his stomach, he passed out.

She moved to his feet, and picking up the left foot, pushed her fist into the sole, into the area she had determined, from practicing on many sufferers in the past year, governed the stomach. As she worked, she watched the man's breathing. Thin as he was, he had good bones, and a good pulse in his ankle. Suddenly, a bold, rash idea came to her. As soon as she could, she would remove this young man to her home. Why? She would never be able to answer with certainty. Was she taken in by his emaciated body? Perhaps. Was it her instinct to mother? She would like to fatten him up, but to what purpose, she did not know, nor did she care in her haste to have him safe in her home, safe from the priests.

"This man needs constant tending. You must bring him to my house in one hour. I will go now to make preparations to receive him." Ah-mah thanked whatever gods might be watching for her good fortune. The high priest was absent, and these priests were so used to taking orders, they did not think to question her. The high priest would have. His ambition to control others was as palpable as Rahotep's.

She patted the man's stomach, relieved to see it less distended than before. If her luck held, his bowels would release before the priests brought him to her and they would have the pleasure of cleaning him up. She called over her shoulder as she left, "Mind you, be certain to bring all his belongings as well."

What had gotten into her? Her mood was so strong, she realized she might have said those words in the presence of the high priest. Dangerous. She must calm herself.

As Ah-mah returned from the temple, she remembered her encounter with Khufer, the high priest, at the recent harvest festival. Khufer and Rahotep had greeted her with respect, but something was not right to Ah-mah's eyes. She sensed secrets hidden in the words he spoke to her and to Rahotep who sat beside him. When Ak-hu and Gedju arrived and the people exuberantly welcomed them, Ah-mah was stunned by the malice evident in Rahotep's eyes, and the ambivalence in Khufer's. Surely, she must be more careful of her words.

The village of Nubt was not large, and even though the house where she and Sept lived stood away from the rest, Ah-mah covered the distance quickly. Most of the houses bordering the path had gardens in the back. Knowing how much she loved gardens, Sept, who fancied himself a kind of designer of houses, created space for a garden both in front and in back of their house. The back was more private, enclosed with a high mud-brick wall, but the front had been Ah-mah's showplace, sporting riotous color and delicious fragrances. A low wall marked the boundaries of the front garden but did little to keep out disrespectful feet.

Paying no attention to the garden's disarray, Ah-mah rushed into the house and stirred the coals, adding more dung. Before the flames subsided she hung a pot filled with water on the hook above the fire. She would put the boy in the room she kept for Ak-hu's visits. She need not have hurried. The priests did not bring the young man for several hours. Ah-mah's prediction had come true, and the priests had done their best to clean him. They looked quite disheveled when they finally arrived, sweating profusely.

"Bring him into this room and lay him on the bed," Ah-mah

said. "Gently, gently. Do you not see he is still in pain?"

The priest who had first come to her door said, "We will pray to Ra for this man's recovery. We are grateful to leave him in your capable hands."

"I am certain of it," Ah-mah thought. To the priest she said, "Did you bring all his things, as I asked?"

"Yes, Lady, they are all here."

"Good. I will take care of him now," she said.

Ah-mah brought more of the mint in a bowl of hot water and set it beside his bed. She did not intend to lave the young man or make him drink more of the mint water, but was content to let him sleep now that the mint, the priests, and his own body had done their best. His color was much better, his abdomen no longer a rounded lump of agony, but flattened to what she suspected was near normal. She sat in the chair and closed her eyes, letting the aroma of mint pervade her senses. Its freshness brought joy to her heart and made her think of Aletha. "Where are you, my dear friend, sister of my heart? Why will you not speak to me?" No answer, but Ah-mah had become used to that. Still, she waited, hoping, ready to welcome Aletha's teasing wit.

"Have they gone?" the young man asked.

Startled, Ah-mah said, "Hmmph?"

"The priests. Have they gone?" he repeated.

Ah-mah's eyes were open now, and she saw deep brown ones staring back at her from a well-formed, proportional face.

"Yes, they are gone. How are you feeling?"

"Weak, but without pain. Lady? What is that wonderful smell?"

"Mint. To heal your spirit and restore your health, although I imagine a steady diet of decent food would do just as well."

"I eat quite well, and every day," the young man said, eyes flashing.

"That might have worked with priests, but not with me. What is your name?"

"I am called Lord Kaliph by my subjects."

"Forgive me, Lord Kaliph, if I do not bow." Ah-mah tried to look sternly at the young man, but knowing his vulnerable state, she softened and said, "You are safe here. You were not safe in the temple. Tell me, what is your real name? And are you slave or free?"

In a low voice he said, "I am slave."

"And your name?"

"My master called me Secono, but my mother named me Nefer."

"Nefer. That is a good name, and rings true for you. You will be called Nefer in this household. May you bring us the good luck your name implies."

"Am I to stay here then, Lady?"

"First, where is your master?"

"In the desert, dead."

"Did you kill him?"

"No, Lady. Raiders did."

"Why did they not kill you as well?"

"I had left the camp to make water, and when I heard the raiders, I stayed hidden in the darkness."

Ah-mah looked hard at him, then clasped her hands together in her lap and closed her eyes. He thought at first that she slept, but soon her eyes opened and she said, "A last question and I will leave you in peace. Are you marked as slave?"

"No, Lady. My master did not believe in it. On the sole of one foot I have a red mark from birth, but it is not something I ever showed to my master."

"Then, if you will, you shall stay here in my employ. I cannot pay you, but you will have food daily and a place to sleep. In return, I would ask that you help me in my garden, and with the people who come to me for treatment. If you are clever enough to make priests think you are nobly born, perhaps you can devise a way to keep people from trampling my plants while they wait. What do you think?"

Nefer's tears were answer enough, but he fell on his knees before her, grasping her hands in his, thanking her over and over again.

She suffered him for a time, but then she bade him return to his bed. "You embarrass me with your gratitude, Nefer. You must save your strength for your duties, and I must remember my need to be your healer at present and fetch some broth for you." When Ah-mah returned, she sat on the bed with Nefer and held the cup to his lips. His stomach did not rebel this time, as she knew it wouldn't, and very soon, his eyelids drooped and he fell asleep.

Ah-mah got up as though to leave, but instead sat in the chair once again, watching him. As his face relaxed, she saw that he was younger than she had thought, probably not yet fourteen. He reminded her of those honest field hands. Nefer had lied, but only for survival, and not because it was his nature. Ah-mah knew in her heart that this boy, as she now thought of him, would be to her and Sept as a son, the son he desired, but that she could not give him. She smiled and reached over to lightly stroke his brow. His relaxation seemed to deepen at her touch, and a faint smile lifted the corners of his mouth.

When Sept returned home in the late afternoon, Ah-mah was treating feet and Nefer still slept. He stood at the back doorway of their house, as he always did, to let her know he was home. Anticipating Sept's arrival, Ah-mah told the waiting people that the woman she currently treated would be the last of the day. She finished with the left foot, having already treated the right, and sent the woman on her way.

In the house, Ah-mah took Sept's arm and said, "Come with

me. I have something to show you." She led him to the doorway of the room where Nefer slept.

"Who is he?" Sept asked.

"A gift from the priests," Ah-mah said.

Nefer awoke, and seeing Sept, rose quickly to stand beside the bed as if awaiting judgment. Ah-mah would not have the boy feel unwelcome, nor unsafe. She went to him, and putting her hand on his shoulder, said to Sept, "This is Nefer. He is going to help me keep people out of my front garden. Nefer, this is Sept, my husband." Before either could say anything, she continued, "The evening meal is ready."

After the meal, Ah-mah and Sept went for a walk along the river. "You believe this boy?" Sept asked. "You believe that he did not kill his master and rob him of his belongings?"

"My heart does, Sept. I cannot prove his story, nor can I disprove it. Proof may lie in the desert, but I have no wish to go there. I trust Nefer. I have told him he is to be in our employ."

"What are you going to do about the high priest? Will he not be told about the boy when he returns? Will he not want the boy to be his?"

"If I take the clothes and rings to the priests and tell them that this boy found them and tried to pretend he owned them in order to get food, maybe that will be enough booty for Khufer. Nefer should be with us, Sept. I feel it in my heart."

Ah-mah's eyes held such pleading, Sept knew he could not object.

"What else does your heart tell you about this boy, my wife?"

"He will be as a son to us, Sept. I cannot explain how I know this, but I do. We will not be sorry we have trusted him and given him a home."

Thus, Nefer became part of the household of Sept and Ah-mah. From that first day, when Ah-mah fed him sips of broth, he loved her. She became his mother, and Sept, his father, but the full price for keeping Nefer was yet to be exacted.

Khufer, the High Priest of Ra, returned the following week from a journey down the sacred river, and hearing the tale from the priests, sent one of them to fetch Ah-mah. She had harbored a fool's hope that the priests would not tell him, or that he would ignore the incident, but in her heart, she knew he would not. She went with the priest, stopping just long enough to fetch a small bag she had prepared earlier.

When the priest ushered her into the same room where she had first treated Nefer, Khufer was nowhere to be seen. She stood quietly, knowing the confrontation was inevitable, and armed with her decision to tell the truth insofar as she knew it, was not afraid. The sooty smell of sacrifices pervaded the room. She moved toward the opening that led to a wooden deck overlooking the river, hoping to breathe fresh air.

"The river is particularly beautiful at this time of day." The high priest stood at the edge of the deck, waiting for her. Ah-mah nodded and went to stand with him.

For a time Ah-mah and Khufer watched the river, golden in the light of the setting sun. Soon he would be called to perform the ritual demanded by the god at his setting. Ah-mah, who had difficulty thinking of the great radiant sun as god, could not fathom such ritual. Sept had schooled her in the sacrifices she must perform, the rituals required of anyone living in Nubt and under the protection of both Rahotep and Ra. Ah-mah obeyed them with reluctance, her feet often straying to the river once she left the temple. These rituals were new, as the temple was new, and she had not needed to perform them when she was Mistress of the Land.

"I understand you have a new servant in your employ, Lady Ah-mah," Khufer said.

"Yes, my lord." Better not to volunteer information.

"My priests have told me of the peculiar circumstances under which your new servant arrived. Would you care to tell me what you know?" Not a question, but a command.

Ah-mah did tell Khufer, holding nothing back, including the knowing in her heart that she could trust Nefer. Khufer listened carefully, aware that Ah-mah spoke honestly, and without guile. Secretly, he admired her, finding her old-fashioned wisdom refreshing, but he wanted something from her, and felt his god had dropped this incident into his lap, so to speak, that he might obtain what he wanted.

When she had finished her tale, he spoke the words he had rehearsed. "Lady Ah-mah, you know that, by rights, the boy should be returned to the temple where he first sought refuge. I thank you for returning the rings and clothing of the boy's master to us, but if I speak to Lord Rahotep, you will be powerless to keep him. I find myself upon the horns of dilemma, caught between duty to the law, and the dictates of my heart. How do you think this dilemma might be resolved?"

Ah-mah had anticipated his question, having learned much of the art of dwelling in Nubt, of paying for everything either with goods or service. She abhorred the need for cleverness, but Nefer had won her heart.

"I would not presume to have the answer, my lord, but perhaps if I came once each ten days to wash my lord's feet and rub them with oil scented with herbs, the burden would be eased."

"The priests of Ra have wished for your ministrations, Lady, but they were hesitant. I believe this matter could be resolved if you were to allow them to come to you four afternoons each month, with perhaps an hour reserved for me. The young man could assist you, and thereby learn more of your art."

"One afternoon each month, and I would come to you for an hour as well."

"Two afternoons, and you would need to see me no more than twice each month."

"Agreed. And Nefer will stay with Sept and me."

"As of this moment, Nefer is yours. When can you begin?"

"I can begin now, my Lord." So saying, Ah-mah indicated a chair and lowered herself to the floor to rub Khufer's feet with scented oil from her bag, silently thanking the river for this happy moment, this small price to pay for Nefer's freedom. In that moment, she almost thought of the great liquid ribbon as a god.

CHAPTER ELEVEN

Ah-Mah Hears a Voice

The priests started coming to Ah-mah's house the next week, two one day, and two another. She asked that they not come until after midday, and they scrupulously adhered to her wishes, not because she asked, but because the high priest commanded it.

On the days the priests were to come, Ah-mah finished with the people before the sun was high, and Nefer told the ones who waited to come back the next morning. News of Ah-mah and her treatments had spread beyond the village so that those who waited included people from other villages. Nefer had solved the problem of Ah-mah's garden being trampled with Sept's help. Together they had added bricks to the low wall surrounding it, making it waist high, so now the people gathered outside that wall and did not come inside until Nefer beckoned. In addition, Nefer checked the line each morning, asking those whose feet had been treated in the past week to go home and not return until ten days had passed. Soon, except for those few who seemed to always take advantage where they could, all obeyed the new rule.

With so many people wanting her treatments, Ah-mah asked Nefer to wash the feet of those who came and to oil those whose calluses might interfere with the treatment. Thus, Nefer handled each pair of feet first, washing them and drying them with a rag. He caught Ah-mah's eye as the first priest entered her treatment room beneath the two young nehets. Sept had placed them in the walled-in garden at the back of the house so that one shaded in the morning, the other in the afternoon. She soon understood the meaning of the look on Nefer's face. The priest's feet were soft and spongy, the slightest touch bringing perspiration. Nefer brought her a rag, and she wiped the man's feet during the treatment to keep her hands and her thumbs from slipping. What could make his feet sweat so? Her mind reviewed what she knew of his activities. He participated in the daily rituals, he ate, he slept. That was all she knew.

"What are your duties in the temple?" Ah-mah asked, hoping his answer would help her find the cause of all the water seeping from his feet.

"I am responsible for the care and feeding of the god Ra."

When the priest said nothing else, Ah-mah blurted out, "Is that all you do?"

"No, Lady. I accept the gifts of the people to their god. I tally them, I sort them, and I present them to the High Priest for distribution."

"Do you ever walk?"

"I walked here."

"Do you walk every day?"

"My duties keep me too busy for walking."

"What do you do when you are not required to serve Ra?"

"I always serve Ra, Lady."

Ah-mah was quiet for the rest of the time, working the toes, then wiping, working the heel and wiping, working, wiping. The feet had a sponginess similar to the feet she had treated of those who were dying. This man held too much water in his body. In a dry land with a river to hold water, the people must be dry as well.

When she finished the treatment, the priest thanked her, and went to sit on a bench nearby to wait for his fellow priest to be treated. Ah-mah stood and stretched. As the next priest was about to lie down, she noticed puddles of water on the mat. Reaching past him, she gathered it up, shaking off the water, and turned the mat over to present its dry side.

"Do not sit on the mat yet," she said to the priest, and went into the house where she poured water from the jar into her cup. Nefer joined her.

"I do not understand how I can be thirsty after treating such sweaty feet."

"What causes the feet to be that way, Ah-mah?"

"My mind searches for an answer, Nefer."

"Is it because they are fat?"

"I do not know. My heart tells me it is because they do not move very much. They do not walk or do many of the things we do daily. Even their food is brought to them by people who think they bring food to a god. Bring a dry mat and follow me."

Nefer, at Ah-mah's direction, took up the damp mat, and put down the dry one. The second priest lay down on the mat, and Ah-mah began the treatment. Prudently, she had brought a dry rag with her. This priest was a little taller, a bit slimmer, but still, liquid poured off him. She noticed that his skin had a strange, unhealthy hue. For perhaps the ten thousandth time, she wished for Aletha. As she worked this priest's feet and wiped them, worked and wiped, she spoke to Aletha in her mind. "I miss your teasing, Aletha. You could always make me laugh. What would you think of these feet? Of these men who do nothing but take in the name of service? Would you see their unhappiness, their restlessness, their silly pride? Or would you think I am the silly one? Am I, Aletha? Do I think I know something of these priests because their feet reveal it? Do I tease myself?" No answer. Ah-mah could have cried with frustration.

Suddenly, Ah-mah was no longer beneath the nehet in her garden, but flew high over water that covered the earth from horizon to horizon. She had never imagined such water, but she was not afraid. The sky held her and would not let her fall. Beneath her, fishes, larger than any she had seen, leaped from the water, sending geysers of it toward her as they dove beneath its surface. Her dream-self flinched and would have flown away but for the voice that spoke. "Dolphins," it said.

Her thumb slipped and brought her back. "Dolphins," she thought as she wiped. Only after the priests left did she recognize the voice as Aletha's. In her joy, the priests and their sweaty feet were forgotten.

CHAPTER TWELVE

The Keepers of Atlantis

Made entirely of crystals fused together, the Crystal Room glowed softly and held sound as a living thing. Everything in the room was crystalline except the Keepers, their robes, the brazier with its eternal fire, and the tiny silver bell that Seronak used to bring their attention to one matter or another. Nestled in the center of the Temple of the Keepers, it could be entered only by passing through one of eight rooms that surrounded it like the spokes of a wheel. From the time of its building in the earliest days of Atlantis, each of the rooms had been made sacred to a Keeper's purpose, serving both for meditation and as a place of preparation for entering the sacred center of the Temple. Each room had a door at either end; one to access the central crystal room, and the other to exit the Temple.

As the Keepers entered the Crystal Room, their whispered chants echoed from the hard crystal walls. When all were seated in the crystalline chairs, the whispering stopped. Seronak voiced a deep bass tone and the other Keepers pitched their voices one or two octaves above his. The octaves grew in strength and depth, bringing a powerful thrusting energy into the room. Then Karon and Volin held the octave above Seronak's tone, but Uljas and Locan shifted to sing the fifth. Suddenly, Belel's voice soared above the others in a haunting melody that became ever more whimsical and playful. With voices pitched three tones apart, Melida and Aletha added harmony and an undulating rhythm above the men's droning octave and fifth, creating the infinitely diverse, yet constant Song of the One.

The music ebbed to a quiet humming as, one by one, each Keeper spoke the ritual words. "I connect us with the beginning," said Belel, Keeper of Origin. "I give knowledge voice," said Volin, Keeper of Wisdom. "I exercise the power of crystals," said Locan, Keeper of Energy. "I dance in rhythm with the planet," said Karon, Keeper of Earth Matters. "I listen with my heart," said Aletha, Keeper of Language. "I bring forth the new," said Uljas, Keeper of Ideas. "I give ideas the means to merge," said Melida, Keeper of Thought. "I bind us to each other," said Seronak, Keeper of the One. The humming returned, amplified a thousand fold by the crystalline room. By the time the last echoes died away, the Keepers were infused with an energy that caused stars to be born and plants to push through soil.

Seronak rang the silver bell. "We are One," he intoned. "The Keeper of Language will speak first."

Into the expectant silence, Aletha said, "In Mu, energy was experienced differently. Instead of invoking energy, we accepted and used what was present in the earth, the trees, and each other. Loneliness was unknown to us, for we were connected, rarely seeking the silence of our own thoughts, content to be known to all. All things felt the connection: animals, plants, rocks, and trees. When Mu was swallowed by the sea, I was hurled into loneliness and grief. For a long time, I confess I did not want to live, for life without the others, my others, seemed barren. In my heart, I longed for the kind of complete absorption I experienced with my people, my trees, my gardens.

"In my grief I sent my desolate soul wandering, and was drawn to a woman, kneeling by a great river, nearly to term with child. The unborn child, restless in her mother's womb, took me in immediately, thinking me to be herself, and for many years of her life, I was her other voice, her internal self, and my loneliness eased. She became the sister of my soul, my other voice as well.

"All was well until my husband from Mu, born again into a different body, came to this woman, Ah-mah. When they found love together, I broke the connection, for I did not wish to intrude on their intimacy." A rustling pervaded the room. "Now I cannot seem to reconnect, and I do not understand why.

"When Mu was lost, I was saved because dolphins found me and carried me to an island. I learned dolphin language and spoke with them freely for a time. While I was on the island of Seronak's birth, I swam with dolphins again, and experienced events which had no definite time or place. Through dolphin dreaming, I saw Ah-mah so vividly that her feet were mine, and together we walked the dirt paths of her land. Dolphins showed me other scenes, one of which was Seronak, lying on a table, a great crystal beside him. I learned one dolphin's name that day. When the dreaming was over, Hukuhu spoke to me in my mind. He asked me, 'Will you be dolphin?'

"The power in this room is great. I would ask the Keepers to consider the dolphins and what their words to me might mean."

In a lower voice, almost a whisper, Aletha continued. "With your help, I would try to reach Ah-mah, not as a voice inside her mind, but as someone from another time and place. I want her to know me and the motherland of Mu, and I want her to know each of you. I want her to know that we have lived." Aletha folded her hands in her lap, and bowed her head.

"Can we see anything of her life thread?" Belel, Keeper of Origin, asked what all were thinking.

"I can see it, but she must want the connection as much as we do," Seronak said.

"Is this woman important in her world? Will she be interested in knowing our history, or be able to record it? What do we expect from her?" asked Karon, Keeper of Earth Matters.

"She is inventing a new method of healing," said Aletha. "I confess I have not thought of whether she is important in her time. I only want to feel she knows mine. I am reminded that she did connect, even as a preborn, so there must be some similarity between us. Her soul is strong, as is her curiosity."

"A new method of healing?" asked Uljas, Keeper of Ideas.

"She has begun to treat feet, to use feet to access the ills of the body through a method she has devised herself," Aletha said.

"Then that is the way to reach her," Uljas said.

"What do you mean?" asked Seronak.

"Feet are the area where she is breaking with the customs of her time," said Uljas. "She will be open to the unexpected when she works on feet. That is the time for contact."

"Then you think we should try, no matter her circumstances?" asked Volin, Keeper of Wisdom.

"I do," said Karon, Keeper of Earth Matters. "Atlantis is doomed, and so, at present, are we. It is no accident that Aletha has come to us at this time, or that she alone, of all of us, is able to contact this woman of another time. I believe that if we focus our energies on this woman of the future, this woman who is inventing something new, we will open ourselves to ideas, some of which may enable us to use our energies in ways we cannot see today. The connection across time and space will affect us as much as it does the woman, Ah-mah."

"I agree," said Uljas. "And I am intrigued by this idea of dolphins."

Melida, the small brown Keeper of Thought, said, "The fabric of the Universe was set in motion long before our time. Should we intrude on this woman's life for any reason?"

In a low voice, Aletha responded. "I have experienced the energy of this room, the energy of the Keepers. Something has drawn me here after causing me to survive what I would not have chosen to survive on my own. Something has given me the ability to send my essence into another's life in another time. I cannot help but wonder if that same Something is not urging us to connect with Ah-mah, and perhaps others? Urging us to consider how we might share what we know with future beings."

Seronak rang the bell again, this time to signal silence. "Aletha, hold the image of Ah-mah clearly in your mind," he said.

The Keepers' energy bathed Aletha and the image she held, until of its own accord, the scene shifted to her dream of Hawk, sailing on sky currents toward the dolphin who had spoken to her through Hawk's dream.

Thus, Ah-mah saw dolphins for the first time. It happened as Uljas had predicted, as Ah-mah searched for a reason for sweaty feet, stretching the capacity of her thinking to encompass this new problem, her mind so involved that the energy sent over time and space slipped into her consciousness naturally, and almost undetected. Almost.

CHAPTER THIRTEEN

Aletha is not Me

"Such beautiful sandals," Ah-mah murmured as she hurried home along the dusty path. Ali, the sandal maker, had drawn the mark for cutting on the leather around each of her feet in turn causing them to fit perfectly. Seeing that the sun was about to rise, she stopped and stood facing the brightening sky. Just before the giant orb rose above the mountains in the east, it seemed the whole world held its breath, never completely certain that the great Ra would favor this day with his presence. A small breeze touched Ah-mah's face as Ra in all his glory began his sky journey and she let out the breath she, too, had been holding. The world would have sun for another day. With a chuckle, Ah-mah continued her hurried steps.

In the year since she had made her agreement with Khufer, Ah-mah had become used to the priests of Ra and did not find them as fat or oily or offensive as she once had. Interestingly, their feet did not sweat as much and some of them had lost weight. Privately, she wondered if the treatment could be the cause.

"Ouch!" A pebble had been scooped up under her toes,

creating a flash of pain. She squatted, putting her weight on the other foot while removing the culprit, and stole a glance at her new sandals. Ali was reputed to be the best sandal maker in Nubt, and it was through the generosity of the high priest that she was the recipient; his way of paying her for her treatments. "When I was Mistress of the Land, I would not have accepted sandals from a priest. Indeed, there were no priests of Ra until Rahotep came to Nubt," she thought. Another thought surfaced, one that had nagged at her. Rahotep had not offered to buy the lands of her ancestors since she joined with Sept and came to live in Nubt. What should she make of that? Her heart must not lose its wariness.

She groaned inwardly when she saw the line of people awaiting her, many of them strangers. The priests still came to her twice each month, and the high priest was treated as often as he required it, but the rest of the time belonged to the people. No matter what she did for them, when she treated their feet, they seemed to feel better. She often used an abbreviated treatment to enable her to see more people. Most were satisfied just to have another wash their feet, thus Nefer had become quite popular with them. Some days she wished for the freedom of a life without so many feet, but most days she was grateful for the skill of her hands and the ability to share it.

Entering her home, she poured a cup of water, and began the rituals she now found necessary. Removing the new sandals and tucking them into a corner, Ah-mah automatically recited the Prayer for the Feet, the Prayer for Healing, the Prayer for the Body, and the Prayer for a Clean Heart as she washed her hands. Each of the prayers had come from Ah-mah's own heart and served to focus her. If there had been a Prayer of Thanks for New Sandals, she would have recited it as well.

"Where are you, Aletha? I miss your teasing. Instead I have prayers," she thought. After that one word, "dolphin," Ah-mah had not heard Aletha's voice again, although she listened for it constantly. She remembered the words that had come unbidden to her when she first began treating feet beneath the nehet, and added them quickly to her prayers: "Where there is Desire. Where there is Need. (I do need you, Aletha!) Where there is Consent."

Taking up position in her treatment room in the back garden, Ah-mah took a deep, cleansing breath, and nodded to Nefer. The man who came first had been given the name Whiner in Ah-mah's private thoughts. He bowed to her briefly before lying down on the mat. Nefer adjusted the cushions to fit his body, one beneath his neck for support, one beneath each knee, a slightly rounded pad to fit the small of his back. Ah-mah began her work. Whiner would require the full treatment.

She twisted the ankle from side to side in her palms to loosen the foot and allow the blood to flow freely. Bringing her left hand toward her from the ankle, she grasped the foot to support it, and began the inching movement, recently discovered, across the ball of the foot with her right thumb. Her thumb dug in, released, moved slightly, dug in again. She usually started with the toes, and thus the head, but recently she had been drawn to the place of breathing. "A man must breathe, as I must breathe,' she thought, as she released the breath she had been holding. "Why?" she wondered, silently. "Something will happen today. My body knows it is coming and stills my breath, afraid it might not hear and be warned. Is it something so terrible? No. Not terrible. But life changing all the same."

Ah-mah moved to the toes, working the largest first, inching the thumb from top to base, top to base, until she had thoroughly worked it before moving to the next toe, and the next. A whimper from Whiner brought her back abruptly from mind wandering, and she grabbed his heel with her left hand, shaking off the pain in the toes with her right. "His head hurts," she reminded herself. "Too filled with all his whining, no doubt." Immediately she was sorry and determined that she would treat him more gently. "I do not know his circumstances, or whether I might not be the same if I were to have to endure them," she thought. She worked each toe, and moved to those tender areas between the toes and under them. Carefully, her powerful thumbs tested each area before entering, much as one might walk through an area of the desert reported to have pockets of quicksand. Working the feet reminded Ah-mah of the desert, especially when she broke up the tiny grains of sand, embedded by the body just under the skin, or deep in the muscles of the foot. For a while she was successful at being gentle with Whiner, but soon her mind wandered into memory.

The river was golden, colored by the late afternoon sun as she and Sept neared it. Out of habit, she removed her dress and waded into the water. Sept stripped to his loin cloth, and waded in after her. She turned around just as he stepped into the water.

Their first lovemaking was cradled by the river. He was gentle with her, careful, holding himself back. She was grateful for his gentleness. It gave her time to remember her body and its needs. Afterward they rested at the water's edge, reluctant to leave.

Suddenly, a surge of energy seemed to come to Ah-mah from deep within the earth beneath her. A hunger for Sept's hard body ignited in her, a hunger that could not be denied. All sense of reason left her as the energy propelled her to a sitting position and clouded her eyes with desire. She thrust her body toward him, ready to devour him or have him devour her. Their bodies interlocked, as Sept matched her mood, and touched her here and there, in the fashion he had learned from an experienced woman from the fabled land of Ur. Her arousal reached a fevered pitch, and she moaned with longing. He entered her, thrusting his manhood over and over. Her body surged toward him as his seed exploded. It was over. They lay, panting for breath, exhausted, glowing.

Brought back to the present by a sigh from Whiner, Ah-mah saw that the lines in his face had eased. "I have not lost my touch," she thought, and moved to the middle of the foot. She inserted a cushion beneath the heel of the now completely relaxed foot so she would not have to hold its weight. "I am getting old," she mused, and knew it was not true.

She set her mind to her work, moving the right thumb across the middle of the foot, and then the left thumb back over the same area. The foot was callused from walking, and in early years, her thumbs were raw at the end of the day from pushing through the tough, thick skin. "Thank you, Nefer," she thought for the thousandth time, as she felt a touch of the oil he had applied after washing Whiner's feet. She had reached Whiner's heel which was hard as a stone in spite of the water and oil. From a small basket, she took a river tumbled stone, smooth and round, and gently but firmly, used her palm to push it against the outer edge of Whiner's heel. Some kind of connection existed between the back edge of the heel and the relaxation of the body. Putting the stone back into the basket, she moved her hands to the large tendon that reached from the heel up into the back of the leg and worked it thoroughly. Ah-mah was pleased to see Whiner relax more deeply and begin softly snoring.

Each of the people who came to her regularly had his or her own quirks. A few of them had wanted to talk to her, to share their lives. One or two still persisted with this, and had to be reminded each time of the need for Silence, for Rest, for Openness to the Treatment. "The Rules must be followed in order to achieve Results," she admonished. With few exceptions, they now napped during the treatment, or at least held their tongues. "Rituals and Rules? When did that happen? And why?"

The pain reached her heart before it reached her mind. Ah-mah held Whiner's foot as she stopped both the treatment and her own breathing in order to listen. The spirit of someone called to her. Leaving Whiner to his nap, she rose and went to search, Nefer following. Looking down the line of people, she saw a small girl lying on a cot at the very end, her anxious mother hovering, helpless hands twisting and untwisting a small square of cloth. Ah-mah went to the child and knelt beside her. Her body was covered with sweat from fighting the pain.

"Where do you hurt?" Ah-mah asked. The girl touched her upper abdomen. Placing one hand on the child's forehead, in the place of the all-seeing eye, the other hand on her own heart, she whispered, "Where there is Need. Where there is Consent." The child opened her eyes and looked at Ah-mah. The look was steady. Consent had been given.

To Nefer, Ah-mah said, "Bring a bowl of water and a clean cloth." Nefer ran to obey and soon returned. Ah-mah dipped the cloth into the water, and after wringing out the excess, handed it to the still hovering mother. Grateful for something to do for her daughter, the mother began to wipe the sweat from her body.

Ah-mah sat at the girl's feet. She held both heels in her hands, closed her eyes, and went inside the girl's body with her inner sight, to a lump, red and swollen, deep in the girl's midsection. Ah-mah took the left foot in her hand and began to work the area in the center of the foot, gently at first, then more and more strongly. When she saw the girl could not stand more, she moved to the right foot to work the same area, and then back to the left. Nothing seemed to help, and the pain did not ease. Finally, she stopped and held the girl's heels once more. "I have received Consent, what else do I need?" she thought, eyes closed. Suddenly, in her mind's eye, a great sword swept down, severing the girl's torso at her waist.

There was no blood, just two parts with a space the width of a finger in between.

Without thinking, Ah-mah opened her eyes, rose to a kneeling position, and crawled to the girl's side. With a finger of one hand, she touched the point of pain on the left foot, and with the fingers of the other, she touched the center of the child's body. "Aletha!" she cried from the depths of her soul. Immediately, a spark of energy ran from fingertip to fingertip through her body, causing intense pain. Only by force of will did she keep her fingers in place. The pain subsided, replaced by warm, wet energy and a large blue-green stone. Ah-mah focused on the stone, looking into its depths, forgetting everything else. It drew her into a calm such as she had never known. "This is my Source." The thought came from she knew not where. Suddenly, the world was aquamarine, filled with sunlight and warm breezes. Ah-mah saw a Lady sitting on a stone bench looking at water that spread from horizon to horizon. She seemed to have such strength of mind and purpose. When the Lady turned to gaze at her, Ah-mah gasped, and fell backward, unconscious.

She awoke to find Nefer's anxious face above hers. "Have you recovered, Ah-mahsis?" His pet name for her. He was frightened.

"What happened?" she asked.

"A miracle," Nefer continued. "The girl is resting, Ah-mahsis. She has no pain."

The girl? Why was she not sitting on the bench, the delicious odor of the Obelon tree pervading the air she breathed? Where did that come from? Anxious to send the still hovering Nefer on his way, Ah-mah said, "I am well, Nefer, but I need to be quiet."

"I will tell the people to come back tomorrow," Nefer said.

Ah-mah lay back, eyes closed. With the room on the other side of her eyelids, it was easy for her mind to drift, and then to sleep.

She awoke much later just as Nefer entered the room with a cup of water.

"Ah, that is good," Ah-mah said, as she drained the last drop. "Were the people angry with me for deserting them?"

"No, Ah-mahsis. They were relieved to find that you were not dead, as they had thought."

"Dead?"

"What happened to you, Ah-mahsis? I watched, but I do not understand what I saw."

"What did you see?"

"You worked the girl's feet, first the left, then the right, then the left. I could feel your frustration when she did not improve. Then you moved to her side and touched her foot with one hand, a spot on her body with the other. Your eyes were closed and beads of sweat stood out on your forehead. Suddenly, you stiffened and your forehead wrinkled. Your eyes remained closed and your lips started moving, as though you were speaking, but no sound came out. For just a moment, I looked at the girl. Her breathing had deepened, and color was returning to her cheeks. I confess I had forgotten you until you fell over backwards. I should have been there to break your fall. You were so pale, and your eyes had sunk back into your head. I raised your lids to look, Ah-mahsis. I laid my head on your chest to see if I could hear the beating of your heart. Such a great, steady heart you have, Ah-mahsis. Even then, the beats were strong and regular."

"Poor Nefer. I am sorry I frightened you."

"What happened, Ah-mahsis? Do you remember anything?"

"When I touched the girl, I saw something, Nefer. Something of which I cannot yet speak because I do not understand it.

"Are you afraid, Ah-mahsis?"

"Something draws me. I am too curious to be afraid. Besides,

I sense nothing to fear."

Whiner was first in line next morning. Ah-mah felt sorry for him, knowing he had spent the night feeling one foot alive and the other like stone. As he settled himself on the mat, she broke the Silence and asked, "What is your name?"

He looked at her, startled that she spoke to him, and answered, "An-hept."

"Well, An-hept, I am sorry you had to go through the night without having a full treatment."

Shyly, An-hept smiled.

True to her own integrity, Ah-mah began her treatment with the same right foot, knowing it had hardened somewhat since yesterday. She loosened the ankle and began working on the lungs. Soon she had done the toes and started to work the middle of the foot. Across with the right thumb, back with the left. Across with the right thumb, back with the left. By the time she reached the heel once more, her mind was far away roaming lush, green lands with flowers perfuming the air and birds filling it with song. A breeze cooled her face, but did not blast it. She worked first one side and then the other side of the ankle, as she walked through jasmine in full bloom. Her thumbs inched their way from under one ankle bone across the great divide between foot and leg and under the ankle bone on the other side. With her left hand she made a kind of collar over the divide and pushed the foot up into it with her right hand to drain poisons from the body. Her mind lingered in the jasmine as she worked the arch, deftly restoring suppleness to the spine. When her hands moved to the other foot, An-hept sighed and his breathing eased. The lines across his forehead smoothed and the furrow between his brows lessened.

Ah-mah had finished the lungs and moved to the large toe when she saw the Lady of the Stone, as she thought of her, gazing across the sea to the far horizon. As Ah-mah approached, she turned and spoke to Ah-mah's mind.

"Do not be afraid. We have known each other for a long, long time, and I have been waiting for you."

Ah-mah's thumb stumbled as she nearly cried aloud, "Aletha? Aletha!"

"Yes, dear Ah-mah, it is me. Come sit on the bench with me."

Ah-mah's dream self moved to sit on the bench beside Aletha while her thumb worked An-hept's heel, steadily, carefully. Suddenly, a thought came to her, a thought that could not be ignored.

"You are not me, Aletha."

"You are the sister of my soul."

"Where are we?"

Once again, the river stone did its work, finding its way through the callused heel to the softness beneath.

Ah-mah could hear joy in Aletha's voice as she said, "We sit on a bench in the Gardens of Mu. We are from different times, dear Ah-mah. Different places. We meet again because people from my time have joined their energy to mine to help me be with you in yours."

"I did not imagine you were so beautiful."

Just then she hit a particularly tender spot and An-hept involuntarily cried out. Quickly, Ah-mah grabbed the heel and toes to shake off the pain. Time to pay attention to feet.

CHAPTER FOURTEEN

Intimacy

The first time the Keepers focused their energies on Aletha, they had all seen Ah-mah. It was the only time thus far. What had seemed easy was proving to be impossible to duplicate. The energy in the room was thick with frustration. For the twelfth time in as many nights, the Keepers met in the Crystal Room to meld their energies with the purpose of contacting Ah-mah, but this attempt was no more successful than the preceding eleven. They were not used to failure, and that fact was taking its toll on their confidence and strength. Seronak dismissed the group by saying, "We will not meet again until the third night hence. Go your way, remembering we are One."

Aletha was devastated. "It is my fault," she said under her breath, forgetting that the chamber amplified all sound. The Keepers stopped, and except for Uljas, turned to look at her. She would have hidden if she could have found a way.

Muttering to himself, Uljas whirled around and walked straight to Aletha. "That's it!" he exclaimed. "The last time we contacted Ah-mah, she was working in her new area of treating feet. Aletha, you must try to find Ah-mah as she works on feet. Until Ah-mah is open to us, we will not be able to reach her. Can you do that?"

"Give me a moment," Aletha said.

Without a word, the Keepers resumed their seats, eager to try again. Aletha sorted through all the experiences she and Ah-mah had had with feet. She had just about settled on one when she and the other Keepers heard a distinctly female voice. "Aletha!"

Seronak began the humming which served to gather the energies of the Keepers. Aletha focused on the sound of Ah-mah's voice calling her name. With the experience of ages, the Keepers sent focused waves toward her, gently at first, and then with greater and greater force, nearly lifting her from her chair.

Aletha walked once more in the Gardens of Mu near the Obelon tree. She also sat beneath a tree in Ah-mah's garden and felt the pain. Her heart nearly leaped from her body as she clearly saw an older Ah-mah walking toward the girl. She heard Ah-mah's words: "Where there is Need. Where there is Desire. Where there is Consent." When the sword seemed to cut the girl in two, the energy thrust through time by the Keepers of Atlantis surged through Aletha and then through Ah-mah, sealing the breach. Just for a moment they were one, but it was enough. Aletha returned to her Gardens, drawing Ah-mah with her.

Sunlight glittered in the great Aquamarine which hung from Aletha's neck. She was about to speak when Ah-mah's eyes widened in amazement, and she fell back, unconscious.

"Her energy is strong and pure," said Melida, Keeper of Thought.

"She is older than I thought she would be," said Volin, Keeper of Wisdom.

"We have made contact with a human being across time and space," said Locan, Keeper of Energy, his eyes shining, his voice filled with awe.

"We were able to help her heal another with our energy," said Belel, Keeper of Origin.

"Go now to rest," Seronak said, "and return here the third night from this one. We have made a beginning."

"Aye," whispered Aletha, through tears of joy, "a beginning."

When they returned, only long-practiced ritual kept them from speaking the multitudes of thoughts and ideas the experience with Ah-mah had brought to each. Instead, they entered the crystal chamber whispering the ritual of Oneness, having cleansed the feet and hands, having rinsed the mouth, having performed all the rites sacred to themselves and their offices as Keepers.

Aletha had placed fresh roses in crystal vases at the foot of each chair, their scent, so similar to that of the Obelon tree, filling the room. Seronak intoned his deep bass and the Keepers sang with him, building the thrusting energy and focusing it on Aletha and her search.

Ah-mah treated the feet of a man. She had loosened the right ankle and was working the lungs. Very soon, with Aletha and the Keepers aiding her, she was drawn in her mind to lush gardens smelling of jasmine and roses. She came once more to the high place, overlooking the sea, the place of Aletha's stone bench. "Do not be afraid. We have known each other for a long, long time, and I have been waiting for you."

Then Ah-mah did know her, as Aletha wished to be known, not as an internal voice but as a separate being in a different time and place. "You are not me, Aletha" she said, calmly.

"You are the sister of my soul," Aletha said.

Ah-mah asked, "Where are we?"

Aletha was answering when…

"Aletha?" A voice, not Ah-mah's, not female, called to her.

She tried to wave the voice away, knowing it could break the connection.

"Ah-mah is gone, Aletha." The voice would not stop talking. What nonsense! Gone? Her eyelids flew open and she saw Seronak, smiling broadly.

"We made the connection, Aletha. You made it. Ah-mah made it. We all connected, and so deeply that you did not realize when the connection was broken."

Aletha looked around as Seronak continued to babble in his excitement. She was in her room with no memory of how she had gotten there.

"Seronak, be still," she said. "Be still and let me come back completely."

Seronak, who had left his chair and was pacing around the room in his eagerness, now gathered himself and sat again, saying nothing, but gazing keenly at Aletha.

With a sigh, Aletha closed her eyes and let her inner vision wander the Gardens. She inhaled fragrances, tempted to follow their scent into an untroubled dream. The Obelon tree stood tall before her, beckoning. She went to it and put the arms of her inner vision about it, as her body reached out arms as well, beginning the Ritual of the Body. Forgetting Seronak and concentrating solely on this daily rite of acceptance of her body, she moved the energy down her left arm, and then her right, and centering her hands over her heart, brought her awareness fully into her body.

When Aletha opened her eyes and smiled at Seronak, he seemed huddled into himself. "Thank you, my friend," she said. "I did not want to come back from my Gardens. It helped to know that you were waiting for me."

Seronak's eyes glistened with unshed tears. "We Keepers have our rituals, our prayers, our rites, but except for the Ritual of One, we do not perform these rites in the presence of another."

"Have I offended you? I did not intend…"

"No, Aletha. Of course not. But you have allowed me to witness something personal. I am overwhelmed by the intimacy of it."

"Intimacy?" Aletha closed her eyes again, trying to understand. She reviewed his words. "We do not perform these rites in the presence of another." Always separate, always declaring that they were one, but never experiencing it except in the Crystal Room, and then only through ritual. Was this the gift she had to share with the Keepers? Intimacy? Did Seronak not realize the depth of intimacy the Keepers inserted into her being when they helped her seek for Ah-mah? No, somehow he did not. Intimacy, so natural in Mu, remained a foreign concept to the Keepers.

She opened her eyes and sat up, gracefully lifting her legs over the side of the bed so that her feet touched the floor. Looking steadily at Seronak, Aletha smiled and said, "Perhaps we have made another beginning."

CHAPTER FIFTEEN

A Second Bargain

"Ah-mahsis, a man from the temple comes!"

Taking a last bite, Ah-mah went to the door to see for herself. One of the high priest's minions walked toward her, the Staff of Office topped with the golden disk of Ra in his hand. The Staff of Self Importance, Ah-mah often termed it privately.

"May I be of service, Holy One?" she asked, with more humility than she felt.

"The High Priest would like to see you when you have finished your treatments for the day. He would like you to share the evening meal with him." Surprise at what he had to say leaked through his voice, causing it to crack embarrassingly. Ah-mah was surprised as well. "Dust clouds on the horizon," she thought. "Nothing good can come of this." Then, she softened. Since their bargain had been made, Khufer had kept his word. Not wanting to interrupt her time with the people, Khufer usually called for her ministrations in the late afternoon, taking his turn last. She had not seen him this week, and to be summoned via this self-important child of a man did not bode well. She nodded her understanding, and message delivered, he left.

The first pair of feet belonged to a fat man, seemingly a person with few limits to his appetite. His feet were small for his size, but Ah-mah knew that carrying all that weight would make them tough and flattened. "Ah, the day continues its downhill run," she sighed.

As a rule, Ah-mah did not speak during a treatment. In fact, the only one to whom she said anything was Nefer, and even those words were sparse, since Nefer had trained himself to anticipate her needs and the needs of the people. Prayers finished, hands washed, Ah-mah sat down at the man's feet. Holding both heels in her hands, she pulled gently. She was about to move her hands to the right ankle, when in her mind's eye, she saw a young boy being pummeled by other boys. She heard the terrible names and felt their impact in her own body. Finally, the picture faded, but not the taunts. She moved to the man's right foot and twisted it to loosen its tightness.

The treatment progressed through the right foot and on to the left with no more pictures, no more taunts. Ah-mah began to believe that her imagination had taken over, or perhaps a bad dream from snatched sleep the night before had surfaced. When she reached the center of the left foot and moved upwards toward where she imagined the heart could be accessed, her mouth opened, seemingly of its own accord. "What is your name?" she asked.

"Nabi," the man said, as though from a distance.

"You are a man, Nabi. You no longer have anything to fear. You are safe." The words came from deep within her. For a moment, she glimpsed Lady Aletha, aquamarine blazing in the sunlight. It was just a glimpse, but Ah-mah could see that she was smiling. She opened her eyes to see slow tears rolling down Nabi's cheeks.

When she had finished both feet and applied another coating of oil, this time scented, she used a rough cloth to wipe off the excess.

The man opened his eyes and rose from the mat, knowing the session was ended. As he passed by Ah-mah, who had also risen to rinse her hands, he bowed to her.

Never-satisfied was next to enter her cubicle. Her feet were quite familiar to Ah-mah, as were her complaints at the end of each session, although, since being admonished to be silent and receptive to the treatment, they had been reduced to mumbles as she left. Gratefully, Ah-mah settled into the routine and allowed her mind to rest.

The last person to be treated that day was an old, old man, his skin so fragile, it seemed nearly transparent. Certainly it had reached that stage of translucence that often presages death, when the veils of life are lowered and the spirit is revealed. As Ah-mah pushed her thumb over the ball of the foot to begin the treatment, she could feel the sponginess of the skin. No longer firm and elastic, it had the feel of death, which Ah-mah could sense was close. She wondered if the old man knew.

"What is your name?" she asked, and looked into his eyes.

"Djosef," was the whispered reply. Yes, he knew.

"Do you need something from me?" Ah-mah asked.

"No, lady. I am ready," he said, and closed his eyes once again.

Tired as she was after this long and arduous day, Ah-mah handled the old man's feet with great tenderness and affection. After rubbing them with scented oil, she held them for a while, tenderly, much as a mother would hold a child. "Blessings on you, Djosef," she whispered, watching gratefully as his son, and a woman she assumed was the son's wife or sister, gently supported the old man, matching his feeble steps, and helping him leave the garden with dignity. The son would have carried his father if that had been needed, so great was the love between them.

Ah-mah was tired. She just wanted to lie down on her bed.

Turning away from the site of the old man and his family, she headed for her bed, intending to rest before eating.

"Do not forget you are dining with the High Priest," Nefer said.

She stopped mid stride, jerked back into an unpleasant reality, and stared at Nefer, a pleading look in her eyes. He raised both arms, palms out, in that universal gesture that was always said to mean, 'it is out of my hands,' but usually meant, 'better you than me.' Ah-mah snorted and stalked off. At least she could remove some of the sweat of the day and put on a clean dress. She longed to see Sept, to feel his arms around her, but he would not be home until later. Someone would have informed the high priest that she had finished her work and he would be expecting her.

She arrived, somewhat out of breath, clean and hastily scented. Two tall young men, standing guard at the door, stepped back to let her pass.

A small table had been positioned on the wooden deck overlooking the sacred River. Only two chairs. "Not a good sign," thought Ah-mah. Khufer, the High Priest, walked toward her in greeting. She bowed to him, and together they took seats at the table.

He asked of the small things in her life. How were her treatments progressing? Did the sandals fit well? Was there news from her daughter and grandchildren?

She answered each in turn, as beer was poured and copper plates set before them, grateful that at the last minute she had remembered to put on the sandals. Two strong slaves entered the room carrying a table loaded with enough food for six or seven. Khufer dismissed them with a gesture, and began serving her from the rich offering. The aromas had already reached her nostrils and started her mouth watering. The food was delicious, making it difficult to enjoy and keep her wariness at the same time.

Once they had eaten their fill, Khufer refilled their cups and stood up, taking his cup with him. Ah-mah stood as well, and together they moved to the edge of the deck to stand in that same place where once they had bargained for Nefer, to watch the river and the traffic that moved on it. Behind them, Ra neared the far western edge of the world, and soon would be obscured as he slept.

"The river supports and sustains us," Khufer said.

"Blessed be the river," said Ah-mah, not automatically, but from a heart filled with love for this lifeline of her people.

"The river also brings us news from other lands, and sometimes visitors," Khufer continued.

"Here it comes," Ah-mah thought. "The price for the meal."

"You have been treating feet for several years now. Your skill is respected in Nubt, but is also known throughout the Land of the River. Did you know?" Ah-mah shook her head.

"Ah-mah, we have visitors. They have come from far away, from across the great sea beyond the sacred river, bringing a young girl, royal by birth, to learn everything you know about rubbing feet."

"I will be happy to treat this royal girl, but I could not teach her."

"You underestimate yourself as usual. The fact of the matter is that their country has trees, and we always need more. It seems their king is willing to trade access to those trees if you will go to their country for a time to treat his first wife, the queen, who seems to have some ailment that has defied her snwn."

Ah-mah did not know what to say. How could rubbing feet have become so important? Would there not be some other trade? At last she spoke, "Surely rubbing someone's feet is not enough for trees."

"We will gain access to trees, Ah-mah. Of course, a fair

exchange of goods and gold will be necessary as well. I spoke with your husband earlier today and found him eager, especially since he would accompany you if you agree to travel to the land of the princess. He and I will meet with Rahotep tomorrow. Thus, I must know your answer tonight."

For a time both were silent, watching the river. Ah-mah did not trust this priest, no matter how much she respected him, and she had never trusted Rahotep. Something else was behind this sudden importance of her treatments. With brutal honesty, she asked, "What if I fail?"

Khufer looked at her thoughtfully. "Once before we made a bargain, you and I, and although it seemed to favor you at first, all, including me, have benefited. Will you not consider another bargain, this time seemingly in my favor?" Khufer paused, and smiled broadly. "You were once Mistress of the Land, Ah-mah. Remember that, and have no fear," Khufer said, and taking her arm, he ushered her to the door and opened it for her. "Princess Medi will come to you tomorrow."

The next morning the line waiting for her was long but orderly. Ah-mah had discussed the proposal with Sept well into the night, and she still felt uneasy about it, no matter Sept's eagerness. Something was not being said, something important, but she could not discern what it was. Secretly, in her heart of hearts, Ah-mah was pleased to have a pupil and eager to meet her.

Ah-mah did not see the Princess at first. She sat in the shadows of the tree's branches and was dressed simply, not like a princess at all, but more like an apprentice, "which," Ah-mah mused, "I guess she is." She folded her hands together and, bowing to the Princess, began her morning prayers. Then, with a nod to Nefer to bring in the first to be treated, she began the long day with its procession of feet.

CHAPTER SIXTEEN

The Student

"What is beneath your knee?"

"Ah, the princess does have a voice," thought Ah-mah, her hands busy with the feet of the princess' personal guard. Her accent was slight, no more than what Ah-mah often noticed in the speech of those who came from other villages.

Ah-mah finished the right foot and moved to the left. For three days, Princess Medi had stayed in the shadows beneath the tree, her handmaiden so close one might question whether they were two people. Not having been introduced to the servant, Ah-mah thought of her as "Shadow." The guard, Malloch, whose foot Ah-mah held, accompanied the two women to Ah-mah's house every morning, stood guard silently all day, and returned them to the house next to Rahotep's before sunset. Each day the princess watched intently, seldom looking anywhere other than Ah-mah's hands. These were her first words.

"It is a pillow, my lady, to cushion my knee as I work," Ah-mah said, deftly turning the ankle in her hands. "Small comfort for old bones," she added.

"Is it like the cushions you use in your treatments?"

"It is smaller, lady."

"May I see it?"

Ah-mah handed the tiny cushion to the princess with one hand, securely holding Malloch's foot with the other.

The princess turned it this way and that, feeling its weight, noting the crude stitches. Ah-mah had made the cushion herself, as she made all the cushions she used. "With what is it filled? It is firm, yet pliable, soft, yet hard."

"Seeds, my lady. Seeds from the same flax that gives us linen to wear," replied Ah-mah. Having loosened the foot, she began to work the lungs.

"Flax seeds! Of course," she said, handing the pillow back to Ah-mah, who restored it to its position beneath her knee. "They are tiny, smooth and slippery, so they would make the perfect filling for a cushion. How did you think of it?"

"By accident, lady. Often the people I treat bring me little gifts. Usually it is food, a bunch of dates, a barley cake, but once, a grateful man brought me a small bag of flax seed." Ah-mah moved her skills to the guard's toes. The princess wore a passive, yet interested face, a face which continually startled Ah-mah, no matter how often she saw it. The almond-shaped eyes, the creamy light brown skin, the small, hawkish nose, were very different from what she normally encountered, and forever unexpected. Ah-mah continued, although she was uncomfortable with talking during a treatment. The princess had asked and she would answer.

"Once I had followed the pattern for treating the feet enough times, my hands seemed able to work without needing all my attention. Thus, after I received the bag of seeds, I often thought of how flax seeds are planted in the soil of my land by the river.

I remembered the joy of seeing the first green sprouts and, in my mind, I eagerly watched the growing plants as I worked one foot or the other, until, finally, I remembered the harvest."

The guard frowned with pain. Ah-mah felt the knot in his foot as she saw the frown and stopped speaking. She worked and worked, first one way and then the other, then back again. The knot would not release. Ah-mah pushed her thumb into the knot and slowly moved it back and forth. Repositioning the thumb slightly, she attacked it again, moving her thumb back and forth over the area all around it and then over the knot itself. At last she felt it softening. She shook the toes to release the pain and the frown disappeared.

Continuing her story, Ah-mah said, "One day, Nefer asked me what thoughts ran through my mind while I worked. I told him of the flax crop, planted and harvested over and over in my mind. For some reason after that people brought me more of the flax seed, for the most part in single handfuls. Soon I had to make another bag to hold them, and then another. What to do with so many bags of seeds? I thought they might ruin and be of no use to anyone. What a waste that would be," she said, as she pushed her thumb over the back of the guard's heel.

"In the midst of my dilemma, my daughter came to visit bringing my grandchildren, and in my haste to create a space for them, I tossed the now five bags of seeds into a corner, covering them with mats to make a pallet for the children. The next morning, my grandson said he felt more rested than when he slept in his own bed at home. The bags of seeds had cushioned him."

For a moment, the princess thought the story had ended. Instead, the treatment had come to a close, and Ah-mah, ever vigilant with the people she treated, spent time finishing the treatment with the ritual pulling of the heels three times, and the

Prayer for Health, which she mumbled aloud. She finished with little flicks of her hand, returning energy that had been pulled into the feet back to the body.

When Malloch rose from the cushion and was about to pass Ah-mah, she said to him, "You should be more careful of how you stand. The knot comes from pressure you are putting on one foot over the other. Stand equally on both feet and you will not have this problem."

The guard frowned at Ah-mah, and said something to the princess in his own language. Rising, the princess also spoke in her native language, illustrating Ah-mah's words by standing equally on both feet. With a nod and a slight bow to Ah-mah and the princess, the guard took up his position near the princess. Ah-mah's gaze followed him. Sure enough, she could see him test his stance, bending his knees slightly, and shifting his weight until he stood equally on both feet.

In the language of the Land of the River, Medi asked, "How did you know, Ah-mah?"

"I do not always know the origin of the words I speak, my lady, but this time, I used common sense. Your guard does favor one foot over the other, much as we tend to use one hand more than the other. Often we are not aware of it, just as we are not aware of how we stand. He knows about his tendency now. He has shifted his stance and will be mindful of it."

Tired, Ah-mah dipped her hands in the water and splashed weariness from her face. She dried both face and hands on a cloth held for her by Nefer, and signed to him that she was ready for the next person, a woman Ah-mah had not treated before.

She sat at the woman's feet and began her ministrations, even as she continued her story.

"It took a long time to collect enough seeds to make the small pillows and even longer for the cushioned mat. I also had to find the linen. That was a little easier, since I just had to gather what others had discarded. You will notice that the mat is made of smaller pieces of cloth rather than one long length."

"Yes, I had noticed, Ah-mah," Princess Medi said. "But I want to know when you will teach me the pattern for working feet."

"I have been thinking of that, my lady. As you know, I am not a teacher, but I have thought of a way we might work together so you can learn the pattern. I hope you will not feel I place myself above you, for that is not my intent." Ah-mah looked at the princess to register any change in her face or body as she said, "I believe I will be able to tell if you are following the pattern if you work it on my feet."

"Does anyone treat your feet, Ah-mah?" the princess asked, softly.

"No, lady."

"Could we begin today?"

Ah-mah nodded. "When I finish with this woman, come sit in front of me and I will teach you the inching motion your thumb must make."

The woman had no sooner risen before, in one swift movement, Princess Medi sat in the spot she had vacated, eyes dancing in anticipation. With one hand, Ah-mah grasped her arm and began inching her thumb up from wrist to elbow. The princess flinched, and the ever-sensitive Ah-mah stopped.

"Continue, please," the princess said. "The pressure is more than I had imagined, and it startled me. It feels as though your thumb is climbing up my arm."

"Show me," Ah-mah directed, holding out her arm.

The princess took Ah-mah's arm and tried to move her thumb just as Ah-mah had. The process was much more difficult than she had imagined. Ah-mah chuckled, as she remembered pushing her thumb into Sept's feet beneath the nehet years ago. She, too, had been awkward at first.

"You are doing well," Ah-mah encouraged. "This is your first lesson, and one you must practice over and over to build strength in your thumbs and your arms. It will be difficult for a while, but one day, it will seem as if you have done it forever."

Ah-mah sat down to the evening meal, much relieved. A thorny problem had been solved, and not in a way she had anticipated. Now the first step had been taken, easily and naturally. She hoped the rest of the instruction would go as well.

"Nefer, today I began showing the princess how to move her thumb to treat the feet. I would like to have you practice with her. You know enough about the process to help her, and by helping her, you will help yourself. One day you will leave me to treat feet in another village."

"I would never leave you, Ah-mah!" Nefer protested.

"I am teasing you, Nefer. You are my son, but you are also my friend." Impulsively, Ah-mah continued, "Nefer, will you hear a secret? One you can never tell?"

"Are you sure you can trust me?" Nefer teased back. "I am about to leave you, and I was born a thief, or so you have told me."

"Then you really are leaving me?"

Not certain she still teased him, Nefer came to her and put his arms around her. "You are the mother I lost, Ah-mahsis. I would never betray my mother, nor would I willingly leave her. You can trust me with your secret."

"It is a long story, Nefer. Perhaps we should have our evening meal first, and then a little beer."

They ate in silence. When the meal was finished, Ah-mah cleared the plates and Nefer rose to fetch the jug and two cups. He returned to the table and poured a little of the beer into each cup.

Ah-mah let the foamy liquid flow from her throat all the way to her stomach, feeling the warm glow that resulted. She sighed, heavy with memory, wondering where to begin, or even if she should.

"By rights, I should be telling Sept first."

"Telling me what?" asked Sept, as he entered the room.

"You are home early!" they exclaimed.

"By two days. The threat was greatly exaggerated. But I see I have returned just in time. My wife is telling something she thinks I should hear, besides drinking all the beer," he said, grinning

Nefer hastened to bring another cup to the table as Sept removed his sword and his knife and stowed them in the corner of the room.

"I am dusty and weary of the road, but I will drink with you and eat a little if there is food left."

Anticipating Sept's hunger, Nefer set a filled a plate before the man he called father. For a while, the only sounds in the room were of Sept's eating.

"Now," he said, through a mouth full of food, "it is time to listen."

Ah-mah sat up straighter on her stool and swiped the back of her hand across her brow. Looking at Sept and Nefer, she said, "From birth I have had a companion who could not be seen by others for she lived in my mind. We spoke together at will, playing when I was a child, discussing ideas and problems as I grew to adulthood. She stayed with me when I married Khmet and shared my joy when Ak-hu was born. She comforted me when Khmet died and went with me to Remtu's hut. When you came to me, Sept, she and I worked to understand the dream I had of you, and to find a way to treat your feet.

"On the day you asked me to join with you, my companion left me. In my joy I called to her in my mind, and for the first time, she did not respond."

Ah-mah stopped, her story apparently finished. Both Sept and Nefer were silent, Sept full of thoughts, Nefer not knowing what to say. Was this Ah-mah's secret? That she had an unseen companion? He started to ask, but Sept spoke first.

"Why are you telling us this? Has something happened?"

"Aletha has returned."

"Who is Aletha?" Sept asked.

"My internal companion. But now she tells me she is from a different time and place. When I see her in my inner vision, she sits in a garden unlike any in this land. Water stretches to the horizon in front of her and a mighty tree filled with fragrant blossoms stands beside the bench on which she sits."

A strange look crossed Sept's face. "What is it, my husband?"

Not willing to reveal that his wife's description of the lady and her garden overlooking the sea felt oddly familiar, Sept said instead, "There is more to your story, is there not?"

Ah-mah nodded. "She returned to me as I worked with a young girl who was in pain so terrible I was afraid she would die. In my mind's eye, I saw a sword cut her in two, and a way came to me to try to reconnect her. When I did so, a strong current of energy passed through my body into the girl's body and my inner sight showed me the lady I have described to you, the lady I now know to be Aletha, my companion from before."

"I remember, Ah-masis. You said something drew you."

Ah-mah nodded. "I never imagined Aletha separate from me, but this beautiful woman in her garden speaks with the voice of my companion. When I was a child, I told my mother of my companion and she cautioned me to keep the knowledge to myself. But now I wonder if the energy that healed the girl was mine or my companion's. That is why I tell you of her."

Sept sat quietly, staring at the bit of beer left in his cup. He shrugged his shoulders, as if to rid himself of inertia, then brought the cup to his lips, draining it.

"If Aletha's energy healed the child, it did so by passing through you."

"And for that to happen, I had to be willing," Ah-mah said. "But what if she causes me to speak or do things I otherwise would not?"

"Do not be troubled, my Ah-mah. Nefer is clever and knows how to be wary. If you are tempted to forget where you are and speak what you should not, he will interrupt or somehow create a distraction. And Ah-mah, I would protect you with my life." Sept pushed back from the table and held out his arms. She came willingly, curling into his arms like the child she wanted to be in that moment. Nefer witnessed the intimacy quietly, grateful for both this man and woman, thanking whichever gods might be watching.

CHAPTER SEVENTEEN
The Keeper of Ideas

Uljas, Keeper of Ideas, joined in the whispered chanting as the Keepers took their seats, but just beneath the surface of his calm exterior, his skin suddenly itched in one spot or another and a lump resided just below his breastbone.

Aletha, beautiful Aletha, had once again filled the crystal vases with roses, but tonight their scent was too much for Uljas. By the time the meeting ended, he was spent, although his body remained tense to the point of rigidity. He rose stiffly, went to his room, and without removing his robes of office, collapsed onto his bed and into a fitful sleep.

When he awoke, the room was as dark as his thoughts. To lose Atlantis… To lose everything he held dear… To know that nothing might remain of this great civilization… He wanted to lash out, but there was nothing at which he could strike. He wanted to shout a grand, violent "NO!"

A soft rapping at the door shook his mind loose from the chaos controlling it. With effort, he rose and went to the door. Opening it, he saw the tall, unquenchable figure of Seronak.

"May I enter?" The voice was soft, steady, a rock to anchor him.

Unable to speak, Uljas backed away from the door, feeling the illusion of normalcy return as Seronak entered the room.

"I have come to remind you of who you are, old friend," Seronak said. "You may think it presumptuous of me, but I sense that the certain doom of Atlantis has overwhelmed you."

Somehow Seronak's words released Uljas' tongue and lips. "I feel frozen. My mind stands on the edge of the abyss and I am terrified to move. How can this be?"

"When we are shocked with our mortality, wisdom and truth flee. You are threatened with the death, not only of yourself, but of all you hold dear, all you thought was solid and unmoving.

"In the beginning was the Void, and the Void was All, until the Cauldron of Time infused it with energy and caused it to become Universe. Now the Universe pulses and breathes, ebbs and flows. Atlantis ebbs, and the cities of Atlantis will soon not exist, but the energy that is Atlantis remains in the Universe forever. Atlanteans may or may not survive what comes, but the impact of our existence cannot be denied."

"But I want more!" Uljas shouted. "I want Atlantis to be real to future generations, not just as energy, but as something tangible. I want this great civilization to have meaning. I want my life to have meaning!"

"Then use your skills to find a way for that to happen." said Seronak, and abruptly withdrew.

Uljas paced the length of his narrow room, up and down, up and down, muttering as he went. Suddenly he stopped, looked at the door through which Seronak had exited, and laughed. The Keeper of the One had restored his sanity, absolving him from the grip of terror. He knew what to do next.

With ritual developed from long practice, Uljas sat in his

meditation chair facing the representation of the sun on the wall and chanted, "I am all. We are One." His gaze focused on the crystal centered in the sun sculpture as he stilled his body and allowed his mind to drift, to roam, the chanting reduced to a whisper.

Into his mind came a picture of Aletha standing among fresh roses in the Crystal Room. "Ah-mah must see more than Mu," he thought to the image of the woman who had sent her energy into the future. "She must know Atlantis."

Aletha's image smiled at him, and said, "Will you be dolphin?"

Warm water caressed his skin and made swimming effortless. He heard something call to him, not with words, but with clicks and whistles. Turning toward the sound, he saw a magnificent, glowing dolphin swimming toward him. The dolphin's eyes were Seronak's.

A knock at the door interrupted him once again. He took the time needed to return from his dream/vision before rising, instinctively knowing that whoever was at the door would wait. Opening it, he was not surprised to see Aletha. She did not come in, but said, "Ah-mah will know of Atlantis and Atlanteans, Uljas. You will not be forgotten."

Uljas leaned against the open door and watched her leave. Then he closed the door, removed his robe and hung it, turned down the covers of his bed, and slipped beneath them. Composing his body for sleep, he drifted into the world of dreams, the great fear banished.

The idea that humans could be transformed into dolphins was born in Uljas that night, and when shared, triggered the Keepers to search for ways to bring the concept into form. Not long afterward, he conceived the idea of the memory disk, which he kept to himself for a while, turning it over and over in his mind. At last he shared it, and this time the response surprised him. At least two others, Karon, Keeper of Earth Matters, and Belel, Keeper of

Origin, had a similar idea. Very soon, they added its construction to their plans.

Never again did Uljas succumb to fear's seduction. Even as the ground trembled, he and the others worked toward three great goals: to preserve the people and artifacts by removing them to higher ground; to preserve the Keepers by transforming them into dolphins; and to preserve the most significant moment in each Keeper's life on the memory disk. They did not forget Ah-mah. The fact that she knew of them served as immediate comfort to each, but especially to Aletha, to Seronak, and now, to Uljas, for Ah-mah spoke of a future that lived, even if he would not. Aletha was right. He would not be forgotten.

CHAPTER EIGHTEEN

Sefra

Ah-mah felt easier in her mind after sharing her secret with Sept and Nefer. She still could not speak with Aletha at will, but thought she felt her presence from time to time. "Probably because I wish it were so, and not because it is," she thought.

Princess Medi was proving to be a diligent student. On the second day after she showed her how to move her thumb by pressing a spot, lifting, moving slightly, and pressing again, Ah-mah noticed her student's thumbs were red and swollen.

"No practice today," Ah-mah commanded. "Today you will watch only." Ah-mah knelt in front of the princess. Dipping her fingers in a bowl of flax oil, Ah-mah smeared some of it on both Medi's thumbs. The throbbing lessened slightly, and she looked at Ah-mah with gratitude.

"Flax seeds are good for more than cushions," Ah-mah said. "When your thumbs have healed, you can practice again, but only for a little while, and only three times in a day. In the meantime, I have something to show you."

Ah-mah placed a flat stone in front of the princess on which she had drawn the sole of a right foot and a left foot. On each foot were islands of color (rubbed in from the cosmetics box) and symbols. Nefer watched the two, bending over the stone, heads together and noticed he liked both heads equally. Ah-mah motioned for him to join them.

"This is a picture of the feet and the important areas to work. It is the beginning of knowledge, the beginning of the pattern." Realizing that the princess in her eagerness to learn would stay up all night memorizing each detail, Ah-mah continued, "Feet have a pattern only time will give you. Pictures are good beginnings, but that is all they are. Tomorrow we will begin learning the pattern."

Accompanied by her guard, Malloch, and her Shadow, Medi came to Ah-mah's house every morning. As part of their routine, Nefer washed Medi's feet, and she washed his, while Ah-mah finished her breakfast, being slower and more thorough with her eating than the two young people. Once their feet were clean, Ah-mah had them take turns pulling and twisting each other's feet. She watched them, but was not hard on either, knowing they needed to get used to handling the foot, to feeling where the hands were comfortable and where they were awkward. Then with Medi at her side, she worked Nefer's feet, talking the girl through each step. On alternate days, Medi would be the one on the mat, with Nefer watching.

Ever mindful of all the people around her, Ah-mah noticed that Medi's maidservant did not hide as completely as she had in the beginning. One morning, Ah-mah asked Medi, "Has your maidservant eaten this morning?"

"She eats before she wakes me."

"If she eats so early, perhaps she would enjoy some refreshment now. There's plenty of barley porridge this morning for her and for Malloch as well," Ah-mah said, all the while aware that Shadow's eager eyes had understood what was said. Malloch stood tall and silent (on both feet equally), as though he had not heard or porridge was beneath his notice.

"Come, Salla. You may eat with us if you like," the princess said in her own language.

Ah-mah was surprised at Medi's seeming indifference to her maidservant, but she held her tongue, remembering that she did not know the customs of Medi's land. After all, the girl was a princess, and no doubt, anyone who was not nobility in her land did not warrant the same consideration as she commanded. Still, the heart of Ah-mah was not to be denied, and as Nefer and Medi continued to practice treating each other's feet, Ah-mah spoke to the maidservant.

"Ah-mah," she said, pointing to herself. Putting her hand on the girl's shoulder, she said, "Salla." A faint smile flickered across the girl's face. Encouraged, Ah-mah pointed to herself and looked at Salla with raised eyebrows.

"Ah-mah," the girl whispered.

"Eat now," Ah-mah said, and made motions of lifting an imaginary spoon to her mouth. Without another word, the girl set to and ate every bite including the dates Ah-mah had liberally scattered on her porridge. Malloch did the same and then returned to his post. From that day, Ah-mah made sure there was plenty of porridge for everyone.

On her own, the princess began to help Nefer wash the feet of those who came for treatment. At first he was reluctant to see someone so high born performing such a menial task, but she seemed to enjoy it. Salla, on the other hand, dropped any pretense of hiding and watched Ah-mah's treatments avidly, inching closer to see more clearly. One day, she whispered a request. Ah-mah, leaning close to the girl to hear her better, smiled and nodded. When Salla would have gotten up, Ah-mah touched her arm to stay her movement. Then she said, "Princess Medi, would it be permissible to have Salla wash the people's feet? That way, you and Nefer could observe the treatments more closely."

"Would you like to do that, Salla?" Medi asked.

Salla gave a quick, determined nod, and looking at Ah-mah, who smiled her approval, went to sit at the doorway with the bowl of water and the cloth. As Ah-mah suspected, Salla proved to be good at any job given to her and quick to learn Kem-T, the language spoken in the Land of the River, since her request had been whispered completely in that language.

No longer needed to wash feet, Nefer and Medi sat behind Ah-mah, watching her every move. Often she would point out a particular callus, or explain to them why she treated in a particular way. The people followed her explanations with interest. Completely unaware of the effect she was having, she chanced to overhear a conversation between two who waited in line.

"Ah-mah says to rub here to help the neck. No, not there. Give me your foot, and I will show you."

She had gone to get a cup of water, and to stretch her back and legs. So surprised was she that she went to look over the wall. The two, a man and a woman, were so engrossed they did not see her. As she watched, others in the line showed interest, moving to stand or squat beside the two. Ah-mah did not know whether to be troubled or grateful that the people would try to help each other. It seemed everyone wanted to learn to rub feet.

"What is it, Ah-mah?" Nefer had joined her.

"Look at those two. They are rubbing feet." Ah-mah sounded dismayed.

"It is good, isn't it?"

"I suppose so, "Ah-mah replied.

Nefer threw his shoulders back, and said, "It is good, Ah-mahsis. I know it."

As he did, a chill passed through Ah-mah's body, and she shuddered. She had a terrible foreboding that she would remember this insignificant incident and wish she had done something about it. With a heart made suddenly heavy, she signaled to Salla that she was ready for the next person.

A stocky man entered the garden, smiling broadly. "Do you remember me, Mistress Ah-mah?" he asked.

Ah-mah looked at him closely, and then at his feet. Certainly slimmer than they had been, but still the same feet. She would know them anywhere. "Nabi! You have lost your extra pounds," she said.

"I feel safe now, and I no longer need the weight to protect me. Is there anything I can do to repay your kindness?"

Still filled with dread at what she had witnessed in the line, Ah-mah asked, "What is your position?"

"I am assistant to the snwn, Ke-ptah," Nabi said.

"Does that one know you come to me?"

"No, Mistress. I have not told him," was the embarrassed reply.

Taking a deep breath, Ah-mah said, "Nabi, what do you think Ke-ptah would say about rubbing feet?"

Nabi chuckled, "I do not have to speculate about that. I heard him say to the high priest only yesterday that he did not think anything good could come from trading foot rubbing for trees."

Ah-mah stiffened and stopped rubbing Nabi's feet. She held them and bowed her head before she trusted herself to speak again.

"Who is trading foot rubbing for trees, Nabi?" she asked.

"Why, everyone knows, Mistress. You are teaching the princess so that her father will allow access to his forests."

This was too much for Ah-mah. She withdrew into silence and went to work. In fact she said no more all day, nodding to Salla for the next person, and the next. When the last pair of feet had been finished, she said her prayers silently and walked out of the house and into the street. "I need air," she thought. Nefer, having heard what Nabi said and sensing her mood, let her go.

Ah-mah walked and walked, letting her feet find their own path. She felt locked in fear, knotted, terrified. "Everyone knows." Why had she thought she could be as private in this village as she had been with the people who came to her treatment room beneath the nehet tree by Remtu's hut? But she had not thought of it. She had never had anything to hide. Well, that was not exactly true. There was her internal companion, hidden for years from all but her mother. Suddenly, her mind showed her the ququ-lined path to the river, the path she had walked almost every day of her life. "I want to go home," she muttered. "I want to sleep in the home of my childhood, to see my daughter, to play with my grandchildren. I am tired of the Nubtians and I am doubly weary of politics."

Quickening her pace, she was soon beyond Nubt and on the levee that formed the western bank of the river. Ququ palms towered over the path with long spaces and a few nehet between them. "I cannot go home. I cannot go back on my bargain with Khufer. What is the matter with me?" She was almost running. Suddenly, she stopped as she remembered the wise woman who lived down river. She ran back down the levee and through the streets of Nubt, halting only when she reached her doorway. Walking straight to the room where she and Sept slept, she picked up the beautiful pillow Medi made for her. The tiny stitches must have taken hours. The pillow would be enough. It must be.

Next morning, she rose before dawn. Telling no one where she was going or when she would return, Ah-mah stepped quietly out of the house and walked briskly toward the river. A pale moon served to light her way.

Lamplight shone through the open doorway of the old woman's hut. "Good," thought Ah-mah, "at least I will not wake her."

The voice was sharp and demanding. "No visitors. Go away."

"I have come to ask a question." Ah-mah had come this far, she could not turn back, no matter how gruff the woman seemed.

"No questions. Go away."

Ah-mah sensed interest in the woman's words and her voice was less strident. "I brought you a gift."

Silence. Then, "A question and a gift. Well." The woman opened the crude door, a lamp, smoky with bad oil, in her hand. She walked up to Ah-mah and stuck the lamp in her face. "Why you are not so young either! It does not show in your voice. Where is the gift?"

Ah-mah extended the pillow to the woman. Medi's skilled fingers had fashioned it of linen dyed purple, and then embroidered the sun upon it with colored thread, some of it wrapped with gold. "She will make me another when she finds this one gone," Ah-mah thought.

It was a magnificent gift and the woman knew it. Her fingers twitched in anticipation, but she was not quite ready to give up the game. "Pshaw!" she spat. "I have seen a hundred like it."

"No," Ah-mah said quietly, "You have not seen even one other like it because there is none. Now, will you answer my question? You will not own the pillow until you do."

"All right. All right. Ask your question."

"May I not have something to drink? I have walked a long way, and I am cold."

"Sit, then," said the old woman, indicating a rock. "I will bring beer for both of us."

Ra had begun to color the rare clouds overhead. Ah-mah tilted her head back and raised her eyes to feast on the sight. Before long, the old woman reappeared carrying two cups in one hand and two flat pieces of bread in the other. Ah-mah had not seen her clearly in the dim lamp's light. The woman's skin was black as night, and her white hair stuck out in all directions, uncombed, wispy, framing a face that held black eyes in pools of milk under jutting, white eyebrows. She was taller than Ah-mah, and in her youth, must have been statuesque.

Something about the beer must have civilized the woman. Her movements approached grace as she handed Ah-mah a cup and one of the pieces of bread, still warm.

"Will you tell me your name?" Ah-mah asked.

"I am Sefra in my country, which is far, far to the south of this place."

"Thank you, Sefra, for your courtesy."

"You may ask your question now," said Sefra, still eyeing the pillow.

"It is not an easy question, nor a simple one," Ah-mah began.

"You want to know if rubbing feet will cause harm to come to those you love."

Startled, Ah-mah could not speak for a moment. Sefra continued, "Stories come to me, and the story of how the Mistress of the Land went to live alone in a hut and then joined with the Master of the Guard has been told to me by more than one person. Why would you think that rubbing feet could cause harm? Something else is in your mind. Tell me."

Ah-mah opened her heart to Sefra, telling her of the political situation she was being forced into, of how she did not trust the high priest or the ruler of Nubt, of how the people had started rubbing feet and how everyone knew her treatments were being traded for trees, of what the snwn had said. She told her everything, and the woman, Sefra, listened, sometimes with eyes closed, sometimes peering intently at Ah-mah, often nodding in agreement. Finally, there was nothing left to say.

As Ra climbed up into the heavens, Sefra remained still and silent. Ah-mah, freed from her burden for the moment, rested, her eyes drinking in the beauty of the day. The humming brought her back. When the humming stopped, Sefra opened her eyes to look at Ah-mah.

"You were born with the gift of healing. When you decided to study feet, you set your own feet on an unknown path. In truth, you agreed to these adventures before you entered this life. Your first adventure involved people you knew. Safe. The second involved more risk, taking you to live in the village, bringing you priests from the temple. Now you have been told you must go to another land, to have your skills traded for trees. You do not know if you will ever return. Perhaps you will find a hut by a river and become an old woman of that land. You are afraid your family will not be safe while you are away. But Ah-mah, your choice to go or not to go has been set before you, not by high priests and rulers, or kings from other lands, but by your own soul.

"Aletha has come to you from another time, another place. Have you wondered how she found you? Was it because she had the energy to look, or did you draw her to you? Like seeks like, Ah-mah.

"If I had one wish, I would wish to see you before you die. I would like to see how you have been changed by your adventures. Trust your path, Ah-mah. That is all I have to say."

Ah-mah rose and solemnly placed the pillow into Sefra's hands. Sefra held the pillow for a moment before rising also. Without knowing why, except that she wanted to give this woman something of herself, Ah-mah placed her hands on Sefra's shoulders and inclined her head slightly. Sefra responded, drawing closer, her forehead meeting Ah-mah's in a gesture, a bonding, more ancient than the Land of the River, as old as life itself.

CHAPTER NINETEEN

The Keeper of Origin

The whispering brought her back from her dreams. "My lady, my lady." The voice was insistent.

The Keeper of Origin opened her eyes to the wizened face. "What is it?"

"Men are here from the city. Someone is hurt. They ask you to come."

Reluctantly, Belel left the warmth of the bed clothes and shrugged into the robe old Melias held for her. Taking the Emerald from the altar, she clasped it at the nape of her neck and slipped her feet into sandals even as her hand grabbed the small cloth bag which held medicines and supplies. She hardly noticed the men as she stepped into their midst. At her coming, they turned as one around her, escorting her rapidly into the poorest quarter of the city.

The man on the bed drew ragged breaths, his chest abnormally flat where a great building stone had broken loose and struck him. The trickle of blood from the corner of his mouth was not a good sign.

Whispering the sacred mantra, Belel sat on the stool by the bed and closed her eyes, going deep within. She gathered energy and prepared to focus it through the Emerald to give what comfort she could to the injured man. Whispering the sacred mantra, "I am all, we are One," she thrust healing energy toward the man only to be stopped by something that felt solid and impenetrable. She opened her eyes and saw nothing, but she could feel the wall that had raised itself around the man. Stunned, she tried to force her hand through the invisible wall and succeeded in touching him, but to no avail. Her energy could not reach his body.

His eyes opened, alert with that clarity which often precedes death, and his lips parted as though he wished to speak. She bent closer.

"Look at me, Great One," he whispered. "I am your death."

Belel drew back in horror as the mouth stretched into a hideous grin and the man drew a last shallow breath, expelling it in laughter as he died. Startled out of her body, she floated above the man, seeking reason. Her body's energy seemed to be encased in a transparent bubble, the man's similarly bound. Wherever the two bubbles met, they did not join as droplets of water do, but bounced violently off each other, jolted by their disparity. Even in death, his energy was alive and vital, ready to continue without him, if only it could.

Belel reentered her body and left the room and the house, forgetting to speak words of comfort to the family, forgetting to speak at all. She dismissed her escort with a wave of her hand and walked to keep chaos in check, passing many, speaking to no one, indeed, not noticing that anyone was there. At last she reached a hill overlooking the sea. One small, sturdy tree stood sentinel, its roots clinging to the rocky soil. She lowered herself to a perch beneath it, worn smooth over the centuries, a spot she often sought when troubled. The Emerald remained clutched in her hand. Cradling that hand with the other, she stared with unfocused eyes at the sea, her true gaze inward. Methodically, she calmed herself, detaching, tentacle by tentacle, from all except the laughter which was permanently imprinted on her psyche.

With her inner vision, she looked at the man. Shorter and darker than others, with stocky, muscular strength, cunning as any animal, the powerful, swirling core of him stretching not, as she would have expected, toward the heavens, but deep into the earth. As she saw him expel his last breath in laughter, it seemed that an entire civilization of short, dark, energy-filled people surrounded him, gobbling up everything in their paths and leaving a trail of destruction. She saw Atlantis, at first neglected and filled with debris, then falling, great stones, tall temples, into the sea. A soundless scream was torn from her as the energy crystals exploded into fragments.

She opened her eyes to rid herself of the terrible vision and awakened to pain. Her hand had been cut by the healing Emerald as she gripped its sharp edges. Tearing a strip from the hem of her robe, she bound the hand tightly to stop the bleeding and sought comfort from the sacred mantra. Over and over she said aloud, "We are One. We are One. We are One," desperately trying to create a bridge between her bubble and that of the man in her inner vision.

On silent wings, an owl brushed her shoulder. Flailing her arms to ward off the unseen attacker, she lost her balance and rolled down the hill, slamming into a tree near the bottom of it with such force that she lost consciousness. She awoke to morning clouds colored by the dawn. Slowly she sat up, rubbing her head and her side where she had hit the tree, hungry and thirsty, battered and bruised, unable to do more than witness the arrival of day.

In the rising sun, she saw a great Wheel which held images of people. As the Wheel turned, an image became sharply defined, then faded as a new image came into view. She watched and watched, surely long enough for the images to repeat themselves, but they never did. Her breath caught when she saw a Muan, very much like Aletha, so real she felt she could touch her. As her hand reached forward, the image was replaced by a new image. "Oh!" she whispered, as someone as grand as Seronak, the Keeper of the One, came into focus. "No!" she cried, as the image began to fade, replaced by one that was short, dark. As she turned her head, unable to bear the sight, she heard his laughter a final time.

"But, we are One." She clung to the words as to a rock in a storm.

"Yes, we are, Belel."

Startled, Belel looked up and saw an image so like herself, she wondered if she might be, once again, out of her body.

"I am the first Keeper of Origin," said the image. "I lived at the beginning of Atlantis when our energy was young and vital. You are at the end. I was eager and filled with ambition, ready to embrace the unknown. You are filled with desperation, afraid of the unknown."

"I cannot forget his laughter," Belel said.

"I laughed as well in the beginning. The Wheel turns, Belel. Change comes. It is a Truth. Tell me, you who are at an ending, what do you know of cycles?"

Set abruptly into a different mode by the question, Belel said, "I am original energy drawn to one conclusion, bearing the seeds of many others. The Wheel seems one-dimensional, but it is multi-layered with depths and heights and breadths only guessed at, just as I am multi-layered, multi-dimensional. As I am, so is every one of my people, whether brightly and vividly so, or in faded, diluted form."

"Beginnings and Endings," said the first Keeper of Origin.

"Beginnings and Endings," echoed Belel. "Two sides of the same coin."

"Ah, but the coin has more than two sides," said the first Keeper. "Even the face one sees is not as clear and bold as imagination declares. Atlanteans began much as the Conquerors, filled with energy. Nothing stood in our way for long. Not only were we interested in things of the mind, Belel, but we wanted a place big enough to house our energy. We took this land from its original inhabitants, and we did not ask permission. Our energy was too strong, too demanding.

"Even though we are One, Belel, we are also many. Each of us, Muan, Atlantean, Conqueror, perceives that he is purely Muan, purely Atlantean, purely Conqueror. How limiting, if true!" The first Keeper flashed a brilliant smile at Belel as her image began to fade. "Many are One. Diversity will ensure the survival of humanity. The race may no longer be ruled by tall, graceful Atlanteans, but it will survive."

CHAPTER TWENTY

Partings

Shemu, the season of harvest, had gone on too long, becoming the season of drought. Smoke from sacrifices hung over the village, adding a sooty layer to the dust, and making everyone short-tempered and irritable except for Ah-mah. Since her time with the old woman, Sefra, Aletha had returned to Ah-mah's dreams, showing her tall buildings perched on rocks overlooking a body of water without end and a room made entirely of clear rocks, which Aletha called 'crystals.' In her joy at her companion's return, Ah-mah sailed through her days of treating feet.

She was preparing a fish stew for the evening meal when Sept stormed in, his face split by a huge grin. "We are leaving!" he exclaimed.

Ah-mah added more herbs to the stew and stirred it. "Leaving? Who is leaving?"

"We are, Wife! Nefer and the Princess, too. We are going across the great sea to Byblos, the Land of Trees," Sept said, never noticing that Ah-mah had turned several shades paler. Nefer hastened to slide a stool beneath her as she sank on buckled knees. "Nefer, my boy, we are going to Medi's land, and we are leaving as soon as the river rises the length of this hand," Sept said, thrusting his hand at the roof.

Nefer saw the impact each word had on Ah-mah. He knelt beside her and took her hand. She sighed out the breath she had been holding. Abashed, Sept knelt and took her other hand in his.

"Who will treat the people's feet? I should have trained others besides Nefer and the Princess Medi." Ah-mah slipped her hands from theirs and placed them on either side of her face, as though to hold it steady.

"You have trained others, Ah-mahsis. As you taught the treatment to us, you also taught it to the people. They will treat each other until we return, and they will appreciate us all the more for our absence," Nefer said.

"I cannot leave without seeing Ak-hu and my grandchildren."

"There, there, my love. We are not leaving tomorrow. You have time to take care of matters that are important to you. Medi's people have come on a grand boat to take her home, and Rahotep is outfitting a boat for us to return with her. I have spoken with Akban, Master of the boat from Byblos, who said the trip took six tens of days. You can tell Ak-hu that we will return before the time for planting." Sept grinned at Ah-mah, unable to suppress his excitement. "We are going on an adventure, wife of mine, an adventure into the unknown!"

For the next few days, Ah-mah's world was turned upside down. Even meals were too haphazard to set a routine. She and Nefer scoured both her gardens in Nubt and the one by Remtu's hut for herbs. They cut and sorted and tied into bundles all Ah-mah thought they might use on the trip. Remtu's hut was used for drying what came from that garden, with bundles hanging from every conceivable peg. The same was true for the house in Nubt, with multitudes of drying bundles hanging everywhere a space could be found. Ah-mah made linen bags for each herb, with one large bag to hold them all. The little cosmetics box Sept had given her was replenished so that she might paint her face for their meeting with Medi's father, the King. The box which had held it became her medicine box. It would not hold all she wished to have close at hand, but she could put small bundles of the medicinal herbs and some of each tonic and unguent into it, adding to it from her stores in the bag as needed. Clean rags, jars of flax oil and honey, the box of salt, and ququ twine were added to the box for good measure, along with the flat and rounded stones she used to grind herbs for her tonics. Her leather bag, worn and patched, was filled with what she needed most often. That bag and the medicine box she would keep close. Now that she had two sources at hand besides the large bag which Sept said could be put into the space below the deck, she felt better.

In the midst of her preparations, an old man came to ask her to help his wife, Iret. Unable to refuse, Ah-mah went with Khent, the old man, pausing only to grab her leather bag and sling it over her shoulder.

The sweetish smell of death greeted them as they entered the door. Ah-mah knelt by Iret's bedside, surprised to see bright eyes looking at her. "Bright with fever, no doubt," she thought.

"Are you in pain?" she asked, gently touching the woman's arm.

Iret nodded and closed her eyes, using much of her remaining strength to keep from drawing her arm away from Ah-mah's touch. Ah-mah felt the light flinch and withdrew her hand. "I brought a potion to help you depart this life." Iret nodded weakly.

Ah-mah rose and motioned for Khent to join her outside. "The potion is quite strong. You will want to say farewell." The old man nodded and went into what was no longer a home to him, but a house of death.

From the bottom of her bag, Ah-mah took a tiny jar. Removing the clay stopper from it she poured a measure of the contents into a cup. "It will make a dying person sleep until death can take the body," the slant-eyed, yellow-skinned man who sold it to her had said. Ah-mah took the cup to Iret's bedside. Khent sat, his hand lightly touching his wife's, his eyes drinking in a last vision of her. As Ah-mah knelt beside the bed, Iret whispered, "I am ready."

Holding the cup to her lips, Ah-mah raised it ever so gently until a bit of the mixture could enter her mouth and be swallowed. The man had said that very little was required. Ah-mah allowed for two swallows and removed the cup. She went back outside to return what was left to the jar, seal it, and place it in the deep recesses of her bag before going to sit with Khent.

It was nearly an hour before Ah-mah noticed that Iret no longer took a breath. She rose and went to the old man. Placing her hand on his shoulder, she said, gently, "She has gone."

"I know. I want to sit with her a while longer."

Always practical, Ah-mah asked, "Do you have someone who will wash her?"

"I have made arrangements."

As she returned home on the dusty path between the houses, Ah-mah observed the village, drinking in its sights and sounds, knowing that she, too, was about to pass into another life, knowing that she would never see the village in quite the same way when she returned.

The next morning, Ah-mah entered one of the many small boats oared by men who ferried people from one side to the other. Instead of crossing the river, the man oared the boat down river to the stone dock where Ak-hu waited with Menes, grown tall with eight summers, and Ah-nah, now a child of four.

The day was spent slowly, carefully, thoroughly. Ah-mah told Ak-hu more than once how much she would miss her, how she loved her, prompting Ak-hu to exclaim, "Mother, you act as if you are not coming back!"

"I shall return, my daughter, but Ak-hu, I have this terrible feeling of dread in my heart. I wonder if it is fear because I have never traveled so far, or if there is some other reason. Could there be something in our future that would separate us? I think of my return and I cannot find you. In my dreams I call out to you, but the house is empty."

Ever practical, Ak-hu put her arms around this woman who was so dear to her, and said, "We have this day."

Not content, Ah-mah said, "Do not trust Rahotep, my daughter. I think he still wants this land."

"I will be wary, my mother, and I will remember the love we share today. Now go, and do not fear for us." As she stepped back from Ah-mah, a radiant light seemed to emanate from deep within her. Ah-mah drank in the light, determined to hold it in her mind and heart forever.

Leaning down, Ak-hu whispered something to Menes, who raced off into the house, coming back almost immediately, his hands carrying a small, beautifully crafted pillow made of linen dyed the color of rich brown earth. Gold-wrapped thread created the rayed sun in the center of the pillow, a thick, wavy line of blue thread beneath it. Ah-mah would take the earth, the river and the sun with her, but best of all, she would take the love of her daughter. Giving Menes a hug so tight it made him squirm, and kissing Ah-nah on both her cheeks, Ah-mah gave her daughter a look of gratitude and love, and stepped into the small water craft.

Realizing that the last thing Ah-mah would remember would

be clothes for them, Sept gave Nefer a verbal list and watched with pride as he raced off to the marketplace. Rahotep had seen to the clothes they would wear to greet the King and Queen, Medi's father and mother. He remembered the day Rahotep had asked him what color his wife's presentation dress should be. Without thinking, he had blurted, "yellow." The dress was not linen, but made of a soft cotton from Ur, with sleeves that touched the wrist, a skirt that touched the floor. Sept had seen the dress once it was finished and knew Ah-mah would like it. She would represent the sun in this new land. He did not show it to his wife, preferring to surprise her later.

One night, a messenger came to the door to ask for Nefer. "Come with me," was all he would say. Before Ah-mah could protest, Nefer was gone. She tried not to show her anxiety, but before long, she paced the floor and muttered softly. Knowing his wife's habits, Sept said nothing, and in fact, was a little worried himself. "I should have gone with him," he thought.

Both sighed with relief when Nefer's face appeared in the doorway, grinning hugely. "I need your help," he said, indicating a very large cloth bag he was trying to manage, stuffed with something. Sept grabbed hold of the bag and the two men carried it into the house.

"Rosemary! Who would send me rosemary, and so much of it?" Ah-mah asked.

"The old man whose wife you helped, Ah-mah. He sent all he had from his wife's garden. He said it was to help you remember."

"Remember?"

Ah-mah put her arms around the bag and buried her face in its delicious aroma. Immediately, she was in Aletha's garden, surrounded by rosemary. Aletha was sitting on her bench, back to Ah-mah. So close. "Perhaps if I stay here, she will turn around." It was her last thought as she sank to the floor. She awoke to shaking, and Sept's worried face. "Ah-mah, are you ill?"

She smiled her reassurance and got to her feet. "Sept, can we take this with us? Is there room? I may need it." The words came in a rush.

"I will find room, my wife."

Ah-mah had one last worry. Medi did not look well. She seldom spoke, even to Nefer, and her face was drawn as though she was in pain. On a day when Sept and Nefer were busy on the boat, Ah-mah sent a messenger to fetch the princess for a lesson. She came with her guard, Malloch, and with Salla. Ah-mah greeted them, but then sent Malloch to fetch some oil from a few houses away, wanting privacy with Medi.

"Come," she said to the girl. "I have prepared the mat beneath the tree for one last treatment before we leave." An involuntary shudder passed through Medi when Ah-mah spoke of leaving. In silence, she lay down upon the mat, and Ah-mah began her treatment. Salla found her usual spot beneath the tree but in sight of Ah-mah's hands. A constant prayer for guidance ran through her mind, and so intently did she concentrate on the treatment, she did not notice Medi's tears. A sniff alerted her.

"Medi," she said, "unburden yourself. Neither Salla nor I would reveal your secrets."

The comfort in Ah-mah's words and her soothing touch were too much for the girl. She put her hands over her face and sobbed. "I do not wish to return," she finally whispered.

Salla, upon hearing her mistress' words, seemed to curl her body into a tight knot.

"Tell me," Ah-mah prompted.

"In my country, I am daughter to the King. I appear when he commands me. At all other times I live with the rest of the women in his household, unseen, unnoticed, and not missed by anyone."

Salla nodded, tears at Medi's words staining her own cheeks, returning to the person Ah-mah had first seen, Shadow to her mistress.

Ah-mah listened with the ears of a mother, which was how she had come to feel toward Medi, and, to some extent, Salla. "We have many days before we reach your country. Some we will fill with talking, some with treating. I am glad you have told me a little of what troubles you so. Will you tell me more once we are on our journey?"

"How can that be, Ah-mah? You will be on one boat, and I will be on another."

"We will be on the same boat, and often. You have not finished your training, nor have I lost my skill in announcing that fact," Ah-mah grinned at Medi, and reaching over, patted Salla's hands.

In spite of herself, Medi smiled back.

CHAPTER TWENTY-ONE

The River

The river had risen by two hands before they were able leave, a small hint of the full inundation which was seldom less than five tens of hands. In the early morning, oarsmen pushed the boat away from the dock and out into the lazy current. Ah-mah rushed to the bow of the boat, knowing that Ak-hu and Gedju, with little Ah-nah and young Menes, waited on the stone dock. As the boat passed the dock, the family waved, and Ah-mah waved back, then ran through the oarsmen to the stern, where she strained to see them until they existed only in her imagination. Still she looked, hoping for a last glimpse until Sept turned her around by her shoulders and guided her to the front of the boat. "You do not want to miss anything, my love," he said.

The Byblosian boat led the one on which she stood. A hut of logs had been built on the aft deck, the small hole cut in the back for air and light, barred and curtained. Ah-mah wondered how Medi and Salla could breathe. "Soon, my girls, soon," she thought, and renewed her determination to have them with her instead of in that hot, airless box.

Ah-mah had traveled to the ends of her lands, but not beyond. In both hands she held the representation of the river Sept had carved into a flat chunk of wood. Before this day's end they would reach the great turn in the river which marked the northern boundary of her ancestral lands.

She knew that distance was measured on the river just as it was on land, in atours. Sept told her the boat must travel twelve tens of atours to reach the sea. Most days they would travel five atours. For a while she tried to measure their pace by eyeing the banks of the river. Ah-mah knew the measurements of the lands of her ancestors to the last step, but measuring with the eye from the middle of the river proved difficult and tiring. As though he sensed it, Sept came to her and pointed to the deck. "This is our place, Ah-mah. I have put your medicine box here. See how it fits into the little rails? These are our mats rolled and stacked with your cushions." It was all she needed. One small spot to be her territory. Ah-mah spread her mat and lay down upon it, the rhythmic sound of oars and water soon lulling her to sleep.

She awoke refreshed and took up position in the bow once more, this time looking behind her at the boat and those who propelled it with their oars. The boat was a marvel. She had looked at boats on the river all her life, but had rarely entered one of the larger ones, content with the two-person ferry that took her from one side of the river to the other. Now she stood before the huge, two-legged mast, which Sept said distributed the weight of the sail equally. Much larger than Remtu's hut, the boat had a flat floor or "deck," in the boat language she was acquiring, with storage beneath it, and ends that curved up toward the sky. A knee-high railing ran along either side and the cross beam with its furled sail lay down the length of the boat. It would not be used until they reached the sea. She marveled at the wood from which the boat was made, rare in this land of mud bricks and stone. It must have cost Rahotep dearly.

The Master of the boat had taken his name, Mu-hem, or water rudder, after many years of sailing, and she felt his sturdiness from the beginning. With his feet planted firmly on the deck, he looked as solid as a mountain.

A shout startled her. She looked ahead and saw the river disappear as it made a wide curve. In front of them, the larger boat from Byblos rowed easily around it. Master Mu-hem worked the long oar that acted as rudder and shouted orders. The sailors nearest the left bank oared with all their strength while those on the opposite side lifted their oars from the water. When the turn was completed, the boat headed, not north, but west, directly into the setting sun.

The boats had traveled more than five atours the first day. Master Mu-hem looked pleased as he steered the boat from the main current toward the bank in tandem with the Byblosian one. A sailor from each boat leaped from prow to bank carrying a rope in his arms. Two single palms, near enough to the great river to reach life-giving water year round, stood on the bank. As the sailors knotted the ropes, one around the trunk of each tree, Ah-mah noticed the deep scars and knew they were not the first to use this bank for harbor.

Men lowered half-filled cooking pots over the side to waiting sailors who took them to a great pit, dark with years of use. Others brought dried dung and straw and the pot of embers from the boat. Fires blazed as the hot coals ignited the dung and straw. Soon a delicious aroma pervaded the air. While the stew (lentils, barley and Ah-mah's herbs) cooked, one man scaled a large perch he had caught, skewered it, and placed it over a third fire in the pit. Ah-mah licked her lips in anticipation of the feast to come.

When Medi and Salla did not join the group, she went to Master Akban and said, "The princess needs fresh air." Master Akban did not roar at her or ignore her as she might have expected, given all Medi had told her, so she continued, "Her maidservant and her personal guard will protect her, as they have while she has been in the Land of the River."

Heavily veiled, Medi came to the cooking fires and sat next to Ah-mah, along with Salla, who was once more her shadow, and Malloch, who stood directly behind her to be certain she was safe. Ah-mah wondered if this loyal man ever ate or slept. Only once had he allowed her to treat his feet, but he still paid attention to how he stood. She could see him now, shifting his weight until he felt balanced equally on both feet. Nefer would have taken a place on the other side of Medi, but Ah-mah waved him away.

Soon, but not soon enough for Ah-mah's growling stomach, the men took the fish, the pots, and several flat clay boxes from the fire. "Bread," Ah-mah thought. She still had no real taste for bread, but she knew the others did, including Sept.

The men circled the pit, squatting or sitting, the men from Byblos on one side, those from the Land of the River on the other. Ah-mah's boat carried a crew of ten sailors, Master Mu-hem, six of Sept's guards, Sept, Nefer and herself. The Byblosian boat had a crew of twenty sailors, Master Akban, Medi, Malloch, and Salla. Privately, Ah-mah suspected the sailors doubled as guards for the princess.

They ate by starlight and firelight, and afterwards, with many gestures, facial contortions and laughter, each crew attempted to outdo the other with tales of their travels. Ah-mah listened, content with Sept on one side, and Medi on the other. She could feel Medi's misery through her veils. Nefer, who had found a place on the other side of Sept, radiated a similar gloominess. In the darkness,

Ah-mah slipped her hand beneath Medi's long veil to hold the girl's hand in secret. When Medi rose to return to the ship, Ah-mah stood with her, and quickly whispered, "Be patient. I will ask the Master to let you come aboard soon."

The next morning, after a drink of river water and a bite of leftovers, the ropes were loosed from the trees, and both boats steered into the main current, oars speeding the boat faster than Ah-mah could have imagined down the great river, speeding it toward the sea. The sea! Such magic in that name! She could feel it.

The land they passed through on the second day was dry, the banks higher, the desert closer. "It is coming," she whispered to the few dusty trees on the banks. "Do not worry, the river is rising even now in the south." Ah-mah wondered if trees did worry. They certainly looked worried and tired, their bark crusty with layers of dust. Inside, Ah-mah knew the trees were healthy, with roots digging deep into the bank, reaching the river and drinking year round. "I am being silly." With that thought, Ah-mah went to the bow of the ship, to the copper bucket and dipped her cup into the water one of the men had just drawn from the river. The water tasted wonderful, like the gift it was to parched lands.

Ah-mah's bare feet enjoyed the feel of the wood planks beneath them, the faint thrumming of the boat as it rushed through the water soothing her spirit. The river became her path, the people on the boat her family, although her daughter, her grandchildren, and the princess and her maid servant on the other boat were always in her heart. "Tonight, dear girls," she thought. "Tonight I will speak to the Master. I will make him let you sail with us. Then you will feel the air on your face."

This time she went to Sept, enlisting him to approach Master Akban on Medi's behalf. That night when Medi joined them at the cooking fires once more, Sept called the Master aside, telling him that Ah-mah needed Medi to sail aboard the boat from the Land of the River in order to continue teaching her. The Master was hesitant, as both Ah-mah and Sept knew he would be. When Sept reminded him that Medi's personal guard would accompany her, as well as her maidservant, Akban agreed, his need for caution appeased.

The next morning, Malloch escorted Medi and Salla, heavily veiled, to Ah-mah's boat. Medi was settled quickly onto cushions placed behind the screen afforded by the high prow. As the boats were oared into the current, Malloch, who had grown quite fond of Ah-mah, stood, equally balanced on both feet and clearly visible to Master Akban. Realizing his intent, Ah-mah flashed him a grateful smile and turned to the princess.

"You may remove your veils now, Medi. No one can see and neither your guard nor Salla will reveal it. Enjoy the fresh air while you can. You, too," she said to Salla, who crouched behind her mistress.

Nefer, who was already seated in the bow, took it upon himself to remove Medi's veils. Malloch's eyebrows lifted, but he did not move or give any other sign. True to her word, Ah-mah continued her instruction, working the princess' feet and having the princess work hers. Nefer joined in, letting the princess coach him as he worked on Ah-mah's feet. Before long, muffled laughter consumed them all, except for Malloch, whose stoic stance gave away nothing.

Master Akban did not let Medi sail on Ah-mah's boat every day. On the days when she did not have a student, Ah-mah's hands became restless. Before long she understood what was missing. She, who was used to rubbing the feet of many every day, had not held a foot other than Medi's or Nefer's in her hands since leaving Nubt. Determined to remedy that fact and put her hands to good use, she went to consult Sept.

"I was wondering when you would think of it. I am certain the

Master will be delighted to allow his crew to partake of your healing treatments. No doubt he will want to be first."

Sept was right. Mu-hem gave over his hold on the rudder to Fayin, and came immediately to Ah-mah. As she began his treatment, she wondered if Sept had not talked with him before now. He seemed too quickly persuaded to her mind.

The days passed, one after the other, the river rising slowly. Now in the midst of the month of Pakhon, the flood would not peak until Mesore, three months hence. The village of Abedju, larger than Nubt, sat on higher ground on the west bank. Its dock swarmed with men carrying bundles and baskets to and from many boats. Ah-mah saw smoke rising from one of the larger mud brick structures and made a mental note to ask Sept which god ruled the village. They did not stop, having all they needed stored safely on their boat, and for that, Ah-mah was glad. For some reason, she felt easier once Abedju was beyond her sight.

That night, as they lay side by side on the ground, Ah-mah asked Sept if he had visited Abedju.

"Many times, my wife. It is different from Nubt, depending more on river traffic than goods from caravans."

"Why would I be glad we did not stop, Sept? Is there something in the village to fear?"

Sept thought a moment before answering. "The village does have a ruler more ruthless than Rahotep, but I suspect your feeling has nothing to do with the village, my Ah-mah. You are reluctant to leave the boat."

Ah-mah felt truth in Sept's words. This boat had become home to her, at least for now.

CHAPTER TWENTY-TWO

The Last Days of Atlantis

Locan, Keeper of Energy, knocked on the door to Seronak's room in the Temple of the Keepers. "Come," he heard, and opened the door.

"The transformation crystals have arrived."

"Good. Will they be adequate?" Seronak asked.

"Their songs seem clear and strong. They will be moved from ship to Temple later this morning." Locan hesitated, then said, "I am pleased with the caretakers of these crystals and their training, but since I am last to be transformed, you can imagine that the level of competency has concerned me. I can oversee all of you, but I must trust them to complete my own transformation without my help."

"How are they handling the separation from their families?" Seronak asked.

"A message arrived yesterday. Their families have reached the mainland and are headed toward higher ground. The news eased their minds, as does the ship that waits in the harbor to take them off this island once the transformations are completed. They are concerned about their own safety, naturally, but they are loyal and devoted, if I am any judge. I wish we could guarantee everyone's safety, but I don't suppose our survival, even after the transformation, is any more secure than theirs." Locan sent a piercing look at Seronak.

"We cannot be certain that we will have the time needed to complete the transformations, or that they will work, or that…"

"They will work," Locan interrupted. "These crystals are the largest we have ever attempted. The smallest is twice the size of a full-grown man. Eight crystals, eight days, eight transformations. We will be dolphins very soon, old friend."

That evening, as had become the custom, the Keepers gathered at the home of Aletha, everyone abuzz about the transformation crystals, asking question after question of Locan, until Aletha stopped them with a call to the dinner cobbled together from what each had brought. The resourceful Nyla poured wine from a dusty flask long hidden in the deep recesses of the cellar beneath the kitchen. As they took seats at the table on the stone porch and began the meal, Aletha watched Locan, as thorough and deliberate with his eating as he was with his crystals.

"Locan, when did you first know you were a Keeper?" Aletha asked when she saw that his plate was nearly empty.

He looked up at her, but his eyes stared inward to memory. "I was born with the song. When I was three, my father, Keeper of Energy before me, took me by ship on a journey of many days. At our destination, we stepped onto a path worn smooth by many feet. My father and I followed the path to a huge hole in the side of a mountain where I stopped, hesitant to enter such deep darkness. Father walked on a few steps before realizing I was not with him. He asked if I would like him to carry me.

"Even at that young age, I was stubborn." Quiet laughter rippled around the table. "If Father could enter that dark place, so could I. Just before going in, I halted, this time not from fear but from what I heard. I listened hard, holding my breath. It seemed I heard a melody, but I could not be sure. I entered the hole, my head high, my ears alert for the sound.

"I followed Father down a passageway that led to a great room with a roof that resembled the night sky, studded with twinkling lights. Eight great crystals stood embedded in the center of the room tended by small, dark men. Ignoring the men, I ran to the nearest crystal and pressed my body against its hard surface. Leaving that crystal, I ran to another and pressed my body against it, and then another, and another, until I had completed, without prompting, a ritual as old as the Keepers themselves. In that moment I knew I would be Keeper of Energy after my father.

"Since we have decided to pursue the idea of transforming ourselves into dolphins, a new song has entered my dreams. At first it was a single melody threading its way through my dreaming self, but then, another joined it, and another. Each morning I awakened with the melodies playing themselves out in my mind. When the transformation crystals arrived, I met the ships which carried them and walked with them as they were transported to the Temple of Healing, now the Temple of Transformation. When they had been placed in the Room of Transformation, I stood in their midst, admiring them. I often feel they are my children.

"Suddenly, the new melodies from my dreams entered the room, a multitude of sounds layered into haunting music that darted in and around the crystals. I was terrified that the crystals would be injured, but the music rooted me where I stood. I felt the crystals shift to harmonize with the new music. Subtle shifts, a tone raised slightly here, lowered there. The music became richer in texture and a pulsing rhythm, like a heartbeat, seemed to drive it." Locan was silent. Either his story had ended, or he listened to music only he heard.

"Did you find the source of the music?" Aletha asked.

"Are the crystals harmed?" Seronak asked.

Startled from his reverie, Locan flinched and refocused on the group. "The crystals are not harmed, but enhanced. I have determined that the new sounds came from dolphins."

"Dolphins! How do you know?" Uljas asked.

"I saw dolphins in my inner vision. They had formed a circle and were swimming around and around in it. I heard a distinct whistle, followed by a series of clicks just before I heard the new music. I think the dolphins know what we are trying to do and are helping us."

"I am certain of it," said Volin, Keeper of Wisdom. "I went in search of dolphins in the sea not far from here. Dolphins came and circled me, swimming around and around just as Locan described. From them, I received the dolphin template and was able to see how it corresponds to the human one. It does not surprise me to hear that they are adjusting our crystals."

Karon, Keeper of Earth Matters, spoke next. He cradled a thin metal disk in his two hands. "When we meet in the Crystal Room for the last time, we will etch our memories onto this disk. Seronak will seal it and a ship will take it to the tree chosen as Guardian. It is one last way we might be known in the future."

Ever practical, Melida asked Seronak, "When do the transformations begin?"

Instead of answering, Seronak looked at Locan, eyebrows raised in question.

"The crystals have only arrived this morning, and I need to listen to them once more since the dolphin adjustments. I think we could begin in two days."

Early the next morning, Aletha and Nyla met in Aletha's room. From some unknown source, Aletha had a bit of nearly fresh bread, a few grapes, and some precious water. Nyla recognized it as a parting feast.

"Have you finished packing?" Aletha asked.

"There's not much to take, Mistress. I will be with an established community, thanks to you and the Keepers. If I survive what comes…"

"You will survive, Nyla. I feel it in my heart," Aletha said. Tears filled Nyla's eyes but she blinked them back.

Aletha took the great Aquamarine on its fine chain from around her neck, and stared into its depths. With a slight shudder, she lifted her head. "To you, Nyla, who has been my handmaid, my apprentice, and my friend, I entrust this gemstone and its chain, the single symbol left from Mu. It was given to me by my father who told me that it did not come from this planet, but was his father's mother's in a far off world." Both women rose and Aletha slipped the chain over Nyla's head. As the stone found its place over Nyla's bosom, the two women inclined their heads and touched, forehead to forehead, in farewell.

Within the hour, they hurried down a rocky path, their sandaled feet stirring debris in the unkempt way between the empty houses. Neither looked to right or left, intent only on the goal ahead. All too soon they came to the dock where one of the last ships and all aboard her waited for their final passenger. With a quick embrace, the two women parted.

As the ship hoisted sail and slipped into the sea, Nyla stood in the stern, gazing at the great port city of Atla with its temples, government buildings, and other great stone structures, to say nothing of the multitude of houses. The Temple of the Keepers and the

Temple of Healing were landmarks long identifying Atla to arriving ships, made more imposing by the thought that she would not see them again. The city, once home to thousands, now held only the Keepers and the great crystals' caretakers. Two ships remained at the dock. One waited to take the caretakers to safety, the other waited for the memory disk. With clear eyes, Nyla looked at Aletha, Keeper of Language, dwarfed by the empty city behind her, her dark green gown covered with a dark green cloak, her honey-colored tresses flying in the breeze. Nyla lifted the Aquamarine to flash in the sun as a final salute.

She sailed first to a community of Atlanteans in the mountains to the east. Many days after her arrival, the earth stopped its shuddering, but left Nyla with a restless hunger for the unknown. She located a ship and left the comfort of the familiar, sailing farther east. Before long, the ship entered a great river, with lush, tropical growth on either bank. When the boat stopped at a stone dock, she departed, fascinated by the stone house that stood before the mountain in the distance. A wide path led from the dock to the house, and she followed it. When she reached the house and climbed the steps, an intense emotion seemed to enter her heart from the stones.

Six people, two women, two men, two children, waited in the interior courtyard, but they were not what caused her heart to flutter. The stone house was open and airy, so like Aletha's house in Atlantis that it seemed Aletha waited as well. The dark green of Aletha's beloved Obelon tree and the rich brown of the soil of her Garden were everywhere to be seen. Even the people were arrayed in those colors, the women in dark green, the men in rich brown, the children in paler green and rose.

Nyla found peace with these people, her restlessness quelled. For the rest of her days, she was their healer, gaining a reputation throughout the region as the Lady of the Stone. When she died, the Aquamarine was put into a silver box and placed in a secret room within a mountain cave, a last link with a lost world. It was said that if one stared long enough into the stone, one could see the Gardens of Mu and the wondrous Obelon tree.

CHAPTER TWENTY-THREE

The Humans of the Sea

"It is important to treat the whole foot, and to give equal time to both feet," Ah-mah said to Medi and Salla. The faithful guard, Malloch, stood as always, equally on both feet and in plain site of the Byblosian boat.

Nefer chuckled. When Ah-mah looked sharply at him, he said, "I was thinking of someone hopping on one foot." Then, embarrassed by what he had said, Nefer ducked his head. "I understand, Ah-mahsis. I will not treat just one foot."

Softening, Ah-mah said, "Remember the time I left the man I was treating and went to the girl in pain?" Nefer nodded. "He had to spend the night with one foot feeling awake, one foot feeling asleep. Very uncomfortable. I treated him first the next morning."

"Ah-mah, yesterday when you treated one of the sailors, you pulled on his toes," Nefer said.

"Oh, yes. Give me your foot, Medi, and I will show you." Medi obliged by extending her bare foot to Ah-mah who took it in both hands. Holding the upper part of the foot steady with one hand, Ah-mah pulled each toe with thumb and forefinger. One of the toes popped at the joint.

"Did that hurt?" Nefer asked.

"Not at all."

Ah-mah held out her hand for Medi's other foot. She did the same procedure with the toes, this time eliciting a pop from several of them.

Still holding the foot, Ah-mah beckoned to Nefer to come closer. "I have noticed that when the foot is uneven in temperature, it needs to feel reconnected to the body."

Ah-mah held the foot securely with one hand, and with the other, made pushing motions with her thumb and forefinger along the large tendon that connected the heel to the leg in back of the foot. Shifting to the thumb alone, she continued lower and lower until she had worked all around the back of the heel.

Medi mumbled, "Oh, that is so relaxing. How did you know it was tight?"

"Some parts of your foot are warm, some are cold. Here, give me your other foot, since our lesson today is to remember to work both feet."

"So much to remember, Ah-mah," Nefer said, as Ah-mah worked Medi's other heel and tendon.

"There is no wrong way to work feet, but some ways seem to help more than others. Do not forget that I started with a rag and a bowl of water."

"Can anyone work the feet?" Salla asked, her voice not much more than a whisper.

"How would you answer, Nefer?"

"I think anyone could learn to treat feet, but not everyone would want to learn. Also, not everyone is a healer like you, Ah-mahsis."

"No matter how long I study feet, I will not have Ah-mah's touch," Medi said.

Embarrassed, Ah-mah changed the subject slightly. "Do you wonder if the hands offer the same access?" Three sets of eager eyes looked at her. "I have tried to work my own hands, and I find some touch soothing, some touch painful, much as is true in the feet. Salla, give me your hands and tell me what you feel when I work them."

Unable to keep her voice to a whisper, Salla said, "Ummm. That feels wonderful."

"Ah-mah," Nefer said, "yesterday, I woke up with an aching head. When we worked the feet of some of the sailors, something happened to me." Ah-mah pulled on Salla's fingers much as she had pulled on Medi's toes earlier. "After I finished with the feet of the last sailor, I stood up to stretch and my head no longer ached. Could it be that rubbing the feet treated my fingers and thumb, and thus, my head?"

"I am blessed with bright students," Ah-mah said. "I, too, have felt a difference in my head when I treat feet. Sometimes I feel light-headed. So much to learn, so much to know, and always more to be discovered!"

The landscape changed on the banks of the river; the mountains receded leaving the land flat. For many days they moved through the waiting, dusty land. When at last the river divided and the two boats sailed into the eastern branch, Ah-mah noticed that the narrowed river spread fingers of itself into the surrounding earth, creating a soggy, spongy land. It seemed she also tasted a faint saltiness on her lips. "Are we close to the sea?" she asked Sept.

"Close enough. We will enter the sea before tomorrow's end," Sept said.

"How long before we reach Medi's land?"

"If our luck holds and we do not have storms, we should be

docked on her shores before the sun has set twenty times once we reach the sea."

"It is not so far then?"

"Oh, it is as far as we have already come, but Master Mu-hem has discovered a way to use the sail to catch the wind and make the boat travel much faster than the men can row."

That night was spent on the boat, with a fish soup for the evening meal. Ah-mah spent much of the night roaming the deck, lying restlessly on the mat, or staring at this unfamiliar branch of the great river, saying goodbye, trying to imagine the open sea. She had glimpsed water without end in her dreams of Aletha, but tomorrow she would see it for herself.

The day dawned bright and clear, and soon they were in the river's current, following Princess Medi in her confining box. By early afternoon, the river had widened noticeably and all thought of treating feet was banished. Ah-mah could not have focused on feet. She stood in the bow of the ship watching for the sea.

It came on her unawares. As she looked ahead, wondering what Medi was thinking, her gaze was suddenly drawn to the left where the bank lowered to sand and disappeared. She quickly looked to the right, and then turned around to look behind. The land and the river were behind them. Ah-mah slowly turned back around and saw nothing but the Byblosian boat and the endless water that stretched to the horizon.

Men hauled in their oars and laid them in the center of the boat, while other men raised the crossbar that held the sail into place with poles. The center of the cross bar had been hollowed out to fit over the mast. Ropes attached to either end of the crossbar enabled it to be moved on the mast. Other ropes dangled from the bottom corners of the sail. Using the ropes and Master Mu-hem's guidance, men positioned the sail to catch the wind, then secured the ropes to the rails on either side of the boat.

Ah-mah ignored the raising of the sail, transfixed by the immensity of all that water. Sound intruded. Ah-mah listened. The boat had made a certain sound as it moved through the river, but this sound was different. Moving her gaze from the far horizon to the edge of the boat, she saw white froth as the bow split the water, but more, wind pushed the boat and waves slapped against it, rocking it in a way the river had not. She looked into the water's depths and saw currents, some moving with the waves, some moving crosswise. Closing her eyes she felt the rhythm of the currents through her feet, her body adjusting to the rolling boat automatically.

Too soon for Ah-mah, Master Mu-hem shouted to Fayin at the rudder to turn the boat. Men untied the ropes that held the sail and repositioned them. Now land could be seen from one side of the ship, the unlimited sea on the other side. Ah-mah felt both comforted and disheartened by the sight of land, however distant, wanting instead to feel the terrible thrill of no land in sight anywhere. All that day, she stood in the bow, her back to the land, staring at the horizon and the expanse of water between, her conversation internal.

"There are many such bodies of water you say?"

"Yes, Ah-mah. Is it not beautiful? Does it not draw you?"

"I cannot stop looking, Aletha. It does draw me, but I could not say why."

"The dolphins call it Mother."

"Dolphins?" Suddenly, it seemed she flew above the sea and looked down on huge fish.

"Ah, you remember being with me in Hawk's dream," Aletha thought to her.

"Will we see dolphins, Aletha?"

"One swims in the foam just there. Look!"

Almost directly beneath her, a great silvery fish swam in the bow wave. Its black eye seemed to look straight at her and its mouth seemed to smile. Was the dolphin laughing at her?

Suddenly it leaped from the ocean and seemed suspended in air before it dropped back to the sea, sending water splashing.

"He likes you."

With a giggle, Ah-mah asked, "Is he playing?"

"Dolphins love to play."

"Is he smiling at me?"

"Could be."

"I have never seen such a big fish."

"The dolphin is not a fish, Ah-mah."

"Not a fish? Then what is it?"

"The dolphin is a human who lives in the sea."

"What is a human?" Ah-mah asked, unfamiliar with the word.

"You are, Ah-mah."

"What would I see if this boat sailed toward the horizon?"

"For many days you would see water, and eventually, you would see land."

"Land I had not seen before?"

"Yes."

"With people, humans, I had not seen before?"

"Yes."

"I would not reach the edge of the water and fall off?"

"No."

"Why not?"

"Because the ocean and the land are on the surface of a great round ball like the sun, your Ra."

Ah-mah halted all conversation then, even her internal one She stared entranced at the horizon, trying to imagine sailing toward it. A splash interrupted her reverie. The dolphin. She looked down at him, his smile echoed by her own. He skimmed along in the bow wave, zig-zagging with its motion. Ah-mah watched this creature, at home in so much water, yet looking at her and smiling.

The boats were turned toward shore in the late afternoon. With precision that comes from years of experience, the sailors on each boat gathered the sail, binding it to the mast. The boats were anchored and the things needed for eating and sleeping were carried ashore. Ah-mah had tucked her and Sept's sleeping mats under her arm when a splash alerted her to the dolphin in the water below. In fact, several dolphins swam near the boat.

Sensing Ah-mah's longing before she did, Aletha whispered to her mind, "Go ahead. They will not harm you."

Ah-mah could see that the water was clear and not deep. She dropped the mats, shrugged out of her sack dress, and climbed the ladder over the side, Nefer, her only witness.

She stood in the water, hands out to touch the dolphins. One brushed her hand causing her to gasp and then giggle. Another, possibly the bow wave dolphin, presented her with the fin on top of his body. She grabbed it, letting the dolphin tow her slowly around in a circle, bringing her back to a spot near the boat. As she found her footing, the dolphin backed away from her, dancing on his tail and nodding his huge head vigorously. Then all the dolphins headed for the open sea, flashing silver as they swam.

Nefer held out her dress to her. Seeing tears on her cheeks, he asked, "Ah-mah, are you well? What are those creatures?"

"Dolphins. Wondrous dolphins," Ah-mah said, her voice not much above a whisper. "I have touched them, but more, they have touched me. They are intelligent, Nefer. They are humans of the sea."

"Humans? What are humans?"

"We are."

CHAPTER TWENTY-FOUR

The First Storm

The dolphins stayed with the boat, playing in the bow wave, and Ah-mah swam with them every afternoon after the boat was anchored near the beach. Sept did not like the idea at first, but before long, he and Nefer joined Ah-mah in the water. After Sept's first time to touch a dolphin, he and Ah-mah talked long into the night. He, too, had felt something unusual, something powerful, from the dolphin. The idea of dolphins being sea people, or, as Ah-mah put it, "humans of the sea" made sense to him, once he had touched them and felt their intelligence.

Five days had passed when Ah-mah heard the words in her mind. "Storm comes."

"Aletha?"

"I speak, hu-man."

Looking down, she recognized the dolphin swimming in the bow wave from the patch near his blow hole where his skin had been scraped and scarred to a pinkish white. He had offered her his fin that first time and seemed to wait for her every evening.

"Storm comes. Dolphins go."

In a flash he was gone, his group fleeing with him.

Looking to the east, Ah-mah saw dark, gray clouds moving toward them, obliterating the sun. Could the dolphin be right?

Master Mu-hem shouted orders to prepare for the storm, and sailors scurried to tie down anything that was loose. The crossbeam that held the sail was lifted from the two-legged mast and tied to the deck, the sail lashed to it. Oars were brought out and dipped into the water, a sailor manning each oar, waiting. Ah-mah watched with interest, feeling the tension but not understanding it, until the first huge drops pelted her skin. Her startled scream was drowned by the torrent that followed. Whipped by the wind and lashed by waves of sea water and rain, the sailors rowed hard to keep the boats from crashing into each other, or being driven onto the beach. Headed into the wind, Ah-mah's boat lost ground and then regained it, the sailors following what gestures they could see, unable to hear the Master's shouts.

Terrified, Ah-mah huddled in the bow, clinging to it with both arms. Sept came to her and tied one end of a rope around her waist after looping it around one leg of the mast. Putting his arms around her and the mast, he used his body to shield her. How long they stayed in that position, Ah-mah did not know.

As quickly as it had come, the brunt of the storm abated, leaving in its wake a steady rain. Ah-mah could not stop shaking. Sept untied her and helped her to sit on the deck, holding her close for warmth and comfort.

"Breathe, Ah-mah," he said "Think of the mid-day sun. Breathe in the heat and let it warm you."

Ah-mah tried breathing. She shuddered in a breath and shuddered it back out. The shaking did not stop. She tried to remember the heat of the sun, but could only remember rain, rain, and more rain.

"The rain lessens," the Master observed.

"The storm is leaving, Ah-mah. The sun will be out soon."

Ah-mah did not believe him. The rain still pelted her, still ran from her hair into her eyes. But gradually, the rain did ease, and the clouds broke, allowing the sun to beam through onto the rain-soaked boat and the bedraggled people it held. A fresh breeze sent the clouds scudding across the sky, leaving only memories of the dark, wet morning. The welcome sun warmed her and caused her clothes to steam.

Both Master Mu-hem and Master Akban shouted orders. The crossbeam was remounted. Sails were unfurled, and soon the boats sped through the afternoon with only a morning lost. A splash alerted her to the return of the dolphins. They played in the bow wave just as they had yesterday, as though nothing out of the ordinary had happened. But it had. Ah-mah chanced to look at the Byblosian boat, and for the first and only time, she envied Medi her box. Watching the dolphin she had come to think of as "Patch" and feeling the warm sun on her face, she was able at last to feel restored, the storm a memory.

The heavens were filled with stars when they finally drew near to shore, both Masters wanting to make up the lost time. The next day dawned brightly, with white, luminous clouds holding no threat. Medi was allowed to join them, and the four talked of treatments once more, illustrating this point or that on each other's feet, having no wish to relive the storm. When they came to shore in the late afternoon, the dolphin, Patch, chittered hopefully, but Ah-mah could not bring herself to do more than walk through the shallows to the land. That evening, as they sat around the fire, she asked Medi about her land.

"My father rules the land from a great house with walls of stone and roof of cedar. Many people live in that house and in the houses surrounding it, more people than are in all of Nubt, Ah-mah. "

"Do you have priests?"

"We have gods, and those who serve them. Our gods are different from yours, but only in name. We have gods to make our women fertile so that children are born, and we have gods to make the land fertile so that crops are born. The foresters, it is said, worship the trees, and some go so far as to name them. I have not heard any names, nor seen the worship, so I cannot do more than report what I have heard others say is true."

"How should I act in your father's house?"

"I would like to say that you should act as you always do, but Ah-mah, women are not held in the same regard in my father's house as they are in the Land of the River. You would do well to let Sept speak for you and say nothing yourself."

"Then why did I come?"

"That will be evident when we speak with my mother privately. Women are not to speak at court, but you will be welcomed when we are alone with my mother. Do not look so dismayed, Ah-mah. All will be well."

Ah-mah said no more, but her head was filled with thoughts. Too much had happened for her to process all of it, and now she found that she must keep silent in Medi's father's court.

"You have kept your peace before. What is wrong with keeping your eyes open and your mouth closed?" Aletha's practical counsel comforted Ah-mah. She smiled as she rose from her place beside Medi to look for Sept and sleep.

Her dreams that night were of Aletha. Ah-mah was pleased to see her in the Gardens, and this time, when she looked out at the sea, she had a much greater understanding of Aletha's feeling for it.

* * *

The Gardens were especially beautiful this morning. Aletha walked the paths, knowing the Gardens belonged not just to her, but to all Muans. She could feel the energy flowing in from all parts of the land, as human energy and plant energy danced together, neither leading the dance, both necessary. The delicious odor of the white garden flower, the one with such delicate blooms a touch could spoil them, drew her down the path that led to the cliff above the sea and the precious, glorious Obelon tree.

This morning her thoughts were filled with memories and she heard her father's voice as he told her of the planet on which she stood. He was tall and she was very small, no more than four. "The Earth is a living being, Aletha," he said, more than once, her hand in his, walking through the Gardens. When the ground trembled beneath their feet, he would say, "Do you not feel the Earth shake itself, just as you might fling water off your hand?" "Why do I remember you so clearly this morning, my father?" she thought and then felt the trembling beneath her feet once more. Just a slight shudder, but it reminded her that in the night she had felt the Earth shake violently far away. The memory was buried too deeply to reach her consciousness until now.

An essence touched her heart and set a smile upon her face. Jonat and Paro played together, Paro showing his father the new game his three-year-old mind had invented. Aletha attuned her hearing to them for a moment, reveling in the sound of their voices. She sent a love thought to them both, and then returned to the lure of the garden flower, the Obelon tree, the sea.

Her bare feet took her swiftly to the fragile blooms and she knelt to be closer to them, to drink in their heady scent. She had not expected them to bloom this early. In fact, the Gardens bloomed as though it were the height of summer, and not early spring. Why? The thought flitted across her awareness and was gone as swiftly as it had come.

Another thought, in the form of a brown face filled with great brown eyes and haloed by thick, black hair, invaded her presence. "I am Ah-mah," the face said, and was gone.

Aletha stretched her arms toward the beloved tree. "I salute you, great Obelon, as I salute these Gardens and their beauty." She pronounced these words deliberately, part of some ancient ritual. The blooms nearly shrank from the sound of her voice, so rarely had they heard it other than through the whispers of delicate mind tendrils sent to encourage growth.

"Ma-ma!" The shout was audible to her heart, carried on a wave of other shouts. A terrible fear swept over her people and all the plants and animals of this island and was bearing down on her. Beneath her feet she felt the earth shudder once, and then again, stronger, and then again, stronger still. Suddenly, Aletha knew why the Gardens bloomed. The Why was nearly upon her. She was turning to face it when it found her, ripping the ground from beneath her, and flinging her into the waiting arms of the sea.

So suddenly did it come, Aletha hardly had time to draw breath before she was plunged into the water, the momentum driving her deeper and deeper. As her body fell, the essence of Aletha fled.

She stood casually in the blackness of space, surrounded by stars and gases, comets and planets, supported by nothing. "I am," she thought, and felt the truth of it. Aware of no body with arms and legs, torso or head, she looked instead with cosmic eyes at her universe. "What anchors me? Why do I not blow away?"

No answer. Just the swirling of gases in infinite darkness.

* * *

Ah-mah awoke drenched with sweat, shaking as the cool night air dried the perspiration from her body. She sat up and then rose, carefully stepping over the bodies sleeping around the dying embers. The surf with its irregular rhythms pounded the beach, drowning out the snores of those who slept. Ah-mah returned to the dream, remembering all she could, reliving it in her mind. Aletha in danger? What did it mean? Time to ask that later. Now, she must remember every detail. Why? To tell the dolphin.

CHAPTER TWENTY-FIVE

Dolphin Dreaming

The eastern sky was barely light when Ah-mah approached the sea. With night eyes, she searched for the dolphin. A splash, barely to be heard above the roar of the surf, alerted her. She dropped her dress and waded toward the sound, moving deeper and deeper into the water. A bump told her she had gone far enough. Reaching out both arms, she touched sleek skin. Skin that suddenly disappeared, as a larger object replaced it, knocking the first one away from her and upsetting her balance. She struggled back to her feet, sputtering. The dolphin was right in front of her. Behind his smiling face were stern eyes.

"Hu-man not come in dark time," he thought to her. "Bad. Many creatures want to taste you. That one would have. Why are you here?"

"Dream. Aletha is in danger. I do not know how to help her," she thought back to him.

"Show Aletha. In your mind."

Through the tears that came readily now, Ah-mah closed her eyes and tried to focus. She thought of Aletha's Gardens, of the Obelon tree. The scent of jasmine wafted to her above the salty sea water. She saw Aletha clearly as she lifted her arms to the Obelon tree in salute and spoke those fateful words. She felt the tide of pain and death rolling toward her beloved friend and was about to shout a warning, when the cliff slipped away, Aletha with it.

When Ah-mah opened her eyes, she was surprised at how light it was. The dolphin nodded his huge head vigorously, and as he darted back to deeper ocean, he sent her a thought. "We swim together at end of day."

"Ah-mah! What are you doing out there? It is dangerous to swim when no one is with you." Sept was awake, as was the crew. He stood on the beach holding her discarded dress.

Wading back to him, she called, "Good morning, my husband," reserving any further conversation for when they were closer and did not have to shout.

"I dreamed, Sept. I dreamed a horrible dream of Aletha and I went to tell the dolphin about it," she whispered to him as she donned the dress.

"Sharks live in these waters, Ah-mah. If they found you, we never would, for they would devour you."

"The dolphin warned me as well. I think I may have touched one of them before he drove it off. I will not go willingly into the water when it is not day."

"Thank you, my wife. I confess I do not know what you will do next. You surprise me over and over again." Sept grinned, relieved now that Ah-mah was within arm's reach. "I think the surprises are why I stay with you."

"That is not the reason. We are husband and wife." Ah-mah, all seriousness, looked at her husband and saw the grin splitting his face. "Do not ever forget that we are," she said, and poked his ribs before running off down the beach with him chasing her. He caught up with her easily, and ushered her behind a convenient dune. The sailors chuckled to themselves.

The morning was beautiful and they made good time that day, passing small signs of civilization, a house, a few fallow fields, and once, a man and his ox, plowing. The man waved, and they waved back.

The dolphin, Patch, and his group appeared in the bow wave again in the late afternoon, not long before they reached the place chosen by the Masters for the night. Ah-mah was eager to join him once the boat was halted, but first she looked over at Sept who was coiling sail rope. He smiled and nodded to her. Slipping out of her dress, she jumped into the water. Sept laughed out loud. What would that woman do next?

She soon bobbed in the water along with the dolphins, but as Sept watched, another strange event took place. The dolphins ringed Ah-mah, diving in and then surfacing to breathe, in and out, around and around. Patch stayed in the center with Ah-mah, her hand on his fin.

On dolphin energy, Ah-mah sped to the lost land of Mu, to Aletha, whose spirit roved the universe while her body drowned in the sea. She heard Aletha ask her questions. "What anchors me? Why do I not blow away?"

* * *

"I do." A simple statement, from no one Aletha knew, and yet the voice was familiar. "Who are you who anchors me?" No answer. Just a knowing, a calming, centered in her cosmic heart.

As Aletha continued observing her universe, dolphins came and supported her unconscious body, carrying her for many days until they brought her to an island far enough away from Mu to have been spared. When they reached the shallow water just out from the beach, one nudged her until she awakened to semi-consciousness.

Her feet touched the sandy bottom and walked automatically toward the beach where she fell down, prostrate, and did not move.

Eyes watched her from the bushes and from behind trees, eyes belonging to a small, brown-skinned people. None had ever seen one so tall or pale. It was long before one of them had courage enough to approach her, and longer still before he could touch her. A groan startled him, but proved she lived. Four of them half dragged, half lifted her to a shelter made of palm fronds. Laying her on more palm fronds, they ringed her pallet, and sat back on their heels, waiting. Before long, a wizened female entered the shelter on the arm of a girl. She bent over Aletha, checking her eyes, her face, her body for cuts or some other sign of injury, all the while muttering to the girl. Very soon the girl scurried out, a list of items needed stored safely in her memory. The wizened one hovered, muttering, sometimes waving her hands as though spreading something invisible over Aletha's body.

A delicious fragrance preceded the girl's return. She carried a bowl filled with steaming water and flowers. Kneeling, she presented the bowl to the wizened one, who dipped her hands into the water and brought up one of the blooms, which she placed over Aletha's heart. The dipping continued until few blooms were left in the bowl. One was placed on Aletha's forehead. Others were set on either shoulder, on her abdomen, and one on the palm frond pallet between her legs and just above her knees. The old woman continued her muttering, speaking now to the blooms as well as to Aletha's body.

The people crowded around the pale-skinned woman and watched. As Aletha's skin began to glow with a rosy hue from all the heat from their bodies, they began to nod and poke each other, chuckling behind their hands. All noticed as her body lost its rigidity and she gave a great sigh. As though a signal had been given, the people left, one by one, and returned to what they were doing before Aletha's arrival.

The wizened one, Kalalawalapo by name, covered Aletha with a mat woven from palm fronds and laid more fronds on top to keep the heat in her body. She had healed those before who had been too long in the water. This one, with the delicate skin, she had not been sure about. Too far gone. But the dolphins did not bring the dead to her. She finished a final prayer for healing, and chose a log to lean against for sitting and waiting. Her assistant, with a name equally long, but which was normally shortened to "Popo," brought clear water and fruit to restore her. She ate and drank gratefully, for she was very tired.

Kalalawalapo spent two full days and nights with the pale-skinned woman. Whenever she seemed near to waking, either she or Popo would dip a sea sponge in broth and squeeze it onto the woman's lips. She licked them automatically, and thus received enough nourishment to sustain her.

On the morning of the third day, the woman came to Kalalawalapo in a dream. She was tall and Kalalawalapo had to look up to her, even in the dream. The words she spoke were in a strange language, but somehow, Kalalawalapo understood them.

"I do not wish to live. Let me die."

With a start, Kalalawalapo came to full wakefulness and called for Popo, who came running. "What is it, Lapo?" she asked, using the nickname permitted to her when they were alone.

"We must wake this woman. We must get her up and walking. Go fetch Palo and Malo. They are strong enough to lift and support her." Kalalawalapo said. Seeing that surprise kept Popo rooted, she exclaimed, "Go!" Then she bent over Aletha and began shaking her shoulder. "Wake up. Wake up, woman," she said.

"Ummmh," from Aletha.

Palo and Malo came running, eager to see the woman again. "Help me get her up. Palo, you go to her other side. Start pushing her up. Malo, you do the same on this side. Popo, take her arm and pull."

The three younger people were small but muscles rippled in the young men, and Popo was well-formed and muscular as well. With their efforts, Aletha was moved to a sitting position. "Hold her there," Kalalawalapo ordered. Aletha, sitting up against her will, began to awaken from the deep, trance-like, blissfully forgetful sleep. Her eyes opened of their own accord.

"We need to get her to rise, to walk," Kalalawalapo said, urgency in her voice.

"Stop." Aletha's voice was quiet, but all heard it clearly, the language unknown, the intent obvious. They stopped pushing, but did not release the grip that kept her upright.

"I will stand."

Hands fell away as Aletha crawled out from the shelter and rose to her full height, which was easily half again that of the tallest man in the village. She did not stop, but continued walking toward the beach. Popo followed her at first, urged on by Kalalawalapo, who was fearful of what Aletha might do.

Aletha did nothing except walk, in long, slow strides. Finally, she turned around and retraced her steps, seeking her own footprints and stepping in them. When she reached Kalalawalapo, she stopped and sat down in front of her. She did not speak, but made the motions of hand to mouth of one who was hungry. At a signal, food was brought, and Aletha ate all of it. When it was gone, she stood and reentered the shelter, lying down upon the pallet once more and falling into a genuine sleep instead of the Trance of Forgetfulness.

Kalalawalapo resumed her position in the corner. This woman had risen, had walked, but death was still in her eyes.

CHAPTER TWENTY-SIX

Hawk

Sept saw Ah-mah's hand slip from the dolphin's fin and leaped over the side of the boat. With powerful arms, he propelled his body toward the waiting dolphins, who by this time had lifted Ah-mah to the surface and were holding her there. With perfect timing they bowed their beaks, delivering Ah-mah into Sept's waiting arms. He held her to him and slogged through the water to shore. Ah-mah seemed to be asleep.

Nefer ran to help, but Sept was not ready to release his burden. One of the sailors brought a blanket and put it over Ah-mah's nakedness. She shivered slightly at the touch. Another blanket was laid close to the cooking fire, and Sept carried Ah-mah to it and tucked both blankets around her.

"Is she ill? Did she fall overboard?" Nefer's questions tumbled over each other.

"She sleeps," Sept said, and squatted beside her, on the side away from the fire.

"But…"

"Let her sleep." Not a comment, but a command.

Ah-mah mumbled something, but did not waken. She was still with Aletha on the island.

* * *

For many days Aletha rose, walked the beach, ate, and slept. At last a day came when she did not return to the shelter, but sat beneath a date palm looking out to sea. Kalalawalapo sat with her. Another space of days passed. Kalalawalapo began to doubt she would ever again hear words from this woman. Almost she spoke first. In the dream, Ah-mah could feel the great emptiness in Aletha. She could sense Kalalawalapo's impatience growing as well.

When the bird screamed high in the sky, halting Aletha's steps, Kalalawalapo was watching. She sent her gaze up into the same part of the sky where Aletha looked, but could not find the source of the scream. When Aletha ran to the shelter, Kalalawalapo, and many of the other islanders followed, eager to see what would make this tall woman run. Quickly she fashioned a crude pad from palm leaves and strips of what was left of the shift she wore when the dolphins brought her to the island. In haste, she tied the contraption to her left shoulder and ran back to the beach to stand motionless. A gasp was heard from all except Aletha as the large, reddish brown bird with the terrible beak dropped to her shoulder. Collectively, their eyes widened in awe as they watched the bird dig his claws into her barely protected shoulder, and saw the blood trickle down her sun-burned skin. Kalalawalapo stopped them with hand raised when they would have followed Aletha into the palms. The woman knew this bird. They should be alone.

"Hawk," Ah-mah's dream self whispered. "Hawk," said Kalalawalapo, startling those who could hear with that strange sounding word.

The woman stayed beneath the palms, Hawk with her. To Kalalawalapo, watching from afar, it seemed the woman spoke aloud, gesturing emotionally, sometimes sitting, sometimes pacing, the bird perched on an overhead limb. At last she lay down full length and seemed to sleep. In the late afternoon, the woman stood, and Hawk resumed his perch on her left shoulder. Together they came from beneath the palms, Aletha striding like a goddess. With the waves lapping her toes, she stood looking out to sea, alone with Hawk, except for the many eyes who watched. Suddenly, Hawk leaped from her shoulder into the air, spreading his wings and flapping them, lifting himself up into the nether reaches of the blue, blue sky. Raising her arms to the sky as though to follow him, Aletha spoke, in words all the small, brown people could hear, though only one understood.

"I am Aletha of Mu. I salute you, Hawk."

Hawk screamed.

* * *

On the boat from the Land of the River the next day, Medi resumed telling Ah-mah the ways of her land, the ways of her father's house. After yesterday, when Ah-mah had been brought naked, except for her loin cloth, and unconscious from the sea, she felt an urgency to teach her instructor so that she would not bring herself to harm. The ways of Byblos could be harsh, and especially so to one who had known only a life in which rules were simple and primarily developed from need, which was how Medi saw Ah-mah's world. If asked, Ah-mah might have shared the rituals and rules of her land, but Medi did not ask.

"Ah-mah, I would like to speak to you about removing your dress," she began.

Still with Aletha in the dream, Ah-mah flinched when Medi spoke. With effort, she returned to the present. "I should not do that in your father's house," she said.

"In truth, Ah-mah, you should not do it here either. Women in

Byblos are always covered and do not show their breasts except on high occasions, and then only certain women may do so. You must always remain covered, and it would be good for you to practice that from now on. In my land, women are revered for their ability to bring forth children and for little else. Love between man and woman is rare and not encouraged. Women seldom speak, even when asked a question. The husband or another man speaks for them."

"How silly," Ah-mah said. Then catching herself, she continued, "Our customs must have been offensive to you, Medi. I had not realized."

"On the contrary, I prefer the freedom women have in your village. Ah-mah, I am afraid for you. Some allowances might be made for you as a stranger in my land, but if you sense someone is in pain, I believe you would tend to them before you thought, even though such an act could bring you death in my country. For the sake of all who love you, stay close to Sept and do not speak, ever, unless it is to whisper to him when you are certain you are alone. Let Sept speak for you, Ah-mah. If you break this rule, I cannot vouch for your safety."

Salla, Medi's ever present Shadow, could contain herself no longer. "The rules are not observed so carefully among the people, my lady," she said softly.

"What do you mean?" Medi's voice was sharp, demanding.

"Among the people, men and women speak freely. The only times they do not are when soldiers, priests, or the great King himself, are present. You could not have known, my lady." With that, she withdrew into the Shadow self she normally presented.

Ah-mah was silent, ruminating. "Then I will not be able to treat the feet of the men of the King's household, or of the King himself? From what you have told me, I should not have treated Malloch's feet. I will not break any more rules knowingly, Medi."

"It is only for a little while. Then you and Sept," Medi gulped, "and Nefer, will be on your way back to your land and I will serve my father by treating the feet of the women as you have taught me."

"Why, Medi? Why did your father send you all the way to the Land of the River to learn my simple treatment for feet? I still do not understand."

"For my part, I obeyed my father's wishes, not questioning, but glad of the opportunity to escape my daily life with the women. Before I left Byblos, I heard a rumor that the King had become desperate for a son. I gave the rumor no credence until you asked, but now I wonder if there is not some truth to it. My father has one other child, also a girl. I have seen sixteen summers. Many men in my country have sired more children than I have years, and in less time. My father needs sons to govern in his absence and to succeed him when he can no longer govern.

"It is rumored that my sister is not my sister, having been sired by another man. In Byblos, a woman is blamed for lack of children, so my father must believe the fault lies with his wives and concubines. Perhaps that is why he has so many of them. And now, I am to treat their feet because my father believes it will cause them to bring forth sons."

"Is that what you want?"

Medi was silent, afraid to voice the desire within. Ah-mah sat quietly, practicing how she would be in Byblos. Seeing that Nefer was engaged in conversation with Sept in the stern of the boat, the girl allowed a tear to slip from each eye, having already forgotten Salla's presence.

"What I want, dear Ah-mah, is to find a place where I can be with Nefer for the rest of our lives. Instead, I go the house of my father."

"Does Nefer know you love him?" Ah-mah's voice was quiet.

"I think he does. We have not spoken of it. He respects me

too much to speak."

"Good."

Looking at Ah-mah through tear-filled eyes, Medi asked, "Do you think he loves me?"

"Since the first moment he saw you. He loved you before I did, Medi. I am glad you have not spoken of it. From all you have told me about your father's house, Nefer would be in grave danger if anyone suspected."

"Yes. He would be killed, for no one may touch me other than my father, my mother or my husband to be, even my feet, in my father's house."

"May I touch you in your father's house, Medi?" Gently, gently.

To Ah-mah's surprise, Medi exclaimed, "We will be together in the women's quarters, and almost as free as we were in your house in the Land of the River!" Suddenly a shadow crossed her face and a frown furrowed her brow. "My father's wives are ruthless and report any misstep. We will have to be careful even there."

CHAPTER TWENTY-SEVEN
The First Transformation

The morning after Nyla's departure, Aletha awoke without the crystal bell, the scent of roses in their steaming water also a luxury of the past. As she began her ritual, using her inner senses to remember the aroma of the blossoms on the Obelon tree, rubbing her arms and bringing her consciousness fully into her body, she heard the dolphin's words. "Not form," he had thought to her. Her ritual complete, she opened her eyes, but did not rise.

"I wonder how you like being on the sea, Nyla," she thought, and then, "I wonder how I will like being a dolphin." Tomorrow Seronak would begin the process. She tried to imagine what it would be like, not having hands, or feet, to swim instead of walking, to eat raw fish. Enough! She rose from her bed, and slipping a robe over her shoulders, went to the balcony.

As she looked out at the sea, she thought of all that had happened to her, from the time she fell from Mu into the sea, to Kalalawalapo's island and the small brown people, to the numerous ships that had transported her, willingly or in hiding, to the many people she had met, both friendly and mean, to the discovery that if she told a person what was in his heart he would pay her, to Nyla, and at last to Seronak, Keeper of the One, giver of house and comfort. She examined her feelings for the Keeper of the One, and discovered a clarity she had not possessed while Nyla had been with her. Truth be told, her feelings for him had heightened since their trip to the island of his birth. Her hand strayed to the absent Aquamarine, its impression still strong within her. She placed left hand over right and remembered her last sight of the great stone as Nyla held it high to flash in the light, the last remnant of Mu, safe for now.

Late in the afternoon, the Keepers gathered at Aletha's house for a last meal. As had become the custom, each brought what he or she had. Seronak, in unusually high spirits, laughed at the slightest provocation, his humor affecting them all.

From the other end of the table, Locan, who had drunk no more than water, said, "Seronak, old friend. This time tomorrow you will be dolphin at last! Any final words?"

"Oh, yes, I have many, Locan, but I reserve the very last for the Crystal Room. I do not know when I have enjoyed myself more. There is something about the idea of becoming dolphin that is freeing to me. Truly, I believe it is the cause of my good humor this night."

"Perhaps you are feeling relief," Volin said. "Think of it! What seemed impossible has been achieved. Atla and Atlantis stand emptied of all except our old bones and those of Locan's caretakers, and we have managed to send a goodly portion of the treasures and knowledge to higher ground as well. Tomorrow we begin transforming ourselves into dolphins of the sea. Is it any wonder that we feel disposed to laugh?"

"You are truly Keeper of Wisdom," Melida said. "But the disk, Seronak. Is the disk here?"

Seronak looked at Karon for answer. "The disk awaits us in the Crystal Room. We will fill it with our memories tonight," he said. Then, to everyone's surprise, the usually reticent Karon rose, and hands behind his back, spoke.

"I cannot become dolphin with you, my friends." Immediately, all eyes were drawn to him, his blue robes doing little to hide the strength of his body. "Long ago, I visited the tall trees that live in a far distant land. They are so tall the sun must sneak between their branches to cast filtered light on the ground. Wisdom is kept fresh in their ancient bark, rising with the sap to their lofty heights, sent around the Earth on the wind. As I walked among those giants, I felt young again, for they are ancient, the ground on which they stand, protected."

Aletha, deep in her own memories, asked, "Is their bark rough and brown tending toward red? And do they have needles instead of leaves?"

Startled, Karon could only nod.

"I have seen the ancient ones. My father took me. Their forest borders the ocean that held my island home." Aletha could say no more.

Karon paced back and forth twice before he could speak again. "Last night those trees spoke to me in a dream. They asked me to bring the disk to them once it has been imprinted, to plant it with my own hands beneath the Guardian who is prepared to protect it for ten thousand years. They asked me to come alone and to stay with them, to live out my days beneath their branches." Looking at each of the Keepers in turn, Karon came to Seronak. "I would do as the trees ask," he said, simply.

"It is time, my friends," Seronak said, rising. He bowed to Aletha as he said, "Thank you for the many evenings you have hosted us, dear Keeper of Language," and extended his hand to help her rise, but he did not walk with her. Instead, he fell into step with Karon and put a hand on the man's shoulder.

In silence they walked the mile or so through the deserted city to the Temple of the Keepers. The Temple of Healing, now of Transformation, stood beside it, awaiting tomorrow's momentous event. None paid attention to that great temple except Seronak, who spared it a glance only, for all were deep into their own memories, preparing themselves for the etching of Karon's disk.

Throughout that night, the Keepers told their stories, each in turn, the disk shimmering briefly as it received the memory, the key to that memory etched upon its surface. Now, everyone had spoken except Seronak, and the disk held six keys with Belel's magnificent emerald in its center. The keys were various; a woman with hands stretched toward a bird in the sky, twinkling lights that formed a pattern, a sun with a crystal in its center, a crystal with a dolphin encircling it, a dolphin baby and a human baby overlaid so that one could not tell if the human had fins or the dolphin had legs, and Karon's tall, tall trees, the final destination for the disk.

Seronak beckoned for the disk and held it gently. "Endings and beginnings. I who speak at the end, remember a night long ago."

* * *

The young boy hesitated, senses alert for any sight or sound. He barely had time to conceal himself behind a curtain before the door to the inner chamber opened and the great Keeper of Wisdom stepped into the room. As luck would have it, the Keeper continued his steps and passed through the outer entrance. The air hissed as the door closed. The boy was alone.

He was in the Temple of Keepers, in one of the eight rooms spread like spokes around the tall, central Crystal Room. Each of the rooms had two doors, one for entering and exiting the Temple, and one that led to the central room. He tiptoed to the inner door and placed an ear against it, hoping to be able to hear if the room on the other side was empty. No sounds reached him. With foolhardy courage he grasped the door handle and pulled. Thicker than his hand from fingertips to heel, the door opened without a sound. Directly in front of him was the back of a great crystal chair. Carefully, he peered around it. The room was empty except for the eternally burning flame in the central brazier. Boldly he walked to the center and stood looking at the eight chairs. They were all the same with no markings to distinguish one from the other. How could he find the chair belonging to the Keeper of the One? Would it matter if he sat in another's chair?

Images of the Keepers floated above the chairs as he envisioned them discussing the weighty questions of the universe. Impatient with his youth and the training still deemed necessary before he could join them, he was determined to sit in one of the chairs. Tall and slender, his intense sea-gray eyes burned with desire in his dusky face, framed by the dark curls of his shoulder-length hair. He shrugged the images from his mind and climbed into the nearest chair.

The second he sat, he felt it. The chair was alive with energy. Tempted to leap from it, to race from the room, he did not. Curiosity and determination had drawn him where he was not yet welcome. He would stay for now.

"Perhaps if I chant the great mantra, the chair will accept me," he thought, and began whispering, "I am All. We are One." The chair did seem to subside, but the chamber came alive as his whispers echoed back to him from crystal walls. Once more he was tempted to leave, but a strangely familiar response in his body to the amplified whispering kept him where he was. He had chanted the mantra for most of his brief life, but never with this effect. He settled into the chair and closed his eyes, still whispering the sacred words.

All was dark, black as a night with no stars. The dark lowered, becoming a horizon. Above the horizon, one by one by thousands, stars lit the dark, forming themselves into galaxies and universes, swirling, pulsing into life, fading, dying, only to be reborn.

He noticed that what he saw had dimension. He looked up and realized he could look up forever and never reach the limits of up. Looking down, he lost himself in the depths of what he saw. No horizon, no limit, existed either ahead or behind. No matter where he directed his gaze, infinity met him. "This is you," said a voice. "This is your moment. It is forever, just as you are forever."

* * *

"As a young boy, untried and untested, I saw the energy of the Infinite Moment and knew that part of me which is forever, which is One."

Seronak's great voice rang in the Crystal Room as he continued, "We, who were without hope, have been given Hope. We, who thought our song would be lost, have heard our song blend with the Universe. We, who are soon to join a magnificent species in their watery realm, have heard their song of welcome. There is no fear, only purpose. No ending, but a beginning. No grief, but adventure. I seal this disk as symbol of the Keepers of Atlantis."

The disk vibrated in Seronak's hands and a thread of gold, festooned with tiny flowers, raised itself around the edge. Each flower held a crystal within its center. With great care, Seronak placed the disk over the eternal flame to smother it, and said, "The Age of Atlantis is finished, the New Age begins."

Then Seronak placed the disk into the cloth Karon held in his hands. All the Keepers rose to circle the Keeper of Earth Matters and touch his shoulders. "You are part of us forever, Karon," Seronak said. "We are One," the Keepers echoed. Karon did not look back as he left the Crystal Room to begin his journey to the ancient trees for he felt the strength of his purpose and the energy of each Keeper within his heart.

Next morning, Seronak strode eagerly into the Temple of Transformation. Interior walls had been torn out leaving one large room, the eight crystals standing majestically around a single couch, a caretaker beside each crystal, Locan moving from crystal to crystal, listening intently to each before moving to the next. The making of each crystal had been overseen by Locan with a particular Keeper in mind, and in the days just prior to this one, that Keeper had stood touching the crystal, imprinting it with his or her essence.

Seronak smiled as two caretakers disrobed him and helped him onto the couch, the crystal beside him already humming its familiar song. As he listened, his consciousness was drawn back into the center of his brain, then up and out, rising until he floated above the great crystal, watching his body on the couch below. He thought of rising even higher, above the room and the city itself, but suddenly his vision was riveted upon the naked body beneath him.

The individual fingers on the hands were no longer distinguishable. Wrinkles on knuckles disappeared, fingernails hardened and flaked off, leaving only smooth skin. The hands and arms drew up to the shoulders. As Seronak watched, the feet lost toes, arch and heel, and became flat, thick extensions of the one large leg that used to be two. The torso thickened in the middle and tapered toward what had been the feet, and the head. No sign of the heavy silver curls remained, and the beard lay on the floor as though it had slipped off the face. The mouth stretched and the ears disappeared.

It seemed only a few seconds that Seronak gazed at the body from his high vantage point. Yet, the transformation was complete. What lay on the couch was no longer human. One of the caretakers moved a lever, and a spray of water bathed the creature on the couch.

Aletha looked up, directly at the spot where Seronak's consciousness hovered, and smiled. Then she went to the creature and placed her hand on the thick brow above the beak. At her touch, Seronak was pulled from his high place into the creature with a rush. Then, nothing.

Such pressure on his eyes. He thought they were open, but he could not see anything. He felt movement around him and tried to move himself, but with no success. Blind, he used other senses and heard his heart beating, the blood rushing through arteries and veins. Air came whooshing in through the hole in the top of his head, filling his lungs. Something new touched him. "Water," his mind said. He slid all the way under the soft, enfolding, welcoming water and heard another sound. A quiet whisper at first, then strong as anything he had ever heard. Song. Song that filled him with joy and a feeling of connection.

His vision cleared and he saw some of the Keepers in the pool, others sitting on the side. He half expected to see them singing, but they were not the source of the song. Aletha still touched him, keeping him in his new body. It seemed natural to butt her hand. She backed away, and at her signal, all the Keepers and caretakers left the pool.

Seronak tingled with excitement as he explored his powerful new body. His vision fastened on the other side of the pool and suddenly, he was there, bumping against the wall. Surprised, he squealed, and heard the squeal bounce back to him from the opposite wall. He quickly realized that bouncing sound off walls told him exact distances and helped keep wall bumping to a minimum. For a time he practiced swimming around the pool in a tight circle, aiming clicks and whistles at the walls to determine his location. Soon he was expert. After all, such echo-location was an inherent sense for dolphins, much like touching with fingers, but at a distance.

"My mind remembers everything," he thought. Still Keeper of the One, Lord of soon-to-be-extinct Atlantis, he was also dolphin, at home in the water, filled with a longing for adventure and curious about everything, especially the unopened, unexplored chambers of his new dolphin mind.

And the singing. Since his first recognition of the song, it had not left him. He searched for the source, listening intently. It came from outside the pool! Haunted by the song and impatient to be with the singers, Seronak sped a thought to them with his great dolphin mind. "Soon," he thought. "Soon."

CHAPTER TWENTY-EIGHT

Byblos

For several nights, the boats anchored away from the shore and posted a watch. The land seemed the same to Ah-mah, but it was known to harbor thieves and others hostile to any who set foot on the shore. All stayed on board, cooking over a brazier in the evenings, eating leftovers the next morning and during the day. When they could once again go ashore safely, Ah-mah rejoined the dolphins in their watery world, but she kept her dress on, cumbersome as it was, practicing her version of modesty, unaware that the mere act of swimming where men could see her would be suspect.

One evening around the fire, Nefer said, "Ah-mah, we have treated the feet of the sailors on our boat, including Master Mu-hem, but we have not touched the feet of the sailors on the boat from Byblos. Treating feet is for everyone in the Land of the River, but I wonder if it will be reserved for royalty in Medi's land. To my mind, it would be good for these valiant sailors to experience the magic of your treatment."

"I do not see how that is possible, since women are not

supposed to touch men in Medi's country," Sept said.

Ah-mah had been thinking as Nefer spoke. "Why not have Nefer treat their feet? Can you not speak to Master Akban on Nefer's behalf, my husband? Nefer knows how to treat feet and he is a man. It could be our gift to the sailors," she said.

"I will speak to Akban, but do not be disappointed if he declines your offer."

True to his word, Sept spoke to the Byblosian Master that very night. Master Akban's answer surprised him.

"My men have watched your wife working the feet of the sailors and several have asked me about it. There is a rumor among them, not heard before this voyage, that if a sailor's feet are touched by a woman, that man will be safe in a stormy sea. My men would like to have a foot treatment, but I believe they would prefer that your wife give it."

When Sept asked about the law forbidding a woman to touch a man who was not her husband, the Master laughed. "The King in his great house has many rules. I do not doubt that some came about from the need to keep all his wives and concubines in line. On the sea, we are practical. If your wife will consent to treating the feet of my men, they, and I, will be grateful."

Ah-mah began the next evening right after the evening meal. Just as he had in Ah-mah's house, Nefer washed and oiled the feet before Ah-mah worked them. Medi and Salla watched, amazed at the way Ah-mah affected everyone she met. The princess had learned more about her people on this trip than she could have in her father's great house. She had heard what Master Akban had said about her father's rules. What if he was right?

Their last night before reaching Byblos, Nefer poured his heart out to Ah-mah, confessing his love for Medi, and his grief at their parting. Ah-mah listened with a keen ear, a compassionate heart.

"The meeting with Medi's father will be difficult for all of us, my son. It will be best if you do not come to the King's house." When Nefer seemed about to protest, Ah-mah said, "I will find a way for you to say goodbye."

With the dawn, all thought of dolphins, of swimming, of spontaneity was consigned to memory. Both boats were scrubbed clean and colorful squares of cloth brought forth and attached fore and aft, marking Ah-mah's boat as carrier of representatives from the Land of the River, the other boat as the pride of Byblos. Chests were brought from the hold and opened, revealing, among other things, Ah-mah's yellow cotton dress.

From the moment she saw it, she knew two things: that Sept was responsible for her having it; and that in it, she would be dignified. She hugged the dress to her, then retrieved the small cosmetics box and took it to Medi, who was spending a last morning of relative freedom with Ah-mah.

"Princess, will you abandon custom for a while longer and help me paint my face?"

Medi bade Ah-mah sit, and much as Ak-hu, combed Ah-mah's hair, oiled it until it gleamed and pulled it back, using two of her own beautiful turquoise- and coral-studded combs to hold it in place. Then she expertly used the malachite paste to outline Ah-mah's eyes and eyebrows, rubbing rouge into her cheeks and lips. When she had finished, she held the polished copper mirror up for Ah-mah to see, just as Ak-hu had. This time, Ah-mah merely nodded, no longer surprised at her image.

"May I dress your hair, Princess?"

Medi nodded, already distancing herself from all on this boat, from all those she loved.

Ah-mah combed Medi's hair, and would have oiled it, but Medi stopped her. "We wear our hair unbound and unoiled, Ah-mah."

She watched as Medi applied a thin line of black kohl to outline eyes and eyebrows, and a little less rouge to her beautiful face. When she was satisfied, she stood, and Ah-mah placed the heavy robe over her shift. Before she could walk away, Ah-mah placed a hand on either shoulder. "You are like a daughter to me, Medi."

Deep in her role, Medi merely nodded, but Ah-mah saw the understanding and the gratitude in her eyes.

"There is one other who would speak with you before you leave, Princess," Ah-mah said and motioned to Nefer, who came to stand before her. Knowing it would be his last time to speak with her made him bold and he took her hand in his, not caring who saw.

"My heart goes with you, Medi." With a quick whisper, meant for Nefer's ears alone, she turned, and with the help of Malloch and Salla, descended the ladder and returned to the Byblosian boat.

They sailed within the hour, and soon entered the harbor. Ah-mah stood in the bow, a new, but not unpleasant odor filling her nostrils. Sept said it was from the cedar, the trees they had come to purchase for Rahotep, and he pointed to a sledge that held three huge logs ready to be loaded onto a waiting boat. But Ah-mah was more interested in the mountains behind the village. In the Land of the River, mountains were a sandy, desert color, but these mountains held swaths of dark green where great groves covered them.

Byblos was larger than Nubt or any other village in the Land of the River, its houses in rows around the harbor, with well-defined paths of hard-packed earth running between the rows and wider paths crossing them. On all the paths, people scurried to and fro, mostly on foot, but some led asses burdened with all they could carry. The houses themselves were of different sizes and styles, most being constructed of wood, but some seemed to be sun-dried mud bricks, just as in Nubt. Ah-mah's gaze was drawn to one of the wider paths, already lined with people, and up to a great wall. A sprawling house, partially visible, stood behind the wall, the tops of many tall trees forming a green backdrop that blended with the tree-covered mountains in the distance. "The House of the King and the King's trees," she thought as the boat touched the dock.

A harsh blaring sounded and a gate in the wall opened. Through it marched a group of the King's guards dressed in brown and green with polished bronze shields and spears, gleaming in the sun. Two abreast, they came down the wide path, separating into two files on the dock. Into their midst walked the Princess, accompanied by Salla and Malloch, and followed by Sept, Master Mu-hem, and Ah-mah. Sept's guards fell in behind Ah-mah, carrying the chest of gifts for the King. Two of the King's guards took position behind Sept's men, effectively sealing off any escape. At least that was the way Ah-mah thought of it, having taken Medi's observations to heart.

The people shouted in a language Ah-mah did not understand, and threw blossoms into the path before their princess. She wished she had the courage to look at them, but all she could see was Medi's head turning neither to the right nor to the left. She could only follow suit.

"Do you have room for another in your mind?"

"Aletha! I am glad to hear your voice, but now is not the time. I must concentrate on controlling my impulses to speak or to do without thinking."

"Then I will stay with you, but I will be quiet."

"Your presence comforts me."

The procession passed through the rows of houses and up the small hill. As they went through the gate giving Ah-mah a better look at the huge house behind the wall, Aletha mind-whispered, "Medi's box has grown!" Ah-mah said nothing, although she had

had the same thought, and left all hope of freedom outside the gate that closed behind them.

The Princess was escorted to the wing reserved for women of the royal house; Ah-mah, Sept, Master Mu-hem, and the guards to another wing. Each of the three guests was given a room and told to wait inside, the guards left in an adjacent courtyard. As Ah-mah entered her room the door closed with a bang.

A small table held a pitcher filled with water, a bowl, and a cup. A length of cloth was folded neatly and laid to one side of the table, a single stool beside it. She went to the stool and sat, folding her hands in her lap. After the noise of the sea and the cacophony of the streets, the silence that filled the room seemed ominous.

Moments passed like hours before the door opened again. Ah-mah stood, her impulsive self under tight rein. With dignified steps, she walked to the doorway, tempted to look at Sept, choosing instead to look straight ahead. She missed his wink.

They were ushered down a hall, Ah-mah first, followed by Sept and Master Mu-hem. When they came to some steps, Ah-mah, unused to the length of her dress, tripped on its hem and would have fallen if Sept had not put a hand on her arm to steady her. She did glance at him then, and his smile heartened her. Grabbing her skirt with one hand, she pulled it above her sandaled feet and climbed the steps.

The room that opened before them was vast. Ah-mah nearly stumbled again, this time from the tangle in her mind as it tried to take in the room's enormity. Sept's whispered "Steady," brought her head up, her attention centered on what was before her: a long walk to a throne in the far distance.

Torches illuminated the room. The space around the throne was lit by them, and by a strange glistening circle behind it. As Ah-mah drew closer, she glimpsed what might have been trees through the circle. "You are seeing what is outside. A stone much like the clear crystals of Atlantis, polished and faceted, allows the view and also distorts it." A mental nod to Aletha was all Ah-mah allowed herself. Finally, they stopped, halted by spears thrust in front of them.

Ah-mah tried not to stare at the King, but she had never seen anyone robed so magnificently. The throne itself was massive, intricately carved from dark wood. The man who sat upon it was as massive as his throne. Ah-mah had no doubt he would be taller than Sept if he stood. "It is an illusion," Aletha whispered to her mind. "See how the throne is placed higher than anything else in the room? I think you would find the King to be a little shorter than Sept if they stood together." Ah-mah paid closer attention, and felt Aletha might be accurate in her assessment, but no matter. The King and his throne were impressive, although, in truth, he did not look at all like Medi, but had a darker countenance with dark, nearly black eyes.

Sept moved to Ah-mah's side, as did the Master. Sept's men placed the chest from home in front of the throne and opened it. Ah-mah could not prevent a sharp intake of breath when she saw the bolts of fine linen, beautifully painted pots, and malachite, lapis lazuli and turquoise jewelry. Tempted to swoon from the wave of homesickness that passed through her body, she held herself rigid.

She heard Sept's voice as he greeted the King in the name of Rahotep of the Land of the River, and bade the King accept the gifts offered. A thin man, his very large nose not unlike the beak of a giant bird, translated Sept's greeting. The King inclined his head a fraction, and the gifts were whisked away. Ah-mah felt her heart strain to follow them. She was brought back by the deep, commanding voice speaking from the throne. She had never heard such a voice, nor did she understand one word that was spoken.

The translator with the oversized nose said, "We bid you welcome to our land, and we thank Rahotep of the Land of the River for these gifts." Normal words, spoken in a higher pitch, but expected. Those that followed froze Ah-mah to her core. "We would see the woman you brought as gift to us. The woman who heals through the feet. Is this she?"

"She is not offered as gift, great King."

More deep-voiced words. Ah-mah did not want to know what this King had said, but the translator paid no mind to her unspoken wish and continued. "We would like to hear from this woman. Can she not speak?"

Sept was ready for this, having been coached by Medi. "She speaks through me, great King."

"We would know who you are."

"I am Sept, Master of Guards to Rahotep of the Land of the River, husband to this woman who has taught her skill to the Princess Medi, at your request."

"You may speak for the woman."

"What does the King ask?"

"Can this woman heal our wives so that they give us sons?"

"This woman is skilled in treating the sick, great King. She is not able to affect areas that belong to the gods." Ah-mah recognized the skill with which Sept was handling this gruff man, king of his land, used to striking fear in all his subjects, used to having his way. "Be careful, my husband," she thought to him.

"He is being very careful," Aletha mind-whispered.

The silence that followed stretched ominously until the deep, commanding voice spoke once more, followed by the translator's higher pitched voice. "We would have this woman live with the women of this house for the days that you are here. We would have her treat them and teach them."

"It shall be done," Sept said.

With that, the guards separated Ah-mah from Sept and took her through a side hall to a door which opened, swallowed her, and was quickly locked behind her. She would have panicked had it not been for the face beaming at her, arms outstretched to embrace her. Beside her, Salla whispered, "Welcome to the House of the King, Ah-mah." With Medi's arms around her, Ah-mah tried to smile, but instead shuddered, and then found she could not stop shivering.

"Come with me, brave Ah-mah. The worst is over and you are safe for the moment."

All the women crowded around Ah-mah, touching her hair, her dress, her skin. A cup was thrust into her hands and she heard Medi say, "Drink this, Ah-mah. It will soothe you." She drained the cup and felt the liquid burn her throat, warming her as it traveled to her stomach. The shaking subsided. Medi took her arm and helped her to one of the cushions circling a fire blazing in a pit. All the women found places around the fire and looked at Ah-mah expectantly. One woman found her voice, and spoke for all.

"It is said that you have brought magic so that we might bear sons for the King."

Ah-mah opened her mouth, then closed it. She had no idea what the woman had said and she was still afraid to utter a word. Seeing her plight, Medi spoke to the women in their language. "Ah-mah has come to teach us many things, but the bearing of sons is best left to the gods." Turning to Ah-mah, Medi translated what the woman had asked, and her answer, adding, "I have asked them to allow you time to recover from your audience with my father. You may speak to any of these women, Ah-mah with no fear."

"I would speak, Medi, if I knew the language."

"I will stay with you and act as translator, and when I am not here, Salla will take my place by your side."

"Are all these women the King's wives?" Ah-mah's first question.

"The King has four wives and ten concubines. All live here in these quarters along with six maidservants, and ten manservants."

"Four wives and ten concubines," Ah-mah mused. "He must be a busy man."

Medi could have laughed out loud at this wonderful woman's innocent audacity. She was painfully aware that she had been away from the women's quarters for a long time. The women irritated her, as did her father's treatment of Ah-mah, which she had witnessed through her privileged spy-hole. "How much I have changed," she thought. In her mind's eye, she saw Nefer, still on the boat, and wondered what he was thinking. "If only..." She closed her mind to that possibility once more, each time praying the door would remain closed and she would not remember the beauty of Nefer's face, his tender respect. "I did not know respect from a man before Nefer. I knew obedience. I knew service. But no man had shown me respect." The door would not stay shut.

"My lady?"

Wife Number Four, the newest one, younger than Medi. She shrugged Nefer from her thoughts and turned to face the woman. She studiously would not remember the names of her father's wives, except for her mother, Delia. She did not speak, but placed an expectant look upon her face. "My lady, can you tell us of your travels? Of your adventures? The people you have met, the things you have seen?"

In spite of her resolve, Medi softened. None of these women, including her mother, had left these quarters since entering them. Besides, Medi enjoyed a good tale, and the telling of it came naturally to her. Salla positioned herself right behind Ah-mah and whispered a translation into her ear as Medi spoke.

"Ah-mah's land is far away, many, many days from this house.

I crossed the great water and entered the largest river I have ever seen. Even then, I had far to go to reach that part of the river where Ah-mah lives. The land is parched, but the river is wide during all the seasons. Once a year, I am told, it rises and spreads itself over the land to make it fertile and then recedes, much as a man gives his seed to a woman and then leaves her to tend to other affairs."

The women nodded. They understood the analogy all too well. Medi continued. "Ah-mah lives in a small house at the edge of a village of small houses. One larger house is also in the village and is devoted to the worship of the god Ra, who is the sun. The priests of Ra tell that he rises in the east at the beginning of the day and enters a boat in which he navigates the sky. In the evening, he leaves that boat in the west and steps into another boat in which he travels the dark, only to enter his sky boat once again the next morning. His night trip is beset with enemies, as his day trip is sometimes beset with clouds to cover his face. The priests are vigilant and regularly perform rites to vanquish Ra's enemies and speed him safely on his way. One such rite includes stamping an image of one of the enemies to bits.

"Ah-mah's house has gardens in front and in back filled with herbs and flowers, some of which I had not seen. Delicious smells come from the garden and from her cooking pot. Two rooms are for sleeping, another for the drying and preparing of herbs. A fourth room has a hearth for cooking and is reserved for the gathering of the family and the greeting of guests.

"Throughout the day, people of all ages come to her for treatment, both men and women." The women gave a collective gasp, placing hands to faces in disbelief, eyes wide. "Often they bring her gifts of herbs or food or cloth or flax seeds as payment for her treatments. She makes tonics and tinctures, poultices and other healing remedies, as well as performing her wondrous foot treatments, which she gives in the garden beneath two young trees.

"Some time back, she made an agreement with the High Priest of Ra so that he and the lesser priests could benefit from her treatments." A shadow passed over the Princess' face as she remembered that Nefer had been the reason for that agreement. Ah-mah had told her the story, as had Nefer.

The women did not notice, so eager were they to hear more. When Medi's silence extended longer than they could stand, one said, "The lady treated men? And they brought her gifts?"

Medi nodded. "Yes, Ah-mah treated men, and all the people she treated brought her what they could spare. She is greatly respected in her village for her skills and knowledge. The High Priest, however, asked her to come to him."

"Did Ah-mah's house have a gate? How did she go to the High Priest? Can her travel be protected so that she will not be seen by any man who is not her husband?" The questions came from all quarters. Medi was saddened as she remembered that these women could not imagine anything outside these walls.

"The ways of Ah-mah's land are different," Medi said, finally. "Women travel freely and do not cover their faces. They speak to anyone they like. Some women travel only to the marketplace and back, but many fish in the river, and some, like Ah-mah, have helped their husbands work the land."

"Do they not have royal houses?"

"Ah-mah's ancestral home is very large and the temple is tall and imposing, but no house is as grand as this one. Great houses like the House of the King do not exist in Ah-mah's land."

The women nodded their approval of this story. Finally, Medi had spoken of something they had that Ah-mah did not.

Ah-mah thought the women's interest in the ordinary affairs of her life to be as unusual as they found her story. As she listened to Salla's translation, she also watched the women, seeing the differences in skin color, size, shape of the face, hair color, and the color of the eyes. One thing that all seemed to have in common was a softness. Ah-mah was used to the angular features of people who worked hard every day. These women seemed water rich. She observed that even the young woman, fourth wife to the king and a fairly recent arrival, had blurred edges and the beginning of plumpness. She wondered what story the feet of these women would tell.

A kind of order seemed to exist in the circle of women. Medi sat to the right of the oldest woman present. Ah-mah sat to Medi's right. With a diplomacy Sept would have admired, Ah-mah asked Medi if the eldest woman was her mother, and when Medi nodded, asked her for a bowl of water and a cloth. Medi spoke to a servant who quickly brought both. Then Ah-mah knelt in front of Medi's mother, and not knowing her language, indicated with gestures that she would like to touch the woman's feet. Medi spoke quickly to her mother and the lady allowed her foot to peep from beneath her robe. She reached down to remove the soft slipper encasing the foot, but was waved away by Ah-mah who removed the slipper herself. She dipped the cloth into the fragrant water and squeezed out the excess. Then with sure hands, she held the woman's foot in hers and began wiping it gently but firmly with the cloth. The women moved closer until all were sitting or standing so that Ah-mah's movements could be seen.

Once the foot had been washed, Ah-mah began a treatment. She twisted the foot to loosen it, then pressed her thumb gently into the area beneath the toes. The foot felt soft with little of the musculature or hard calluses she was used to. Her hands kept straying toward the ankle and the sides of the heel. The first few times, she brought them back to the routine, but the third time she left them where they were.

Ah-mah closed her eyes and let the foot speak to her. Her hands began to move very slowly, pushing the ankle slightly one way, then the other. Medi's mother visibly relaxed. Ah-mah's hands moved to the tendon that stretched from the heel to the back of the leg, the same place she had told Medi and Nefer connected the body with the foot. A sigh escaped Medi's mother, and at a word from Medi, servants hurried to place cushions behind her so she could recline with ease.

Ah-mah worked the foot thoroughly, her hands glad of familiar work to do. With a final pat, she finished that foot, and dipped the rag into the bowl once again. Tenderly, she washed the eldest's other foot and worked it, beckoning to Medi as she worked. Medi knelt close while Ah-mah whispered her request. With a smile, Medi went herself to fetch a smaller bowl filled with a deliciously sweet aroma. The women knew this scent. Their maidservants had used it to oil their bodies, not just their feet. Ah-mah dipped her fingers into the bowl and began working the oil into the eldest's feet, first one and then the other. The owner of those feet snored softly, completely at peace.

Every other woman in the room was ready for Ah-mah's ministrations. They all wanted to feel the touch of the exotic looking brown woman, especially since her touch was said to bring sons to the womb. Once again Ah-mah looked at Medi, this time with a quick shake of her head.

"That will be all for today. Ah-mah is tired from her long journey, and must rest," Medi said. To Ah-mah she spoke in her own language, "Come with me, I will show you where you may refresh yourself."

Medi led the way to a nearby courtyard where Ah-mah, to her surprise, heard running water. She followed the sound to an animal's head on the far wall. From its mouth water poured in a continuous stream into a pool beneath it. The pool was a mystery. Ah-mah watched it for several minutes. Why did it not overflow? She asked Medi.

"Because it drains out through a hole in the bottom of the pool. The only time it overflows is if that hole is filled with debris. In truth, Ah-mah, it is a small stream which has been diverted to run through our quarters before returning to the main stream beyond these walls."

Ah-mah splashed water from the pool on her face and hands. She was about to use the new yellow dress as a towel when one of the tall, soft men who acted as guards and servants to the women offered Ah-mah a cloth with which to dry herself.

"Medi, these people are like none I have seen. Can you tell me about them? Are they women dressed as men? Are they men who look like women? If they are men, how can they be here, in the women's quarters?"

"They are men who have lost their desire for women, Ah-mah."

"How is that possible?"

"They come to us as boys, offered for service by their families. It is a great honor to be allowed to serve the women of the royal house. To be certain that they will not desire any woman, but simply want to guard and serve her, the sacs which hold a man's seed are removed. It is a good life, and an easy one."

Ah-mah was silent, letting the words in, allowing them to settle into her mind in hopes that she could understand what Medi was saying. Sacs? That hold a man's seed? Suddenly, Ah-mah's hand went to her mouth. These men were not men. They would never father children. It was not unusual for an animal to be neutered in the Land of the River, especially if it was not needed for breeding, but never a man. "Careful, Ah-mah. You are in new territory. Keep silent and do not show what you are feeling."

Ah-mah coughed to cover her dismay. A Not Man (as she now thought of him) brought her a cup to fill with water from the pool. His hand brushed hers as she took the cup from him and searched his eyes. Deep pools lay in those eyes. As Ah-mah stared into them, she seemed to see sadness, but suddenly, the light went out, as though a veil had been dropped. "This burden is not yours, Ah-mah."

In spite of Aletha's warning, Ah-mah smiled at the Not Man. He returned her smile and inclined his head.

As Medi led her from the room, Ah-mah noticed that a tree grew in its center. She had seen the trunk when she first entered the room, but would have thought it an oversized post except for its odor. The tree was one of the King's prized cedars. Now, looking up, she was surprised to see the intricately carved, wood grating surrounding it, creating a kind of open-work ceiling.

"To keep enemies from entering our quarters," Medi said, following Ah-mah's gaze.

"To keep us inside these walls," Ah-mah thought.

CHAPTER TWENTY-NINE

Escape

The moon woke her. An opening high in the wall, covered with a grating similar to the one surrounding the tree and which, Ah-mah suspected, covered every other opening in the King's great house, allowed the soft light to bathe her tiny alcove. The memory of the moon seen from the deck of their boat the night before caused Ah-mah to remember the tree and to rise when all were sleeping. "I want to see the moon clearly," she thought.

Ah-mah still wore her beautiful yellow dress, somehow reluctant to remove it even though a Not Man had brought her a garment to wear instead. She shuddered as she remembered him. Would she ever become used to the idea that a boy would submit willingly to such an act?

The stone felt good to her bare feet, solid. Hiking her dress above her knees so it would not rustle, she walked carefully through the room still warmed by embers, and straight to the tree, guided by its clean odor. Moonlight sifted through its branches and the grating created patterns on the floor. Ah-mah hardly noticed, being more interested in whether she could climb the tree. A hole, large enough for a tree trunk to expand over the years, had been left in the grating. She might be able to slip between the grating and the trunk.

Gathering up the skirt of the dress and knotting it, and with no intention other than to see the moon and the stars, Ah-mah climbed the rough bark of the tree. She was taller than most women and not conditioned to staying where she was told, which may explain why she was able to reach the grating so easily. Using it as a handhold, she pulled herself up to the branch above it. Climbing higher and higher, she did not think of how far above the ground she was. At last the branches divided to reveal a quarter moon.

Unknotting her dress so that it covered her limbs in the night chill, Ah-mah sat gazing at the partial white orb. Calmness flooded into her body with the moonlight as she determined where she was. The moon was in the eastern sky. The boat would be to the west. She looked for familiar groupings of stars and located Sothis just past overhead. Dawn was four hours away.

A small sound caused her to look down. Someone was climbing up the trunk. Ah-mah froze, hoping she could remain undetected, but whoever it was kept climbing, using the grating much as Ah-mah had. Evidently the climber was headed for the spot Ah-mah had chosen. She could do nothing but wait.

Medi's face poked through the leaves. "What…" she started and stopped, seeing Ah-mah's finger on her lips. Ah-mah pointed and Medi saw it: a shadow that was not a woman. One of the Not Men glided past on soft-soled slippers, a hint of the perfumed water he carried wafting to them as the puff of steam rose from the grated room.

"He takes hot water to my mother to ease the pains in her joints.

She suffers in the night," Medi whispered. "Do you think rubbing her feet might help ease her pain?"

"Perhaps," said Ah-mah, softly. "Fresh air and long walks would help more, but I suppose that is against all the rules in the King's House."

"I did not know, Ah-mah," Medi said. "I did not know that the rules only existed in my father's house. So much have I learned on this journey."

"Now you are here to stay. Will you try to change things?"

"The women do not want change. They have not known another life." Medi was quiet. "I no longer belong here, Ah-mah. My travels have changed me. These women find comfort in the sameness of each day, the little spats and scuffles over the attention of my father, the attention of the servants, the safety of guards and walls."

"They are not alone in that. After Khmet died, I found comfort in the gardener's hut of my childhood. The sameness of the land, with its growing time and harvesting time and time of inundation, served to hold me to life. These women are not stupid, Medi. Your mother is wise; I see it in her eyes. The difference between you is that you have witnessed a different culture. You have lived with people who have different rules."

"It seems there are so few rules in the Land of the River, Ah-mah."

"Not true. Do you think I could neglect my duties at the temple without my husband being called to account? Politics and religion: They did not always rule, but they do now."

"I am glad you found the tree. It has been my favorite hiding place since the first time I found a way to climb it. I was eleven years old then and eager for adventure. The fresh air on my face and the feeling that I was alone with no one to tell me what to do, I felt I could fly."

"Now you have flown, far away to another country. How will you manage with clipped wings?" Ah-mah asked.

"I do not know, but I must find a way," Medi said, and moved closer to Ah-mah on the branch. The older woman put her arms around the younger, and Medi snuggled closer. The tree held them beneath moon and stars until Medi stirred.

"We must go back before it is noticed that we are not where we should be," she said.

"Who would notice?"

"The servants roam at night, watching over all of us. I have wondered whether they were guarding us or making sure we did not escape. That wonder has grown to suspicion now that I have been away. Come, let us return to our beds, but Ah-mah, let us also meet here every night for as long as you are here."

Ah-mah smiled in the moonlight and followed Medi back down the tree.

The next morning she awoke with the ominous feeling that someone was in the room with her, someone she did not know. Peeping from behind slightly raised lids, she saw slippered feet, larger than most. The enormity of where she was came flooding back into her consciousness. She opened her eyes to look at the Not Man who stood before her bed holding a bowl of steaming water and a large cloth. Not having any idea of what was expected, she continued staring at him, raising both eyebrows in question. He was not going to wash her. Of that, she was certain. She positioned both hands as though they held a bowl of water and set it down beside her bed. To her surprise, the Not Man placed the bowl he held in that exact place, and stood holding the cloth over one arm. She shooed him out of the alcove with both hands, whereupon he laid the cloth on the bed, and pulled the curtain across the opening as he left.

A new dress lay at the foot of the bed. It was a deep rose color with a dark green, sleeved cloak to wear over it. The fabric was unusual, thicker than she was used to, but she was glad of the weight since the air coming through the grate was cold, chilling her body. Her teeth were chattering by the time she had donned the dress, the cloak, and the slippers that lay beneath them. Memories of the warm fire from yesterday enabled her to draw the curtain back and enter the large room without any need for courage. A seeming multitude of faces turned as one to look at her. Ah-mah took no notice, but headed straight for the fire and the only cushion unoccupied. She sat and stretched her hands to its warmth.

"Greetings, Ah-mah," Medi said, from the next cushion. "Are you hungry?" Without waiting for an answer, Salla knelt beside her with a plate full of food and a cup of warm white liquid. Ah-mah lifted the cup in both hands and sipped. The wonderful strangeness of fresh camel's milk passed her lips and tongue to flow down her throat and into her stomach, warming her as it did. Taking a bite from a cake on the plate, she looked at the women who sat with her around the fire.

Medi's mother, Delia, still sat regally in the choicest spot, Medi on her right. A woman with a swollen belly, Number Two Wife, sat next to Delia on the other side. Ah-mah listened to the soft chatter among the women. The language sounded different when spoken by women and not the great rumbling voice of the King. Not one word did she understand, but she surmised that these women spoke as her people did of the small things in their daily lives. She wondered if they spoke of the dreams they had in the night, or the child, soon to be born, or the little girl, barely more than a toddler, in the lap of her mother. So intent was she on studying the women, Medi's voice startled her.

"Ah-mah, the women have been talking about your treatment of my mother, and from the sound of their chatter, they want to feel your hands on their feet. Do you think you could work today?"

"I would be glad of the opportunity."

"Good. We will not overtire you. I have suggested that two make themselves available to you this morning, and two more this afternoon. Would you mind if I treated feet beside you?"

"Who will translate for me?" Ah-mah asked.

Medi beckoned to Salla, who came gladly with warm scented water and a cloth and placed them at Ah-mah's side. Then she, too, sat, no longer a shadow but ready to offer any assistance that might be needed. Cushions had been placed in front of Ah-mah by a Not Man, with more before Medi. To Ah-mah, but in a voice all could hear, she said, in the language of the Land of the River, "This is Wife Number Three. She has not long been with us and came from the rugged hills to the south of Byblos. While you treat her feet, I will do those of her maidservant." The women gasped as they saw Third Wife's maidservant lay down on the cushions before the princess. Medi had already determined that she would not treat any of her father's wives or his concubines, just as she would not remember their names. Since her time in the Land of the River and her recognition of her own maidservant's gifts, Medi felt quite comfortable treating the feet of one who was beneath her in status.

With a sense of the need for ritual, Ah-mah dipped the cloth into the warm water and wrung out the excess, all the while muttering the Prayer for a Clean Heart, the Prayer for Healing, and the Prayer for Feet. Normally, she would not have bothered, and had not with the sailors, but this was different. She was an emissary from the Land of the River and she was determined to present herself, her land, and her skill in the best possible light. "The light of the sun," she thought to herself. "That is what is needed here. It is too dark inside this place."

"I agree." Aletha. The corners of Ah-mah's mouth turned up in a faint smile at the voice inside her head, but she concentrated on her work instead of answering. She took both heels in her hands, and murmuring her own prayer, "Where there is Desire, where there is Need, where there is Consent," she pulled on the heels, firmly and gently, once, twice, three times, until the expected sigh escaped Third Wife, and she relaxed. Medi, followed Ah-mah's movements closely.

Aletha spoke to Ah-mah's mind. "You could ask Salla or the princess to tell the women what you are doing as you work."

"Good idea," Ah-mah thought back to her. "Medi, do you think the women would like to hear what we are doing?"

For answer, Medi began speaking in Byblosian. Ah-mah suppressed a chuckle as heads jerked up. The women had bowed their heads respectfully during Ah-mah's muttering, recognizing the ritual in the alien words she spoke. They had not expected Medi's voice.

Ah-mah worked the place of breathing, her strong hands holding the left foot steady, her strong thumbs pushing, pushing, kneading the sole of Third Wife's foot. She did not think about what Medi might be saying, but kept her focus totally on the foot in her hands. A question was asked by one of the women, and answered by Medi. The women crowded closer behind Ah-mah and the princess, spellbound, the only sounds in the room, Medi's voice and the soft snores of the two on the cushions.

Ah-mah and Medi did two pair of feet in the morning, and then after a meal and a rest, prepared to do two more pair in the afternoon. Thus the days passed, with Ah-mah and Medi treating the women's feet, Medi translating as they worked. Each night, they met in the tree, whispering to each other about the day, hands over mouths to muffle laughter. On her fourth day in the women's quarters, Ah-mah sat in front of the next woman to be treated, a concubine, and thus, not worthy of name or title as far as Medi was concerned, when Medi surprised her once again.

"Salla will translate. I must be absent for a while." So saying, Medi left the room accompanied by two Not Men.

Before Ah-mah could react, Salla spoke, "I have watched you, Lady Ah-mah, and I have heard you teaching Princess Medi and Master Nefer. I can tell the women what you do," she said, in Ah-mah's language.

"I am sure you can, my girl," Ah-mah said, and smiled at her.

The sessions went well that afternoon and were followed by a sumptuous meal. Medi returned during the meal, taking her place by her mother. "You are eager to climb the tree again," said Aletha to Ah-mah's mind.

"I want to know where Medi has been. She seems subdued," Ah-mah answered.

Ah-mah thought of making an excuse for leaving, but as it happened, Salla noticed her nodding off, and came to her side. She touched Ah-mah's shoulder and beckoned to her. Gratefully, Ah-mah rose and followed Salla to the alcove. As Salla turned down the bed covers, Ah-mah removed the green cloak and began to remove her dress when a thought struck her.

"Salla? Where is my yellow dress?" she asked.

"The servants have taken it to make it fresh for wearing," Salla said.

"I wish it were here now. Could you find it for me? I confess I want to touch something from home."

"I will bring it to you, Lady Ah-mah," Salla said, and left the alcove.

Ah-mah sat on the bed, prepared to wait as long as needed. In much less time than she had expected, Salla reappeared, the yellow dress in her hands. She draped the dress over a wooden chair, taking down a plain gown from a peg next to the chair, and laying it on the bed.

"This garment will be more comfortable for sleeping, and you can wear your yellow dress tomorrow," she said.

"Thank you, Salla. I will sleep deeply and remember your kindness."

Truth be told, Ah-mah hardly closed her eyes. Aletha was correct. She was eager to climb the tree, to hear where Medi had been and what she had done there.

As soon as the rising moon lightened the sky, Ah-mah rose and slipped out of the sleeping gown and into her yellow dress. The long sleeves of the cotton were warm and reassuring to her, but knowing the cold at the top of the tree, she added the warmth of the green cloak. She stood just behind the curtain and listened. Hearing nothing, she pulled aside just enough of the curtain to slip between it and the alcove wall, making sure the curtain fell normally once she was on the other side. Again, she stood and listened, quelling her desire to run through the large, central room to the tree. A shadow crossed the room on the other side. Ah-mah froze in place until it passed, then walked quickly across the room, her bare feet making no sound.

She halted at the doorway to the courtyard, eyes on the bole of the tree that stood majestically in the center, ears listening for any sound that did not belong. Water still spewed from the animal's mouth into the pool. Other than the water music and the faint breeze soughing through the boughs of the tree, no sound could be heard other than the pounding of her heart. Satisfied, she stepped into the room and went straight to the tree, pausing for a moment to knot both the dress and the cloak before climbing it swiftly. Once again she used the grate as a hand hold, quickly reaching the branch above it. By now, she knew exactly where she was going, and climbed up limb after limb until she reached the place that was open to the night sky and the light of the moon.

Medi waited for her. Ah-mah held onto the tree with one hand, and embraced Medi with the other. "You have seen your father, the King," Ah-mah said.

"How did you know?" the girl asked.

"I did not know," Ah-mah said, "but I suspected. No one else would command you so easily in this house. Was the meeting difficult for you?"

Instead of replying immediately, Medi gathered her thoughts. "You have influenced me more than you know, Ah-mah. I spoke honestly with my father. I told him how women are treated in the Land of the River, how they move freely and command respect. He asked about you specifically, Ah-mah. He wondered how you learned to do feet. When I told him it was from curiosity and need, as you have told me, I saw genuine surprise on his face. To think it might be your idea, and not something you learned from a man, was apparently inconceivable to him.

"He asked me again if the treatment would help his wives bear sons. I had witnessed Sept's answer to him, and I responded as Sept did. My father said that was too bad, for he needed a son, and soon. A powerful man, long a friend to my father, but now his worst enemy, has gathered men to him in a remote corner of our land, and my father's spies warn him that this man is planning to challenge him. He has become a sneaky man, Ah-mah, with an affinity for shadows. My father fears he will strike soon, perhaps while you are here."

"I am sorry to hear this, Medi. The disruption of authority is hard for any people. Your father may have extreme rules for the women in his house, but they all seem to love him in spite of that, and the rules seem to be working."

"Ah-mah, something extraordinary happened today. My father thanked me for going to the Land of the River. He put both his hands on my shoulders and looked into my eyes when he said it."

So caught up in the scene Medi painted, Ah-mah almost did not hear the sound, a hollow thump as though something had been dropped. Both women looked through the branches at the floor below. Medi touched Ah-mah's arm and pointed. Ah-mah had already seen it. A shadow that moved.

Suddenly, shouts could be heard and torch light seen flickering. The shadowy figure lost his hiding place as servants and women rushed into the courtyard, Medi's mother, Delia, at their head.

The servants surrounded the man, now revealed to all.

"Who dares enter the royal house this night?" Delia's voice was strong and demanding, her language unfamiliar to Ah-mah, but not her intent.

"I have come to claim your daughter." The man's voice was equally strong.

"The King has not granted you his daughter. By what right do you claim her?"

"I do not explain myself to women," the man said, his voice a sneer.

Delia ignored him, drawing her robes around her in a regal gesture. To the servants, she said, "Escort this man to the door and give him to the guards. Be certain they lock the door once he has left."

Strength lay beneath the softness of the Not Men. They laid hold of the man to escort him to the entrance to the women's quarters, thinking a light touch would be all that was needed. He shrugged off their hands and, drawing a dagger, let out a shout. Six men came running, daggers unsheathed. Before anyone could cry out warning, the Not Men lay in heaps on the floor, their blood forming pools around them. Delia stepped toward the man, determined to stop this horror. She was cut down before she took her second step.

Medi watched transfixed as the terrible event played out below her, her eyes wide and dry. Carefully, so as not to make a sound, Ah-mah leaned over and put her arm around Medi, bringing her mouth up close to her ear. "We must flee this place." Medi turned her head toward the sound of Ah-mah's voice, and would have answered her aloud, had not Ah-mah clamped a hand over her mouth. Recognizing that Medi was in shock, Ah-mah held her close and did not remove her hand.

"You!" the man shouted, pointing to one of the women. "Take me to Princess Medi. You men, follow me."

Within seconds the room below was deserted, the bloody heaps mercifully hidden in the darkness. Ah-mah whispered frantically in the girl's ear with all the force she could muster. "You have seen great horror this night. You are not safe. Before long, that man will know you are not where you should be. He will remember this tree and he will be back. Do you hear me, Medi?" Medi nodded. "We must leave now! Follow me, and stay close."

As she whispered, Ah-mah drew her skirt up again and knotted it and the cloak. She climbed back down the tree, not waiting to see if Medi would follow, ran along a branch that extended over the grating, and dropped to the roof. Ah-mah's sense of direction and her bare feet carried her steadily west. Medi's light footfalls could be heard behind her.

"Ah-mah, wait!"

Ah-mah slowed, but did not stop, and Medi caught up with her.

"If we continue this direction, we will reach the high wall. There is no way down. Come with me, I know another way."

Medi led them north, to roofs that were lower and lower. At last they climbed down a trellis into a garden filled with heavenly scented flowers. Medi picked up the pace and raced toward a gate hidden in a wall of bushes. The gate opened at Medi's touch and both women fled through it and into the woods behind the great house.

"Where do we go, Ah-mah?"

"Back to our boat. I know of no other place."

"That is the first place they will seek for us. Let us go to a place I know from childhood. The woman there would give her life for me and ask no questions."

"Is it far? I confess that my courage is outlasting my strength."

"Not far. No one will have suspected such daring from women, Ah-mah. We can slow our steps a bit, or rest for a moment in the shadows."

"Rest," said Ah-mah, holding her waist and breathing hard.

The princess stopped, secretly grateful. "It all seems like a dream," she said.

"Do not speak of it. We must first find safety. Let us walk for a while," Ah-mah said as she stepped off at a brisk pace. Best to leave that horror behind for a while yet. What about Sept? And Master Mu-hem? Best not to think of them either. Just walk, and then, when her heart stopped pounding, run again.

They continued their northward trek, pausing several times in the darkness, wishing silently for water. When they had to cross a small stream, both dipped cupped hands into it and drank deeply, but not long. Ah-mah could not escape a sense of urgency. Dawn was showing its first lightening of the eastern sky.

"How much farther?"

"Not far."

"Will we be there before the dawn?"

"I do not think so."

"Then we must run now."

They reached the woman's hut just as the morning light was casting clearer shadows on the ground. Medi did not knock, but went in through the open door and squatted quickly just inside, breathing hard. Ah-mah followed suit. Both had smelled cooking.

A woman sat, back to the wall near the hearth, a long spoon in her hand dangling loosely. Her soft snores and the fire's crackle were the only sounds in the room other than Ah-mah's and Medi's panting.

Medi recovered first and went to the woman. Kneeling down beside her, she gently shook her shoulder and called, "Mama?" Touched by the scene in a way she had not expected, Ah-mah muttered softly, "Mama." When was the last time she had spoken, or heard those words? An image of Ak-hu, followed by one of her own mother, and then her dear grandchildren, brought tears on a wave of homesickness.

The woman opened her eyes and smiled. "I have been expecting you."

"You have?"

"I dreamed last night that you were coming to me, and my heart sang in gladness. See? The pot holds your favorite porridge." The woman took a rag, and much as Ah-mah when she had cooked by Remtu's hut, picked up the lid and set it aside. Delicious odors filled the room and made Ah-mah's mouth water in anticipation.

"I have brought a friend with me, Mama."

"Then I will need three bowls. Will you get another from the shelf, Medi?"

Ah-mah could not understand the words that were said, but she understood three bowls and she saw the ease with which the two women interacted.

Medi motioned for Ah-mah to draw nearer. "This woman is

Ah-mah, and she comes from a land far away."

"You are welcome in this house, Ah-mah."

Medi translated Mama's words, and Ah-mah bowed her head slightly and smiled in greeting.

"By what name should I call this Lady?" she asked Medi.

When Medi translated Ah-mah's question, Mama laughed.

"I am no Lady. I have been Mama so long, I would be hard pressed to remember any other name."

Ah-mah waited for the translation, and then asked, "Why do you call her Mama, Medi?"

"Mama nursed me when I was a baby. She is more truly my mother than the woman who bore me."

"Why does she not live in the King's great house since she performed so valuable a service?" A shadow crossed Medi's face as she remembered her mother no longer lived. Ah-mah reached over to touch her arm in sympathy. Mama saw, but said nothing.

"When I was six summers and my mother had shown no signs of bearing my father a son, the King saw Mama one day when he visited the women's quarters. His eyes filled with desire for her and my mother became jealous and afraid. After my father left, she raised a stick to Mama, breaking her arm and marring her face, and then, without pity, she turned her out. I knew Mama would have difficulty caring for herself with her wounds, so I bribed one of the guards with a necklace I stole from my mother. He found a place for her and someone who would set the arm."

Mama had been listening, and now she smiled and nodded as though she knew Medi was telling her story.

"Medi has taken care of me ever since," Mama said. "I require little and I always have much. What joy it is to have the opportunity to share my abundance."

Medi translated Mama's words and then said to her old nurse

and friend, "We cannot stay long, Mama. Ah-mah and I have witnessed a terrible event and I am sure men search for us even now. We would be pleased to share a bowl of your delicious porridge, but we must find a safer place soon."

"What has happened?"

In quick words, fear ever present in her eyes and gestures, Medi told how the man had come looking for her, and not finding her, killed all the servants and her mother.

"Oh, Medi! How terrible! But why did they not find you?" Mama asked. "Were you in the tree?" Chuckling, Mama continued, "I remember the first time I could not find you. You gave me quite a scare until I heard the rustling in the tree. Those were happy days. Who could have known then that the desire to climb a tree would save your life?"

"They will not think to look for you here. Anyone who remembers me thinks I am dead, as I should have been, were it not for you, Medi," said Mama, and handed them each a bowl of porridge and a wooden spoon.

The porridge was even better than the delicious aroma proclaimed it to be. Ah-mah tasted plump dates and figs nestled within, the cause of its sweetness.

"You will want water," Mama said, as she bustled about.

The morning light brightened the little hut, exposing the woman's face and the true reason for her banishment. She was beautiful by anyone's standards. Younger than Ah-mah by some years, Mama had thick black hair and brown skin, and nestled in her face were the most intense green eyes. It wasn't until Mama extended the cup of water to Ah-mah that she saw the long scars on the woman's face. Ah-mah took the cup, staring with unabashed honesty and not averting her eyes. Mama smiled, revealing in that act how the scars puckered and contorted her face.

Sipping the water even though her thirst invited gulps, Ah-mah said, "Medi, will you ask Mama if she can remember another name? One which she was called at birth?"

This time, when Medi asked, the answer was immediate.

"Laskella."

Medi, who had never heard this woman called anything but Mama, watched these two she loved most dearly of all women.

"A beautiful name for a beautiful lady," Ah-mah said, reaching over to touch Laskella's face and beaming a smile at her.

The action required no translation. "Beautiful? Perhaps once, but no longer," Laskella said.

Still looking at Laskella, Ah-mah said to Medi, "Tell her I was born by a great river to people who worked the land. We did not think of personal beauty, but only the abundant generosity of the river and the land, and the goodness of the people. Tell her she has goodness and she has given to us generously from her bounty. How is she not beautiful?"

Medi quickly translated, but before Laskella could respond, Ah-mah continued, "I thank Laskella for harboring us, for feeding us and giving us comfort in her home, but my heart is troubled by what has happened in the King's great house. I fear that more death than what we witnessed has taken place. What if they were able to reach the King?" Then, as the horror of what she had envisioned reached her mind, she exclaimed, "If they could reach the King, what about my husband, and Master Mu-hem? We must warn them, if it is not too late!"

To Medi's translation, Laskella responded, "It will have to be done carefully. Let me think. Waron usually comes each day to bring fresh water. He would take a message to Ah-mah's husband. Are you certain he would be in the King's House? Would he not have returned to the boat?"

"Yes, Sept and Master Mu-hem and the guards returned to the boat the same day Ah-mah came to the women's quarters. My father told me when I saw him," said Medi.

Hearing Sept's name, Ah-mah grabbed Medi's arm when a translation was not immediately forthcoming. "Where is Sept, Medi? Do you know?"

"Yes, Ah-mah," Medi said in the language of the Land of the River. "They are on the boat. They are safe."

"Still, they must be warned," Ah-mah said. Then, as the truth of the situation dawned, "They will hear of what has happened. They will think we are dead, Medi. We must get word to them, but it must be in a way that will not alert others or place anyone in greater danger."

Now it was Laskella's turn to grab Medi's arm, begging for translation. When it was given, the three women were silent, thinking of how they could warn Sept.

Suddenly, all three began talking at once, and then, struck by the absurdity of trying to reach one solution with three voices, they laughed. The fear brought by the terrible events of the night receded, for the moment, and as the hilarity subsided, Ah-mah spoke.

"My mother said that laughter heals the wounds of the heart. I feel better than I have since I last swam with the dolphins. My head is clearer, and I believe I know what must be done."

"Tell us, Ah-mah," Medi said, "and I will translate for Mama."

"We must get a message to Sept on the boat."

"Why not just go there?" Medi asked.

"You heard that man, Medi. He wants you for his wife! You are not safe, nor is anyone who is with you."

When Medi translated, Laskella said, "Waron is perfect for the job of messenger except that he cannot speak Ah-mah's language."

"We can write the message! Ah-mah, you can write the message to Sept. He can read, can't he?" Medi asked.

"Yes. He has taught himself, and I have taught him a little," was Ah-mah's response.

Medi and Ah-mah tried to settle on a sentence or a phrase that would alert Sept but not cause his position to become vulnerable if the message were somehow intercepted. More than an hour had passed before they could agree. Laskella provided a scrap of cloth and a tiny pot of black kohl. With her finger Ah-mah drew a picture for day, a picture for three, and then signed her name in pictures. They rolled the cloth around a stick as soon as it had dried and tied it with another strip of cloth. Just in time. Someone came up the path whistling. Medi and Ah-mah hurried to the darkest corner of the hut, crouching down behind bags of grain and drying bunches of herbs, for they did not want any harm to come to the messenger. The less he knew, the better.

"Hello, friend Waron," Laskella called, and waved.

"Hello, Laskella. You are looking beautiful today."

"I thank you both for the water you bring for me to drink and the water you pour on my soul. You are a good friend, Waron."

Blushing in spite of himself, Waron quickly changed the subject. "The new growth in Jared's field is nearly to my ankle. There will be good harvests this year."

"Can you stay for a moment? I have made a tea for you and I would hear more about the crops."

A rag rug had been placed beside the opening. Waron often sat on that rug sharing with Laskella news of the people of the area, a birth, a sickness, a death. Inside, Medi felt she was intruding on a long-established intimacy, her eyes filling with tears as she felt the depth of Mama's loneliness.

"I have a favor to ask you this morning, friend Waron. Have you noticed the new boat in the harbor? The one from far away?" Waron nodded. "I need you to take this message to a man named Sept just as soon as you can. He will be on that boat."

"Do you require an answer?"

"It would be good to hear that the message was delivered."

So great was Waron's trust of this woman, he simply took the rolled cloth from her and said, "It will be done." Then he rose, and hurried off, eager to please the woman who had stolen his heart.

CHAPTER THIRTY

Messages

The message came to Sept in the early afternoon, the first of two. By nature a cautious man, Waron stood at the end of the last row of houses facing the harbor and watched the foreign boat. Two men stood by the double mast, talking. Waron approached the boat and climbed the rope ladder. When his head cleared the railing, he saw both men looking at him. Holding onto the railing with one hand, he held out the rag bound stick with the other. In a soft voice, able to be heard by the two men, but not on the dock, he said, "Sept." The taller of the two men came to him and took the roll of cloth. The man said something to him that he did not understand. Waron shrugged his shoulders and climbed back down the ladder.

Sept untied the rag and slipped the cloth off the stick. Spreading it out, he read its cryptic message.

"Who is it from?" asked Mu-hem.

"Ah-mah."

"What does it say?"

"Three days."

Mu-hem waited.

"There are other clues here as well. This cloth is crudely woven, not something that would be found in a royal household. I suspect both Ah-mah and the princess are no longer in the King's House but I do not know why."

As soon as Sept voiced his thoughts, he saw the head of the big-nosed translator. The Master went to help the man to board, Sept quickly tucking the message into a fold of his robe.

Before the translator could speak, Sept blurted out, "Is everyone well in the King's House?"

"That is not for me to say," said the translator. "The King asks that you join him immediately. Will you come with me now?"

Without waiting for answer, the translator climbed down the ladder and headed for the King's House, both Sept and Mu-hem following. This time, instead of the huge audience hall, they were led down one passage and then another, upstairs and through yet another hall to an ornately carved door in front of which stood two guards in the brown and green of Byblos, polished, bronze-tipped spears barring entrance. At their approach, both guards lifted their spears. With a slight push, the translator caused the door to open inward, revealing the king sitting at a table, looking much less regal, an empty chair ready for a guest on either side. Sept and the Master stood at attention before the king and bowed. The king indicated the chairs, and Sept and Master Mu-hem sat. The translator went to stand behind the king.

At a signal only he perceived, the translator clapped his hands together and servants entered with cups, wine and the water to dilute it. Quickly, they poured wine and water into the cups and backed out of the room. Sept and Master Mu-hem did not touch their cups, waiting for the king to drink first. He seemed weary to Sept, his face drawn and mottled, his deep voice lower and softer in the smaller room. The wine stayed untouched.

"The King asks if you slept well on your boat."

"Our sleep was deep and undisturbed," Sept said. "Did the King sleep as well?" He suspected that the king understood more than he let on, a suspicion that was confirmed when he rumbled before the translator rendered their words in Byblosian.

"There was no rest in this house last night. An attempt has been made to seize my throne and the Princess Medi," said the translator.

Sept's response was immediate. "The Princess Medi? Surely you will tell us she has not been harmed."

Again, the rumble before the translation. "As far as we know, the Princess has not been harmed."

"As far as you know? What do you mean?"

"The Princess cannot be found in the King's House."

"My wife, Ah-mah? Where is she? I must see her at once."

This time, the King allowed time for the translation and he did not answer immediately. When he spoke at last, Sept chilled to the core as the translator said, "The Lady Ah-mah is not in the King's House."

"Will you beg the King to tell us the full story?"

At a nod from his master, the translator said, "A powerful man, long known to have ambition to replace the King, entered the women's quarters last night with a group of men. They killed most of the servants and the Queen. The King is greatly distressed. They would have captured the Princess Medi, but when they went in search of her, she was not to be found."

Interrupting, Sept asked, "Where is this man? I will wring answers from him. If he has harmed my Ah-mah..."

The translator said, "Calm yourself. The traitor and those who accompanied him are under guard and will be dealt with in due time. No doubt they will be killed, and most unpleasantly."

"Then the threat is over for now?" Without waiting for answer,

Sept continued, "We must leave. We must return to our ship. Ah-mah may be trying to reach it."

"She is not there, nor is the Princess Medi." The reason for the cryptic message was clearer now. Medi and Ah-mah had anticipated that the boat would be watched. "You may return to your ship, but do not leave the harbor."

"How can you think I would leave without my wife?" Then, remembering his position as emissary from the Land of the River, Sept turned to the King. "Master Mu-hem and I are filled with sorrow at the Queen's untimely passing. We will return to our ship, but we beg the King to send word should the Princess or my wife be found. We will offer prayers to our gods for their safe return."

As the translator spoke, the King rumbled. "We will watch for your wife and inform you when we find her."

Sept and Mu-hem rose, bowed to the King, and left with the translator. He led them to the front gate, where he promised once again to send a messenger should Ah-mah or the Princess be found.

The two men walked out of the gate, feeling a flash of freedom as they left what they, too, felt was more to keep people in than to be a barrier to those without. Neither broke the silence as they followed the wide path back to the boat. When they were on board at last, Sept ran to uncover the hold and climb down into it. He half expected to see Ah-mah sitting on the bag of rosemary waiting for him, but no one was there. The note had said three days. He would wait.

"Anyone there?" The Master stuck his head into the hold.

"No. I will stay for a while. I need to think." Sept tried to imagine what had taken place in the women's quarters. What had made Ah-mah leave and take Medi with her? How did she manage to leave the King's House? She must have felt they were in danger, and no wonder, with servants killed right in front of them.

In front of them? If that had been so, the traitor would not have had to go looking for them. Did someone warn them? Try as he might, Sept could not draw any conclusions other than that Ah-mah had sensed they were in imminent danger. And why the cryptic message? Sept slapped his knee. Ah-mah must think they were still in danger. Were they? How could he reassure her? Was there a way?

Suddenly, Sept was filled with terrible dread that he might never see Ah-mah's precious face again. His eyes filled with tears that spilled down his cheeks unchecked. He leaned forward from his perch and put his arms around the huge bag of rosemary, hugging it, as he could not hug Ah-mah. Great racking sobs were muffled by the bag as his tears were absorbed. The pungent scent of rosemary, released as his weight crushed the dried branches, brought a vision of Ah-mah sharply into focus. In his mind's eye, he saw her in her garden at home. Home. The very word threatened to bring more tears, but he drew himself up, away from the bed. He knew the signal to give Ah-mah now. He knew how to tell her the boat was safe.

CHAPTER THIRTY-ONE

The Summons

On the morning of the third day after receiving Ah-mah's message, Sept and Mu-hem were called to the King's House. Until the summons, they had received no word from the king or either of the two women. Sept felt in his heart that Ah-mah was alive and that the princess was with her, but he worried as he tied the strip of yellow cloth to the railing, his signal to Ah-mah that the boat was safe. With foreboding, he and Mu-hem arrayed themselves carefully and made their way for a third time to the King's house. Once more they passed through the gate, and wondered if they would be allowed to leave. They climbed the same narrow steps and crossed the same lofty hall to the spot where the guard's spears had dropped in front of them the first time, and now did so again.

The King sat on his throne as before, but Sept noticed the darkness beneath his eyes and knew that, no matter what he said, he had suffered. Sept bowed his head toward the King who rumbled in his language, with high pitched translation, "Rejoice with me, Sept, Master of Rahotep's Guards in the Land of the River and

Mu-hem, Master of Rahotep's boat. This day the gods have given us a son. We have an heir!"

Sept raised his head, and spoke directly, "We do rejoice in your great good fortune, my lord."

"Today we give thanks, but we do not forget that we have lost a Queen and the daughter you returned to us. We believe she has been killed. We mourn her loss and that of her mother, the Queen. We regret that we have found no trace of your wife since that fateful night. Have you had word of her?"

"No, my lord," Sept lied, "although I pray daily to our gods for her safe return."

"May your prayers be answered, Guardian. In our joy, we would grant a boon to you. What will you ask of us? We cannot restore your wife, but perhaps there is something else you would want?"

Seizing the opportunity, Sept said, "My master would be grateful if the King of Byblos would allow him to purchase several boat-loads of cedars, with one to accompany us on our return voyage, and the rest to follow later."

"In anticipation of your request, we have prepared documents for you to take to your master and we have begun hauling the first load to the dock. We had thought you would want six loads. Would you want us to change the documents?"

"No, my lord. The King is most generous."

"We expect payment in gold."

"Which the King shall have."

"Is there nothing else the Guardian would desire? Our women are said to be lovely and skilled in the art of pleasing a man. Although we would not presume to replace your wife, we would be pleased for you to take one of our women with you." At that, the King raised a finger and a girl whose beauty would have rivaled Medi's came forward. Sept was shocked, but recovered quickly.

"I am grateful for the King's generosity, but our ways are different. I have but one wife, be she dead or living." The finger lowered, and the girl stepped back into the shadows of the cavernous room. Sept continued, "If the King will hear of it, I would ask that the servant to his daughter, by name, Salla, be allowed to return with us."

The translator raised his eyebrows before translating the request. The King did not answer, but moved his hand slightly in an apparent signal, for very soon, Salla came to stand before him. Sept could see how frightened she was. He admired the courage it must have taken for her to stand so quietly before the King. His rumble produced an immediate effect. The translator went to Salla, and with his hand on her shoulder, guided her to stand beside Sept. Nothing else was said, nor sign given, Salla not being worth the effort.

Realizing that the business of the day had been concluded, Sept said, "The people of the Land of the River will offer prayers for the King's son, that he become a mighty warrior."

"We are grateful for the prayers of your people. We shall continue to offer prayers for the safe return of your wife, and a voyage free from ill winds."

The audience was over. The guards turned around smartly, Mu-hem and Sept with them, now accompanied by Salla. Together they marched across the hall, down the steps, and out through the gate. A smile played with the corners of Sept's mouth. If he understood what had just happened and if Ah-mah and Medi were both living as he suspected, Nefer would have reason to rejoice as well. Salla said nothing. Sept glanced at her, wondering if she understood how her fate had been changed.

If possible, the odor of cedar was more dominant than before. In his absence, several sledges of logs had arrived and more were coming. A long line of them snaked up the road toward the tall trees. Sept saw that they were being loaded onto the same boat which had accompanied them to Byblos. Master Mu-hem's boat had been moved some distance away from the Byblosian one and was now moored to the other end of the dock. Master Akban looked worried as the first logs were brought on board. The weight, no doubt. Certainly they would hug the coast on the return trip.

The guards who had accompanied them from the King's house departed, leaving only two who would stay to watch over the cedars at night. No one guarded the boat from the Land of the River.

Sept, Master Mu-hem and Salla boarded the boat, taking places around the brazier that would put their backs to the dock. Salla smiled through her tears when, in a soft voice, Sept told her about the note from Ah-mah. She had not thought Sept would want her as concubine, but she could think of no other reason she had been asked to accompany him. "You think Princess Medi and Mistress Ah-mah still live?" she asked him.

"I do, Salla, and more, I think we will see them tonight."

"Is that why you have tied the yellow cloth to the railing?" she asked. He nodded.

She started to ask the husband of Ah-mah whether he expected they would all return to the Land of the River, but she did not. No longer was she in the House of the King. It was enough.

After the evening meal, Sept took up position in the bow of the boat. To anyone who cared to notice, it seemed that he watched the loading of the logs. Actually, he was looking for all possible hiding places, paying careful attention to anyone who came into the area. By dark, all activity had ceased, the two guards having boarded

Akban's boat to eat with the crew. The moon, near to half full, made spying easy for one used to watching at night. Before long, Nefer joined Sept and watched with him, the yellow cloth moving faintly in the breeze.

What was that? Something moved. Sept elbowed Nefer and pointed with a slight shift of his head. Several shadows darted cautiously through the wide street that led from the dock to the King's House, keeping close to the walls of the houses. The two men slipped over the side of the boat and down the ladder, moving quickly. As they neared the houses, Sept whispered, as loud as he dared, "Ah-mah?" Two shadows froze against the wall, one taller than the other. "Ah-mah," Sept said softly, moving closer. "We must board the boat." He put his hand where her arm would likely be and hurried her along, Nefer having done the same with the other shrouded lump. Suddenly, Sept was aware of two other shadows following them. "Hurry! We are being followed."

"They are friends, Sept. I will explain once we are all on the boat," Ah-mah whispered.

"Then let them hurry!"

Master Mu-hem helped the two men and their four shadows board, the crew bunched behind him. As the hoods of their cloaks were thrown back, Sept and Mu-hem recognized Waron as the man who brought Ah-mah's message to them. From the comfort of Sept's arms, Ah-mah introduced Laskella and Waron. Hesitantly, Nefer put an arm around Medi and drew her close, surprised when she came willingly. On orders from the Master, the crew poured beer into cups and handed them around. When all had drunk, Sept said, "My friends, fortune has favored us. Both my wife and the princess have returned to us unharmed. Earlier today, Master Mu-hem and I learned that the King has a son and heir. He thinks his daughter has joined the Queen in death. We shall not cause him to think otherwise. He has given me documents for six boat-loads of cedar and I have given him gold. Further, the King is sending Master Akban's boat back with us, to carry the first load of cedar logs. We begin our return voyage with more than we had hoped for, including two newcomers who wish to live with us. Tonight we sleep but in the morning and for the days to come before we reach the open sea, our women and our newcomers must stay below out of sight of prying eyes. Is this agreeable to all?"

Sept's men slapped chest with hand in salute for answer. The Master said, "I speak for my crew. We welcome Ah-mah's safe return, and the Princess Medi. If Ah-mah vouches for these other two, they are welcome."

The crew and the guards dispersed to find mats for sleeping, but Ah-mah wanted to be sure she had heard Sept correctly.

"Sept, are you saying that Medi is dead to her father?"

"That is exactly what I am saying, my wife. Of course, if Medi would rather stay here than go with us, that is her choice."

"I love my land and my people. But those I love most dearly are on this boat. A time may come when my people will want me to return, but I do not foresee it. I will come with you to the Land of the River and there I will live the life that is given to me."

"I have a surprise for you, Medi," Sept said, and motioned to Salla. The girl ran to Medi, and kneeling in front of her, bowed her head before her mistress.

"How can this be?" Medi asked.

"Your father wanted to give me a beautiful woman to replace the wife he thought I had lost. I asked for Salla instead. I hope you are not displeased."

For answer, Medi took hold of Salla's shoulders and helped her to rise. Before all, Medi declared, "You are free, Salla, no longer servant, but a woman in your own right, free to go or to come as you choose." Then, she hugged the girl.

* * *

A hooded creature had watched and heard all. He slithered through the shadows and back to the King's House where he did not go through the main gate, but around to the side and through a hidden way into a secret garden, the same garden through which Medi and Ah-mah had escaped. The King waited for him beneath the moon. He, too, was cloaked and hooded. The watcher conveyed what had happened on the dock. He spoke concisely and finished his tale quickly. The King pulled at his beard. Then he said, "It is as we thought. We gain a son and lose a wife, the sweet Delia. Further, we must allow the daughter we love to leave us to remove the temptation she represents to any others who have designs on our throne. We would not question the gods, but it seems a hard bargain. Go now, and tell no one else what you have said to us this night. The people of the Land of the River will leave in a few days, taking our daughter and her maidservant with them, and if you saw right, her nurse as well. Laskella deserves some happiness. She would have given us sons, but for an accident of birth."

"Pardon, Lord?"

"She was not nobly born, although, by rights, such a beauty should have been."

The King said no more, but his spy knew better than to leave first. They sat together on the bench, one deep in thought, the other awaiting his pleasure. Finally, the King sighed out the breath he had been holding and reached into his cloak. Pulling out a rolled cloth, he held it, still seemingly undecided. Just when the spy thought he would put it back into his cloak, the King handed it to him, saying, "Find a way for this to reach my daughter's hands."

A small bag lay on the bench beside the King. He did not offer it to the man, but business concluded, he rose and walked back toward his Great House. When the King disappeared within, the hooded man reached down and plucked up the bag and the payment it contained, melting into the darkness as he left the garden.

CHAPTER THIRTY-TWO

Medi's Gift

The next day, Ah-mah, Medi, Salla and Laskella stayed beneath the deck. Waron, in unfamiliar garb from the Land of the River, became one of Sept's soldiers and watched the dock for any sign that things might be amiss. When the stars came out, so did the four women, sleeping on the deck or talking quietly, often dangling their legs over the sea side of the boat.

Medi seemed drawn into herself.

"What troubles you, my girl?" Laskella asked.

Medi's head jerked up, startled, and then went back down, as she hid her face once more.

"Medi, do not hide from me. I am Mama, remember?"

Medi did not answer. Ah-mah whispered something to Salla who ran to find cushions. Placing the cushions on the deck, Ah-mah said, "I have not yet given Laskella a foot treatment."

Hearing her name, but not understanding the meaning of the words or the cushions, Laskella looked to Salla for translation. Excitement colored her voice as Salla told the woman about Ah-mah's healing foot treatments. Puzzled, but willing, Laskella lay down on the cushions. Ah-mah held both heels and pulled three times before she turned her attention to the right foot. When she finished the lungs, she began working the toes, big toe first.

"Ow!" Laskella exclaimed, a word understood in any language.

Medi scooted to Ah-mah's side. "Where are you working?" she asked.

"I have just started the largest toe and I just pressed here," she said, indicating the inside of the toe near its base. "Ask Laskella if she has pain in her neck?"

Laskella's eyes widened with surprise. "How did you know?"

"Mama, if you can stand the pain in your foot, Ah-mah will see if she can relieve the pain in your neck."

"She can do that?" Medi nodded. "Then, I can stand the pain."

"Tell her it will be better if she relaxes and breathes deeply. Tell her if she does that the pain will be less," Ah-mah said.

With complete trust, Laskella began to breathe deeply and her limbs softened as she relaxed. Ah-mah waited a few moments before beginning again. She had felt a sharp, hard something like a large grain of sand. Instead of returning to the spot, Ah-mah worked around it, working all the toes, stretching the big toe and pulling it out from the foot, hoping to break up the sand. Finally, she returned to the spot of pain and pushed, gently at first, then deeper, moving her thumb back and forth slightly as she worked. The sand was still there. She pushed her thumb into its center, hard. Laskella gasped and Ah-mah grabbed her foot by the toes to shake off the pain. When she went back to the spot, the sand was gone, exploded into a thousand pieces by her strong thumb. Ah-mah continued to work Laskella's feet, Medi beside her, reluctant to leave the focus the treatment gave her mind. With the worst of the pain gone, Laskella drifted into sleep.

"Do you think your father knows you are still alive?"

Ah-mah asked. The startled look in the girl's eyes told her she had hit the mark.

"I wish…"

Before she could complete her answer, a commotion was heard on the dock. Sept spoke with someone. "You cannot come aboard," he said clearly. A muffled response could barely be heard. "All right. I will come down."

"Be careful, my husband," her heart said as Sept climbed down to the dock, returning almost immediately, a hooded, cloaked figure with him. He went to the one lamp still lit, bringing it to the group of women.

"What are you doing, my husband? We will be seen!"

"It seems that someone knows you are here, Medi."

The man, if man it was, could not be seen clearly, his face completely in shadow. He handed a rolled up cloth to Medi. She drew in a quick breath when she saw the seal it bore. Message delivered, the hooded man vanished into the night.

"Open it, Medi," Sept said. "We must know what it says."

The girl spread the cloth on the deck, Sept holding the lamp so she could read what was written and so he could see her face. Quickly her eyes scanned it.

Laskella was first to speak. "What is it, my child?"

"An answer. From my father. Here, I will read it to you all, for what he says to me concerns you." She bent back over the cloth and read, "Fornas tells me you are on the foreigner's boat and that Laskella is with you. I do not have a way to hide you from danger other than to send you back with these people to their land. You cannot return to Byblos, but must make your life as you can. You will always be my first born. If only you had been a son."

Medi's eyes shone in the lamp light. "I am a most fortunate daughter."

CHAPTER THIRTY-THREE
The Death of Atlantis

Locan was last to join the Keepers in the pool, brought by the loyal caretakers. The others, accustomed to the powerful strength of their new bodies, tried to be patient as they waited for Locan to feel comfortable in his. Suddenly, a stream of clicks and whistles reached them from the other side of the gate.

"The wild dolphins warn us. It is time to leave," Aletha mind-spoke to the others.

Seronak dove for the underwater lever designed to open the gate and gave it a mighty push with his beak. A violent tremor shook the earth as the Keeper dolphins slid into the sea and the wild dolphins who waited.

"Swim! Swim for your lives!" Seronak's thought cried to the others.

The wild dolphins surrounded the Atlantean ones, herding them away from the destruction. When they surfaced to breathe, they choked on air that was thick with dust and debris.

Only once did a break appear in the clouds of dust and ash, and for a single moment, Atla was visible. Flames devoured what was left of the city. Buildings crumbled as the rock on which they stood gave way. The two Temples, symbols of Atlantean culture for longer than anyone could remember, hung in the air, then slowly fell. The break closed, mercifully cutting off the view, but not the groaning roar of stone and earth.

Seronak wanted to stop, to ponder, to try to make sense of what he had seen. He wanted to spend the rest of his life wondering why. Something kept interfering, nudging him, trying to get his attention. CRASH! The abrupt entry of a huge foundation stone not a dolphin length away forced him to remember his danger. Together with the wild dolphins, he and the Atlantean dolphins fled, staying underwater as long as possible, surfacing only when their lungs were ready to burst.

But underwater was no safer. The ocean floor was lined with dangerous, fiery cracks. One spewed liquid fire, taking one of the wild dolphins with it. A sudden upthrust sent the dolphins rocketing away on the wave it spawned, then plunged them into the deep as the ocean floor sank beneath them. They fought through the violent water, survival their only goal.

After days of struggle, they reached water that did not writhe and heave in torment and they rested, letting the water support them, too exhausted to eat the tiny fish that swam past. The wild dolphins recovered more quickly than the others and moved among them, nudging them, clicking and whistling to them, shoving tiny fish at their beaks. Instinct took over and beaks opened, crunching the fish or swallowing them whole. With bellies somewhat sated, they let the natural motion of the waves gently rock them.

After a time, a few of the wild dolphins drifted into a circle. One by one, the others swam with them, diving into the water and then surfacing, in and out, in and out, around and around. Curious, Seronak joined them, as did the other Atlantean dolphins. It seemed the wild dolphins wove mind pictures, creating vivid scenes with the energy of thought. Soon the Atlantean dolphins were swimming in warm waters, mating, birthing, being born, dying, until many generations had been experienced. With an ease that would have surprised them had they still been human, the Atlantean dolphins merged their minds with those of the wild dolphins, blending their energy into the weaving. Seronak felt a request brush his mind and responded with an image of the Atlantis he knew so well. The wild dolphins picked up the thread he had given them and wove it, adding memories from Belel, Uljas, Melida, Locan, Volin and Aletha, until it was a tapestry rich with color and meaning, a tapestry of history more accurate than any book or scroll. The seven Keepers added their memories of Karon to the tapestry, knowing it would not be complete without him.

Not only did the dolphins record Atlantis in all its glory, but also they added its terrible ending, as well as the grief felt by all of them. Then, at the wild dolphins' urging, the Atlanteans pictured their lives as Keepers and the energy melded once again, the story of Atlantis richer still. At last all the dolphins drifted, caught in the memory of what was, what had been, what would never be again.

A nudge interrupted Seronak's reverie. Immediately, he knew Aletha, but did not understand the desire she aroused in him.

CHAPTER THIRTY-FOUR

The Great Storm

The rosemary bed cradled Ah-mah until late afternoon when she awoke to the gentle rocking of the sea. They had left the harbor while she was sleeping! Ah-mah leaped off the bed and ran up the ladder to the deck. The breeze, moist and slightly salty, caressed her face and blew her hair back as her gaze was drawn to the endless expanse of water, horizon touching sky in the far distance.

"Your love of the sea grows, Ah-mah. Can you be content with one river?" Aletha's question brushed her mind.

Ah-mah did not answer. Sure footed, she moved toward the bow and looked down into the water. With a feeling of joy so great she thought her heart might burst, she recognized the scarred, pinkish-white patch on the dolphin who swam in the wave. She sank to the deck, utterly and profoundly content. After a while, Nefer joined her.

"Patch has returned," she said, indicating the dolphin swimming with the boat.

Nefer made a half-hearted effort to look over the side.

"What is wrong, my son?" Ah-mah asked.

"I love a princess. I have seen her land, her father's house, her fine clothes, the way the people greet her. I was a slave, Ah-mahsis. I am not worthy."

"How does having been torn from your mother and father and sold into slavery make you less than Medi? She has lost both mother and father as well as her land, her status, her fine clothes and her people. I would think you have more in common than most."

Startled, Nefer looked at Ah-mah.

"Medi loves you, Nefer. Remember what she has lost and do what you can to cheer her."

When Medi emerged from below the deck, Nefer went to her. Ah-mah smiled when she saw Nefer take Medi's hand.

As Ra slipped toward the western horizon, the two boats turned toward shore and anchored for the night. Ah-mah slipped over the side and into the water where the dolphins waited. Medi and Nefer watched with Laskella. They wanted to join Ah-mah, but that would mean leaving Laskella alone. Sensing their desire, she motioned them into the water, whereupon both dived into the midst of the dolphins, laughing and playing with abandon. Waron, returning to retrieve something from the boat, saw Laskella and came over to her.

"What are you watching?" he asked.

Laskella pointed to the melee of humans and dolphins in the water below.

This voyage was proving good for Laskella. He had not seen her so radiant. Stealing a glance at her still beautiful face, Waron noticed tears. He squatted beside her and put his hand on her arm. "What is it, dear one?"

"I wish… I wish… I wish for the impossible, Waron."

"What do you wish, Laskella?"

"I wish to be with the dolphins, but I cannot swim."

Waron stood up and held out his hand. "Then you shall," he said.

Love filled her eyes as she took his hand and let him pull her up.

"There is a rope ladder here, do you see?" Laskella nodded. "I will go down the ladder first, and you shall follow. No harm will come to you because I will not let it. Are you ready?" Laskella gulped and nodded again.

Waron climbed quickly down the ladder and dropped into the water. He watched Laskella, her hands clinging, a foot testing each rope rung before trusting it with her weight. When she reached the last rung, Waron called out, "Let go, Laskella. Let go, and I will catch you." With trusting heart she did just that, falling into the water, feeling his strong arms around her, supporting her, and something else…

A sleek gray dolphin waited for her, as did Ah-mah. She had released his dorsal fin, which he now inclined to Laskella. When she took hold of it, the dolphin towed her away from the splashing and cavorting still going on between the younger humans and dolphins then brought her back. Feeling Waron's hand on her back supporting her, she let go the dolphin and leaned back into the water, feeling as safe as she had in her mother's womb. Waron floated Laskella close enough to shore that she could walk out through the surf and onto the beach. The water seemed reluctant to give her up and the sand sucked at her feet.

During the evening meal, Salla came to Medi, and knelt before her.

"Why do you kneel? You are a free woman, an equal."

"Do you speak truly, Princess Medi?"

"I spoke truly when I freed you and I still say you are free."

Salla rose and said, "Then I would join the boat from Byblos."

For a moment, she lost her courage and bowed her head, unable to look at her former mistress while she said, "I have found true love on that boat."

"I am not surprised, Salla," Medi said, and put her arm around the girl. "I thought I noticed one of the sailors eyeing you as we traveled from the Land of the River."

"Your eyes did not deceive you. Lothan and I stole a few moments together before we returned to Byblos. We thought never to see each other once we arrived. Now we would declare our love. But, first, I thought to be certain that my coming and going could be farther than your sight."

"Go to Lothan with my blessing. Master Akban can perform the rite of joining." Then, in the enthusiasm of the moment, Medi exclaimed, "Bring your Lothan here, Salla. Let us array you as a bride, and without further delay, let us see you joined."

Salla ran to obey, her heart running before her. Ah-mah, Medi and Laskella searched for an appropriate dress, then painted the girl's face and dressed her hair, while the men from both boats stamped a circle in the sand with their feet and gathered driftwood for a fire. Soon wonderful odors flavored the night, where, under the stars, Lothan and Salla were joined by Master Akban according to the traditions of Byblos. The couple feasted with the rest of the company until, at last, they returned to the boat for a night alone together.

The next day dawned with clouds of rose and orange against the deep blue sky. They sailed before the sun was fully risen, Ah-mah already at her post in the bow. About mid-morning Sept came and stood with her, watching the dolphins playing in the wave.

"Ah-mah? Come with me. I wish to show you something."

When they reached the stern, Sept pointed to the boat from Byblos which followed. Ah-mah saw nothing amiss.

"She rides too low. Look, Ah-mah, her deck is barely above the water. Master Mu-hem and I saw it yesterday and spoke to Master Akban last night. He is worried as well. The logs are weighing her down. I fear for her if a storm comes."

For many days the weather held, but one morning they awoke to no wind and a strangely calm sea. All that day the sailors rowed, those on the boat from the Land of the River faring better than the Byblosians on the cedar-laden one. Often the sailors on Ah-mah's boat lifted their oars and waited for the other boat to catch up. When they did, Ah-mah and Medi went among them offering water from the copper buckets. Sept, Waron, Nefer and the rest of Sept's men rowed as well. At the end of the day, the Byblosian men stood in the water, letting the sea cleanse open blisters on their hands. The women treated the palms of the oarsmen from both ships with flaxseed oil to which Ah-mah had added honey, binding the hands lightly with strips of coarse linen.

The next day brought no breeze, nor did the day after, the hours filled with the incessant dipping of oars into the sea, pushing the water back, the boats forward. When the boats turned to shore and dropped anchor, the women took the cloths and washed the blood from them in the sea, reusing them to bind the hands again with oil and honey.

That night, Ah-mah woke to feel a breeze kiss her face. Sighing with relief, she turned over and fell into a deep, restful sleep. The breeze blew through the night, filling sleeping hearts with hope. Next morning as they broke their fast, sailors spoke of sailing toward their goal, laughing at some ribald comment, pain eased by the promise of time to heal.

Some distance down the beach, Master Mu-hem and Master Akban stood staring out to sea. Ah-mah sent her gaze in that same direction and saw nothing save a hint of clouds on the far horizon, the only ones to be seen in the brilliant morning sky. Sept watched the two masters as well, finally walking over to them. He was grim-faced when he returned to help Ah-mah carry their mats and blankets to the boat.

"We must hasten with the wind this day. A storm lies on the horizon. The Masters fear it is headed this way. The calm of the last days and the cloudless sky portend a great storm. They hope to be in the shelter of the river before it strikes us."

"How close are we to the river?"

"The best guess is two days of good sailing, and even the wind cannot make the Byblosian boat go faster, laden as she is."

All that day, Ah-mah stood in the bow of the boat, feeling the wind at her back pushing the boat forward. If she could have, she would have willed it to fly. She watched the dolphins playing once again in the wave generated by the speed of the boat. In her mind she asked them about the coming storm, but received no answer.

The threatening clouds could not be seen when they stopped for the night, both Masters tempted to sail through the darkness despite the danger. The moon and stars in the clear sky seemed sent to reassure them, but when Ah-mah looked eastward, she saw flashes of light where stars should be. Before dawn, the boats sped before the ominous clouds that drew ever closer. Ah-mah sensed what was not said, that this storm was huge, and that none might live to tell of it. The dolphins were not to be seen.

She did not know Sept was behind her until he spoke in her ear. "When the storm comes, Master Mu-hem asks that you and the other women take shelter in the hold."

At first Ah-mah was relieved, for it would keep her from the pelting rain, but then truth dawned. "What about you? And Waron? And Nefer? Will you not join us?"

"No, my Ah-mah. We are needed to keep this boat afloat. I am new to sailing, but I have strength in my body and I would help the Master keep us alive."

Horrified at Sept's words, Ah-mah could only mutter, "Then I might never see you again."

"Courage, Ah-mah. If it is within our power, we will keep you and this boat safe from harm," Sept said, and then returned to help the others tie down what they could.

As they sped before the storm, Ah-mah stood in the bow, her attention riveted on the shore, seeking the river and its relative safety. The squalls came first, teasing the boat with showers. Ah-mah almost believed their teasing, almost believed that they were the storm, but the clouds behind them were black, tinged with green. Shafts of light followed by great booms continually announced their formidable presence.

Sept came to her, saying only, "It is time."

A sudden surge sent a wave over the boat, nearly toppling them. As they struggled toward the entrance to the hold, Ah-mah shouted at Sept, "Be safe, my husband." Sept grinned at her and winked. With the other three women she watched as the cover was put in place, shutting out any light, pegs driven in to hold it there. As they sat on the rosemary bed and held tightly to each other, the full fury of the storm broke over them. What followed was a nightmare of crashing waves and darkness. Tossed about like straw in the wind, the women clung to whatever seemed stable as the ship rocked and heaved in the terrible dark. Ah-mah put both arms around one leg of the mast. The storm-tossed boat threw her into the mast, and then away from it, with such violence her arms were nearly wrenched from their sockets.

Ah-mah clung to the mast until her arms were numb, her body bruised, her face bloody. She clung, for the only alternative was death. Once she heard a shout from above, then nothing but the noise of wind and water and the rolling of the boat in the all consuming dark. Ah-mah tried to remember the sun, to remember the paths she had walked, tried to remember the river. As she felt her consciousness slipping, she locked her hands together around the mast and gave herself over to the dark.

When she came to, her hands were still locked around the mast, and with her dark-adjusted vision, she could see them. The wind still blew and she could hear the rain, but the ship did not heave and roll as it had. The greatest blessing was the lessening of the all-consuming dark. Unable to unlock her fingers, Ah-mah looked around. In the gloom, she saw jars and chests and bags flung every which way.

"Ah-mah?"

"Medi!" she croaked. "Are you unharmed?"

"A few bruises, and a memory I wish was not there."

"I cannot seem to move my fingers."

"I will help," Medi said, her shadowy figure crawling over a chest to reach Ah-mah. "Oh, your hands are very cold. Here, I will warm them." Medi wrapped Ah-mah's hands with her own, not much warmer ones, and began to rub warmth into them. Carefully, she loosened the fingers, one by one, until Ah-mah could unclasp her hands.

"Ah-mah, you are bleeding! Oh, your poor face!" Medi grabbed a cloth from a pile and rubbed Ah-mah's face hard in her fear that the woman was gravely wounded.

"Ow, Medi! I am not hurt, only bruised. Give me the cloth and I will finish the job. Have you seen Laskella or Salla?"

"No."

"Look for them, Medi. We must find them."

Medi found Laskella, an unconscious mound atop the rosemary bed which had been shoved into the stern.

"Mama?" Medi shook Laskella gently, and then, when she did not respond, continued with more vigorous shaking.

"Careful, Medi. She may have some injury we cannot see," Ah-mah said, coming up behind the girl, still rubbing her hands together to help restore circulation.

"Ummmm," from Laskella.

"She is alive! Mama, wake up. The storm is over and you are safe."

Something caught Ah-mah's eye. It was Salla, crumpled in a sodden heap, not moving. Ah-mah went to her, and with numb fingers, tried to turn the girl over to see her face. Medi crawled over.

"Does she breathe?" Ah-mah asked.

"Her chest does not move. Salla? Salla! Wake up, my girl." Medi gently shook her shoulder, but the girl did not move or give sign of life.

The screech of pegs interrupted their efforts as the cover to the hold was pried loose and light flooded in. The women raised hands to shield their eyes, squinting in the brightness.

"Ah-mahsis? Medi? Do you live?"

"We need help with with Laskella and Salla," Ah-mah said. "We need to get them into the sun."

Nefer leaped down the ladder, with Waron and Sept close on his heels. Ah-mah looked tenderly at her husband, shyly reaching to touch his arm. Sept grabbed her, exclaiming, "We are alive, wife! We have survived the greatest of storms!" Releasing her, Sept hurried to help Waron and Nefer lift the two women up through the hole and onto the deck. Medi followed, but Ah-mah looked for her medicine bag and her box of herbs. She found the bag where it had come to rest beneath broken pots and several bags of barley and lentils that, remarkably, were not soaked. No boat could have withstood such a storm and not retained some water, but this one, she suspected, had done better than most. Retrieving her medicine bag with hands still stinging from restored circulation, she slung it over her shoulder and climbed the ladder.

The storm could still be seen in the west, flashes of light and fainter booms reminding them of its power, the boat confirming it. One leg of the mast had snapped in two and dangled precariously. Men lay everywhere groaning with their injuries. Nefer seemed unscathed, as did Sept. Waron wore a blood-stained piece of cloth around his head, but seemed jovial and unharmed otherwise. With rapt attention, he tended Laskella who now sat against the bow. Ah-mah would check on them later. She knelt by Salla to see if, by some miracle, she lived. A dark bruise at her temple worried Ah-mah. She put her head on the girl's chest to listen for a heartbeat. It seemed a very long time before she heard the faintest of beats, but it was enough. Ah-mah pulled the girl into her arms and held her, putting her mouth over the girl's own and breathing into it. Salla coughed and some water trickled from her mouth. With an audible sigh, she began to breath again, but she did not open her eyes.

"Cover her," she said to Medi, "with something dry, if you can find it." Then she went to the nearest man and began working to clean and bind the gash in his shoulder.

Medi found a dry blanket, and after tucking it around Salla, worked alongside Ah-mah. Nefer, and the rest of the men who could, brought sea water for washing wounds. Two men set up the brazier for cooking, the wonderful aroma of garlic and onion reminding Ah-mah of the bags of barley and lentils that were still in the hold. When Nefer brought her more sea water, she told him to bring everything up from the hold onto the deck so what was dry could be separated from what was wet. Any lentils or barley that had gotten wet would soon spoil and contaminate the rest. Sept saw what Nefer did and went to help, dumping any wet barley and lentils into the sea. When all had been sorted through, they still had nine bags of lentils and five of barley. Supplemented with fish, it would last them until they reached Nubt.

The medicine box had escaped the water and the large bag of herbs was mostly dry. Sept carefully inspected the smaller bags as he removed them. Any that were damp he brought to Ah-mah to determine if the contents could be saved. Lastly, he and Nefer labored to remove the water in the hold.

Ah-mah sat by Master Mu-hem as she sorted through the herbs. He had been struck in the head by the leg of the mast when it snapped and had not regained consciousness. Something tickled her mind, something she should ask, something she should know. The other boat. Where was it? Ah-mah scanned the area around them, shading her eyes with her hand to scan the horizon. No other boat could be seen anywhere.

Sept put his arms around her. "They are gone, Ah-mah. We do not know if they are lost, or if the storm took them a different direction."

"We must look for them, Sept. Surely they will not be very far away."

"You remember how much faster we traveled after the logs were loaded?" Ah-mah, eyes wide, nodded slowly. "If they still live, they will find us."

"How will they know where to look?" she asked, and then brightened, as the answer came to her. "Master Akban will know that we were lighter and would have traveled farther. He will sail toward the setting sun to find us."

"We can hope that he will."

"How long did the storm last, my husband? It seemed endless when I was awake and I do not know how long I was not awake."

"A day, a night, and half the next day."

"It is a wonder that we were not lost."

"We did not carry the logs, Ah-mah."

As soon as they could, the sailors turned the boat toward shore. Master Mu-hem and Salla were carried to the fire, the Master still unconscious. Salla seemed to be resting, although she had not opened her eyes. Ah-mah directed that the Master be covered with another blanket, and then feeling his forehead, asked for a third blanket. "We must keep him warm," she said. All night she stayed with him, bathing his forehead and his arms, speaking to Aletha in her mind about what should be done. In the darkest hour before moonrise, Ah-mah woke Sept. "We must take him to the sea."

"Is he dead? We could bury him if he is."

"No, he is not yet dead, but if the fever does not break, he will be. The blankets are not working. I do not know what else to do but let the sea cool him."

Sept woke Jasoth. Together they carried the Master into the sea and held him there, Ah-mah at his side. The moon rose and dolphins came to keep the four protected from sharks. Ah-mah thanked them in her heart. When dawn spread its morning glory, the Master stirred and gave a great sigh. As though the sigh were a signal, Ah-mah directed the weary men to carry him back to the fire. They stripped his wet clothes from his body and covered him with more blankets.

"He will rest now. The fever has broken and he sleeps."

Men were up, stoking the fire, adding any driftwood they could find. One man carried a large piece of wood to the fire that caught Sept's eye. He called out to the man and went over to examine it. The faint odor of cedar brought hope to Sept's heart. Maybe the Byblosian boat was not lost. He looked up, half expecting to see the crew walking toward him on the beach.

Sept called the others to him and showed them the log. A gloom settled over them all, with some who had spent time with the men from the other ship weeping openly. Sept thought a moment, then asked two of his men, Jasoth and Kopt, to search the beach in the direction from which they had come for any signs of the boat or its crew. The two took a jar of water and some food and started out at a trot, determined to cover as much ground as possible before nightfall.

All that day the wounded rested, glad to be on shore, while others started repairing the boat. The broken leg of the mast was its greatest wound, but hours were spent restoring order to the rest of the boat. Ah-mah, not having closed her eyes since coming ashore, gave over care of Salla to Medi and slept through the day, waking to eat, walk a bit, and then sleep through the night. Salla had wakened not long after the men left on their search, but was still weak. Medi tended her like a mother and let no one mention the suspected fate of the other boat. The evening of their second day on shore, the two men returned, having seen nothing. On the third day, Sept gathered Waron and another man and set off to explore the area inland. They returned with a tale as grand as the storm, but filled with marvels instead of horror.

Waron, his tongue loosened by what his eyes had beheld, told of a vast lake filled with water, sweet to the taste and surrounded by grasslands and a few trees. As he spoke and Sept translated, his face shone with the delight of what he had seen. "A man could live here and be content," he said, and went to sit by Laskella.

Sept gathered all the men who were able to walk and carry jars for a return trip to the lake. Ah-mah, weary of tending the wounded and knowing all were mending, placed a jar on her head with remembered grace, and took her place among them.

The lake was not far. They soon reached its shores and filled their jars, but the beauty of the lake would not let them leave. Sept and Ah-mah sat apart from the others, having found a knoll that afforded a sweeping vista.

"Waron is right," Sept said, breaking the silence. "We could live here and be content."

"It seems so, my husband. After the horrors of the storm and the uncertainties of Byblos, it is good to have such beauty to restore us. But I long for home, Sept. My heart wants to see my daughter and my grandchildren."

"And I must report the loss of Rahotep's cedars to him."

"I had forgotten that. He will be angry, but perhaps not so angry when you show him the document for five more loads."

Sept did not answer.

"You do still have the document?"

"I do. Sea water has made it illegible. Even the King's seal has been washed away."

"What will you do?"

"What can I do, other than report what has happened and hope that the next load of cedars has a better fate?"

"We could stay here. We could send a messenger to Ak-hu and Gedju, asking them to come here." So great was the power of the lake and its beauty, Ah-mah nearly spoke the truth. The lake drew her. The river, her ancestral home, Remtu's hut, her home in Nubt, all had been familiar, accepted, part of life and living, but the lake… Ah, the lake. That was a different feeling altogether.

"And it is near to the sea."

"Not yet, Aletha. Do not make me return to those memories just yet."

"Not the memories of horror, Ah-mah, but the dolphins. Remember the dolphins. They would be delighted to have you close."

Ah-mah let out the breath she had been holding. "It is not yet time for us to be here, my husband. You have your duty and I want to see my family again. And soon. When can we leave, Sept?"

"I think that may depend directly on knowing where we are."

The Master knew as soon as he woke and saw the first stars. Still weak, he sat propped up by a log of driftwood and spoke to Sept and Ah-mah as they ate.

"I believe we have been blown farther west than I have ventured. The great river has two main branches to the sea, and I think we may be west of the westernmost of the two. We should see that western branch within a day's sailing, if I am correct."

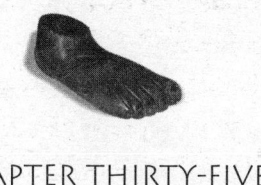

CHAPTER THIRTY-FIVE

The Bennu

Ah-mah may have been ready, but neither the Master nor his boat were. Three more days passed before Master Mu-hem could stand alone, and then he was wobbly. Ah-mah used the last bits of her store of mint to make teas for him and he did seem better for it. At least his spirits were lifted and he laughed more often.

Salla was more of a concern. To other eyes, she appeared recovered, but Ah-mah noticed that she stood looking out to sea more often than not. Medi often stood with her, as she did now. Ah-mah was not surprised when Medi took the girl's hand.

Trips were made daily for fresh water from the lake. On one such trip, Sept found a small group of tall, fair people who seemed to be waiting for him and those who came with him. The language they spoke was not one Sept or any of the others had heard, but they made do with gestures and signs, the new people at last making Sept understand that they were being invited to a village. His words tumbled over themselves when he told Ah-mah.

"These people are tall and pale eyed, their pale skin tanned by the sun. They seem gentle and good, and Ah-mah, they want to take us to their village. I want to go and I want you to come as well."

"We come?" Laskella asked, her first words aloud in Ah-mah's language.

Waron, who had been more diligent about learning the language, chimed in, "We would stay here. We must ask."

"Stay here?" Ah-mah asked. "But I thought you would go with us to the Land of the River. I have so much to show you both."

"We want see your land. Storm frighten Laskella. Make her weak. She need time…to heal."

"Stay here, Ah-mah. With new people," Laskella said. "You come back."

Ah-mah had grown to love Laskella and Waron. Disappointment must have shown in her face, for Waron continued, "You return, Ah-mah. You need this place. Medi stay."

"Nefer?" Ah-mah's world had been turned upside down.

Waron answered. "He go with you. He come back. You come back."

"How do you know?"

"My heart," Laskella said, touching her chest.

The next day, when the three couples went to the lake, one of the new people waited for them. He wore a white, sleeveless robe, and his arms, though tanned, were not as brown as Ah-mah's. She heard a gasp in her mind. "What is it, Aletha? What is wrong?"

"I know this man," Aletha thought to her. "Ah-mah, he is Muan! Or was. Or his ancestors were. The blood runs true in him."

"Will they welcome us?"

"Yes."

"Could we be happy here?"

"I could be happy here."

The man, taller than Sept by a head, looked at them with clear gray eyes and used his arm to gesture toward the other side of the lake. Sept nodded and they fell in step behind him.

That first trip seemed long because they did not know its end. After a while, Ah-mah saw hills in the distance. She sensed that in them lay their destination. Tiny signs of civilization appeared to her as she glimpsed paths, barely the width of two feet side by side in the tall grass. When their leader reached a similar path, undetectable to most, he took it into the hills and they followed.

Topping a slight rise, they were surprised to see nothing before them but more rocky hills, with green grass growing at their bases. When the man continued down the path and into a slender valley between the hills, people appeared before them, a family group here, another family group there. The man halted in front of one of the family groups. "How clever!" Ah-mah thought, as the family moved aside, revealing an entrance that for all intents and purposes looked to be a crack in the rock. To enter, Ah-mah and the rest had to turn sidewise, take a few steps, then round a corner.

Inside the hill, it was cool and much less bright, a pleasant change from the strong sun. If Ah-mah had stood on tiptoe and stretched her arms above her head she would have touched the low ceiling. The floor seemed solid, like stone, the room long, but no wider than twice the width of Remtu's hut. Curtained doorways were spaced evenly on either side. She was reminded of the cave of her ancestors in the mountains behind her home, the cave where her mother and father were buried, along with Khmet. She wondered if this was a similar cave.

"You are close to the truth," Aletha spoke in her mind.

The man gestured to low benches placed around a brazier near the center of the room and indicated they should sit. Young people moved among them with trays holding cups of cool drinks, delicately flavored.

Later Ah-mah would wonder why she did not see the old woman when they entered the room, but suddenly, it seemed as if the wall in front of them disappeared and she was revealed, a person of authority. She waited until all had returned her gaze before she spoke.

"You are welcome here."

Astonishingly, they understood her words. She spoke the language of the Land of the River.

"We are the Bennu, for our legends say that we came from the sea as a gift. I am called Mother, though I have borne no children. It is a term of honor among us," she said. "I was named Thera, and that is what you may call me. You are a long way from the Land of the River and many of you have been injured. Will you not tell us your tale?"

Sept would have spoken for all, but Thera raised her hand to stop him. "I would hear from this woman," she said, pointing to Ah-mah. "How are you named?"

Ah-mah stood and moved closer to the woman, drawn to her. "I am Ah-mah, called Healer by some."

"Will you speak of your travels, Ah-mah the Healer?"

"We are from the village of Nubt on the great river. We journeyed to Byblos by way of the sea to return a princess to the King, her father, and to secure trees for the ruler of our village. A storm blew us off course and we are unable to find the boat from Byblos or any of its crew. The Master of our boat believes we are west of the westernmost branch of the great river, and when we have healed, we intend to return to the Land of the River."

"A fine tale, but there is much you do not say. Is there more you would tell?"

"Only that some of us have found peace by the lake. They would like to stay, but they do not wish to take land that is not theirs."

"Who would stay? Are they here now?"

Waron rose and extended his hand to Laskella to help her rise. Ah-mah's heart cried out when Medi joined them. Nefer did not stand, nor did Sept.

"They are welcome to live with us, but we are a hidden people. Any who stay must learn our ways of hiding and swear never to reveal us willingly."

Waron spoke for himself, Laskella and Medi. "We learn ways. Not reveal to others."

"What about you, Ah-mah the Healer. Do you not wish to stay?"

"I have family in Nubt, Mother Thera, and my husband has duty to the ruler of our village. I confess I am tempted to stay, but I must return to the Land of the River."

"Then you shall, but, Ah-mah, you and your husband are welcome to return."

"I do not foresee how that could be."

To Waron and Laskella, Thera said, "Will you stay with us now? We have places for you. I sense the young woman will not want to return until the boat leaves."

"Laskella will stay. I will stay. We from Byblos. Princess Medi come back after boat go."

"Princess? The same princess Ah-mah the Healer spoke of returning to her father, the King?"

"The same," Ah-mah said.

"There is more to your story as I suspected. Very well, Princess Medi. We welcome you now and will prepare a place to await your return."

"I am princess no longer, Mother Thera. I am Medi."

Thera looked intently at Medi for a moment before replying,

"I think you always were." Then, her gaze encompassing them all, she said, "You are far from your boat and if you start back soon, you will arrive in time for a meal, if I judge aright. Refresh yourselves, eat and drink, and then be on your way with our blessing." Just as suddenly as it had disappeared, the wall reappeared, and Thera was gone.

One of the women was about to lead Laskella and Waron to their new quarters when Laskella stopped and turned back. She went to Ah-mah, holding out her arms. Ah-mah embraced her and the two women touched forehead to forehead. Then Laskella went to Medi and hugged her. "I will be waiting for you," she whispered.

The return trip was long, but somehow, with landmarks more familiar, did not seem so. They soon recognized the tree where they had met their guide, and stopped to fill water jars before beginning the last leg of the journey. The savory aroma of fish and lentil stew greeted their return.

Ah-mah was grateful to hear Mu-hem say they would sail with the dawn. Medi blanched at the news and turned to Nefer, eyes wide with the enormity of separation. Ah-mah watched them walk away, seeking solitude beyond the fire, Nefer's arm around Medi's shoulders. Sept stayed with Mu-hem telling him everything he could without betraying the Bennu, but Ah-mah could not join them. Something about the meeting with Thera made her aware of a knot of fear residing in her chest. She hardly touched her food, unable to swallow. With no reason other than a need to be in motion, she walked away from the fire and down the beach.

The sun had not yet set, but sent its rays toward the clouds, coloring them incredible hues of orange and coral. A flash of silver caught her eye, and without thinking, she pulled her dress over her head and waded into the water. She swam a few strokes toward the chittering dolphin, then let him tow her to deeper water. Other dolphins ringed them, and began the in and out, round and round swimming that signaled dolphin dreaming. Ah-mah gave her lonely, fearful self over to the dreaming, letting it take her where it would.

The group formed the sleep circle, all but one shutting down half the brain. All was quiet, if the sea could ever be called quiet, with its currents and fish and plant creatures always in motion. Ah-mah rested with them, a deep rest, complete, half of her brain shut down as well.

Deep in the dreaming, they awoke refreshed and swam through schools of sardines, eating as they swam. Ah-mah enjoyed the taste of the raw fish, crunching tiny bones in her powerful jaws. One of the other dolphins poked her with his beak, inviting her to play. He dove deep into the water only to race back toward the surface, exploding into the air and landing with a great splash. Ah-mah took a massive breath through her blowhole and dove deep, following him. With powerful tail flukes, she pushed herself toward the surface, feeling the water slide off her sleek skin, feeling powerful and free as she broke through the surface and almost touched the sky before crashing mightily into the water, sending a jet of it skyward.

She awoke in Sept's arms. He had seen her follow the dolphin and waded in after her. Now he carried her out.

"I can walk, Sept."

He put her down, but stayed close. She reached out her hand to him and he held it tightly. "I have been dolphin, Sept."

"Oh, Ah-mah, my beautiful, impulsive, Ah-mah."

She saw the love in his eyes, and still in a playful dolphin mood, pulled her hand from his and ran down the beach. Looking back once to be sure he followed, she raced behind the dunes, Sept close on her heels.

That night she dreamed of Aletha. They were both dolphins swimming, eating, sleeping with their pod. To her dream self, Aletha said, "I am dolphin now, Ah-mah. You are dolphin in the dreaming, but I am no longer human, although I retain my memories." Ah-mah opened her beak to widen her smile.

CHAPTER THIRTY-SIX
The Return to Nubt

They made ready to sail with the dawn. Ga-lek, who had guided them to the Bennu village, arrived with Waron as they gathered their belongings. Ah-mah was glad to see them, for she had worried about Medi finding her way back to the village alone. Medi seemed relieved as well and went to stand with the two men while the boat was boarded. Ah-mah and Nefer hugged Medi one last time before boarding with the others. All too quickly for Nefer, the sail was put in place atop the double mast whose broken leg had been patched with as sturdy a piece of driftwood as could be found. The sail caught the wind and the boat sped faster and faster away from the three on the beach.

Ah-mah stood in the bow with Salla, the girl searching for any sign of the Byblosian boat and crew. Before long, the dolphin, his pinkish-white patch glistening in the sun, reappeared to play in the bow wave, slipping in and out, eyeing her. As they neared the westernmost branch of the river, she spoke to him in her mind, "I will not be coming back."

"You are Ah-mah-Aletha. You will return."

It was the last she saw of him for the boat soon entered the westernmost branch of the river, speeding her away from the sea. She thought of all that had happened since she had left the river, a clear picture of Sefra entering her mind. She would visit the old woman and soon. When Sefra saw how she had been changed by her adventures, she would laugh.

"Have I been changed?" she asked silently. "Am I not the same as the one who started this journey?"

"You had not felt the moist wind on your face." Aletha's voice. "You had not swum with dolphins or climbed trees or run over roofs or sent secret messages."

"Or met people who look like you."

"Or endured a storm and survived."

"Yes, all that has happened, events I would not have witnessed in the Land of the River. The question remains, have any of these events changed me? Am I still Ah-mah the Healer?"

"You will always be Ah-mah the Healer. Do you think you have changed?"

"I do not yet know. Maybe when I reach familiar surroundings and engage in routine matters I will know. There is something else I would ask you."

"What?"

"Who is Ah-mah-Aletha?"

"We are."

"We have been two voices, speaking in my mind. We have been two people walking in your Garden. How can we be one? Are we one?"

Nefer interrupted her, needing to talk about Medi.

"Ah-mahsis?"

She turned to look at him, irritated at being drawn away before Aletha could answer until she saw the pain in his face.

"Will I ever see her again?"

"Do you want to?" she asked.

"More than anything."

"Why did you not stay with her, Nefer? You are a son to me, but sons leave home when they wish to take a wife."

"I wanted to, but I could not. Ah-mahsis, do you feel something is not right at home?"

The knot of fear, temporarily forgotten during her swim with the dolphins, returned with a vengeance, rising from the pit of her stomach to lodge in her throat, causing her to gag. Nefer saw, and helped her sit, squatting beside her.

"We must watch the banks of the river, Ah-mahsis. The warning will come from one bank or the other."

Suddenly, Ah-mah saw Sefra's face again. What she had thought was a laugh became a scream. Sefra crumpled to the ground. Ah-mah's hands began wrapping themselves around and around each other, as though she continually washed them.

"There is nothing we can do except watch. We will not be close to Nubt for many days," said Nefer.

Ah-mah hardly heard him, so great was her fear. If Sefra, a lonely woman in an isolated hut, was in danger, how much more so Ak-hu and her family?

Nefer left her to fetch water and a rag. He placed a bag of lentils behind her and gently pushed her shoulders into it. Carefully, he pulled her legs toward him and began washing her feet. The action served its purpose. Ah-mah released the tight anxiety enough to look at him.

"You always know how to bring me back from the deep desert, Nefer."

Nefer worked Ah-mah's feet thoroughly and carefully, just as she had taught him, glad of a task to pass the time, to speed them on their way to whatever lay in wait for them in Nubt, to hasten the time when he could return to Medi.

The river was deep, the current no longer as slow. Grateful for the strong breeze that filled the sail, Master Mu-hem tried to keep the boat to one side or the other of the current and posted a man in the bow to watch for any new sand bars. Soon they reached the place where the westernmost branch joined the main river. Although the river was not yet at its peak, it had filled its banks and spread a thin layer of itself over the fields. When water was drawn from the river, it was dense and barely drinkable. Ah-mah and Salla poured the water through cloths to take out some of the silt.

At night they tied the boat to whatever trees they could find, sometimes stopping early because the Master knew no trees were to be found in the near distance or sailing on past sunset to reach trees he remembered. They ate and slept on the boat instead of the muddy banks. The wind held, blowing them past the village of Abedju and around the first bend in less than a week. When they reached the two tall palms near the great bend in the river, Ah-mah knew they were close to Nubt. She caught Nefer's eye and voiced what both were thinking. "It is time to tell Sept."

To their surprise Sept said he felt a similar uneasiness, but had thought he was anticipating the reaction of Rahotep to the loss of his cedars. He motioned to Master Mu-hem, who gave the rudder to Fayin and came to listen to Ah-mah with a keen ear.

It was Sept who saw the black-skinned woman waving to them in the early morning. She stood ankle deep in water and mud on what passed for the west bank, two brown children with her. He shouted to the Master and pointed, whereupon the Master turned the boat toward the bank where the woman and the children stood. One of the sailors jumped from the boat to the bank, slipping in the mud to the delight of the onlookers, but managing to tie the boat to a tall palm. Ah-mah was already over the side and swimming toward the woman before anyone could stop her. She had recognized Sefra, and thought she knew the children as well, although they were taller than she remembered. The two confirmed her suspicions with cries of "Na-na!"

She reached the bank, slipping in her haste to reach her grandchildren. "Menes, Ah-nah, my dear ones," she said over and over, kissing them and patting them, leaving mud wherever she touched. Looking up at Sefra, she said, "How do you come to have my daughter's children?"

"The story would best be told on yonder boat and not in this mud."

Sept had come ashore, as had Nefer. One of the sailors secured the boat to another tree to steady it. Ah-mah carried Ah-nah, and Sept, Menes, while Nefer helped Sefra as best he could. All were muddy and soaked by the time they reached the deck. Ah-mah doused herself and the children with water to rinse away the mud. The rest followed suit. Dry clothes were found and the brazier lit, not for food, but for comfort. Sailors, soldiers, and the rest sat around the brazier, all eyes on the tall black woman with the bushy, white hair that framed her face and formed her eyebrows. She looked directly at Ah-mah as though the story was hers alone.

"This tale is one I did not witness. It was told to me by your servant, Bo, and to some extent, by your grandson.

"You had not been gone three days before Rahotep declared your house in the village to be his. A beeswax seal was affixed to the door announcing his ownership. Bo, who had come to check on the gardens, was told to leave. When Rahotep made no other move, most thought the trouble was over, when in fact, it had just begun.

"Rahotep, with his guards, came to your daughter not long

after. From what your grandson has said, it was not the first time." Ah-mah nodded. "He told her he brought gold to purchase the land. When she refused, he said he would give her time to reconsider, but that when he returned, he expected her to turn over ownership of the land to him.

"Your daughter considered gathering the field hands and standing up to Rahotep, but she knew they were no match for his men, and especially the new men who had joined him, fierce men with fierce weapons. Instead, she and Bo started gathering cuttings from each of the plants in her garden, rooting them in water, and once they had rooted, putting the roots in soil wrapped in coarse linen. The wrapped plants were stored in the cave. Bo said you would know where. A store of seeds for planting was also taken, enough to begin again, should the need arise. That store was placed with the plants.

"On a night when the quarter moon showed its face late, Ak-hu dreamed a bloody dream. She saw soldiers entering the fields with swift swords and fire. The next morning, she gathered the house servants and told them to go, one by one, across the river to the huts of the field hands and not return. Bo and the children she took to the inner room of the cave, telling them to wait there for two days and nights, then leave by the north exit. She told Bo to bring the children to me by back ways, to travel at night, and to trust no one."

Sept, who sat behind Ah-mah, placed his hands lightly on her shoulders. She held herself straight, and her gaze did not falter as she waited for Sefra to continue with the tale she had known would be told as soon as she saw her grandchildren with the old woman instead of their mother.

"Bo and the children waited for two days. All was quiet when they left the cave by the north exit in the dark of night. They crept across the fields to the river where a man waited to ferry them across. On the other side, Bo found a cluster of nehet with bushes at their bases, and she and the children crawled beneath the bushes and slept the rest of the night. When they awoke, she allowed the children to play quietly with the colored stones and painted sticks their mother had included in the little bag of clothes and food, while she watched for any sign of danger. She played finger games with them and told them stories, and thus, they passed the day.

"During that afternoon as the children napped, Bo received the only foretelling of her long life. In a dream during a brief sleep, she saw soldiers coming, and knew she might not be able to keep the children safe. The three began walking again when night fell, Bo often carrying Ah-nah when she tired. As soon as the moon rose, she hid the children and herself, this time in an abandoned hut. The children slept, but Bo did not. When they awoke, she used a stick to draw the way to my hut in the dirt and made Menes show her over and over again how he would follow it. Finally, she erased the drawing with her foot and asked him to tell her again how he would find me. The boy is wise beyond his years."

Ah-mah, both children sleeping in her lap, drew Menes closer. The boy shifted, but did not waken.

"They had not gone far the next night when Bo heard voices. She hid the children and herself and waited. When the voices came closer, she whispered her goodbyes to Menes and Ah-nah and left the hiding place, circling around the voices and coming up on the other side of them. She walked boldly into their campsite, knowing from the dream that they were two of Rahotep's men.

"Suspicious of anyone out late on a seldom used path, they grabbed her, one holding her arms behind her while the other smothered the fire. They put her between them as they marched off, little Menes watching with his sister from the bushes.

"He found me the next day. I have not heard from him the terrors he must have suffered, but although muddy and tired, he and his sister were unharmed. I left the two children sleeping one night and went to find Bo. It was she who told me what happened to your daughter and her husband, having heard it from a house servant who hid in the bushes, unable to let the event pass unwitnessed."

"Where are my daughter and her husband?" Ah-mah asked.

"Rahotep's men killed them as he watched. They were murdered in front of your ancestral home," Sefra said, steadily, looking directly at Ah-mah as she spoke.

"Your daughter was brave, Ah-mah. She saved your grandchildren and enough herbs and seed to begin again. Bo is dead, killed when she would not reveal the location of the children." Sefra folded her hands in her lap and bowed her head, her story finished.

Voices erupted, with sailors and soldiers alike asking, "How can this be?" Master Mu-hem silenced them with a raised hand.

"What is the state of Ah-mah's ancestral home now? Do you know?"

"It lies empty. Rahotep plans to build himself a grand house of stone on the land across the river from Nubt, a house grander than that of Ah-mah's ancestors. He speaks of the cedar you bring as though he had sailed himself to fetch it. Once the cedar has been unloaded, your lives will be forfeit."

"We have no cedar. The boat carrying it was lost in a great storm," the Master said.

"Then your lives are forfeit already."

Mu-hem thought for a moment, then spoke. "Let us stay here for the night. In the morning, we will decide what to do. For now, I am hungry. Let us put food on this brazier and cook it."

The sailors set to work filtering water and soaking lentils and barley. In the meantime, Mu-hem, Sept, Nefer and Sefra gathered in the stern. Ah-mah spread mats for her grandchildren and covered their precious, sleeping bodies with blankets before joining the others. Salla stayed with the children, glad of something she could do.

"I do not think it will be safe for us to enter Nubt," the Master ventured.

"It will not be," Sefra agreed.

"Then we must leave this place. But where will we go?"

Hearing them, Ah-mah, her voice husky with unshed tears, said, "We will return to the Bennu. Waron and Laskella said they would make a place for us. It will be sooner than any of us expected, but we can make a life there, and my grandchildren will be safe from the Murderer of Nubt."

Sefra went to Ah-mah then, and pressing her forehead against Ah-mah's, she said, "Your daughter would want you to take the gift she left for you in the cave."

Ah-mah clung to Sefra, and for a moment, she shed tears into the older woman's shoulder.

Sept the Warrior, ready to fight his former employer to the death if Ah-mah asked it, said, "Draw the way for me, Ah-mah. I will go to the cave."

"There is too much for one to carry. Bo said it," Sefra said.

"I will go. A secret way winds through the hills and avoids the river paths. I am the only one who knows it. Two of your men should come with us, Sept."

"Can you find the path in the dark, Ah-mah?"

"The moon is full this night and will light the path for us," she said. Then, to Sefra, "Will you watch over my grandchildren for a while longer?" Sefra nodded. "And will you come with us when we leave? We go to a beautiful place, a fitting place for your wisdom. I could never repay the debt I owe you, but you have a place on this boat if you wish it."

"There is no debt owed, but I will go with you. My heart will not let me stay."

CHAPTER THIRTY-SEVEN
Darkness Takes Ah-Mah

The moon had not yet risen when four shadows slipped over the side of the boat, now anchored on the east bank. They slogged through the muddy fields, their goal the hills which rose as dark lumps backed by even darker mountains beneath the starlight. Ah-mah led them onto ground not yet flooded by the river. They were a good distance north of the stone house and the cave and she was not certain the path extended this far, but she had heard it did. Up into the hills they climbed, breathing hard with the exertion, afraid to stop for fear they would not be able to reach their goal and return before the rising sun revealed them.

They had crested the hill and were descending when the moon rose above the mountains, its reflected light glittering on small stones below, stones far apart, yet spaced evenly, ancient markers of an ancient path. Ah-mah was heartened by the path, and hurried her steps, the other three following closely. The path wound around and through the hills, and they walked briskly for several hours before Ah-mah halted them. No reason for stopping was evident until Ah-mah ducked under a clump of chest high bushes and crawled through a hole hidden behind them in the rock face. This opening into the cave, the north exit used by Bo and the children to escape, was low, requiring the men to kneel before crawling through.

Once they were inside the dark cave, Ah-mah whispered, "Take my hand, Sept, and give Ja-soth yours. Ja-soth, hold to Sept and to Kopt. We must not speak beyond this entrance, since anyone in the cave might hear us. Stay close and do not stumble."

Further and further into the cave they went, Ah-mah leading them from memory, for she could see no better than they. At last, the dark lessened, revealing a faint light ahead of them. But Ah-mah turned away from that light and into more darkness, the men following. They were in a narrow passage, with shoulders scraping walls until, suddenly, there were no walls. Ah-mah halted them, whispering, "Stay here." They could barely hear the touch of her feet upon the floor of the cave as she walked away from them.

Ah-mah hoped the stone was still there. She had been fascinated by it when her mother brought her to this inner sanctum long ago and showed her its treasures. "I do not know the origin of this stone," she said. "My mother said it was here from the beginning." Ah-mah held the rock carefully and inspected it, finding nothing out of the ordinary. She said as much to her mother, who said to her, "Close your eyes. Feel the weight of the stone. Let it speak to you." The stone felt solid in her hand, heavy for its size, as though it was filled up with something. Suddenly, in her mind's eye, she saw the stone as a shell filled with something that moved within its confining walls. The deeper she went into the stone, the thinner the shell became. From a distance, she heard her mother say, "Open your eyes, and see what the stone has become." The light nearly blinded her with its brightness. She almost dropped the stone in her surprise, then closed her fingers over it. "Will it stay this way forever?" she asked. "No, but it will stay lit for the rest of the day unless you dampen it." "How do I do that?" she asked. "How did you cause the light?" her mother asked in return. "Oh," Ah-mah said, and closed her eyes. Within seconds, she had caused the outer surface of the stone to thicken, feeling the stone solid once again in her hand.

As the memories flooded into her mind, Ah-mah's fingers found the stone. Holding it, she pictured the shell of the stone thinning and soon there was enough light to see the three men across the room. Once she deemed the light strong enough for their purposes, she replaced the stone and turned around, her vision encompassing the good-sized room, and the many, many linen-wrapped plants and bags of seeds.

"What is this place?" Sept whispered, unable to contain his curiosity.

"This is the room of my ancestors. It holds all that is left of our origins. Now quickly, we must gather everything and divide it for carrying," Ah-mah said, keeping her voice barely above a whisper.

The men did her bidding, but Ah-mah, still in the midst of her memories, went to the glowing stone and reached behind it, pulling out a box so small it fit in the palm of her hand. She felt Sept behind her and turned to face him, the box visible in her hand. "My mother once told me that this box contained a treasure from our distant past, but I have never opened it, nor seen its contents. Do you think we have room to take it with us?"

For answer, Sept took the box from her, surprised to feel cold metal in his hands, and slipped it carefully into the small bag that hung from his neck.

Ja-soth found large, sturdy bags lying next to the plants. He and

Kopt laid the plants into the bags, trying to divide the load equally among the three men, with fewer plants in the bag Ah-mah would carry. The seeds were placed on the bottom so they would not crush the plants. Ah-mah picked up the stone which gave light but not heat, and the bag Ja-soth handed her, and took one last look around. "Sleep well, my ancestors," she whispered. "I shall not forget you."

Sept wondered at how easily she left. He had thought she would want to see her daughter's body, but she said nothing and neither did he, knowing time was precious and not to be wasted.

Ah-mah thickened the rock so that it emitted only a faint glow, but with even that small light to guide them, their return seemed easier and quicker. At the north exit, Ah-mah made the stone solid and would have left the cave, but Sept placed a warning hand on her shoulder. He had heard something. Setting his bag on the floor of the cave, he inched his way out through the opening and peered through the bushes, alert to any sound. Hearing nothing, he ducked back into the cave and whispered to the others. Pushing the bags carefully in front of them, the four crawled through the bushes and disappeared down the path and into the hills.

In the early dawn, Ah-mah, Sept, Ja-soth and Kopt came down out of the hills and through the fields to the boat. Master Mu-hem watched for them, as indeed did most on the boat, the children having been the only ones who had slept through the night. As soon as they were on board, sailors untied the ropes from the trees and oared the boat into the current, rowing Ah-mah ever more swiftly away from the place of her birth a second time. She did not look back, for there was no Ak-hu to see, no Gedju. In fact, she could not have looked back, for she was already on her mat, sleeping the sleep of exhaustion, her husband beside her, Ja-soth and Kopt not far away.

She awoke in the afternoon. Menes saw her move and hastened to her side. His face was the first thing she saw when she opened her eyes.

"Menes. Come to Na-na," she said, and smothered him with kisses as he fell into her arms. Not to be outdone, Ah-nah, holding one of the painted sticks in her hand, joined them, plopping herself down on Ah-mah's legs and rocking her bottom back and forth. Sept swooped her up into his arms and planted a huge kiss on her cheek. Whereupon she kissed him back, squealing her delight.

As the boat sped down the river, a man in the bow constantly watching for sandbars, Ah-mah acted as though nothing had happened, playing with her grandchildren, talking with Sefra, eyes dry, a smile on her face. She let Salla help with the children from time to time, but she never let Menes or Ah-nah out of her sight, and she did nothing else all day other than see to them, play with them, hold them. At night she sometimes slept for a few hours, but mostly she paced the deck, her bare feet silent, but those who loved her knew, and few slept any better than she did.

"Will Ah-mahsis ever come back to us?" Nefer asked Sept one day.

"What do you mean?"

"There is no light in her eyes."

Nefer spoke the truth. Ah-mah's eyes no longer danced, but had a haunted, hunted look to them. Sept had seen it in men who had been too long in battle, afraid to fight more, afraid not to fight.

The next morning, he found her standing at the bow staring into the water, her grandchildren with Salla. He stood behind her and put his arms about her. She slipped from his grasp and looked at him as though he were a stranger. Plainly, she did not recognize him.

"Ah-mah? Ah-mah, it is me, Sept, your husband."

"Oh," was all she said before her gaze turned to her grandchildren.

Before he knew what he was doing, Sept took hold of Ah-mah's arm, drawing her back to him, to the comfort only he should provide her. To his surprise, she pummeled him with her fists, beating his chest with fury. He put both arms around her and held her to him, both to stop her fists and to feel her body close, as he had not felt it for all too long. She struggled and would have slipped from his grasp, had his strength been less.

"Let me go!" she shouted in a voice he did not recognize.

He held on as she writhed. She would have bitten him if Sefra had not come up behind her and pulled her head away by her hair.

"We must tie her. You," she said, pointing to Salla, "take the children into the hold." To Sept, who looked at her, unbelieving, she said again, "We must tie her. It is the only way."

Nefer made a place for her by the wounded mast, piling cushions together, while Kopt brought strips of cloth left from Ah-mah's store of those she had used to bind blistered hands. Sept and Sefra bound her wrists and ankles with the strips, and with the strong rope used to tie the boat to the bank, they circled her waist, adding padding beneath the rope wherever possible. Sitting her, still writhing and shouting, now incoherently, on the cushions, Sept tied her to the mast.

She screamed and tried to break her bonds all that morning. Her raving would have continued longer, but her throat was so raw, she had no voice left. Still she opened her mouth and strained, the cords standing out rigidly on her neck. As the sun westered, Ah-mah gave up her struggle, seemingly all at once, but Sefra who sat with her, had noticed her tiring. When Ah-mah's eyes closed and Sefra saw that she slept, she motioned for Sept.

"We can untie her from the mast, but do not unbind her wrists and ankles. I will watch her and see that she comes to no harm."

"I will stay as well," Sept said.

"No. You will sleep. She will need you tomorrow, and for all the days that follow."

"Why, Sefra?"

Sefra looked at him.

"Why does she grieve so?"

"She has lost a child," Sefra said, so softly Sept almost did not hear.

"I have seen women lose children before, but never have I witnessed what Ah-mah has done."

"She loves deeply, Sept. For that you should be grateful, for the depth of her love includes you. She will be Ah-mah tomorrow. Go to sleep."

But she was not Ah-mah the next day, nor for many days after, and she did not seem to need Sept. She did not speak, having no voice, but more, she did not see or hear or feel when someone touched her. The Ah-mah who had sustained them all, that Ah-mah was gone.

Sefra sat with her, and when she would take it, fed her spoonfuls of porridge, or sips of water. Nefer and Salla took charge of Ah-nah and Menes, playing with them, telling them stories, and answering the boy's endless questions. Sept took Ah-mah's place in the bow, unable to stand her rejection.

One afternoon, Menes came to sit by Sefra. She was about to put her arm around him, thinking he wanted to be held close, when he turned toward her, and with a direct stare, asked, "Where is my Na-na?"

Sefra thought of six different responses to give the child, and chose none of them. She had not hidden the truth from him and she would not start down that path now.

"Na-na has gone on a journey," she began.

"Where has she gone, and why did she not take her body

with her?"

"The journey is inside her body." Sefra bowed her head for a moment, gathering her thoughts. "I have been on this journey. It is a hard journey and lonely, and equally hard to tell. Will you hear it?"

The boy's ancestry showed in his bearing. "I will hear it."

"Then sit beside me and do not stare at me. To understand this story, we must close our eyes and go within."

Menes took his place beside her and leaned into her shoulder, a little boy once more.

"A long, long time ago, I lived in a place that is very far from here. My family had lived there since anyone could remember in a round house made of twigs, with fowl in our yards, and cattle in the land surrounding us. We had no fields for we were not farmers. We were very happy with our lives, in harmony with the earth, our mother, dancing to welcome rain and sun, birth and death."

"What is rain?" asked the boy, since in his brief life, no rain had fallen on the land.

"Open your eyes. Do you see that cloud?"

"Yes."

"In the country of my birth, clouds are not always white, but sometimes turn gray, or even black, and water falls onto the ground from them. The water, when it falls, is called rain."

"Oh."

"Now, back to my story." Sefra peeked at Menes. His eyes were already closed.

"I lived with my husband and my son and daughter, my mother, my mother's brother and sister, and my mother's father. Eight of us in our round house, eight houses in our village. Every day, my son and daughter, along with other sons and daughters, would take the cattle to green grass, for that is what they ate. When they brought the cattle back in the evening, the other women and I would squeeze the milk from the full udders. In the dry season, green grass was difficult to find, and one day, our sons and daughters took the cattle farther than they had ever been from our village. The women gathered for milking in the evening, but the cattle and the children did not return. Night fell and still they had not returned."

"Why did you not go look for them?"

"In the place where I lived, many wild animals, big and ferocious, prowled at night, hunting for food. It was not safe to go."

"I would have gone, if my children had been lost," Menes said, voicing the words Sefra had spoken that night.

Tradition and fear of more than the animals kept the men in place. They feared the spirits of the dead which tradition said walked in the night, seeking the unwary, entering their bodies and taking over their minds. A foolish tradition when the lives of her children were at stake, but she was female and no one listened.

"You would have gone, but they did not, and they would not let me go, for I would have. I would have, and my children might still live if I had."

Sefra bowed her head, unable to speak through the raw grief returned by the telling of the tale. Menes put his small brown hand over her large black one.

"The next morning, the men transformed themselves into warriors with paint on their faces and bones and feathers in their hair. If any animal lurked, it would be frightened by this display, or so they believed. I wanted to go with them, but it was forbidden."

"You followed them."

"Yes. I followed them for a while. They went slowly, looking for signs of where the cattle had passed, plain to see to my eyes. Using senses I did not know I possessed, I struck out on my own, and looking neither right or left, followed a trail that seemed etched into my heart and my inner vision. I found them in the late afternoon. The vultures alerted me, a flock of them circling high in the sky, marking the place.

"I will not tell you everything I found, Menes. It was too horrible for anyone to see. My children were dead. The cattle were gone. Not slaughtered by animals in the night, but taken by another tribe. My children died because they would not give up our livelihood and fought to keep the cattle.

"I sat by my children and gathered their broken bodies into my arms. I held them, for it seemed to my tortured mind that they still lived. I held them and felt them in my womb. And then everything went dark, and I knew no more.

"What I remember of that long journey is fragmented, even now. I wandered on a treeless plain with no landmarks, always searching. I could feel the object of my desire, but I could not reach it. Some days it would throb, an answering pulse taking over my body, and that day I would not search, but would sit on the vast plain and feel the awful thing that hid just beyond my reach. One day I saw it in the distance, blood red, nearly black, a great lump on the horizon.

"At last, I came to it. I sat in front of that bloody, beating lump, staring, unable to understand its purpose or why I wanted to enter it, but I did. There was no purpose, no reason, just the lump and me on the plain with no trees. I stood up, and extending my arms, I embraced the lump and was drawn into it. Much as quicksand draws in its victim, I sank into the lump, all the way to its core. The smell of blood, the feeling I could not breathe, threatened to overwhelm me, but I had given myself willingly, and finally, I passed through.

"I remember clearly the first sound I heard when I came to myself again. It was the night call of the whoop-whoop bird. I listened, for I had not yet opened my eyes, and heard crickets and frogs and the soft snores of those who lay nearby. I smelled food and my stomach rolled with hunger. My eyelids lifted, revealing a sky lit with stars beyond counting. I lay on a mat beneath them, as did the others, the night being hot. I rose and went in search of food. Finding it, I ate a little. Inside one of the round houses, I found a cloth in which I wrapped more of the food.

"What I saw in my darkest hour I have not seen again, nor do I have clearer memory of it, but I awoke changed and no longer connected to my people or their traditions. I took the food and a warrior's traveling skin of water and slipped into the night. I have never returned."

Sefra's eyes flew open and she looked to see the boy's response. He was fast asleep, his hand still over hers. She smiled. "What a brave boy you are," she said, and deep into her story, decided to continue its telling. She did not see the flicker of interest in Ah-mah's blank stare.

"I walked for a long time, finding food in roots once my food was gone. I would have starved and given my bones to the land, had I not come to the river, the same river on which this boat travels. By chance, a boat was tied to trees for the night beneath the hill upon which I crouched. There was no moon, and when the night reached its darkest, I left my hiding place and climbed into the boat. Stepping around those sleeping on the deck, I found where they had stored food from the night's cooking. The hole in the deck was right where I suspected it to be, having watched the boat carefully while it was light enough to see. I slipped into it and found a dark corner beneath the deck, where I made myself a kind of covered nest. All day I would stay in the nest, leaving only in the dark of night, passing my days in sleep, or listening to the water rushing by the boat. The boat brought me to your land, Menes: The Land of the River.

"I recovered, my boy, and so will your Na-na. Ah-mah has a

strong spirit. She will come back to us in her own time."

Ah-mah continued to stare at a world only she could see. When pressed, she did swallow the spoonful of food, or sip of water Sefra held to her lips. Sept tried talking with her and once he touched her, tentatively, for he did not want to make her scream again. She did not respond to him, nor did she seem to be aware of anyone or anything else. Menes watched her, his young mind thinking its own thoughts. Ah-nah seemed unaffected by Ah-mah's insanity, but Menes had seen it, for Ah-mah's pain echoed his own. Unknown to old Bo, who would have prevented it had she not fallen asleep with Ah-nah, he had crept out of the cave's north entrance and circled around through the garden to the bushes beneath the trees that lined the path from the house to the river. He had seen his mother and father cut down by the soldiers at Rahotep's order, a wound that festered in him. In the afternoon, as Ah-mah stared into her blessed nothingness, Menes approached her.

"Na-na?"

Ah-mah did not move. Menes almost lost his courage, but he had inherited his strength from his mother as well as his grandmother. He sat down by her and stared into the river. Sefra's story had touched his heart, and given him hope that his grandmother would return from her long, lonely journey. Sefra had returned. Na-na would also. His small brown hand stole over hers.

From that day, Menes hardly left her side. At first he sat and stared with her, lost in thought, but soon his irrepressible spirit grew bored and he related stories of his own adventures. He had explored the hills around the cave much more than he would have if his mother had known what he was doing. In between stories, he sang to her, and sometimes, when Ah-nah knew the song, she joined in.

Ah-nah had not approached her grandmother, but she watched her. Sefra had seen her, seemingly intent on her painted sticks, her head down, eyes peering past her shoulder at Ah-mah. One day, Sefra overheard her playing with the sticks. "Ma-ma is sleeping," she said, and laid one stick down, covering it with a bit of cloth. "Da-da is sleeping." Another stick was placed down with cloth to cover it. "Na-na sleeps with eyes open." Ah-nah laid a stick down but did not cover it. "Menes is awake. Ah-nah is awake. Pa-pa is awake. Sleep, Na-na," she said, as she patted the stick. "Sleep, Ma-ma. Sleep Da-da." Each stick was patted in turn. Then suddenly, she stood up and jumped up and down on the sticks. "Wake up! Wake up!" she shouted, and ran off to find Sept, leaving her sticks to their own devices.

Gradually, Ah-mah improved, sitting up and feeding herself, with the light flickering in her eyes now and then. Menes continued to tell her stories, mostly the same ones over and over, and to hold her hand with his when he did not need it to illustrate the story. Often he sang a little song he had made up.

> "Na-na steps upon her path.
> She does not look to right or left.
> I hope her feet will lead her soon
> to Menes' house and her own room."

Sefra called Sept's attention to the song one evening when he sat with her and Ah-mah, the boy and Ah-nah asleep in his lap.

"Will she come back to us, Sefra?" It was not the first time they had talked. In fact, Sefra had listened to Sept's fear and longing many times. He no longer spent his days in the bow, but seemed resigned to his wife's sickness, though he no longer tried to approach her. In truth, seeing Menes with his grandmother had shamed Sept. Surely he could be as loving as a small boy. But as the days passed with no sign of her return, Sept gave in to his need for reassurance.

"She will come back to you, Sept. She may be changed as I was, but she will return."

"What do you mean, changed?"

"Do not worry yourself. She is better. Do you not see how she feeds herself? Yesterday, I thought I saw the beginnings of a smile."

As though she heard, Ah-mah turned her eyes toward Sept and did smile. Then she resumed her stare. Sept was heartened by Ah-mah's smile, fleeting though it might have been. Sefra started to tell him that Ah-mah was relearning how to act among people, relearning the rules of civilization. At present, she mimicked or followed the directions she understood, her recovery as far away as the farthest horizon. It was as though she had been washed clean inside, clean of all previous experience, and had to recover not only her health, but her memories. But she said nothing of this to Sept.

"Have you and the men come to an agreement concerning Rahotep?"

"We will take you to the people we found when we were blown off course. You will be safe there and Ah-mah will have the time she needs to recover fully. When all of you are safe, we will decide what we need to do about recovering Ah-mah's land."

"Have you thought of letting him have the land?"

"I have thought of it, but Sefra, Rahotep must be stopped. He has taken what is not his, and he has murdered."

"Times change, and people with them," Sefra observed.

"Perhaps. But the rules for living do not. When I know that Ah-mah and her grandchildren are safe, we will teach him a lesson he will not soon forget."

CHAPTER THIRTY-EIGHT

A Spirit Cradled

All the Atlantean dolphins mourned the death of their island home, but to Aletha it seemed especially poignant. Try as she would, she could not lift the dark, oppressive cloud that settled over her mind and heart. Belel and Melida nudged her with their beaks and sent comforting thoughts to her. She tried to respond, but could do no more than surface for breath. In desperation, Belel thought to her, "Tell us of your friend from the future."

Immediately, Aletha knew the source of the oppressive feelings. They did not come from her own grief but from Ah-mah's! "We need dolphin dreaming!" she thought to the other two.

Quickly, they gathered the Keeper dolphins and the wild dolphins, and explained what they wanted.

Soon the wild dolphins and the Atlantean dolphins circled Aletha, swimming in and out, around and around, creating the dreaming. Aletha pictured Ah-mah on the boat as it entered the river on the return trip, and the dreamers took the picture and made it real. Deep in the dreaming, Aletha felt anxious with Ah-mah as she sailed up the river. She saw Ah-mah's grandchildren with Sefra on the bank, and knew as she did what story would be told. She followed the glittering stones to the cave and lit the stone with Ah-mah. She returned to the boat, falling deeper and deeper into grief, but pulled away as the rope bound Ah-mah to the mast and she slipped into darkness.

When the Great Dark had taken Aletha after the destruction of Mu, she had welcomed it. So different to be on the other side, to witness Ah-mah's mind, nay, her whole being, collapsing in on itself, becoming smaller and smaller until her essence was barely to be found.

The dolphins still circled her, still kept the dreaming alive.

Aletha did not know what to do for Ah-mah and neither did the dolphins, until two things happened, simultaneously. The dolphins saw Ah-mah, sure footed on a sea-rocked boat, and Aletha heard the song.

As the dolphins cradled Ah-mah's spirit, rocking it with the irregular rhythms of the sea, Aletha recalled Ah-mah's mother holding her infant child close to her heart. The song was ancient. Aletha could remember her own mother singing it. The memory of singing the song to her son, Paro, threatened to intrude, but she blocked it, knowing she could not afford the grief. In the dreaming, Aletha held Ah-mah, and sang.

> "Le-lo, my baby
> Dream of the tree
> Dream of the river
> that leads to the sea"

Across time and space, Aletha sang as the dolphins rocked the essence of Ah-mah the Healer, infusing her with their passion for life. At last, they felt her essence flame. The image of a sleeping Ah-mah came to the dolphin's minds then, the lids suddenly opening.

"Where am I?" the image asked in the dreaming.

"You are here," Aletha answered.

"Why am I?"

"Your life is not complete."

The image seemed satisfied to close its eyes again in sleep, the essence strong. The image disappeared. The dreaming stopped.

Afterwards, still captured by the dreaming, Aletha swam away from the other dolphins, wanting to be alone. Deep in thought, she was surprised to feel another dolphin brush against her. Seronak! Her body tingled in response.

"Will Ah-mah live?" he asked.

"Yes, although her journey back will be long." Abruptly, she asked, "Do you feel different since becoming dolphin?"

"I feel young again," he answered with his thought, "and I wonder if it is just this body."

"I dream of mating, of producing young ones, of taking care of them. When I lost Mu, I vowed I would never take another mate, or have another child, but now…"

Seronak nodded his huge head. "As Keeper of the One, I felt ancient. Now I feel newly born. I desire a mate, Aletha, but only if that mate is you."

Her body reacted to the joy in her heart. She dove deep, then shot skyward, sending a geyser of water into the air as she fell back into the welcoming sea.

CHAPTER THIRTY-NINE
Ah-Mah Returns

They entered the west branch of the river, having left Salla at a tiny village just below the place where the river branched. Sept and Mu-hem were reluctant to leave the girl, but she insisted, having heard from the villagers that a great boat had been seen near where the eastern branch of the river reached the sea. Sept dug into the gold he had left to pay for her passage on a boat that sailed down the eastern branch.

"I would go with you, Salla, if it were not for these children and my wife."

"If it is Master Akban's boat, I will persuade him to sail to you," the girl said, with a determination he had not heard from her before.

The spark within Ah-mah, cradled by the dolphins and Aletha's lullaby, continued to bloom, but Ah-mah's conscious self was aware only of a softness, a quiet protection around her heart. Today she walked with her grandson from one end of the boat to the other. Menes chattered, encouraged by her smile and the way she squeezed his hand from time to time. When she suddenly returned to her cushion, he worried that she was ill again, but she looked up at him and smiled. With a raspy voice she croaked, "Drink?" Not waiting to be asked twice, Menes raced to find the copper water bucket and a cup. He shouted as he passed Sept, "Na-na spoke!" Sept, seeing that the bucket was too heavy for the boy, went to help him.

Ah-mah's recovery was remarkable after that day. As she healed, she told Menes of her adventures, delighting in the boy's wonder although speaking tired her and her voice did not lose its raspiness. Of all her tales, he seemed most intrigued by the new people they had found, the ones Ah-mah called the Bennu. He asked her to repeat that story over and over, never tiring of it, asking astute questions beyond his years. One afternoon after she had told the story yet again, he said, "Na-na, we are going home." After that, he seemed satisfied and no longer asked for the tale.

Nefer triggered Ah-mah's return to the treating of feet with an accident. He was just taking position on the prow to watch for sandbars when the boat hit a pile of floating debris and lurched, causing him to fall overboard. Menes shouted and Master Mu-hem turned the boat out of the current. Sept dove into the water and swam toward where he had last seen Nefer's head. Every so often he shot out of the water and took a quick look around, searching. The crew shouted and pointed to help. Nefer was still in the current, moving faster than Sept until a sandbar caught his body, holding it until Sept could reach him. A wound in his hairline bled freely and he was not conscious. Sept held Nefer's head above water and swam toward the boat. Ja-soth threw a rope to him, and he looped it around Nefer's chest. The men pulled both of them to the side of the boat where the ladder had been lowered. Ja-soth and Kopt took Nefer from Sept and handed him up, Sept following.

Ah-mah bent over Nefer, unsure what to do. "He is cold! Bring blankets to warm him," she croaked.

Master Mu-hem intervened. "No, Mistress Ah-mah, he does not need blankets. We must get the water out of him first."

So saying, he knelt by Nefer and pushed his hands into the young man's chest, rhythmically, five, six, seven, ten times before Nefer coughed and water came out of his mouth. Still the Master pushed, bringing more water from Nefer until he protested with his own voice. "Walk him," Mu-hem said, and two of the men hauled Nefer up and began walking him around and around the deck. He threw up water several times more before they brought him back to Ah-mah. "Now you may warm him."

Ah-mah took the blankets that had been brought and covered Nefer with them. He smiled at her weakly. "I am not a very good sailor, Ah-mahsis," he said.

"Rest now. Someone else can watch the river."

Nefer slept, and when Ah-mah felt beneath the cover, his legs felt warm to her, but she did not like his color. His brown skin had a grayish cast to it.

"Menes? Come to Na-na. I want to show you something."

The boy came quickly, glad to be included and hoping he could help Nefer. "Pa-pa is very brave," he said, referring to Sept. Then, seeing Nefer's color, he put his hand over his mouth and great tears threatened to spill from his eyes. "Na-na! Will Nefer die?"

"Watch as I work his feet."

Intrigued, Menes watched the way Ah-mah pulled on Nefer's heels, twisted foot and ankle to loosen it, and then began the slow pushing of her thumb into the sole of each foot. He asked questions continually and she answered with the patience of a grandmother teaching her favorite grandchild. She remembered that Ak-hu had said that Menes was most like her. The pain in her heart at the thought of her dead daughter no longer took her breath.

Nefer was young and improved rapidly, joining Ah-mah in treating the feet of all the men on the boat within a day of the accident. Menes plied them both with questions and tried to treat his sister's feet, but she would have none of it, screaming for him to stop tickling her.

"Come, Menes," Sefra called to him. "Come and work my feet."

The boy came willingly, fascinated with Sefra's skin, the top of her foot black as night, the bottom, pearly white. He took the foot she thrust at him and tried to mimic the movements his grandmother had made so easily. Sefra closed her eyes and leaned back. After a while she said, "Little hands and big feet make for tired boys. Would you like to rest?" The boy nodded and moved to sit by her. "My foot feels better, Menes."

The tall, black woman felt solid to him, safe, and he had grown to love her. He snuggled closer, and she put her arm around him, for her love of him had grown also.

Menes and Sefra stood with Ah-mah in the bow the morning they left the river. Ah-nah sat on the prow, Ah-mah's protecting arms securely around her. She had asked them to be with her, wanting their first time to see water stretching all the way to the horizon to be memorable. She did not speak, but watched them, remembering her first time. Ah-nah was too young to notice the loss of the land or to care, but she enjoyed the attention from her grandmother.

"Na-na! The river is gone!" Menes exclaimed as the banks slid behind them. A gasp from Sefra told Ah-mah that she beheld the far horizon with nothing but water in between. No other sound escaped Sefra's lips, but her eyes hardly blinked, so intent was her gaze on that far horizon.

"I have wanted to travel the sea between. I have wanted to know what was on the other side," Ah-mah said.

"Does land exist there or would we be lost forever on all this water?"

"I have heard there is land, but none on this boat can confirm it."

"Perhaps one day I will go to find out," Sefra said, a hand immediately covering her mouth and her surprise.

As though Sefra had spoken of eating and not of an outrageous adventure, Ah-mah said, "Perhaps you will."

"Na-na, the boat turns, and look, Na-na, look! The dolphin comes."

How Menes recognized the dolphin, or how the dolphin with the pinkish-white patch knew her boat, Ah-mah did not stop to consider. This remarkable boy was much like the equally remarkable dolphin.

That evening, she introduced Menes and Sefra to the dolphin. Sept held Ah-nah, and with Nefer, watched from the deck of the boat, not ready to let Ah-mah too far from his sight. Nefer reveled in the sight of the sea. He could almost feel Medi in his arms.

"Look, Pa-pa! Menes is in the water!" Ah-nah exclaimed.

The water was deep and Menes was not a good swimmer, so Ah-mah held him. Sefra came into the water as far as she dared, but when the water reached her chest, she could go no farther. "I do not swim," she said, when Ah-mah looked at her questioningly.

"Sept? Sept! Is the floating ball still on the boat?" she asked. "Sefra does not swim and Menes would feel safer with it."

"I shall fetch it," Sept said. Ah-nah ran ahead of him. "I find it!" When he caught up to her, Ah-nah had found the ball and was tugging at it. Sept swept her up into his arms, holding her as he did not dare hold Ah-mah. She squealed with delight. He still felt awkward with Ah-mah and did not know how to bridge the gap he felt growing between them. Transferring Ah-nah to one side, he picked up the ball with his free hand and tossed it into the water, watching as Sefra took hold of one side, Menes the other. The dolphin gently nudged the ball out into the sea, Ah-mah swimming beside it. Just the dolphin called Patch joined the humans, with the rest of the pod staying some distance away.

After the swim and the evening meal, Ah-mah left her grandchildren in Sefra's care and went to find her husband. He sat in a group of men, not talking, not really listening, just attempting to assuage his loneliness. She squatted behind him and whispered in his ear, "Walk with me."

As though no time had passed, no days filled with darkness and terrible fear, the two walked off down the beach hand in hand. For many steps neither spoke, but finally, Sept could contain himself no longer. "I have missed you, Ah-mah."

For answer, she said simply, "I am here now." Then she took off, running with the feet of a girl, dashing behind a dune where she had hidden a mat earlier. Sept followed, hard on her heels, still afraid to trust her moods. When he saw the mat, he understood and his fear dissolved.

Borne on fair winds, they arrived the next day at that same beach which had harbored them after the storm. Alerted by those who watched the sea, several of the Bennu waited for them, including Medi, eyes shining when she spotted Nefer. Their reunion was much different from their parting, Medi having thrown off the last vestiges of her royal bearing. She ran across the beach and into the water, and Nefer risked drowning once more as he jumped in to join her. The men laughed, elbowing each other and shouting encouragement to Nefer as his feet touched bottom and he plowed through the water to hold her close.

"Where's Salla?" she asked, as they walked arm in arm. Nefer told her of the boat sighting, and Salla's journey to find it. Medi smiled. "Master Akban is a great sailor. I hope he found a way to save everyone."

The Bennu had built a welcoming fire and prepared food, more diverse and abundant than they had tasted for some time. They ate heartily, talking quietly together, hardly wondering at the ease with which the Bennu spoke the language of the Land of the River. Sept noticed. "How is it that you speak our language?" he asked. "We have been gone less than fifteen days."

"Medi taught us and Mother enhanced the learning," Ga-lek, the man who had led them to the hidden village, answered.

"Mother Thera, the lady behind the wall in your village?" Ah-mah asked.

"Mother is also Thera," he answered.

There was more here, Ah-mah sensed it, but tonight was not the time to ask. She turned to Nefer and asked, "Have you told Medi how you saved our boat from sandbars and nearly drowned for your trouble?"

"Yes, Nefer. Tell the story. We would hear your version." The men chuckled. They all loved Nefer, and since he was youngest, it was only right they should tease him.

The stars came out during Nefer's tale. Sept slipped his hand over Ah-mah's, and she leaned into him as she had done all the years of their life together, until... Best not to remember. She was back and that was all that mattered.

They slept well that night, all but Ah-mah. When the moon rose, so did she, walking toward the water, but not into it. The sand felt good to her feet, but that was not her purpose. She walked the beach until she was ready, and then, she spoke aloud to her daughter.

"I miss you, my child. I remember when your father died. You were brave then, too.

"I remember your first steps, your first smile, your first words. I remember you once told me you were plain like your father. You were not plain to me, my Ak-hu. You were beautiful. More beautiful than you could ever imagine.

"When you married Gedju, he became my son. When Menes was born, I could not have been prouder if he had been my own child. He is bright as the sun, Ak-hu, just as you were, and he and Ah-nah give me joy.

"I should not have left you. My heart knew it then, or at least I think it did. Why did I not warn you? Would it have mattered if I had?

"Were you and Gedju brave, or foolish, my precious girl? You could have hidden in the cave as well. You knew its secrets. You could have saved yourselves for your children. Did you know something I cannot?"

All the rest of that night Ah-mah talked with her daughter, until, at last, as the sun lit the morning clouds, she was ready. The dolphin, Patch, waited, his silver tail flukes flashing in the foam. She pulled the yellow dress over her head and dropped it, swimming to the dolphin as soon as the water was deep enough to bear her. Patch offered his dorsal fin which she grasped gently. Forming a circle around the two, the pod swam in and out, in and out, around and around. Ah-mah closed her eyes and gave them her daughter, letting them thread Ak-hu's life through dolphin dreaming. Deep into the dream herself, Ah-mah held Ak-hu tightly, and said goodbye.

"I am here forever, Mother. The dolphins hold me. You do not have to say goodbye," Ak-hu said in the dreaming.

"Is it true?" Ah-mah asked.

"Yes," Patch thought to her.

The dolphin towed her to the beach. With a full heart, she

slipped her arms around him as far as they would go.

Sept waited with a blanket to cover her, the yellow dress tucked under his arm. "I am reborn," she thought.

"It is a new day, Ah-mah," said a voice in her head.

"Aletha! If you are here, I must be sane again," Ah-mah thought back to her.

Sept put the blanket around her and held her to him.

"When I woke to find you gone, I was very afraid."

"I will not frighten you again, my husband. I have given Ak-hu to the dolphins and they have placed her securely into their dreaming. Her memory is safe and I am alive once more."

He kissed her then, long and thoroughly, finally believing every word she said.

CHAPTER FORTY

The Need to Kill

Next morning they made plans to unload the boat so that a log of acacia wood, purchased in Abedju, could be used to replace the second leg of the mast. Although she had several dresses besides the yellow one, all water stained from the storms, Ah-mah chose to wear the one Sept had given her when she still lived in the gardener's hut. She could still remember Ak-hu's face when she took the dress from its box so long ago. "The dress of a healer," Ak-hu had said. Sept noticed the dress and smiled, reassured once more that truly, Ah-mah had returned.

When he took Ah-mah into the hold and showed her the bags of plants and seed, she wondered aloud about their origins. "We went to the cave to get them, Ah-mah. Do you not remember?" Sept asked.

"Cave? What cave?"

Unsure of what he should say, of what might trigger the return of Ah-mah's terrible grief, Sept chose the truth. "Ak-hu prepared the plants and this seed and hid them in the cave of your ancestors. You and I and two others retrieved them by way of a secret path through the hills. You led us there, my wife."

"Ak-hu did this?" Ah-mah's eyes filled with tears, and Sept's heart nearly stopped.

"Ah-mah?"

"Thank you, my daughter, for your great gift," Ah-mah whispered. She squatted beside one of the bags and opened it, pulling out one of the rooted plants. Inspecting it with a gardener's eye, she said, "We must pour water on these bags, and plant their contents soon, or Ak-hu's efforts will be lost."

Sept let out the breath he was holding. Ah-mah did not hear, but went in search of water.

Master Mu-hem and his sailors were in the midst of a discussion as to what they should do. All agreed that they should not leave the boat unguarded. Ga-lek listened to the discussion with interest, at last disclosing the existence of a bay a short distance further west. "Tall dunes protect it from sight, and one man could give warning of any approaching vessels. It was from those heights that we saw your boat approaching. My people often visit the bay, and a way from it to the lake, through the hills, is known to them. If you will allow me to travel on your boat, I will act as your guide."

Mu-hem was delighted with the news that he could keep his boat hidden and have warning of any who approached. The beach felt too naked to him, too exposed.

Just as Ga-lek had said, the bay was not visible until the dunes abruptly disappeared revealing a narrow entrance before continuing on the other side. They sailed through the opening between the dunes and into calmer waters, the Master choosing a spot well inside for anchoring.

Sept and his men, Ah-mah, Medi, and Nefer, prepared to take Ak-hu's children and her plants and seeds to the village.

Ga-lek left the food his people had brought. With that and the fish they could catch, the ship's crew would eat well. Several sailors accompanied them, bringing empty water jars.

The path through the hills was barely discernible to Ah-mah's eyes, but Ga-lek followed it unerringly and soon brought them back to the valley with its hills and hidden caves. Ga-lek led the sailors to the lake to fill their jars, and then set them on the path to return, the sailors uncomfortable if too long away from the sea. Ah-mah watched them go with mixed emotions, eager to see Laskella and Waron, reluctant to leave the dolphins and the image of Ak-hu they now held, reluctant to leave the sea and the promise of adventure it held.

"And Sept, Ah-mah? What does Sept feel? Can he be happy planting seeds and harvesting them?" Aletha asked in her mind.

"Why would he not?" she thought back to her unseen companion.

"He is a warrior. It is all he has known."

Ah-mah did not comment nor did she say anything to Sept, but she watched him from that moment. He grinned at her often, grabbing her hand at the slightest provocation, touching her shoulder with his. In her mind she heard Aletha once more, "You were gone a long time, Ah-mah."

"Gone?"

"Into your grief. We worried that you might not come back."

"How long?"

"Many days."

"I do not remember."

"I know. It is a blessing."

In the midst of this internal conversation, some of the Bennu appeared, Laskella and Waron among them. When Laskella saw Ah-mah, she quickly masked her shock at Ah-mah's thinness and the darkness still evident beneath her eyes. Struggling somewhat with the way words in the language of the Land of the River felt on her tongue, Laskella greeted Ah-mah. "I am glad you back," she said and opened her arms wide.

"Laskella," Ah-mah cried in her raspy voice, and hugged her. "It is good to see you again. And you, Waron. This is Sefra, a friend to me and to all in this group, and these two... These are my grandchildren. Menes, Ah-nah, give greetings to Laskella and Waron."

"Greetings, Laskella. Greetings, Waron," Menes said boldly. Ah-nah looked up at Laskella and raised her arms. Laskella picked up the girl, who promptly touched the scars on her face with her little hand, and then, impulsively kissed all she could reach.

With eyes glistening at the warm meeting between those she loved, Medi came to Ah-nah and said, "Waron is tall, and if you ride on his shoulders, you will be able to see better than if you walk."

Ah-nah took Waron in with a look, and satisfied with what she saw, let him lift her up to his shoulder, squealing her delight. From that moment, Laskella and Waron thought of Ah-nah as their own. Menes would have liked to have ridden as well, his heart suddenly lonely for comfort, but a boy of eight years was too old for such. Sept noticed the shadow that seemed to cross the boy's face. Without saying a word, he lifted Menes up over his head to sit on his shoulders. The boy laughed with delight.

The valley was smaller than she had remembered. "You compare it with the endless sea. Unfair," she heard in her mind.

"I fear I shall compare everything to the sea, Aletha. Why do I feel it is my home now?" Startled by her thoughts, Ah-mah stumbled and would have fallen had not Sept grabbed her elbow to steady her.

Ga-lek led them to a rock face and through the concealed opening into the room behind. "There is room here for all of you.

Rest and enjoy. Tomorrow Mother will speak with you."

"Will you stay here?" Ah-nah asked Waron when he took her from his shoulder and put her on the ground.

"We live here, Ah-nah, and now, so do you."

"Stay always," she said, an impish grin on her face.

"Ah-nah, you are a shameless flirt," Ah-mah said, swooping the child up into her arms and kissing her.

Soon all the newcomers had found empty cubicles behind cloth-draped openings and stored their belongings. Some of the cubicles were larger, intended for two people or a family group, some were smaller. Sefra chose a small cubicle deep in the cave, one that afforded as much privacy as possible.

"What in bags?" Laskella asked Ah-mah. Then, changing the expression on her face to a hopeful one, she asked, "Rosemary?"

"Yes, and many other herbs besides. They have been rooted, but they need water, and to be planted. Is there a place for growing in this village?"

This was too many words for Laskella, and in her dismay, she asked Medi in her own language for help. When she understood that Ah-mah had brought the means to plant an entire herb garden, she said, with Medi translating, "I have dreamed of planting herbs since I came here. I miss my garden and tending my plants. Waron and I have wandered all over these hills, and I believe there are many good places for planting."

With Medi acting as translator, the two women continued the conversation.

"Let us ask Thera for one of them. If she agrees, we can begin digging tomorrow! I hunger for digging and planting and tending, although I did not know until you said it."

"We will need all the places, Ah-mah. Planting is done differently here in order to keep us unknown. Have you not wondered how we have food to eat, but no fields to be seen?"

"I had not, but I do now. Tell me more."

"Each of these plants must thrive on its own, tended and watered carefully to look as though it were not tended, so that a stranger, coming upon it and recognizing it, would think a bird had dropped seed from which the plant sprouted."

"The food is grown in the same way?"

"Very nearly. We grow lentils and barley among the grasses. The harvest requires more labor, but the plants seem to thrive whether they are planted on the hillside or near the lake."

"How should we begin?"

The rest of the afternoon was spent sorting through the plants, separating them, grouping them, a task that required little more than the few words Laskella and Ah-mah had in common. Sefra watched them, as did Medi.

"I know of roots, fish, cattle and fowl, but I know nothing of planting," Sefra confided to Medi. As the only other women in their group, the two had formed a kind of bond through their ignorance and sat together on the other side of the room from Ah-mah and Laskella and their plants, Nefer content to sit with them, Medi's hand in his. "Sefra? What happened in Nubt? Why are Ah-mah's grandchildren here and her daughter is not?"

"Ah-mah's daughter is dead, as is her daughter's husband. Do not show your distress," she cautioned Medi. "Ah-mah is recently returned from the darkness of her grief. You have noticed how thin she is."

"How? Who would do such a thing?"

"Rahotep. He seeks to rule all of the Land of the River, and will if no one calls him out."

"I wonder if the high priest was not behind this," Nefer said. "Do you know the story of how Ah-mah bargained with him for my life? I think now that he had his eye on her land even then."

"Will we never be rid of politics?" Medi asked. "How were Ah-mah's grandchildren saved?"

"That story is more involved. Their mother had a foretelling and made sure they were safe in the cave of their ancestors. They were left in the care of a nursemaid, Bo, and they came to me because Bo drew a map and made Menes remember it. I cared for them until Ah-mah came in the boat."

"What happened to the nursemaid?"

"She was captured and killed."

"How awful! But look how Ah-mah works. She seems restored except for her weight."

"Aye, but this time I do not believe she will find consolation in her plants." Once they had reached the sea, Sefra and Ah-mah had shared their longing to sail to the far horizon and not look back. "The dolphins call us both," she said to Medi.

Mother Thera and the Bennu were quick to give Ah-mah and Laskella permission to plant, the morning meeting cut short by the women's eagerness and Laskella's assurance that she had taught Ah-mah the way to place the plants so they appeared to have grown on their own. Seemingly, Thera understood the women, no matter which language they spoke.

The plants were sorted into twelve smaller bundles. The group gathered around them included gardeners from the Bennu as well as Laskella and Waron, Sept and Ah-mah. They would go two by two into different areas, one to plant, one to carry water and watch for danger. In her eagerness, Ah-mah grabbed a digging stick from the pile of tools that lay on the ground and would have left immediately for the area where she was to plant, but Laskella stopped her with hand on arm.

"We ask for blessing," she said.

Raising both arms as though to encompass all the land, she said, Medi translating, "We come to you from afar, bringing plants that are strangers. We ask you to welcome them and bless them with the richness you hold within your soil." To Ah-mah, she said, "Now we plant."

All that day was spent finding places for each of the plants, digging a hole, setting the plant, covering the roots and tamping the soil down, watering, and then placing rocks and tufts of grass at random so that the plant seemed to have been there from birth. The process took longer than Ah-mah anticipated and she was very tired by day's end, as was Sept, who had made countless trips to the lake for water. When the last cutting, a rosemary, had been planted and the last rock placed near it, Ah-mah sat back on her heels and wiped the back of her hand across her brow. As she had done with all the others, she spoke to this plant. "Grow, little one, grow strong. Dig deeply into the soil. Be brave in your new place and remember who plucked you."

She awoke on a morning not long after to see Sept looking at her, his head resting in his hand, propped on an elbow. He asked if she would like to see the sea. The light which flashed in her eyes was answer enough.

They filled a water skin and gathered food into a bag, for they planned to be gone all day. When Ah-mah would have taken the path to the bay, Sept stopped her, taking her instead a different direction into the hills, climbing a short way to another path.

"Where does this lead?" she asked.

"To the sea, my love. It is a shorter way."

Ah-mah was amazed at how easy the path was to follow. Many feet had come this way. The path disappeared when she saw the first dunes, and heard the crashing surf in the distance. The boat was nowhere to be seen.

"Where is the boat?" Ah-mah asked.

Sept pointed back over his shoulder where nothing could be seen but tall dunes. Ah-mah understood that they were on the open sea, the boat hidden behind the dunes which framed the bay. Sept said, "I would be alone with you this day, Ah-mah."

They spread a blanket and rested, Ah-mah content to listen to the comforting surf, Sept wondering how to tell Ah-mah what he must.

"Look, Ah-mah. There is the dolphin we know."

She looked at him, and then at the dolphin. "Shall we?"

For answer, he stripped off his clothes. She was up in a second and out of her healer's dress, running with him toward the surf. They dove in and swam to Patch, playing with him, nudging each other, feeling his sleek skin, diving together, and finally floating, rocked by the currents. At last they said goodbye and slogged through the water and sandy beach to fall onto the blanket and sleep.

When they awoke, they drank a little and ate a little, neither hungry nor thirsty. "Ah-mah, you truly do not remember our trip to the cave?" Sept asked after a while.

"No."

"What do you remember?"

"I remember leaving this place and journeying up the river. We tied the boat to what trees we could find, eating and sleeping on the boat, and we stopped before we reached Nubt because Sefra and my granchildren waited on the bank. The next thing I remember clearly is walking with Menes, and knowing Ak-hu was dead, but I do not remember how she died."

Sept told her then, holding nothing back, filling in the empty space for her. He had talked long with Sefra about his timing, finally deciding he must tell her now, even though Sefra advised against it. He must tell her before he left.

Ah-mah was dry-eyed and quiet. When there was no more to say, she stood up and extended her hand to him. He rose and took it, and together they walked the beach, in the opposite direction from the bay. Neither spoke, and when Ah-mah's need for movement was satisfied, they walked back.

Sitting once again on the blanket, Ah-mah broke the silence. "Did you bring the stone and the box?"

For answer, Sept dug into the leather bag that hung from his neck and brought out both. He placed the stone and the tiny box into her waiting hands. She stared at them, and then looked at Sept. "This is all that is left of my ancestors."

"No, Ah-mah, it is not. It is all you took with you, but the land of your ancestors and the cave which holds their bones is still there, as is the great stone house."

"I have no need to return, Sept." Suddenly, Aletha's words returned to her. "Sept is a warrior." Insight came with the words, and she asked him, "Do you?"

"What Rahotep did was wrong, Ah-mah. He took what was not his, and murdered your daughter and her husband. He must be stopped. Do you see that?"

"I confess I do not, Sept. Ak-hu and Gedju are dead, my grandchildren are alive. Is it not my place to take care of the living?"

"There is no doubt of that, my wife. You do take care of the living, be they human or plant. It is your nature to do so. I am a warrior, trained to protect, to fight. You nurture and heal, I cut away. Rahotep must be cut away."

Ah-mah gathered her thoughts before speaking. "I believe we each follow the path appointed to us."

"I do not believe it is anyone's path to take what is not his and murder those who would stand in the way. I must go. I trusted this man when he employed me. I sailed through storms and navigated the treacherous rocks of diplomacy for him. An entire boat filled with people I knew and loved may have been lost because he had to have logs to build a house greater than yours. I must confront him with his evil. Whether you return to your lands or not, I must make him see that he did not have the right to take them."

"If he does not see? What will you do then?"

"I will kill him, Ah-mah. I will kill him because he killed Ak-hu and Gedju and Bo, and he had no right to do so."

"Will that not make you a murderer?"

Sept hesitated before answering, but his voice was strong when he spoke. "I am a warrior. Killing is what I do."

"No, my husband, it is what you have been trained to do. It is not in your heart to kill. I saw that the first time I looked into your eyes."

"I will not argue with you, Ah-mah. When Mu-hem is ready to leave, my soldiers and I will go with him. You will be safe here."

"I will be safe, my husband, but you will not."

With heavy hearts, Ah-mah and Sept picked up the blanket and every scrap that might reveal the day spent there. Thera had been adamant about her rules in allowing them to stay. Using grasses growing in the dunes, they whisked away any sign, holding the broken grass loosely in their hands when they finished to let the wind take it.

Their argument surfaced several times in the next few days, with the same results, until finally, Ah-mah said to her husband. "My heart knows that you will go on this foolish errand. I can do nothing but send my heart with you. Know this, Sept, and believe it: the need to kill is not in you." After that, Ah-mah said no more, but helped Sept prepare for the journey he was determined to take.

CHAPTER FORTY-ONE

The Aquamarine

The sky was brilliantly blue and cloudless the morning Sept left. Waron and Laskella had come with them, Ah-nah riding in her favorite place on Waron's shoulders. Sept touched her little cheek and smiled before scooping Menes up and holding Ah-mah and the boy close to him one last time. "Take care of your grandmother," he whispered to the boy, who nodded solemnly.

"Come back to me, Sept," Ah-mah whispered.

As the boat disappeared behind the tall dune, Ah-mah walked back to the village with the rest, already thinking of how she would establish the routine that would carry her through the days of Sept's absence. When she entered the cave, she went directly to Sefra's cubicle.

"Would you go with me to tend the plants, Sefra?"

"What could I do other than keep you company?"

"I ask nothing else, my friend, unless you would carry water."

"That I can do."

Sefra did accompany Ah-mah that day and for many other

days, water jar in its leather harness slung over her shoulder for easier carrying as they climbed to the plants. From the many cuttings Ak-hu had rooted, all but one or two thrived.

Often Menes went with them, but Ah-nah preferred the freedom of running about the cave, delving into nooks and crannies, or devising new games to play with Waron. Ah-mah was grateful to Waron and Laskella for the love and attention they gave the child. She did not seem to miss either her mother or father, but Ah-mah noticed that Ah-nah never left the cave by herself.

On a day when Menes did not go with them, Ah-mah asked Sefra, "Have you ever taken a mate?"

"Once, years ago, I had a husband. It is not something I care to remember."

"I have had two husbands. One died and one keeps leaving me. What does that say about me?"

"That Sept has his own thoughts, and that you have not bent him to your will." When Ah-mah's eyebrows lifted in question, she continued, "You are strong, Ah-mah."

"How can you say that after the miserable way I behaved on the boat?"

"Sept told you?"

"Everything."

"I thought he might have. He is strong, too, Ah-mah, but he was deeply hurt by what happened."

"I was lost for a time."

"That is not what hurt him. You did not turn to him in your grief."

"I do not know what I did or did not do, only what Sept says."

"I think you could not turn to anyone living for help, but had to go deep inside yourself. For a time, you did not want to live, Ah-mah. I know this, for I felt the same when my children were lost."

"Your children? Lost?"

"I told Menes the story on the boat to help him understand what was happening with you."

"Tell me, Sefra. If you can bear it."

They talked long that afternoon, Sefra telling her story, Ah-mah connecting with Sefra's feelings as she expressed her terrible loneliness and guilt, her helplessness, how she would have given her life for her children. Finally, she spoke of leaving her village, of her struggles to stay alive, of finding the river and hiding on the boat, of making her home in the abandoned hut, of the days and days of solitude which at last brought a measure of peace to her heart. When Sefra stopped speaking, the two were silent, Ah-mah filled with a new respect for her friend. The sun was low in the west when they gathered their tools and the water jar and returned to the cave that was now home.

As part of the new routine, evenings were devoted to feet as Ah-mah continued her lessons with Nefer and Medi. A few of the Bennu joined them from time to time, but none had volunteered feet for treatment as yet. Menes sat next to her and watched everything she did, his smaller hands imitating her movements. Laskella joined them, as did Waron, she out of eagerness to learn, and Waron because he loved her. Often, Nefer or Medi would do Ah-mah's feet, and once, she allowed Menes to rub them. Sept was never far from her thoughts, but in spite of his absence, she felt a peace that had been long in coming. She often retraced the hidden path they had taken to the open sea, at first accompanied by Sefra. As the days passed, Ah-mah often left before dawn, choosing to greet the morning alone from the dunes. She felt she waited for something, she knew not what. Aletha went with her on these solitary journeys, Ah-mah never tiring of the tales of her adventures as a dolphin. When Aletha confessed she had mated with Seronak, it was

Ah-mah's turn to whisper, "I told you!" At last, Aletha revealed Ah-mah's darkest hour and how the dolphins entered dolphin dreaming to cradle what was left of her essence. Ah-mah understood then the depth of her insanity.

Sometimes, Ah-mah slipped out of her healer's dress, which had become even more dear to her since Sept's leaving, and went into the water alone, swimming with Patch, or joining with his pod. She began to stay longer, not returning to the cave until the mid-day meal. She did not go every day, and it was on one of the days she stayed in the cave that a young Bennu came to her one morning as she was eating her porridge.

"Mother will see you now," he said, and took a step back. When he did not leave, Ah-mah understood that "now" meant he would wait for her. She finished her porridge and cleaned the bowl with sand, just as she had in her hut, this time flinging the used sand into a large wooden trough. When it was filled, the men would carry it to the beach and scatter it. Smoothing her dress, she nodded to the boy. They left together, the boy leading her from one rock face across the valley to the other side and into the concealed entrance within another. The old woman was alone and sat in the center of the room, an empty chair facing her. Ah-mah went to the chair and sat. The boy vanished.

"I would speak with you, Ah-mah."

Ah-mah nodded and said, "And I with you, Mother."

"You are different. The blood of our ancestors runs true in you. Do you know this?"

"No, Mother. How does my difference show you the blood of my ancestors?"

"Our ancestors, Ah-mah. We are the last of a race bred on an island in the sea. Can you not feel it? You who were born in a dry land with one river, you who had never seen the sea, do you not feel it draw you?"

"I feel it, but..."

"But?"

"I thought the dolphins drew me."

"Ah, the dolphins. You have swum with them?"

"Yes, Mother."

"You have dreamed with them?"

Ah-mah nodded, wondering if the old woman had ever dreamed with dolphins.

"I understand you brought things with you from the cave of your ancestors. Sacred things besides plants and seeds and grandchildren."

"I did."

"I would see these things."

"Now?"

"Do you have them with you?"

"No."

"I will wait for you to fetch them."

Ah-mah walked quickly across the valley and into the cave, her thoughts tumbling over and over in her mind. "Can I trust her?" she asked the companion in her mind. "She and her people have given us safe harbor. Is it because she knew I had the stone and the box?"

"You can trust her, Ah-mah," Aletha thought to her.

Ah-mah entered her cubicle and took the tiny bag from its place on the shelf carved into the wall. She clutched the bag to her bosom and walked back to the cave where the old woman waited. Still holding the bag close, she sat. Thera, her face lined, her gray eyes faded but not dimmed, her silver hair pulled back to a knot at her neck, turned her hands palms up and placed them on her knees. Slowly, Ah-mah brought the bag to her lap. She drew the stone out and held it. Thera did not move, nor did her fingers twitch. The stone seemed comfortable where it was, fitting into Ah-mah's hand as she closed her fingers over it. "Give it to her, Ah-mah," Aletha's thought commanded. "Put it in her hand." In one quick motion, Ah-mah placed the stone in Thera's hand, then clutched the bag and drew it back to her bosom.

Thera cupped the stone in her hands, closed her eyes and murmured unknown words, whereupon the rock filled the room with blinding light. One word more did Thera speak, and the stone returned to its former state.

"You know this stone?" asked Ah-mah.

"Long ago, we had such a stone, or so legend says. My mother said the stone would return to us, and against that day, taught me the words for lighting it. Do you know the words?"

"No."

"Can you light the stone?" she asked, holding it out for Ah-mah to take.

Ah-mah held the stone in her hands and imagined its shell becoming less dense. The stone glowed, brighter and brighter, until the room was lit once again, not so brightly as when Thera held it, but with no corner left untouched.

"Is that as bright as you can make it?"

"I can make it brighter, but I do so only at need."

"You did not say words to the stone."

"I spoke to it with my thoughts."

"Keep the stone, Ah-mah. You are its owner if it has one."

Thera watched as Ah-mah tenderly put it back into the bag.

"May I see the box?"

This time, reluctance gone, Ah-mah pulled the box from the bag quickly, forgetting to wonder how Thera knew the bag contained it, and handed it to the ancient woman, who brought it with both hands to her heart. Her eyes closed and she seemed deep in thought.

"Do you know what is in this box?"

"I do not."

"Nor do I, Ah-mah, although I have tried to open it in my mind. I believe it may hold something you will recognize, though I do not know how that is possible. Will you open the box now?"

"I never thought to, Mother. The box has been closed for all my life. I do not think my mother opened it, or her mother before her. Why should I open the box now? Are we not guardians of this treasure?"

"Are you afraid, Ah-mah? Are you afraid it will be empty?"

Ah-mah was taken aback. "I believe I am afraid, Mother," she said, and laughed. "What nonsense." Thera handed her the box, its silvery lid covered with an intricate design that glinted in the soft light. But as Ah-mah started to slide the cover back, the old woman snatched the box, startling her.

"I will open the box, Ah-mah, for I now know it holds a gift, and I would be presenter." With that she removed the cover of the tiny box, and with her gnarled fingers, lifted a finely linked chain of metal. Dangling from that chain, sparkling as it reflected the light, was the great stone, the beautiful Aquamarine Ah-mah had last seen cradled by the bosom of Aletha. The gasp she heard internally confirmed it.

Thera stood, and with great tenderness, slipped the chain over Ah-mah's head, the Aquamarine dropping to rest between her breasts and settling as though it had been there forever. "You are Ah-mah the Healer," she said, placing her hands on Ah-mah's shoulders and kissing her brow.

Closing her eyes, Ah-mah felt the blessing in the old woman's hands, even as she felt the powerful energy in the Aquamarine. The old woman, tall no longer, was just Ah-mah's seated height. She leaned her forehead toward Ah-mah's, touching it as Sefra had touched her, and Laskella. A picture flashed through her mind, her first glimpse of Aletha in the Gardens, the great gemstone over her heart glistening in the sunlight. Aletha's thought joined hers, "When you touched the young girl who was in pain. Yes, Ah-mah, I remember also."

"Were you healer, Aletha? Did you use this stone to heal others?"

"Not a healer of the body, Ah-mah, but a listener to hearts."

The old woman stirred and returned to her chair. "What do you feel?"

"From this beautiful jewel? A great energy, Mother Thera. It is too dear a treasure to hang from my neck."

"Nevertheless, it has chosen you. I feel it," she said. Thera sipped from the cup which rested on a small table beside her chair. A similar table and cup were by Ah-mah's chair, although she had not noticed them. She took a sip from her cup as well and found the contents to be cool, delicious and refreshing. Thera leaned back in her chair, closed her eyes and steepled her fingers. "Tell me what you know of our origins," she said.

The rest of the day was spent with the telling of tales, the asking of questions, with the young boy bringing food and drink from time to time. In the afternoon, the boy and a companion brought cushions and they rested, Ah-mah sleeping deeply, dreaming of the jasmine in Aletha's Garden, Thera resting, her head too filled with all Ah-mah had said for sleep. "She does not understand that she is the jewel," the ancient woman thought.

When Ah-mah awoke, Thera said, "I have a story to tell you about the jewel you wear.

"Some say that another woman wore the jewel, a woman who had great renown in the Land of the River a long, long time ago. It is said that she lived with our people but came from another island in the sea which held a great city upon its rocks. That island, too, was destroyed, and she escaped, so the story goes, carrying the very gem you wear."

Ah-mah's eyes stared at nothing for a moment as she listened to the voice within. "Nyla. I wondered what happened to you."

"Who is Nyla?" Ah-mah silently asked her mind companion.

"She was my maidservant, my apprentice, and my friend. She left us right before we Keepers began the transformations."

"How do you know of Aletha and her Gardens?" Mother Thera asked, surprising Ah-mah, for she had not mentioned her mind companion.

"Aletha has been my inner voice since birth. This jewel was hers, and her mother's before her. She once told me that it is not from this planet but from another, far away. She said it was brought here by her grandfather."

"My head is full of all you have told me, and still there is more to tell. We will speak together again, my daughter. Your coming brings the old stories to life and assures us of their truth."

"One last question, Mother. Is the wall that disappeared when we first saw you and then reappeared, is that wall like the stone which holds light?"

"A very astute question, Ah-mah. The energy within that cubicle is what sustains me, and I can no longer leave it for very long. I have been away today longer than I should have, and my old bones feel it."

"You thinned its walls so we could see you, and then thickened them again?"

"I spoke words in my mind, ancient words, but I had not thought of thickening or thinning the wall. Still, that was the result, was it not? More to ponder. You are such a gift, Ah-mah. I fear you will not be with us very long, for your heart seeks adventure."

Ah-mah wore the gemstone openly when she was in the cave, and beneath her dress when she left it. Ah-nah was fascinated by the Aquamarine, continuously asking to sit in Ah-mah's lap so she could finger it. Menes was drawn to it as well, but more because he felt it as a link to his mother. She was often in his thoughts, and those thoughts were often troubled. One night his dreams of her were so violent, so filled with blood, he awoke screaming, waking everyone in the cave. All rushed to his side, but Ah-mah waved them away. She bundled him up in a blanket and, grabbing one for herself, took him with her to sit beneath the stars.

Under their brilliance, he told his grandmother how he had waited for Bo to fall asleep with Ah-nah, how he crept out of the north exit, slipping cautiously through the fields, until he reached Ah-nah's hiding place beneath the bushes. With halting words, he told her how his mother and father stood on the steps, how Rahotep marched with his soldiers to stand in front of them, how he asked again to buy the land. Sobs threatened to choke him as he spoke his mother's reply, and saw the daggers, drawn and plunged so swiftly into his parent's bodies. He ended his tale with chilling words, "I hate him."

"He is not worthy of your hate, Menes. You have honored your parents by daring to witness what you should not have, and you took care of your sister. You are a brave boy and I am a foolish grandmother. I should never have left you, Menes, never have gone away with Sept. If we had been there, Rahotep would not have dared to do what he did."

Looking up at her, Menes said clearly, "No, Na-na. If you had been there, you would be dead, too."

As the truth of the boy's calm statement reached her, Ah-mah was surprised at his wisdom. He was right, she and Sept would have been killed by this power-hungry man. "Some of them would be dead as well," she thought, with a mirthless chuckle.

The sky lightened in the east. Impulsively, Ah-mah said, "Menes, could you survive without porridge this morning?"

"Yes."

"Then let us go!"

"Where?"

"To see the dolphins."

Ah-mah went back into the cave long enough to retrieve a water skin and some day-old bread. Folding one of the blankets, she draped it over her shoulder. The skin she tucked under her arm, the bread she gave to Menes to carry. They arrived at the beach just as the sun bloomed from the water on the far horizon. Ah-mah was not surprised to see the flash of silver a little way out into the water. "The ball, the floating ball. I knew I had forgotten something. Oh well, we will have to make do," she thought.

Sept had been teaching Menes to swim. The boy was not yet confident with his skill, but he knew enough to survive. The dolphin swam lazily around them and then rolled toward the boy, extending his dorsal fin. Ah-mah lifted Menes so he could grab hold, his small hand hardly to be noticed on the fin. She took hold of the fin behind his hand, her other hand on her grandson's waist, letting the dolphin tow them both.

In her mind she thought to him, "Would you bring my daughter to her son?"

The big dolphin emitted a series of clicks and whistles, and soon the pod was circling them. Menes laughed with the joy of seeing them. "Close your eyes, Menes," said Ah-mah. "Let the dolphins take you to your mother."

The boy obeyed, but soon opened his eyes, too excited by the dolphins. He watched them swimming, in and out, in and out, around and around, until his eyes closed of their own accord and he fell into dolphin dreaming.

"Menes? Menes! Where are you? Come here right now."

The day was warm and dry. He was playing his own private game of hiding and letting his mother search for him. A particularly dark corner seemed to be the perfect hiding place. Unfortunately, it was also dusty. Before long, he could not stop the sneeze. It erupted from his nose, immediately revealing his whereabouts to anyone in the house. Before he had a chance to wipe his nose on his sleeve, his mother had found him and swooped him up into her arms.

"There you are, you rascal. Why do you tease your poor mother so?"

The scene played out, with the little boy playing around his mother throughout the day. When she put him to bed that night, holding him close before blowing out the light, the scene faded, and was gone.

The boy's hand slipped from the dolphin's fin, and Ah-mah caught him, floating him in the water, her hand beneath his back for support. "How did you know about this part of Ak-hu's life?" she thought to the dolphin, Patch. "I did not tell you."

"The boy did."

With gratitude, Ah-mah floated the boy to shallow water, and stood him up, helping him walk out. She spread the blanket and fell asleep beside him.

CHAPTER FORTY-TWO

Sefra's Warning

Sefra spotted the cave on a day when she and Ah-mah took water to the plants. A bird's flight had drawn her gaze from the plant Ah-mah watered to a spot farther up the hill, revealing a narrow darkness that was not shadow. She climbed the hill, Ah-mah close behind, and entered a small cave.

"This is my new home," Sefra announced.

"You would leave the village?"

"I am a person of solitude, Ah-mah. Old habits die hard, and I have wanted to be alone for some time. I will visit as I am able, but I prefer silence to talk."

"Menes will miss you. He counts you as friend."

"Menes may visit me every ten days. You must blindfold him when you bring him. I know him. He will spy on me if he knows where I am."

"He is likely to find you anyway," Ah-mah said with a chuckle.

"I suppose he is. Well, until then, I will enjoy my solitude."

The women left the cave intent on returning to their task when, abruptly, Sefra said, "Sit with me on this ledge, Ah-mah."

When they had both settled, Sefra said, "There is something I have not told you. When Rahotep took your house in Nubt, I wondered what else would be stolen from you. After a while, I went to Nubt dressed as a desert wanderer, a good disguise since the villagers are wary of such. I saw nothing amiss in the marketplace until my steps took me to the Temple of Ra. I watched closely. A villager gave the priest who sat behind a table a gift which he tallied. Another priest took the gift away. Then the villager sat on a mat behind still another priest, and placed his leg alongside the priest's leg. That priest took the villager's foot in his hand and offered prayers aloud. He twisted the foot and shook it, and made a few other motions. Then he did the same with the other foot. I would not have known the intent had I not witnessed your treatments."

"The priests have stolen my treatments?"

"Worse. They make them into something that brings more wealth into the temple, but does not serve the people as your treatments did. I believe this is another sign that you no longer belong in the Land of the River."

"You may be right. I love my land, the people who work it, my ancestral home, the cave where my ancestors are buried. I needed my years in Remtu's hut, but, Sefra, I have been changed by my encounter with the sea and the dolphins. Nothing else has changed me so."

"I feel it also. Ah-mah, I, too, long for Sept's return, but only because he brings the boat and the possibility of adventure on the sea."

"You long for solitude, my friend. How can you think of being confined to a boat?"

"I would not be as long as I could see no land on the horizon. The water itself is solitude enough."

"If it were not for my grandchildren, I would have sailed with Sept."

"When Sept returns, we will persuade him and Master Mu-hem to take us to the far horizon. Menes will go with us."

"You believe Sept will come back?"

"Yes, and soon."

"My heart misses him so. But Sefra, how could I expose Menes to such danger?"

"Danger is everywhere. How long do you think the Bennu can remain hidden? Do you not feel change in the air? What do you want for your grandson, adventure or a lifetime of hiding in caves?"

Sefra returned with Ah-mah to the Bennu cave, having cautioned her not to speak of their discovery. After all were asleep, Sefra gathered her few belongings and left for her new home.

Ah-mah was hard pressed to explain Sefra's preference for solitude to Menes.

"Why, Na-na? Why would she leave us? Is she in danger? Is she ill?"

Finally, Ah-mah said to him, "Do you remember Sefra's telling you about her children?"

The boys eyes got big. "Sefra has not died, has she?"

"No, she is well and safe. When her children died, Sefra lost part of herself. Since that time she spent all her days alone until you and Ah-nah came. She took care of you both for a long time and I know she loves you, but Menes, she is not used to being around people who chatter."

"I would be silent, Na-na, if only I could see her."

"She has asked that you do, but not yet. In the meantime, I have something for you." Ah-mah pulled the little pillow from behind her back that Ak-hu had made and given to her before they left for Byblos. "Do you remember this?" she asked the boy.

"Mama made it for you, Na-na."

"Would you know how to keep it safe for me?"

"Certainly, Na-na. I would keep it next to my heart."

"Then do so," Ah-mah said, handing him the pillow. As he tenderly pushed it inside his shirt, she said, "Menes, Sefra told me you could come to see her in ten days."

"I will start counting today!"

Sefra's cave had awakened something in Ah-mah. She continued to leave the larger cave early every morning, but now she walked in starlight up into the hills, their height enhancing the glory of the sun rising from the depths of the sea. Often Aletha joined her, and they spoke of adventures, and feet, and healing, and Sept, always of Sept.

"Can you see him, Aletha?"

"No better than you."

"He has just a few men to Rahotep's many. I am afraid, Aletha. I fear he will not return."

Sefra saw them first. Sitting outside her cave, she spied three boats on the far horizon, each sail, a cloud clinging to the mast, colorful squares of cloth proclaiming the richness of the boats' inhabitants. She watched them turn toward the beach, dropping anchor all too near the path through the hills, but still east of the bay. The Bennu had cleaned the beach, sweeping away all traces of human use, but what if they had been careless?

She watched until Ra had set, memorizing the layout of their camp, noting Rahotep's tent. From the time she saw the first sail, she wondered what she should do. Should she tell the others or just observe? If they did not suspect anyone lived here, the boats would move on in the morning. But why were they here? What drew them so far west? If they started searching, she would be hard pressed to reach the caves before they did. She headed for the hidden village.

"Sefra!" Menes spotted her the minute she entered the cave. All eyes turned to her, Ah-mah hastening to her side, concern in her eyes.

"Are you well?"

"I have news."

"Come join us. Will you eat?" Ah-mah asked, and before she could answer, food and drink were put in front of her as she sat in the circle with the rest. She took a sip of water before she spoke.

"Three boats have come. They are camped on the beach. I believe they are Rahotep's boats, and that he is with them. I thought you should know."

"Nefer, go to Mother Thera and tell her. Now!" Ah-mah was surprised at how cold she felt inside, cold and clear. She gave more orders.

"Laskella, you and Medi must keep the children safe, but for now, everyone should go with Nefer to Mother Thera. She will want to oversee all plans for observation and defense. Go! I will be along shortly."

Menes was indignant. He should not stay with the women. He should find the man who took his mother's life and the life of his father and slay him. Drawing himself up to his full height, he said, "Na-na, I will stay with you."

She almost laughed in spite of herself, but seeing the earnestness in the boy's face, thought better of it. "Menes, I have to ask you to make a terrible sacrifice. These two women must be protected, as must your sister, and Sefra. I have no one else I can count on to guard them. Will you do this for me?"

"No one else?"

"No one else."

"Be careful, Na-na. We need you," Menes said, seeming to know that Ah-mah was not going to Thera's cave, but somewhere else.

"I will be careful and I will come back," she said, softly, for his ears alone, and entered her cubicle, letting the cloth fall behind her, shutting her away from the view of anyone who might be watching. She removed the Aquamarine and returned it to the safety of the box within the bag. From a more hidden recess she retrieved the sheathed dagger that Sept had left her for protection. For a moment, she held it to her heart, and allowed herself to consider that her husband might be dead. Blinking back the tears that threatened to overtake her, she slipped the hide thong over her head and left the cave.

The brisk night air restored her resolve as she followed the path to the sea, a mere shadow. When she crested the last hill, she stopped to observe. Yes, Sefra's assessment was accurate. Those were Rahotep's boats. Was he here? She searched for the greatest number of men still awake, and found four, huddled around a fire. Rahotep's guards.

She ran beneath the stars to the last dune and halted, catching her breath. Then she crept to the top of the dune, laying flat that she might not be detected. As she suspected, Rahotep slept near its base. The men who guarded him sat facing the fire, expecting any danger to come from the sea and not the dunes. Ah-mah thanked the stars for her good fortune.

"Ah-mah? What are you doing?"

"Not now, Aletha."

"You are not thinking clearly..."

Ah-mah ignored the voice in her head and concentrated on the vulnerable man below her. Quiet as a breeze, she crept down the dune toward him. "Murderer," she thought and drew the knife from its hiding place. A few more steps and she would have him.

Snap! The driftwood was dry and brittle, its breaking loud in the night. Ah-mah froze where she was.

CHAPTER FORTY-THREE

Rahotep

He was not asleep; merely thinking with his eyes closed. Why had they come so far given the ridiculousness of the scrap of information? No one sailed west of the westernmost branch of the river. But he had chased his former Master of the Guard too long to stop now. And his wife, he reminded himself. That Ah-mah. A formidable Mistress of the Land. She and that first husband of hers, what was his name? Kh something. They were worthy opponents. Revered by the people, even the Nubtians. When she married his Master of the Guard and came to live in Nubt, he wondered if she would oppose him. But she observed all the local customs, seeming to be content with her husband and her foot treatments. Surely her daughter had told her of his attempts to buy her land.

Would Ah-mah have become friend to him, as she seemed to be to Khufer, if he had left Ak-hu and Gedju alone? If he had not taken her lands? He would never know now. Until this voyage, he had not slept well since their deaths. The river soothed him in a way the land could not. Maybe if he went back to the boat to sleep?

Snap! His eyelids flashed open and he stared up into stars and a shadow. Men flew past him, grabbing the shadow and bringing it to the fire. Another man came to him. "Are you unharmed, my lord?" he asked as he helped him to rise. Without answering, Rahotep went to see who this shadow might be.

Walking directly to the person who sat on the sand in front of the fire, he demanded, "Identify yourself!"

Angry eyes looked at him. What most surprised him was the hair, and the yellow dress, so familiar. By all the gods, this was a woman!

"Do you not recognize me, Rahotep?" the woman asked. "I am mother to one you murdered. If not for a twig, you would be dead now."

"Ah-mah?" What good fortune had brought her to him? But wait, what had she said, 'dead now?' "You were going to kill me? You, Ah-mah? A woman?"

"Here is the dagger she carried, my lord," said one of the men as he handed Ah-mah's knife to Rahotep.

When the blade touched his hand it catalyzed something in him. He stomped away from the fire. How dare this woman! By what authority did she interfere with the inevitable? Did she not know that the people wanted him to rule them? Not her, but him! At last his rage settled into cold fury, leaving him as determined as the wind to be rid of this woman, this last Mistress of the Land.

Returning to the fire, he said, "Bind her wrists and take her to my boat. In the morning, when all can witness, she will share her daughter's fate."

CHAPTER FORTY-FOUR

Sept

The Bennu watched from hidden places, unable to counter so large a force. In the night Ga-lek saw another boat some distance out slip around Rahotep's camp and into the bay beyond. He ran to meet it and those he knew it carried.

"Sept! Sept!" he called as he approached the boat. A head popped up above the railing.

"Ga-lek! Come up. We are all awake."

As the tall Bennu reached the deck, many hands helped him over the railing. "Come, sit. Tell us why you have come."

Beneath the starlight, Ga-lek spoke of the coming of Rahotep's boats and how Sefra warned them. The next words he spoke chilled Sept to his core. "Ah-mah is no longer with us. She is on Rahotep's boat, bound and guarded. He says he will kill her at dawn."

Sept was on his feet. "How?"

"We think she intended to kill him. The jewel she wears is in its box in her cubicle, and the dagger you left with her is missing."

Unable to bear the thought of Ah-mah captured, Sept cried, "We must go immediately, Mu-hem! Back to the sea."

Mu-hem stood and put a hand on Sept's shoulder. "We must consider everything, my friend. We cannot afford to endanger the Bennu. There is much more at stake than might be seen at first glance."

"I will not lose my Ah-mah," Sept said, his eyes angry.

"There is something else. Ah-mah's grandson cannot be found," Ga-lek said.

"Is there a place where we could watch the beach without being seen?" asked Mu-hem.

"Come with me," said Ga-lek.

Leaving two men on the boat, they followed Ga-lek into the dunes between the bay and Rahotep's camp. As soon as Jasoth saw the swarm of men on the beach, he put his mouth close to Sept's ear, and whispered, "We could take them. We could surprise them in their sleep and rescue Ah-mah before Rahotep knows he no longer lives."

Sept knew his few brave men were no match for the force on the beach, sleeping or no, but Jasoth had triggered something in his mind. Suddenly, he felt certain of his own path. Telling no one his intent, he turned and quickly retraced his steps to the bay. He did not go near the boat but ran swiftly toward the sea.

CHAPTER FORTY-FIVE

Ah-Mah

Ah-mah shivered in the sea breeze. Sept would be furious when he found out about her foolishness. At least Rahotep had not asked how she happened to be here alone. The Bennu were still safe for the moment. She inspected the single guard, thinking she might persuade him to release her. The man was not from the Land of the River. Most likely he did not speak her language. Clever of Rahotep, if true. She decided to test him.

"The moon will rise late this night," she said, and smiled at the man.

He whirled around, hand on the hilts of his dagger, a look in his eyes she had not seen before in any man. Truly, this man had been well chosen.

She sat in the center of the boat, her only comfort, the railing against her back. Her guard paced the length of the deck, always watching her. Absently, she rubbed her wrists where the rope chaffed, as her mind sped through any possibility of escape. Surely her guard would tire soon. When he eventually dozed, she would be ready. For what? Why, to overpower him. Perhaps the man was like Rahotep and saw only that she was a woman. The plan had its flaws, but it was the only one that came to her.

The stars moved slowly overhead. Just as slowly, Ah-mah realized that this could be her last night of life. The guard showed no sign of tiring or even sitting. She shuddered and drew her feet beneath the yellow dress.

"Death comes to everyone," she thought. "There is no need to fear what comes." But, she was not ready. Khmet had not been ready either. Unless he had some warning he had not told her. No. The gany's strike was a surprise. Ak-hu had known she was going to die. She had prepared for it. She had prepared plants and seeds, and she had prepared her children. Ah-mah remembered the last time she saw Ak-hu, bathed in light that came from within. Now the dolphins held Ak-hu's memory in their dreaming. Would they add her to their dreaming once she was dead?

Ah-mah did not know how to prepare herself for death. She could not gather plants nor could she speak to her grandchildren. "I cannot say goodbye to anyone," she thought. "Not even Sept."

The moon rose, making her more visible to the guard who did not tire. If she could have hugged herself, she would have. Her heart felt as cold as her body.

"Ah-mah?" Aletha's voice conveyed her concern.

"Oh, Aletha! I am going to die and I can see no way to prevent it."

"Your plan to overpower the guard will not work, my Ah-mah. His heart is cruel and he is strong."

"Then I am already dead, for I can think of no other means of escape."

"It is not your time to die."

"How can you say that? My hands are bound and the guard does not sleep. The sky grows lighter in the east."

"Listen."

Ah-mah almost smiled when she heard it, but she wanted to give nothing away to the guard. A dolphin chittered softly in the water directly below her. She watched the guard pace and noticed that he often hesitated when he reached the stern, his gaze caught by something on the beach. She would have to be quick.

The guard looked at her as he passed, almost as though he suspected something. When he reached the stern, he did not hesitate, but pivoted on one foot and passed her again. She had been about to rise but caught herself just in time. He strode to the bow and back to the stern, where he halted. Ah-mah rose on unsteady legs. Hearing her, the man turned. As she reached for the railing with her bound hands and launched herself over the side of the boat, he whisked the dagger from its sheath and threw it. Pain seared her shoulder as she fell.

The guard ran to the railing and searched the water for any sign of the woman in the yellow dress. Waves glittered in the soft moonlight, but revealed no woman, no yellow dress. Knowing the swirling water held death for anyone foolish enough to enter it at night, he was not tempted by it. Rahotep would kill him when he found the woman missing, of that he was certain. But he would have a death he could see coming, a death on land and not from whatever lurked in the dark waters.

The dolphins carried her below the water until she was out of sight of the boat. When the blood from her wound attracted sharks, two dolphins broke away from the pod and drove them off. The dolphins who carried Ah-mah lifted her head out of the water as they bore her through the break in the dunes and into the bay, not releasing her until she was in shallow water near the shore. Ripping off the yellow dress, she flung it out into the bay, preferring to be chilled rather than wear anything connected with

Rahotep. She staggered out of the water and toward a man she had not expected to see.

"Sept!" she cried. "Did you send the dolphins?"

"I wanted to come myself, my Ah-mah, but they would not let me."

"Oh, Sept," she said, and buried her head in his shoulder, suddenly unable to stop trembling. He picked her up and carried her to the boat.

The two men on the boat were surprised to hear a woman's voice. Both recognized Ah-mah in the early dawn and scrambled over the side to assist Sept. Fayin helped lift Ah-mah onto the boat while the other man ran to tell Mu-hem and Sept's men. The rudderman saw Ah-mah's wound.

"Careful, Sept," said Fayin. "She has been injured."

"Where?"

"Her shoulder. I will get water to wash it."

Sept examined the wound with a warrior's eye. It was deep, but she would heal. Fayin washed the wound thoroughly with sea water, then bound it tightly with linen.

Ah-mah was exhausted and her shoulder throbbed, but she remembered the host of men on the beach and the man who led them and said, "We must watch. We do not know what Rahotep will do when he learns of my escape. Come, my husband, I will take you to a place where we can see everything."

No one slept on the beach. Rahotep bellowed and the men scurried, some with purpose and some aimlessly, not knowing what would satisfy their master. The body of the guard lay where it had fallen, having paid the expected price for Ah-mah's ingenuity.

As Ra in all his glory rose higher into the turquoise sky, Ah-mah saw the dolphin and whispered to Sept, "Look there!"

The dolphin had something on his beak. He tossed it into the air and let it land in the water, only to slip his beak beneath it to toss it again. Over and over he performed his act, drawing quite a crowd. One of the men waded into the water. The dolphin gave one last toss and disappeared. The object landed right in front of the man. He bent over and picked it up.

Ah-mah and Sept saw it at the same time. It was yellow, and when allowed to blow in the breeze, looked very much like a dress.

Gripping Sept's arm, she whispered, "They will know we are here! Sept, we must do something."

"We must watch, my Ah-mah. I believe the dress will make Rahotep leave."

"Leave? How could that be?"

"Watch."

The man brought the dress to Rahotep who fingered it for a moment, then shouted orders. A chest was brought and the dress placed in it. More orders. The men took down the tents and began loading the boats. Two of the men lifted the guard's body from the beach and flung it out into the sea.

"They are leaving! Why?"

"Rahotep has proof that you are dead, proof he can show the villagers and your people. He will tell them that our boat foundered on the sea and all were lost. The people will believe him."

"But was he not chasing you and Mu-hem?"

"You were always the one he feared, Ah-mah. To the people, you are still Mistress of the Land."

Sept hugged her. "Would you have killed him, Ah-mah?"

"I would have tried."

Unknown to either adult, Menes hid nearby. He had followed his Na-na when she left the cave, his much smaller frame lagging behind. The loud snap of the twig had startled him. When his Na-na was taken to the fire, he was sorely tempted to stand with her, the thought of losing her more terrifying than his own death. When they bound her hands and took her aboard the boat, he curled his body into a tight ball and sobbed himself to sleep. The cold pre-dawn air woke him, and with no purpose other than to warm himself, he retraced his steps. Suddenly, he turned aside and climbed into the hills, unable to allow his Na-na's death to go unwitnessed.

By some strange fortune, he chose a hiding place close to his grandparent's. He heard their whispering and watched as they did while the dolphin played with his Na-na's yellow dress. When the man who had murdered his parents placed the dress in the chest and gave orders to leave, he was as surprised as she was. He heard Pa-pa ask her if she would have killed the terrible man, and he heard her answer. As the last of Rahotep's boats set sail, Menes' eyes flashed. "One day I will return to the Land of the River with many men," he whispered. "Then, my mother, you will be avenged." He hugged the little pillow to him as he spoke, still a child hurting from his loss of her. The pillow, faded and water-stained, swallowed his tears.

THE HEARTMIND CHRONICLES CONTINUE:

BOOK TWO
the White Crown

BOOK THREE
Heartmind

BOOK FOUR
the Last Dolphin